H. Peacocke

A Simple Life

ROSIE THOMAS

A Simple Life

HEINEMANN : LONDON

First published in Great Britain 1995
by William Heinemann Ltd
an imprint of Reed Consumer Books Ltd
Michelin House, 81 Fulham Road, London sw3 6rb
and Auckland, Melbourne, Singapore and Toronto

Copyright © Rosie Thomas 1995
The author has asserted her moral rights

A CIP catalogue record for this title
is available from the British Library
isbn 0 434 00183 x

Typeset by Intype, London
Printed and bound in Great Britain
by Clays Ltd, St Ives plc

For Paul and Jane

The author wishes to thank Sir David Phillips,
Dr R. H. Jones and Mrs S. Abraham for generously
sharing their expertise in connection with
certain aspects of this book. Thanks are also due
to Mr and Mrs John Clayton and colleagues in
Amherst, Mass. and, as always, to Ellen Levine.

One

It was a pretty street in a good neighbourhood. The Stewards had seen that right away, as soon as they turned the corner from Pleasant Street into Kendrick, at the beginning of their first year in New England. The houses were a friendly distance apart, with mown grass and tidy trees between them. There were basketball hoops over the garage doors and children's bicycles on the open porches.

'Looks okay,' Jack said from the back of the car. 'Looks good, in fact.'

In fact was one of his sayings. *You see* was another of them, and both were copied directly from his father. Jack used them in his careful explanations of the world for his younger brother's benefit.

'I know that already, you don't have to tell me that,' Merlin would retort, conscious as always of his position as the youngest and least well-informed of his family.

'It's kind of neat-looking,' was Merlin's verdict on the house as they drew up. From the beginning he was the most determined to fit into this new world. He spooned up the language as if it were ice-cream.

'So, what do you think?' Matthew Steward asked his wife, after they had seen around. He was eager for her to like it. They needed a home to settle into in Franklin, a real home not a rented apartment, and Matthew wanted to have all this fixed up so that he could be free and comfortable to concentrate on his work.

'Oh. Ye-es, I think it's the best we're likely to find,' Dinah answered.

They had moved only a week ago from home in England to this stately tree-canopied college town in Massachusetts. Matthew was a scientist, a molecular biochemist. He had been invited here by the university to set up a prestigious new department and his wife and children followed behind him, bobbing in faint bewilderment on the wake of his latest success.

Dinah stood on the porch steps of the house on Kendrick Street, her head tilted as she squinted upwards. She could see snug-fitting window frames and solid timbers. Even so, the house appeared to slide out of focus and then, when she stared harder, it took on an insubstantial quality, two-dimensional, like a family home mocked up for a film set.

Jack looked from one parent to the other. 'I like it. I really, really like it. There's room for everything, all our stuff.'

'Me, too.' For once Merlin did not try to argue the opposite case. The boys also wanted to feel that the decisions were safely made and that they were fixed, taking root in a place where they could leave their bikes and skateboards on the porch like these other as-yet-unknown children.

Matthew nodded his satisfaction. 'Good. That's settled.'

They drove back across Franklin to the realtor's office. Dinah trailed her arm out of the window and felt the concentrated sun hot on her skin. The street had an exhausted, end-of-summer air and the cars and shops were veiled with pale dust.

The house *was* nice. It was white clapboard, with green shutters at the windows and a raised porch that ran all the way round. Inside there were wide pine floorboards and the family room had an open hearth. They could take their

2

belongings out of storage. Their English furniture would look well in the house.

The Stewards became the new family on Kendrick Street.

The Kerrigans next door gave a welcome party for the Stewards, and everyone in the street came, even old Mr Dershowitz from the end house and the quartet of post-graduate students who were renting for the year while the Berkmanns were in France.

Matthew was introduced over and over as the new pro-fessor at the university.

'What is it you do, exactly?' Dee Kerrigan asked him.

'I'm a molecular biochemist. My particular field is protein engineering.'

Matt grinned, the way he did. He talked about his work to Todd Pinkham from across the street and George Kuznik, their neighbour on the other side, telling them what a privi-lege it was to be here to set up the programme for the university.

Dinah ate the chicken with black-eye beans that Linda Kuznik had brought, and listened and smiled. There was a lot of smiling to do, and she felt the kernel of herself shifting within this shell of politeness. These people were so friendly, with their warm questions and welcoming explanations, and in return all she could feel was isolated and estranged. Home was a long way away.

No, she reminded herself, this was not like her, that was not the way to think; *this* is home. She could make it so.

She tried harder to be responsive. There must be a way to direct herself into the current of goodwill on which everyone else was happily sailing.

'I did have a job, back in England,' she said in answer to a question of Linda's. 'In advertising, I don't know yet what I'll do here. Get the house fixed up, the boys into school, do the domestic map-reading for all of us. Matt's going to be too busy.'

'I hear that your husband is very brilliant.'

3

They both looked across the room to Matthew. He was describing something to the postgraduates, and making decisive chopping gestures in the air with his capable hands as he did so. There was a ripple of laughter. At the same time Dinah noticed a rushing stream of children headed by the largest Kerrigan child. Jack was watching a little to one side, rubbing at the frame of his spectacles, where they rested on his nose.

'Yes,' Dinah agreed. 'He is.'

Brilliant was the word that went with Matthew.

'Matthew Steward is exceptional,' people said, colleagues and supervisors and professors. 'He is an unusually brilliant young scientist.'

Dinah had once been eager to hear this praise and had treasured it, adding it grain by polished grain to the glowing heap of her love and admiration for him. She looked down at her empty glass.

'Have you got enough liquor over here?' Nancy Pinkham enquired. Without waiting for an answer she sloshed out more white wine from the bottle she was carrying, and then refilled her own tumbler. She blinked at Dinah over the rim as she drank.

'So. Settling in?'

Dinah could see without looking too hard that Nancy was getting pissed, not angry as the word would mean here and at home would need the added *off*, but simply and eagerly pouring wine down her throat. The distinguishing of terms and the homely associations of the expression itself cheered her up, and so did Nancy's relaxed way with the bottle.

'Yes, thanks. I've found the way to the mall and I know where to buy coffee and the best bagels.'

'And your kids?' Nancy asked.

Merlin had appeared at Matthew's side. His father's hand rested on his shoulder as he talked, but Merlin was looking around for Jack.

'When they get into school, they'll be fine.' That was next

4

week. Dinah and Matthew had already met the elementary school head, and the boys' class teachers.

'Sure. Listen, come over one morning and have a drink. Coffee, even.'

'I'd like that.'

'Mm. D'you know what?' Nancy moved closer, so that Dinah smelt her perfume and the wine on her breath. 'One of the graduate students said to me that you were *kind of surprising-looking. For a professor's wife.*'

The disclosure implied a potential for intimacy between Nancy and herself that Dinah welcomed. The room seemed to change shape, becoming more familiar, enclosing her with all these well-meaning strangers. She forgot her separateness and found that she was laughing.

'No pince-nez or grey hair in a pleat, you mean?'

Nancy pursed her lips. 'Evidently.'

'Which postgrad?'

'Sorry. Not the cute one. One of the others.'

'Well, just my luck.'

Nancy regarded her. She held her glass rakishly tilted.

'I guess you make your own luck, don't you?'

'I suppose.' Dinah directed her thoughts away into a vacuum, and then, once they were neutralised, let them slowly return to here and now. It was a long-practised technique.

'Have some of this carrot cake, Dinah, won't you?' Dee Kerrigan asked.

'Oh, Dee's carrot cake is *famous.*' Nancy wobbled on her high heels.

The party was slowly coming to an end. Mr Dershowitz had fallen asleep with his mouth open and his knobbed hands splayed on the arms of the chair, and there was an ominous absence of children except for the Steward boys. Jack was reading a book in the corner.

Matthew came to Dinah's side. His hand rested on her hip, transmitting the semaphore of partners: *time to leave now, wouldn't you say? I'm ready if you are . . .*

Dinah felt her physical connectedness to him. At that moment he was utterly familiar, solid and intelligible. Her husband. He was her anchor, her compass needle steadily indicating magnetic north. Her signals went back to him: *yes, we should go now. Home to our very, very, very nice house on Kendrick Street . . .*

They summoned the boys and said their joint goodbyes. The Kerrigans' hospitality pursued them out of the front door and into the mild afternoon with offers of sitters and recipes and telephone numbers. As the Stewards walked the few steps across the grass beneath the sugar maple to their own door, Dinah thought that they must look like a neat, bright family in a commercial. For what? Something safe – medical insurance, breakfast cereal, building society? She played with copy lines in her head: *one small step, a big jump, how many miles, miles to go before we sleep, dum dum deedum.* Then she remembered with a shock that she didn't do that any more. No more copywriting, no niche of her own. She was Matt's wife, Jack and Merlin's mother, this was Franklin, Massachusetts. Not London. Not Sheldon, the village in Hertfordshire where they had lived.

The heat had drained out of the air at last. The end of the summer, and the afternoon was cool with a seductive, resinous breath of autumn.

'Enjoy yourself?' Matthew asked her.

'Yes. Yes, I did. I liked Nancy Pinkham.'

'Joey Kerrigan's a schmuck,' Merlin said.

'Is he? Why's that? What does it mean, exactly?'

'Dad, he just is, I can tell.'

Merlin's eyesight was better than his brother's, but the two of them were very alike. Both boys were small for their age, inwardly assertive, externally wary, inquisitive and critical. They were clever, like their father, but as yet without his practised charm. Their hair kinked at the crown in the same way. Their close resemblance and their vulnerability touched Dinah, and made her heart twist with a determination that all should be made well for her children.

6

The front door banged shut. It had an annoying spring closure that Matthew would have to fix. Packing cases and boxes lined the hallway.

'Can we get a dog?' It was Jack who asked, from halfway up the stairs.

'No,' Dinah said, and Matthew, simultaneously, 'I should think so, why not?'

Because a dog is permanent. A dog says this is where we stay. I don't want that, to be so far away, we've talked about it and yet not talked, and Matthew always evades me.

'Yesss.' Triumphant Jack punched the air with his fist. 'Did you hear, Mer? Dad says we can get a dog.'

Only a dog, what difference will it make? We're here now, with this house, neighbours, school for the boys, Matt's big job. What did I tell myself, back at the Kerrigans'? That he's my anchor, my compass needle . . .

Or not?

'I'm not walking it. Not once. Not a single bloody step. Nor cleaning up after it. Right?'

Matthew leaned and affectionately kissed Dinah behind the ear.

'Absolutely right. My lady dog-lover.' Then he wandered away, picking up a stack of scientific journals from one of the half-emptied boxes.

Dinah walked on into the kitchen. The sun shone into this room. There was a view from the window beyond the pine table all the way up the street to Mr Dershowitz's. The boys' footsteps clunked on the uncarpeted boards overhead.

Dinah stood at the window, her hands resting on the sill, looking out at Kendrick Street. Matthew's work had brought him here, and so naturally she and the boys were with him. And in truth it made no difference, did it, wherever they lived?

Using the familiar strategy, she told herself that she had her husband and two children, the promise of novelty and the possibility of new friendships. There were boxes to be unpacked, and books and pictures and familiar pieces of

7

furniture to be arranged in rooms that would accumulate their memories, given time.

And it might even turn out that Matthew and she were not running away at all. That their paths were parallel, not divergent, not leading away into a future she was unable to decipher.

The academic year turned with the seasons through fall and the long New England winter to spring, at last, and the heat of summer. The pattern and measure of university life as it revolved around Matthew was familiar to each member of the Steward family. Matthew appointed his team and began his ambitious research programme. Work took up much of his time, as it had done in England. The boys settled into their school, accepting or rejecting the various customs of this new place with their usual clarity. It was only Dinah, with no niche of her own beyond the house and the family, who still felt an outsider as the months passed. With an oblique view of herself that somehow did not take account of her good looks or good humour, she envisaged a tall, spare and awkwardly reserved Englishwoman who seemed to move through the unmapped thickets and coverts of Franklin in the wrong camouflage, anxious to blend in for everyone's sake, but never quite managing to do so.

And then, twelve months after they had bought the house on Kendrick, at the same turning point of the year after the summer vacation but before the fall semester began, there was another party.

The Berkmanns were back from their year abroad, and the Pinkhams were having a barbecue evening to welcome them home. Dinah had offered to help Nancy make some desserts. In the morning she drove to the Stop'n'Shop and prowled the aisles, moving deliberately out of sync with the remorseless muzak that washed over her like nausea. From time to time a disembodied voice thanked her for shopping at Stop'n'Shop and begged her to check out the week's supersaves. Dinah read the shelf-screamers and placards and

8

found herself thinking of grocery campaigns she had worked on in the past. It seemed very long ago, and distant, and exotic. As she stood at the checkout she wondered if she wore the same drugged look as the other shoppers.

Back home the boys pitched balls outside in the yard while she made lemon tarts and meringues for Nancy.

The house was quiet except for the dog, Ape. Matthew and the boys had chosen a barrel-bodied creature with a rough coat and beady eyes. His toenails clicked on the pine boards as he roamed the house and occasionally his tail thumped meatily against a door. Dinah knew that he stared expectantly at her back as she worked.

'No,' she told him without looking round. 'Go away.'

Her voice cracked the silence. The solitude was oppressive. She looked around; the kitchen was orderly with utensils stacked in the sink and the finished desserts were laid out waiting for the evening. Dinah longed for company, for the solace of talk, with a longing that dried her throat like thirst. But Nancy would be busy with her two little girls and Dee would also be occupied with children. All the children in the neighbourhood flocked to the Kerrigans', even Jack and Merlin. Dinah knew plenty of other people in Franklin now, but there were none she could count on in just this moment of need.

It was three-thirty.

She could drive over and call in on Matt at the lab. She smiled at the thought of surprising him. It was a while since she had dropped in there. She heard his accounts of how the research was progressing, but she wasn't quite sure of the latest developments.

The idea took hold. She could say hi to the team, most of whom she knew, and then perhaps Matt and she might even go for a coffee. Years ago, before the children, she sometimes used to look in on him at his lab in London. Through one of the portholes in the swing doors she would catch sight of the back of his head and his shoulders hunched over a rack of test-tubes or a set of DNA sequences. He would look up and see her and wave her over. Then they would walk downstairs to a canteen, and laugh and drink urn tea at a table decorated with chipped formica and a crinkled tin ashtray.

Outside, Dinah called across to the boys,

'I'm going over to see Daddy for an hour. Don't leave the street, will you?'

'Yeah, Mom.'

They were old enough now. Jack was ten and Merlin nearly nine.

She drove her Jeep along Pleasant and turned across Main under the traffic lights, and from there swung into the central square. There was a wide green with handsome trees enclosed by solid, pinkish brick buildings. Franklin was proud of its history, and there were a number of tasteful shops on the green selling souvenirs and pamphlets about the original settlers and notable sons of the town. The campus of the University of Massachusetts at Franklin extended from the far side of the green, beyond a pair of tall stone pillars and a ponderous statue of the Founder. The buildings were dignified, with stone steps and massive doors and pediments with clocks that reflected the sun in discs of gold. There were libraries and chapels and memorial theatres facing each other across inevitable smooth lawns; this was the face of the university that was featured in prospectus photographs.

Matthew's part of the foundation was housed in one of a series of big, glassy blocks discreetly separated from the photogenic old buildings by a belt of trees. These newer facilities were a world away from the mousy warren of stairs and ancient cubbyholes where he had worked in London, although Matthew seemed barely to notice the difference.

Defiantly she left the Cherokee in a convenient space labelled faculty members only, and strolled across the grass towards the science blocks. The steps and lawns and student parking lots were deserted and somnolent in the sun. It would be another week before the students came crowding back in time for Registration Day. The clock on the James

Randall Hallett Library struck four behind her, triggering a series of associations. The church clock in the village, back at home. Vicarages and English tea. Gardens with roses and honeysuckle. Fields with gates, and white-laced hawthorn hedges.

Dinah walked faster, digging her hands deeper into the pockets of her skirt. Her hair was pulled into a thick plait that felt weighty and hot at the nape of her neck. No, not plait, braid. Bangs. She marshalled the different words, distracting herself by doing so.

The road curved through the shadow of the trees. There were huge, elegant conifers here with branches like trailing skirts that looked black in the bright light.

There was more grass in front of the new buildings, a curving bank of it, and across the grass a scatter of people. The senior members of the various faculties pursued their research throughout the year, so there were more parked cars here, and the doors of the dining commons were open.

Dinah headed diagonally across the lawns. In front of Matthew's building a handful of people were playing frisbee. She watched a boy in a baggy white shirt leap up and twist in the air to make a catch. Several voices called out and then the disc floated on from his hand in a smooth arc. All the figures were leaping now, their hair and clothes rippling and Dinah imagined how a director might freeze the frame to capture a single image, a blurred smiling face in a swathe of hair and an outstretched hand to signify, what, youthful abandon, confidence, freedom?

For the life that *you* live.

Perfume, trainers – *sneakers* – or low-fat yoghurt?

She was smiling with pleasure at the sight of the frisbee players when she realised that one of them was Matthew.

He was wearing khakis and a blue shirt that had pulled loose, and a peaked baseball cap she had never seen before. It was jammed low over his forehead to keep the sun out of his eyes and his hand was reaching up in a salute as he called out,

'Sean! Over here, look.'

Sean Rader had been part of Matthew's old team in London. It was part of the agreement Matt had made that he should be able to bring two of his key people over to New England with him. Dinah had met Sean often, back in London. He was a small, tense man with a corrugated frown. And now he was out in the four o'clock sunshine playing frisbee and shouting. These were all people who worked with Matthew. The boy in the white shirt was a technician, and there was a little dark-haired woman PhD and Jon Liu, Matt's deputy director, and half a dozen others.

The frisbee skimmed again on a long curving path towards Matt. He caught it two-handed and as he leapt in triumph he looked to Dinah so taut and springy, and so unquestionably comfortable within himself and in his place, that the coloured lenses of familiarity fell from her eyes.

The naked vision made her shiver in the afternoon's heat.

How was it that she had driven across town needing to talk to this man rather than that one, or another altogether? She was gazing at a stranger, a man she didn't know in any way, who lived a life with which she was unacquainted.

Disorientation rocked her. She put out a hand to steady herself in the rushing air.

Someone had sent the disc spinning away on the wrong trajectory. There was a chorus of jeers and the players ran after it in an eager pack. The woman PhD stumbled on the bank and landed on her outstretched hands, but she pushed herself up again and ran on, anxious not to be left out. The shadow of his cap's peak cut sharply across Matt's face.

Dinah did not want him to see her here. She could only think of getting away before anyone noticed her. She shrank backwards, two or three steps, then turned and fled for the shelter of the trees.

'It was only a frisbee game,' Nancy said. 'Why are you so angry?'

They were in the Pinkhams' yard, laying out cutlery and

paper napkins. Nancy had had her hair cut in the summer and it stood out in a cottony floss around her face, making her look not many years older than her little girls. 'Even Todd plays it.'

'It wasn't the game. I'm not angry.' Dinah couldn't express to Nancy the failure of recognition and the confusion that had come with it, or the sense of loss at being excluded from a closed circle of shared interest and common purpose that mocked what her marriage had become.

Matt was happy here.

How had that obvious fact somehow escaped her? She was lonely; Matthew was considerate and careful of her, almost as if she were an invalid, but on his own account he was happy.

'Damn it. Nancy, I sound a miserable shrew, don't I?'

'Uh-huh. You don't deserve him. And oh boy, are you a misery. You never come over here and make me laugh when I'm ready to scream, do you? You aren't funny or cute or a great mom or anything?'

'Aren't I?'

'Shit, Dinah, what's wrong? You know you are.'

Simple. On the face of it.

Dinah shook out a gingham cloth and twirled it like a matador cape. The boys were up in the trees hanging candle lanterns from the branches. Todd had lit the barbecue and there was the scent of charcoal. Later there would be a full moon.

'I miss home,' she offered bathetically, trying to explain something away. She patted the cloth over a table and smoothed the wrinkles.

'Sure you do. Anyone would.'

'About Matt, you know? There's all this talk of how busy he is, and the research, and all the other administration work to keep up with and the travelling to lectures and conferences and the pursuit of funds. And then I go round there and they're all playing bloody frisbee?'

'Listen up. That's the way it is. You have to let them have their importance. It's the same with Todd, the hospital hours and the crises and being the only one who can do anything right. They have to show us they're out there hunting and gathering. They're men, aren't they?' Todd was an intern at the local hospital.

Nancy's plump-cheeked face was smooth and shining within the halo of hair. Dinah felt a surge of affection for her and ashamed of deflecting her friendly concern with only a sliver of the truth.

They had not become close friends. Nancy made Dinah feel cynical and partial and foreign. They spent a good deal of time in and out of each other's houses, and Dinah was sparky and ironic in her company, but it was as if with her clothes and manners and eccentric theories of motherhood she was playing the role of a certain kind of Englishwoman to meet Nancy's expectations.

'You're right, darling. Men are men and all too explicable, and woman are supreme beings full of wit and insight and beauty. Now then, where shall we put all this bread?'

'French loaves, if you don't mind. Maria Berkmann has only been back for four days but I think if I have to listen to any more about Lyons and Côtes-du-Rhone and TGV pronounced tay jay vay, I shall start hollering.'

'Thanks for the warning. Otherwise I might have put the noise down to the hopelessly un-Gallic Californian Chardonnay.'

Laughing together, the two women went on laying out plates and knives.

When they finished Nancy said, 'You don't want to worry about Matt. Just let him get on with what he wants to do because he'll do it anyway, regardless.'

That much was true. Matt always got what he wanted. He worked out in his methodical way precisely what it was, and as soon as he had identified it he went ahead and got it. He was never blurred, never impetuous or unconsidered. Dinah knew him so well, and yet he could reveal himself to her as a total stranger.

'You're probably right.'

14

'I know I'm right.' Pleased with herself, Nancy gave a little affirming nod. 'I'll tell you something else. You should do something for yourself, instead of just for your husband and kids. You should get yourself a job.'

'Right. Hillary Clinton could probably use a little help. I'll call her.'

'I'm serious.'

'Nancy, I know you are. Thank you.'

Todd appeared dressed in a lemon-yellow Ralph Lauren Polo shirt. Nancy turned to him at once.

'Todd, are you planning to barbecue tonight or do I have to do everything?'

Dinah went home to change her clothes and tidy the boys.

'Clean T-shirt, Jack.'

'I don't want to change. I don't think it's necessary, in fact. This one's good enough.'

'All right.'

'So if Jack doesn't have to, then I shouldn't have to either.'

'All *right.*'

'When's Dad getting home?'

A minute later they heard his Toyota drawing up, and Matthew banged through the front door. The spring was still not fixed. His blue shirt was tucked in again and he was bare-headed. The boys leapt at him and he looked over their heads to Dinah.

'I like that dress.'

She smoothed the bright yellow linen with one hand. She had dressed carefully, but Matt had seen the outfit a dozen times before.

'Busy day?' she asked.

'Yep, pretty busy. The usual.'

'You've got time to shower before the party.'

We are so careful of each other, Dinah thought. Solicitous, as if we have some sickness between us that is never mentioned, even though the pain gnaws.

Matt groaned. 'I'd forgotten the party.'

He made for the stairs, with a child hopping on either

side. Watching him, Dinah saw that his shoulders were hunched and there was a prickle of grey in his hair. She remembered the lithe man across the grass who had seemed a total stranger to her, and tried to knit together the two images. They made an uncomfortable hybrid. We are Matt's responsibility, she thought. He shoulders the weight dutifully. And work is his resort and comfort. When did it happen, this switch?

She thought back involuntarily and then stopped herself, pinching off the flow of recollection.

The guests arrived, headed by the Berkmanns. Max Berkmann was wearing French workman's overalls. Mr Dershowitz was missing because he was in hospital, and the four graduate students had moved on. Dinah had never really got to know the good-looking one any better than to exchange affable nods across the street.

'Bit of a failure,' she had joked to Nancy.

'Matt's better-looking anyway, and he's got full tenure.'

It was a good party. The moon hung above the trees, heavy and orange-tinged, and the children's candle lanterns glowed amongst the dry leaves. The Kendrick Street neighbours were pleased to see each other after the long vacation and there was plenty of news to exchange.

Jack and Merlin went off with Tim Kerrigan. Dinah caught a glimpse of them in one of the bedrooms, sitting in a line with legs stuck out in front of them and chins sunk on their chests, watching a video. Just lately, her children had stopped making unfavourable comparisons between Franklin and home. They seemed to have stopped thinking about England altogether.

Dinah flitted from group to group, laughing and talking. She had drunk two quick glasses of wine in the kitchen with Nancy. Two or three people told her she was looking well, that her summer tan suited her. She listened to Max Berkmann describing the idyllic year in France.

'I tell you, we would have stayed right there in Mâcon if there was any way I could have fixed it.'

'Here, Dinah.' George Kuznik was partial to Dinah, and he shifted to make a place beside him on the garden seat. The darkness was warm and scented and within it the lanterns made oval patches of fuzzy golden light.

George's voice rumbled in her ear. 'A cold beer and you. What more could a guy ask for? You know, I always think this is the best time of year. After the heat, waiting for the fall, before the cold comes.'

Talking without listening to herself, Dinah said something about not much looking forward to another New England winter. She was overtaken by a sense that this place was still utterly strange to her, and by the mysteriousness of the people around her, even her husband. The landmarks of habit and logic and certainty were dissolving. She was on the outside of all this talk, detached from the physical world even with George Kuznik's bulk pressing against her thigh, and she was losing her ability to decode the messages that were flashed to her.

She was afraid they would notice; everyone would notice her singularity.

With a beat of panic Dinah wondered if she might be going mad.

She turned to George suddenly and took hold of his hand. Anchoring herself. His palm was moist, surprisingly soft. George's domed forehead reflected the lantern overhead. He leaned forward and for a moment she thought he was going to kiss her. A bubble of laughter forced itself upwards but George only asked solemnly, blinking a little,

'You all right, Dinah?'

The garden began to coalesce again around her. The fearful dislocation was passing. Dinah did laugh now, and the laughter eased her throat and slackened her face. She released George's hand and set it back in his lap, registering the flicker of his disappointment. Beyond him she saw a big man emerge from the house and stand on the porch steps, hands on hips, his gaze panning across the garden.

'How much have I had to drink?' she smiled.

'Aw, and I thought it was my charm that was intoxicating.'

Dinah kissed George's cheek then leaned back, separating herself from him. 'You're a good neighbour,' she said truthfully. They both drank, allowing the tiny awkwardness to pass.

'Who's that?' She indicated the big man who was now strolling between the groups of people. His height and commanding manner gave him a seigneurial air.

'A friend of Max's, Todd must have asked him over. Name's Ed Parkes. Have you heard of him? He writes thrillers. Pleased with himself, but a decent sort of guy. His wife's British, now I come to think of it.'

Later in the evening when the party shifted indoors and the children began to reappear and rummage for leftover food, Dinah met the Parkeses. Ed had a huge handshake, and his face creased into affable crinkles while his shrewd, light-blue eyes examined her. He told her that he came originally from Detroit but he and his wife had a house in the woods outside Franklin, and one in London where they spent part of the year, and a chalet in Zermatt. He talked easily, amusingly, but in the slightly overbearing way of a man accustomed to being the focus of attention. At last, but with a suggestion that it was out of good manners rather than real interest, he turned the conversation to Dinah.

'I don't have a job here,' she told him. 'I used to be in advertising, in London.'

'Doing hearth and home for a while?' He was appraising her.

'That's right.' She was grateful for his way of putting it.

'Your husband's the scientist, isn't he? I must have a talk with him. I can always use special expertise.'

Dinah was amused at the idea of Matt's work being good for nothing more than extra colour in one of Ed Parkes's airport blockbusters. She bit the corner of her lip, and then realised that Ed had followed her thoughts as plainly as if she had spoken them aloud. He was grinning down at her.

'You think I'm full of shit?'

'Not at all.'

'Not much. Hey, I want you to meet Sandra. Here she is. Sandy, this is Dinah Steward. You'll like each other, and not just because you talk the same language.'

Sandra Parkes was in her mid to late forties, tall and pale and thin, and very beautiful. She had the kind of flawless finely featured face that make-up artists and cameras fall in love with. Dinah didn't dare to squeeze her hand when she took it in case the pale skin bruised.

'What's he said?' Sandra asked.

'Nothing you can't contradict if you wish, honey.' Ed sauntered away. His made-to-measure shirt sat comfortably across his massive shoulders.

'Nothing worth contradicting,' Dinah told the woman coolly.

Sandra was wearing a complicated outfit of layers of gossamer fine wool and chiffon and slippery satin. Dinah had often wondered, as she flicked through the fashion magazines, what colour greige might be. It came to her now that this was it. It was so subtle and refined that it made her cheery yellow linen look by contrast like the flowering of some tenacious garden weed.

'It's never worth disagreeing with Ed,' his wife murmured. 'He believes that he's right and he almost invariably is. I think it's the act of believing itself that does it.'

Dinah smiled. Surprisingly, but distinctly, she felt herself warming with interest in Sandra Parkes. It was not her clothes, or the way she looked, or even what she said. It was the sound of her faint English voice and the half-swallowed, descending semitones of irony and deprecation.

Ed Parkes might look like a bull elephant and sound like a hick, but he was as quick as a whip. The stirring of empathy was not a matter of sharing a common language with Sandra, nothing as obvious as that. By the bare movements of her lips

19

and the darting little gestures of her fingers, Dinah knew where Sandra came from. She could read the text of Sandra's background just as surely as Sandra could read hers.

Within a few moments the women were perched side by side on the scrubbed pine of Nancy's kitchen table, exchanging the common currency of their histories in a way they would never have done at home in England, or even in New York or Los Angeles. Whereas the links would have been taken for granted there, here they seemed surprising, remarkable. They had both grown up in the Home Counties, the only children of career servicemen. Sandra's father had been in the Navy, Dinah's in the Army. There had been overseas postings, and then from the age of eleven, good safe girls' boarding schools within a sensible radius of London. After boarding school there had been long interludes of rebellion. And then for both of them, marriage to men from backgrounds entirely different from their own.

The Parkeses lived for part of the year in London, Sandra explained. Ed liked to be there when he was writing. Zermatt was for a month or six weeks at Christmas and Franklin was where he claimed to feel most at home.

'But Ed gets bored quickly. In a month he'll be fidgeting, working out a trip to somewhere.'

'And you?' Dinah asked.

Sandra sighed, looking sideways at Dinah through the pale and silky bell of her hair. 'I would like to feel . . .' her elegant fingers shaped a box in the air '. . . located.'

Like me, Dinah thought. Correctly located. It must be this need in both of them that Ed Parkes had recognised. Talking to Sandra had stirred a hundred associations within her. Her Englishness called up the inessential details of home and history, but it was not those details Dinah felt severed from – only what they contained. A secret, embedded in England like a fly in amber. She couldn't explain the severance to Nancy or Dee or George Kuznik or anyone else, nor could she talk about it even to Matthew.

Most of all, not to Matthew.

She couldn't even think about this. She had to keep them sealed away, all the connected threads, or they would snake loose and whip and whistle around her.

'Do you have children?' Sandra was asking.

Yes.

'Yes, two boys. They're here somewhere.'

'Of course. I met them earlier. One of them said to me "You see, dinosaurs had tiny brains relative to their bulk." '

'Jack. The younger one is Merlin. And you?'

Sandra plucked at the filmy top layer of her draperies. An odd wary note sounded in their talk. Each of them heard it and interpreted it for herself, without wondering if the other did the same.

Sandra said, 'One. A girl. She's fourteen now.'

Fourteen.

Dinah felt a jolt, and the tidy focus of her attention scattered like beads in a kaleidoscope. She made herself say smoothly, 'You must bring her over, the boys would like it.'

Sandra's narrow shoulders lifted. 'I don't know. Perhaps. She's quite difficult . . .'

Impulsively Dinah put her hand on Sandra's arm. 'Aren't they all? Listen, why don't you come and see me? One day next week. We'll have lunch, just the two of us. Will you?'

There was some connection between them, not yet identifiable, beyond the mere similarity of their histories.

'Yes. All right, I'd like that. I'll come while Milly's with her tutor. She doesn't go to school just at the moment. Ed travels so much, and I like us both to go with him . . .'

For a second, Sandra's pale eyes held Dinah's imploringly.

From across the room, Matthew was watching them. He saw Dinah touch Sandra's arm. It was okay, he thought. Good. Dinah needed a friend over here and the writer's nervy wife might be the one. He had liked the writer himself, for all his bullshit. But there was a shiver of impatience with Dinah. She was needy, and once she had been strong. He had drawn on her strength, of course. Made himself with her help.

21

The equation was different now. He was concerned for her, for Dinah separately and the two of them together. But still there was the chafe of exasperation, the raw edge of worn-out patience rubbing the smoothness between them.

The boys were in bed and asleep at last. Even Ape had given up his clicking and thumping and settled in his basket in the laundry-room. In her bathrobe, Dinah sat in front of her bedroom mirror brushing her hair. When she was a little girl her nanny had taught her to brush her hair every night, just so, counting the strokes. Not that she did it, then or now. Why tonight? Because of the associations crowding in on her? Dinah remembered her parents coming into her bedroom while she sat at her dressing table, her mother in a cocktail dress with a stole round her bare shoulders, her father resplendent in his uniform. A kiss on the top of her brushed head. A cloud of Arpège and her mother's hands resting on her pyjama shoulders. Their two faces reflected one above the other, a blurred half-formed version under the poised lipsticked one. Eleanor always so perfect. Yet they were alike, hair and eyes and colouring.

That mother-daughter link broken. Eleanor, long-widowed, in England, in a bungalow on the south coast. Elegant, bridge-playing, lonely probably. Herself with her two boys. Tufty hair, their father's, an odd whorl at the back of three heads.

'Are you coming to bed?'

Matthew was already there, propped up with the inevitable scientific journal.

Dinah untied her robe, and slipped under the covers. Matthew put his reading aside and turned out the light.

In the darkness he asked,

'Are you all right?'

'Yes. Of course.'

She had not mentioned the frisbee game. Scientists' wives often feel excluded. Someone had warned her, at the very beginning. The Prof's wife, back at UCL, that was it. *It's like a very exclusive club. The exchange of ideas, the stimulus, the sheer thrill of it all. Most of them enjoy it more than sex, dear.*

It wasn't the obviousness of her own exclusion from the club that had hurt her, though. It was the sight of Matthew's unclouded happiness. And as she thought this Dinah felt a stab of self-disgust like a spike driven into her neck.

He reached out for her now. She knew that they would make love and they did, in their tender and considerate way that masked other feelings nothing to do with tenderness or concern.

Afterwards Matthew mumbled sleepily, 'I love you, you know.'

'I love you too,' she answered. And thought that the divide between love and hatred was a very fine and fragile one.

Dinah dreamed of England. It had become a place of steep hills, each hill revealing another beyond it, all of them with pale roads winding to their rounded summits like illustrations in a child's picture book.

Two

The road climbed as it led deeper into the woods. There were no more houses to be glimpsed between the trees, nor were there any mailboxes at the roadside.

'Have we missed it?' Dinah wondered as she drove, peering ahead to where oblique shafts of sun filtered through the branches. The leaves were showing the first margins of butter-yellow and crimson. In another two weeks the fall would be in full blaze.

In the back seat Merlin looked up from his GameBoy.

'101 was miles back.'

They were looking for 102, the Parkeses' house.

'How do I get to the next level of this? Jack?'

'Give it here. You're so dumb, I've shown you this already. Look, there's another sign.'

A yellow arrow stencilled *102* pointed onwards.

'I wouldn't want to live out here,' Jack said.

'Aw, too creepy for you? The deep dark woods are full of monsters?'

'Too boring, in fact, Merlin. Like you.'

'Stop bickering,' Dinah snapped.

'Mum, we aren't bickering. Can't you tell the difference between argument and conversation?'

Opposition to her was the only factor that united them, Dinah thought. Nothing was new.

'Sandra Parkes complains that Camilla is difficult. She can't be as bad as you two.'

'*Camilla*, what a totally sad name.'

'Sort of like some disgusting pudding, Camilla-and-custard.'

'Pink and wobbly. I bet she's really fat.'

The boys snorted and retched, united also by their unwillingness to make the visit to the Parkeses.

Matthew seemed to hear none of this. He had been silent most of the way, sitting with his eyes turned to the woodland flickering past.

He was thinking about his work; ever since the summer, when the present avenue of speculation had properly opened up to him, the thought of it had never been far from his mind. Even when he surfaced from sleep he was aware of it rising again through the membranes of semiconsciousness.

He was thinking about his engineered molecule now, his inner eye turning it so that it twisted elegantly, three-dimensional, a dense cluster of atoms floating free in black computer space. Which group should he change, to make the molecule more active?

Frustration and excitement simultaneously prickled within him.

The first tests were encouraging. His technicians had demonstrated that the enzyme material he had engineered was beginning to function as it should, partly binding to the surface of IM 9 lymphocytes, and so indicating that it would bind to some extent to insulin receptors on the surface of cells. The question now was which part of the beautiful structure to change, to make it work better, to make it perfect?

His eyes were unfocused but he saw the sign first. And the mailbox beneath it. Matthew pointed.

'There, look. I thought the place would be somewhere at the top of this hill.'

The road was dipping downwards ahead of them. Dinah compressed her lips but said nothing as she swung the jeep sharply into the driveway. There were more trees, conifers and birches pierced by airy columns of sunlight, and then they emerged into a wide space at the crown of the hill. The Parkeses' house rose in impressive stone and timber tiers against a sombre belt of firs.

Before Dinah had parked beside Ed's Porsche a door opened in the bottom tier and Ed himself emerged.

'Great, so you found us okay, no problems? Come on, come on in. Sandy's looking forward to it.'

Obediently they followed him through a hallway and into the centre of the house. The huge room soared up through complicated levels, its cool space enclosed by squares and rectangles of wood and rough stone and shimmering glass. Beyond the glass was blue air and the reckless colours of the trees.

'Cool,' Jack murmured.

'This is an amazing house, Ed.'

'You like it? I designed it myself, with a bit of help from an architect.'

Matthew looked around him, his hands in the pockets of his shabby khakis.

'Is there no end to your talents?'

Ed turned on him, grinning and sharp-eyed.

'Beginning, doesn't the line go?'

Matthew was easy in the company of other men, particularly men as successful in their fields as he was in his own. He laughed now, genuinely amused by Ed's disarming self-satisfaction.

'That's not what I said or what I intended. Hi, Sandra.'

Sandra appeared on one of the balconies projecting over their heads, and then fluttered down some steps to join them. Her hair was knotted close to her small skull and she was wearing a loose cream tunic that revealed the knobs of bone at the base of her throat. She kissed Matt and Dinah in turn, resting her hand for an instant on Dinah's wrist.

Dinah and she had had lunch together the week before.

At Sandra's suggestion they had met in one of the potted-

26

fern-and-scrubbed-boards café-bars that were popular in Franklin. They sat at a window table looking across the green towards the campus. Students streamed past in pairs and groups, on their way between morning and afternoon classes.

'Would you like to be that age again?' Sandra asked.

Dinah made the conventional response without thinking about it. 'Only if I could be forewarned and forearmed against making all the same mistakes.'

'Did you make so many?'

Dinah could not look at her. She felt an instant of fear that this woman was a threat. She might come too close and Dinah would not be able to fend her off in the way that she could keep Nancy and Dee Kerrigan and the others at bay. She heard herself laugh, a false high-pitched denial.

'No, not really. What about you?'

Sandra turned her wineglass full circle on its stem. A spilled drop broke into shining globules on the polished table top. Dinah's deflection of her question had been too sharp. She hesitated, on the brink of offering some truth of her own, and now thinking better of it. They looked at each other, suspecting an opportunity missed before they had even become properly aware of it.

Sandra said, 'Mistakes? I couldn't lay claim to too many, could I? Ed's a good man, as well as a very successful one. I have everything I want. A husband, a daughter I adore . . .'

Family, wealth, travel, ease, luxury, Dinah silently supplied for her. Only Sandra did not have quite everything she wanted, evidently. Not her own freedom, perhaps, from her husband's dictates. Dinah wanted to ask her why they had only one child. But she could not. The ripples that the question would make might stream back and rock her own precarious equanimity.

'How is your daughter?' she tried instead. Sandra had said the child was difficult. *Fourteen* . . .

Sandra drank her wine. 'Milly's quite unusual. Very strong-willed, very certain in her opinions. And we've probably spoiled her. But I expect most of the difficulty is just to do with her age, isn't it?'

'I should think so,' Dinah murmured. 'I daren't think what will happen when Jack gets there.'

That was all. The spectre of intimacy had shivered between Dinah and Sandra and they found that they had somehow brushed it away. After that they talked about missing England, and all the places Ed and Sandra had travelled to when Camilla was smaller and more tractable.

Now, a week later, they were all in the Parkeses' gleaming glass castle in the woods. Ed was herding them towards the drinks.

'C'mon, honey, what's going on? Are Bloody Marys okay for everyone? I don't believe in these orange-juice brunches. Take this glass and let's fill it up for you. Listen you guys, the pool table is through there. You don't have to hang out with us if you can find something better to do.'

Jack and Merlin sidled away, not needing to be told twice. Dinah and Matt were caught up and washed along like twigs in the full flood of Ed's hospitality.

'Now, you want the house tour? Outside or in first? Perhaps we'll do outside after we've eaten, maybe we can get some kind of a walk. The property stretches a good distance, way down into the dip out of sight of here. I want to take you in my study, Matt, show you the set-up I've got in there, maybe you can tell me something about computer modelling, I've got this idea I want to kick around? Dinah, what do you think of this bathroom?'

He led them through his house, flicking taps on and off and clicking remote controls of lights and blinds and screens into choreographed display. There were twin studies, a vast creamy bedroom with twin bathrooms, an exercise suite with every conceivable machine and a ship-sized deck with a spa tub overlooking the descending panorama of trees. There were pictures everywhere, covering the limited wall space, excellent modern pictures. Ed had a good eye.

Matt and Dinah tried not to look at each other because

28

they feared a descent into giggles. They suddenly felt like children, awed and irreverent in the face of such purchasing power. The house was beautiful, but in its sheer opulence and abundance it was also comical.

And yet, it was impossible not to like Ed himself. The energy of him was invigorating.

'Quite a place,' Matt murmured. Ed seemed to expect no more.

One corridor on the upper north side of the building was left unexplored. Dinah glimpsed at the end of it a door, firmly closed, and guessed that this must be Camilla's territory. Because every other nook and cranny had been so freely displayed and demonstrated, she was left with the sense of something brooding, almost sinister, contained within the open geometry of the house.

Ed led them away from the corridor without comment and back to the big room. Sandra was setting out food and cutlery on a huge refectory table in a slate-floored annexe.

'How are the drinks? Here, Matt, let me freshen you. What hardware have you got in that department of yours? Are we ready to eat, baby, those boys will be starving.'

'Yes, everything's ready,' Sandra said.

The boys came in from the pool table at the first summons.

'Where is she?' Ed growled. The creases in his face were no longer genial.

Sandra picked up an intercom and pressed a button.

'Milly? Brunch is ready, darling.' She replaced the handset. 'She's coming,' she said.

The six of them were standing behind their chairs, as if waiting to say grace.

A door slammed shut on another level. A moment later a girl appeared framed in one of the upper windows and stared down at them. There was a silence, and then an awkward clatter as they all pulled back their chairs and hurried to sit down. The girl was coming slowly down the stairs.

There was nothing pink or wobbly or plump about Camilla Parkes. Nothing so familiar or explicable.

She was thin and dark and her small pointy face was dead white. Her lustreless hair was matted and spiked and knotted into dreadlocks that hung around her cheeks and down her thin neck. Her eyes were painted with thick black lines and her mouth was outlined in vicious crayon. Her clothes were layers of shredded knits and torn and faded black drapes, and her spindly legs were thickened by black woollen tights with holes at the knees. On her feet she wore huge Doc Marten boots with steel toecaps. Her right nostril was pierced with two small silver rings.

Camilla did not look at any of them, or at Sandra's scrambled eggs and smoked salmon and bagels and the baskets artfully heaped with raisin breads and croissants. She went to the fridge and took out a small dish covered in clingfilm, tore off the film and screwed it into a ball and aimed it towards the sink. Then she sat down at the far end of the table and began to eat, spooning up a gluey mixture of rice and beans without lifting her eyes from the dish.

'Camilla is a vegan,' Sandra explained. 'Milly, please say hello to Professor and Mrs Steward.'

She raised her head briefly. Her eyes were full of anger.

'And this is Jack, and Merlin. Some company for you.'

Milly didn't favour the boys with so much as a glance.

'Where do you go to school?' Jack asked, refusing to be intimidated into silence.

'Milly doesn't go to school right now. A teaching assistant from UMass comes here to tutor her.'

Milly put down her spoon. There were dirty silver rings on every finger of both hands and her nails were painted black. She turned her burning stare on her mother.

'Why do you answer everything for me, as though I'm a moron? Why do you think I can't speak for myself?'

Her voice was pure glottal North London.

'If you can speak, why don't you?' It was Ed who asked, with surprising forbearance. There was a flush of colour mottling Sandra's lovely face.

Dinah had been watching Milly with terrible fascination,

half-greedy and half-apprehensive. But as soon as the child opened her mouth familiarity embraced her and Dinah smiled, without thinking.

'You make me remember London. It's like hearing a piece of home.'

Oh, what a crappy thing to say, she reproached herself immediately the words were out.

But Milly only shifted her gaze in her direction.

'Where you from?'

'London.'

'Yeah. London's okay.'

'Did you go to school there?'

'Camden. Only I got expelled.'

Dinah and Milly looked at each other. In the child's face as she made her boast Dinah read the habits of defiance and aggression, and also saw from the soft and uncontrollable pout of her lower lip that she was vulnerable, and deeply unhappy. Milly was very young, however hard she might try to pretend otherwise.

'Tough,' Dinah said.

But she was already becoming aware that Milly and her assumed disguise – fourteen-year-old part-punk, part-Goth and part-Dickens street-urchin – called on some hungry instinct ineffectively buried within herself. She was drawn to the child, and she also felt a cold stirring of fear brought on by the intensity of these feelings.

Merlin put down his bagel. 'Ben Burnham was expelled from my old school. He used the phone in the secretary's office to call the Fire Brigade. He told them the science room was on fire, and two fire engines came with ladders and hoses and about twenty firemen.'

The adults laughed and Jack sighed, but Milly gave no indication that she had heard the story. She ate the last grains of rice from her bowl and then left the table as silently as she had come. The tails of her wraps flapped behind her as she mounted the stairs and disappeared the way she had come.

31

'Do you see what I mean?' Sandra murmured to Dinah. 'Somehow it's easier just to let her . . .'

Ed shrugged and ran his fingers through his hair until it stood up in a rakish crest on top of his big round head.

'They're parents as well, honey. You wait, you guys,' he warned Dinah and Matthew. 'They get past twelve years old and all bloody hell breaks out.'

'I'm nearly eleven . . .' Jack said meaningfully.

The adults laughed again and the boys were given permission to go back to the pool table. Coffee was poured and the baskets of croissants passed round, and the mellow Sunday morning talk was resumed. From time to time Dinah found herself glancing upwards to the frame where Milly had first appeared in the half-apprehensive hope that she might materialise again. But she did not, and there was no sound or movement to indicate that she was even in the house.

After the meal Ed proposed a walk. He wanted to show the Stewards the full extent of the property, and some thinning and replanting that was under way in his woodland. Ed liked to be physically involved in the work. He emerged for the expedition in a lumberjack's coat and boots with a bow-saw slung over one shoulder. Sandra had already announced that she was not much of a walker, and would stay behind to have a nap.

Ed was leading the way through his woodland garden when an outer door slammed in the house. They all turned. Milly had put on a man's long tweed coat over her ragbag clothes. The afternoon was mild but she was wearing gloves with the fingers roughly sawn off and a shapeless knitted hat. The Dickens urchin effect was complete.

'Great,' Ed called to her. 'Glad you're coming. Which way shall we go, Deer Path or along the ski trail?'

'*I* dunno,' Milly shrugged. The route was of no interest to her. She stood pointedly waiting until her father and Matt and the boys moved on again. She was not quite looking at Dinah, but almost. Dinah resisted the urge to turn and look at whatever it might be in the air six inches to the left of her own head. Ed's voice faded in the distance. He was explaining something about cross-country skiing. The boys were running, chasing each other, their feet in the years' depths of dead leaves sounding like waves breaking.

'Shall we follow them?' Dinah asked.

'We'll have to, I suppose. I don't know the way, otherwise.'

The lack of familiarity with her own home ground was deliberate, Dinah thought. Milly didn't want to know this place.

They began to walk, not quite side by side, along a wide path through the trees. The air was still scented with resin and leaf-mould. Dinah imagined how if she were to be lifted up over the treetops she would see the undulating woodland stretching in every direction. She had seen a pattern of leaves, a carpet in chemical approximations of these colours, somewhere, a long way . . .

No.

She asked Milly, not waiting to consider her words, 'You live in London for part of the year, is that right?'

'Yeah.'

I won't make her talk if she doesn't want to. She may just want to walk, not necessarily with me. I'm glad she came out. The thoughts skittered through Dinah's head. She wanted Milly to continue beside her, not to frighten her off.

They continued in silence for perhaps a hundred yards. There were birds singing, and silver-barked birches with their leaves turning butter-gold.

'It's very beautiful here,' Dinah said quietly.

'I hate it.' Milly's voice was so low that it was barely audible.

Dinah waited, walking with her head bent and her eyes fixed on the path in order not to intrude on Milly.

'I hate it,' Milly repeated more loudly after a minute.

'Why?' Dinah ventured.

Milly stopped walking. She half turned and made an eloquent gesture of spreading her hands an inch, opening her hunched shoulders, twisting her head against the backdrop of gilded trees and china-blue sky. And at once Dinah had a sense of her isolation in this calendar landscape, sullen and trange, adrift from the chains of healthy high-school kids she had seen dismounting from the dog-nosed yellow State of Massachusetts school buses. Milly fierce and freaky. Lost and longing to be found. And yet, she was not so different from hundreds of kids in London. She was only so different here.

To Dinah's surprise, Milly suddenly smiled.

Her teeth were white and even, startlingly so as they appeared between the dark-painted lips. Her eyes slanted upwards, giving her a completely new expression of sceptical merriment.

'See?' Milly asked.

Dinah nodded. 'Yes. I suppose I do.'

It came to her that she recalled the familiarity of London and home for Milly, just as Milly did for her. They had recognised the exile in one another. They walked on, the distance between them perceptibly lessened.

'It will start snowing soon,' Milly remarked.

'Not that soon. Another two, maybe three months.'

'Then everyone will put on their ski-suits and start poling around the trails like these clockwork people, arms up and down, two, three, legs going like stupid machines.'

Milly's spidery black limbs jerked in cruel imitation and Dinah laughed at the image she conjured up.

'Cross-country skiing is harmless enough,' she protested mildly.

'It isn't just that, is it? It's the woods and the empty fresh air and the *kindness* and *health* and shitty peace and beauty of it all.'

'What would you like instead?'

Milly's second shrug was as expressive as the first.

'Decay,' she murmured gothically.

Merlin appeared ahead. He scuffled back towards them through the leaves and then stood in the middle of the path.

'What are you talking about?' He looked from his mother to Milly with a hint of jealous accusation. His round face was

34

shadowed. Milly ignored him, simply waiting for Dinah to deal with the interruption so they could resume their conversation. She was entirely focused on what interested her, and what was of no interest did not exist. Dinah reflected on this as she dealt with Merlin, and guiltily encouraged him to run on again to look for the men. She wanted to prolong this talk.

As soon as he was out of earshot Milly greedily reclaimed her attention. 'Why don't *you* like it here?'

'How do you know that?'

'Well, you *don't*, do you?'

Dinah sighed. 'I miss . . . threads, connections. Nothing very specific.' She could not explain, particularly she could not think of explaining to this child. Associations began to pile up, like nerve impulses behind the blocked synapses of denial.

'Just plain homesickness,' she offered lamely.

Milly walked with her hands in the pockets of her long coat. Her bottom lip stuck out; her expression was a young-old hybrid of disappointment and dismissiveness. Dinah saw that she had given an inadequate answer.'So what is it *you* miss?' she asked.

'Nothing. Well, everything. People, you know. Mates. That you can just be with and, like, not have to pretend to be someone else for half the time just because they think you ought to be different from the way you are. I've got friends in London, in Camden, who know me all the way through. Better than Sandra and Ed ever will. I'd rather be there with them than stuck here.'

The tone of her voice was withering.

'School friends?' Dinah asked. She felt sorry for Milly, cut off in the glass castle from children of her own age, with only her UMass tutor for company.

'God. I told you. I got expelled from Camden bloody School.'

'Why?'

Milly sniffed in exasperation. 'The usual shit. Smoking.

Language. Defacing school property. Bunking off. Violence to a member of staff. Actually it was only a ruler I smacked her with. Should have been an iron bar, really. Only I didn't have one in my pencil case.' There was a distinct note of pride in this recitation.

Dinah nodded. 'I see,' she said mildly.

Milly's voice softened. 'No, my mates are nothing to do with school. I met them down the Lock. I used to hang round there in the day, not being at school. They just do stuff, like, their own way. They've got a place they live in, near Chalk Farm. Caz, that's one of them, he's fixed it well up so there's water and heating and everything, not like some stinking squat. I'll move in there, soon as I'm old enough.'

'You aren't old enough yet.'

'Yeah. Thanks for the reminder. All I'm old enough for is either being towed round while Ed researches his crap books, or being left behind with some pain in the arse house-keeper. It's no wonder nothing worked out in school, really. I was always being taken out to go somewhere else, that they wanted.'

Dinah contemplated this opposing perspective on Milly's life.

'I can see that would be difficult.'

Milly shrugged. She stuck her hands deeper in her pockets and walked on, looking straight ahead, as if she had already given too much away.

Dinah tried one or two more conversational openings, but Milly did not respond. They walked the rest of the way in silence, but it was a companionable silence.

When they came back to the house, having made a wide arc through the unrelenting woodland, Ed was already waving at them from the deck, the bow-saw hanging over the other arm. Sandra was watching too. Her eyes flicked from Milly to Dinah. Milly veered away from Dinah.

'See you,' she muttered.

It might have been a threat or a promise. Her face was

closed up again, admitting nothing. She went up the steps, looking at no one, and vanished into the house.

The Stewards were ready to leave. The boys were already inside the Toyota and the adults gathered in a loose group beside it to exchange their goodbyes. Sandra stood beside Dinah.

'Thank you for taking such trouble with Milly.' The thanks sounded oddly formal.

'I liked her,' Dinah said.

'Did you?'

It was less than the truth, but even the mild assurance seemed to displease Sandra.

'She doesn't often go out for a walk. You were honoured,' Sandra told her.

'Great, great, we must do that,' Ed was saying to Matthew. 'I'll call you and we'll fix it.' He crossed in front of the Toyota to Dinah's side, taking something out of his wallet as he did so. Dinah watched him, noting the set of his head on his neck and the forward thrust of his chest and shoulders. He was a bully, she thought. An amiable one, but still a bully. She wondered how the Parkeses lived together when there was no call for the polish of hospitality.

Ed was talking to her. 'Di, you said you were thinking of looking for a job of some kind? Sounded like a good idea . . .'

They had discussed it, only very briefly, over lunch.

'Well . . .'

Ed had taken out a card. He passed it to her now through the open window. 'This woman's a good friend of mine, an employment consultant. Now, don't look like that. She's the best, and I'll call her about you. Go see her, won't you? Can't do any harm.'

'No, it can't do any harm,' Dinah agreed. It was not easy to deny Ed.

The car rolled down the driveway leaving the Parkeses with their arms around each other, waving, against the backdrop of their woodland castle. Dinah wondered if Milly was mutely watching from some window slit.

'I rather like Ed,' Matthew said. 'There's something about all that energy.'

Matt liked him because he reflected himself, Dinah thought. Matt was full of his own kind of energy, and he was capable of the same self-absorption.

'Odd child, wasn't she? Why do they let her behave like that? It's almost as if they're afraid of her, of what she might say or do.'

'Camilla-and-custard,' one of the boys murmured from the back of the car.

'Or the wild witch of the woods.'

Dinah thought of the streetwise shell and the vulnerable core she had glimpsed within the carapace of clothes and cosmetics, and suppressed her impulse to jump to Milly's defence.

'What did you talk to her about on the walk?'

'Home,' Dinah said.

Matt sighed. He would not pursue the conversation, and a space of silence admonished them both. Dinah stared ahead at the trees and the dipping road and then the gas stations and parking lots as they drove back into Franklin.

A little later, when the boys were back in school and her days were no longer superficially occupied with their needs and demands, Dinah crossed town in the Jeep on her way to an appointment with Ed's employment consultant. Dinah had concluded that it could not do any harm to see her, as Ed had pointed out at the beginning, and the woman had sounded pleasant and businesslike on the telephone. Dinah's résumé and some examples of her work were in the unfamiliar briefcase on the passenger seat beside her.

The town lay quiet under a pallid, sunless sky. The trees that lined Main Street brandished their fall colours, but less noticeably against the backdrop of dignified clapboard houses and the rosy brick-built façades across the green. The windows of some of the tackier shops were already displaying Hallowe'en masks and costumes. There was little traffic in

38

the wide streets and she arrived too early for her appointment. She parked the jeep and sat waiting, thinking.

There was an uncomfortable pressure weighing on her, and the sense of it made the colours of the day seem sickly and caused the clean resinous scent of the air to scrape in the back of her throat. Dinah felt that the gap between the capable laughing wife and mother she pretended to be and the real woman who crept within herself was growing wider and wider.

Only Matt sensed it, and she could barely talk to Matt at all.

She checked her watch again. Still a few minutes before time, but she needed to get out of the Jeep. She felt shut in, panicked by claustrophobia, fearful of the two women who slid uncontrollably apart beneath her skin.

She scrambled her belongings together and stepped out into the cool air. She dropped her purse and bent down to retrieve it, and as she straightened up again dizziness assaulted her.

Forcing herself to breathe evenly Dinah walked up the shallow steps to the door of the building. It was a new low-rise, with glass curtain-walls reflecting the whitish sky. Two men came out of the doors as she tried to go in and they glanced curiously at her as she edged past them.

The building was multi-occupied, there was a long list of tenants in the small lobby. Dinah searched for the consultant's name, reading the list twice before she located it.

It was a corner office on the second floor. In the little anteroom there were two chairs and a table with neatly arranged business magazines.

'Jenny shouldn't be more than a minute or two,' the consultant's secretary smiled. Dinah opened her briefcase and stared at the typed résumé in her lap. Who was this woman? Was this who she had once been, defined and held in place by these qualifications and this much work done?

She realised that she was looking past the sheets of paper at her own knees. They made bony protuberances under the matt black stuff of her leggings. Solid enough. Yet she was afraid to touch them in case her fingers met emptiness. The fear of it ballooned in her chest like nausea.

Dinah's head jerked up again and she focused on the view from the window. The buildings in the block opposite. A sugar maple, fire-tinted leaves. Back on Kendrick Dee Kerrigan would be laying out after-school bread and cookies in her kitchen. Nancy would be lifting her little girls out of the back of the station wagon, wondering as she did so if it was too early to have a glass of wine. Not knowing that Dinah was out she might well call over to see if she wanted to join her.

Normal things.

Were they normal, or did they seem strange to her only because of her distance from them?

Dinah straightened her legs. Her feet looked odd, disjointed.

Am I going mad?

'Hi. I'm Jenny Abraham.'

The consultant had emerged from her office, was holding the door open for Dinah. They shook hands and Dinah obediently followed her. She sat down in the chair facing the desk, fanning out the paper evidence of herself before handing it over for scrutiny.

'Thanks. That's all very professional-looking. I'll check through it in a moment, but we should talk a little first. It helps if I can get a kind of a feel for the person you are.'

Ms Abraham smiled encouragingly. They began to talk about the kind of work Dinah might do. Dinah knew that her body language was all wrong, but still she could not make herself unlock her knees and arms. She doubted that there was much in advertising outside New York or Boston, and even if there were there would surely be plenty of home-grown talent. Who would want a precarious Englishwoman? She wondered vaguely if she could teach. Almost everyone in Franklin seemed to be some kind of a teacher.

'Good. That's very interesting.' Jenny Abraham managed

to purse her lips and shake her head at the same time. She was writing busily in the spaces on a long form. The little stabs of her pen seemed sharp enough to puncture Dinah's skin. There was a big coloured Peanuts poster on the wall behind the woman's desk.

This was a bad mistake, Dinah was already thinking. Why had she let Ed Parkes bully her into it?

'Let's talk a little bit about the real you, Dinah.'

Ms Abraham leaned back in her swivel-chair and steepled her fingers.

'Tell me, what are you proudest of, amongst all your achievements?'

Dinah started to talk too quickly, to fend the woman off. The words came out jumbled up. She said something about a campaign for a children's charity she had once worked on and then contradicted herself, mentioning her boys, her family.

'And most ashamed of?'

No.

I should have heard that before she said it. I should have guessed it was coming and forestalled her.

Who is she, to sit in her big chair with a smile and eyes like glass chips and ask me about shame? It was only a job I wanted. Some little occupation to divert my mind. Perhaps make me feel fixed here like Matt, even Jack and Merlin, instead of skidding over some huge inhospitable polished surface with no landmark, no harbour.

Only there *is* no diversion. How could I have imagined there would be? I have to get away from here first. Then I can think.

Dinah made an answering smile, just by stretching her stiff lips. She leaned forward and took her papers off the woman's desk, squared them neatly by tapping the edges and slid them back into her briefcase.

She said, 'I'm sorry. I think I've been wasting your time. I don't really need a job. I've just realised.'

Somehow, she was standing up. Ms Abraham's face showed

a real expression, surprise. Dinah gathered her belongings awkwardly in her arms. Anger carried her out of the room and past the secretary in her cubicle, and back down in the elevator to the lobby. The Cherokee was where she had parked it, across the street.

She was driving, unseeingly following the route that led across town, before the fortifying anger drained away. It left her weak and disorientated so that she blinked through the windscreen at the white clapboarding of the Franklin Hotel on the south side of the green, and the line of cars waiting to turn at the lights. The driver of the station-wagon behind her hooted, and Dinah slid the Jeep into a parking space. She was shaking now.

Surging out of the dark place that she kept shuttered all her waking hours came a black wave of pain.

What was she ashamed of? That was what the woman had asked her. Not the woman's fault, of course. Just a crappy pop personality-test question to make everyone think they were getting a slice of a real person in the answer.

Dinah's hands gripped the steering wheel until the bones of her knuckles showed their reddened cleft. Shame and guilt were her constant companions. Sometimes they hid their faces, dissembling as craftily as she did herself, but still they were always with her.

She didn't see the fake-rustic Franklin Inn sign swinging in front of her eyes. Instead Dinah was thinking of home, picturing the rain-smeared streets of a small town in Norfolk. She had never even been there, although to hear its name or see it written made her catch her breath.

I have to go home, she said aloud, knowing that she must look like a madwoman mouthing in the sanctuary of her car. *I have to go back home and start searching.*

Matthew sat at the end of the big kitchen table with some papers spread out in front of him. The boys were in bed and the house was quiet except for Ape snoring and twitching in his basket under the window.

42

Matt liked this time of the evening. The day trailed in a wake behind him and there were still hours beckoning, subterranean chambers below the chipped surface of the working day, before he need think of bed. Matthew never slept before the small hours. There was too much else to do, to think about, to waste time on sleep. Dinah was different, always had been. She needed eight hours and firmly believed, like her mother, that one hour before midnight was worth two after.

Matthew was reading columns of figures, following a pattern through them that was as vivid to him as a picture. He didn't hear Dinah come in, but he looked up when she sat down in the chair opposite him. She was wearing her bathrobe, splashy red print on a white background.

'Hi.' He had been drinking a glass of wine, a Californian Cabernet recommended by Todd Pinkham. 'Want some of this?'

Dinah shook her head.

Resignedly Matt took off his reading glasses. 'Tell me about your day. What did happen with the job woman?'

He had asked the question earlier and she had turned it aside, pressing her lips into a thin suffering line as she did so.

'Nothing happened. I just decided it was a bad idea.'

'Okay, so don't talk about it.'

Irritated, although he had resolved that he would not be, Matt replaced his glasses and began reading again. He wanted to slip away from Dinah and the difficulty that she had become, and re-enter the cool lofty place in which she had disturbed him.

Dinah sat in silence. She was aware of the comfortable structure of their home enclosing them, filled with pictures and furniture and all the insulating drift of their joint possessions. How many things, she wondered, remembering the packing cases in which they had been shipped to Franklin. How many cups, and scarves, and books, and teapots.

Matthew turned a page. She watched the way he reached

43

out unseeingly for his glass, his fingers quivering a little until they connected with the stem.

Dinah looked at her husband and wondered, Do I love him or hate him? Did I do it alone, this thing, or did I do it because it was what Matt wanted?

'Matthew?'

He rubbed the inner corners of his eyes, sighing, working his middle fingers under the lenses so that the frame bobbed over his nose.

'Yes.'

'I'm all adrift here in this place. I want to go back home, to look for her.'

His face hardened. His flexible mouth became a slit and the planes of his cheeks and forehead turned boxy.

'You can't do that, Dinah. Why torment yourself?'

'Why not be like you, you mean? Indifferent?' Her voice whipped him.

'I'm not indifferent.'

The telephone rang. For three, four rings neither of them moved, and then Dinah slowly got up and lifted the receiver. Even from where he was sitting Matt could recognise Sandra Parkes's high insistent voice. Dinah listened as it nibbled on, saying yes, yes okay, nodding as she spoke.

'Of course we can,' she added at length. 'If Milly's happy with that we'd be glad to have her.'

There was another high-pitched torrent of talk. And then Dinah said, 'Friday, then. Yes, yes. That's fine.' She replaced the receiver.

'Ed and Sandra have got to go out to the coast for three days. Something to do with a movie deal for one of Ed's books. Sandra wondered if Milly could come to us.'

'I'm taking the boys up to the cabin in Vermont for the weekend. Had you forgotten?'

Max Berkmann had promised a loan of their summer cabin. Matt was going to take the boys fishing and hiking, although neither of them had shown much enthusiasm for the prospect.

'Yes, I had,' Dinah admitted. 'It doesn't matter. Milly and I will be okay here.'

She hesitated for a moment, but Matt was shifting his papers, ready to immerse himself in them again. He had closed off her plea with his hard face. Not now, she told herself. Don't try to talk about it now.

'I'm going up to bed,' she said at last.

'I'll be up soon,' he told her, although she knew he would not be.

Three

Dinah imagined that to have Milly in the house for two or three days would be to have a companion.

In the muffled, dead-weighted time after her visit to Jenny Abraham, Dinah planned how Milly and she would cook and talk and watch TV together, maybe even go shopping for clothes. Out of the brief affinity that had flickered between them she constructed in her head a temporary daughter and allowed herself awkward, unspecific imaginings in which Milly confided in her in some way, and she was able to offer advice and comfort.

Dinah looked forward to the weekend visit, and when the time came she confidently waved Matt and the boys off at the beginning of their drive up into Vermont.

'You won't be lonely?' Matt asked, as he was halfway into the loaded Toyota. 'You could still join us, you know. Bring the Parkes girl as well.'

'Milly. Her name's Milly. No, we're going to stay here and have a women's weekend.'

Matthew caught her chin in his hand and looked into her eyes.

After a minute he said, 'Good. You look all right.'

'Of course. Why not?'

After they had driven away Dinah went back into the house with the sense of having become someone who sometimes

46

did not look all right, as if another person's face had become superimposed upon her own.

Ed and Sandra arrived with Milly later that Friday evening. Milly unfolded herself from the back of the Porsche and hoisted a very small and shabby black canvas rucksack over her shoulder. She seemed to be wearing exactly the same clothes as the last time Dinah had seen her.

The adults moved into the house, with Milly at a little distance behind them. It was the first time the Parkeses had been to Dinah's house. Looking at his watch, Ed refused her offer of tea or a drink.

'We should get to the airport,' he said. Out of the corner of her eye Dinah saw Milly turn her head to gaze blank-faced out of the window. She had not put her rucksack down.

'Dinah, this is so good of you,' Sandra murmured, but the words were at odds with her expression. She stood awkwardly halfway between Ed and Milly, unable to move closer to either of them. Clearly it was important that she go with Ed to perform whatever service it was he required of her, but equally clearly she did not want to leave Milly behind with Dinah. Torn between the two halves of her family, Sandra's confusion crystallised in hostility to Dinah. She twisted the silver bracelets on her wrist as if adjusting her armour. Her face was cramped with jealousy. 'I wanted Milly to come to LA with us, of course. But she absolutely won't.'

Milly continued to stare in the opposite direction, her rucksack clutched against her chest. Dinah guessed that Milly knew exactly how to cause dismay and discord at home. She wondered what it was the child wanted to punish her parents for.

But she only said, 'I've been looking forward to it. We'll have a good time, the two of us.'

'Sure you will,' Ed said heartily. 'Now, come on, honey. You know the Friday traffic.'

They went out into the street again, Milly trailing in her heavy boots, the embodiment of sulky reluctance. Dinah suppressed a sudden urge to turn round and shake her. The child was getting what she apparently wanted, after all.

Ed and Sandra both kissed Milly, who did not return their embrace. The Porsche cleared its throat, over-loud in the quiet of the street, and swung away towards Boston and the airport.

Milly tilted her head, and the black knotted strands of hair fell back to show her white neck.

'Your house is the same as all the others.'

Without looking Dinah saw the various white wooden houses with green-painted shutters, porches and steps, old Mr Dershowitz's at the end shabbier than the others, and grass dotted with shrubs and trees. She felt no more fixed in this serene suburbia than she had done a year before.

'Similar. We can't all live in fantasy castles in the woods, can we? You're welcome here, anyway.'

'Yeah,' Milly said.

'Is all your stuff in that one bag?'

'Stuff?'

'Everything you need for the weekend.' Change of clothes, washbag, book, cosmetics. Middle-aged baggage, crap, is that what you'd call it?

A shrug. 'Yeah.'

Milly followed her into the house. Dinah led her through the rooms, showing her the place where she would sleep, the boys' playroom, the bathroom. Milly dropped her little bag on her bed and sat down, barely rippling the smooth white cover. She stared out of the window into the steely blue twilight.

'I'll leave you to sort yourself out,' Dinah said. 'I'll be downstairs making some supper, when you're ready.'

Milly reappeared a little later. She leaned in the kitchen doorway with her thin arms wrapped across her chest, defensive.

'There's no TV.'

'Yes, there is. Through there, in the den. I showed you.'

'In my room.'

48

Dinah had forgotten her moment of irritation. She considered her present urge to propitiate this child, to move televisions and rearrange her house, so that in return she would smile and talk and look upon her as a friend.

'No. We don't let Jack and Merlin watch in their bedrooms. If we did, they'd never do anything else. Switch it on now in the den, if you want. Are you ready to eat? It's pizza.'

'I don't eat pizza.'

'Four-cheese and tomato. I know you're a vegetarian.'

'Vegan.'

For God's sake, Dinah thought. 'So what do you eat?'

'Rice. Pulses. Fruit. Tofu.'

There was a distant clicking sound and then a skidding rush as Ape emerged from his lair in the utility room. He stopped short when he saw Milly and his legs stiffened as he launched into a volley of barking. A thin thread of spittle roped down from his furious jaws. Milly scrambled away from him, almost falling, and wedged herself behind the table. Her lips went white, making their dark crayon outlining bloom lividly.

She's afraid of the dog, Dinah thought. She's a scared little girl.

'Ape, quiet. Sit now. Dead dog. He's quite all right, Milly. Ugly but harmless, look.'

The dog subsided, sighing and panting. Dinah went to Milly and put her hand on her shoulder to reassure her, drawing her closer in a half-hug. Her fingers felt prominent bones through the layers of matted wool.

'I hate dogs,' Milly snapped.

'So did I, as it happens. Ape belongs to the boys. Shall I cook you some brown rice? If that's all you eat it's no wonder you're thin, but . . .'

Milly wrenched away from her. Her eyes glittered between the hanks of hair. 'Why do you think you can touch me? What gives you the right to make personal remarks about me?'

An answering spurt of anger burned in Dinah for an instant. They looked at each other, bare-faced, waiting.

'I'm sorry,' said Dinah. She dragged Ape away by the collar and shut him in the utility room. Milly trailed off into the den and watched a game show on television while Dinah cooked her food. She could see through the open door that Milly was curled up with her boots resting on the cushions.

When it was ready she ate the plain rice and then a banana, but she deflected all Dinah's attempts at conversation while she did so. They finished the meal, picking at their opposing dishes in silence.

'Shall we go out and see a movie?' Dinah suggested when the plates had been cleared away.

Milly's black mouth twitched with a suggestion of sarcastic amusement. 'Thanks, but no. You go, if you want.'

'I can hardly go out and leave you here alone, can I?'

She stared. Her eyes were black-painted and the lashes were thickly spiked with mascara. Dinah noticed for the first time the colour of her irises, a pale greenish hazel. 'Why not?'

'Because I told Sandra I'd look after you.'

Another shrug, dismissing her. 'Well, okay. That's between the two of you. I'm going upstairs.'

She went, closing the door with a snap. Dinah sat on at the kitchen table, listening to Ape lumbering about in the confined space between the washing machine and the boiler. She imagined that Milly would be sitting on the unfamiliar bed, arms wrapped around her knees. She wanted to go up and tap on the door, open it and slip into the room and perch on the bed beside her, to twist a blade between the clamped halves of Milly's shell and prise it open so that the child could be reached.

Another voice, a colder tone of her own inner monologue warned her, It isn't Milly who needs that. It's you.

Dinah pressed her knuckle against her mouth. Her thoughts tipped sideways and away from her. Thetford. England. A house, probably on an estate somewhere.

50

Another bedroom, a child's room with animal posters and family photographs. Not her family.

The telephone rang. Dinah lifted it and heard Nancy's voice.

'Hi. Listen, Linda and Maria are coming over for a drink and a sandwich. We thought we might play a couple of hands of poker or something dumb like that. Want to join us since you're a free woman?'

'I can't. I'm not. I've got Milly Parkes staying the weekend, Ed and Sandra have gone to LA.'

'Sweet Jesus, rather you than me.'

Is this what I'd rather? Dinah wondered, as she hung up. Rather a clumsy attempt to bond with another woman's child, who looks at me as if she despises me?

When she went up to bed the closed door of Milly's room confronted her. She hesitated briefly and then silently eased it open. Milly was asleep, lying on her side with the covers pulled tightly up around her. Her face looked younger, smoothed out by sleep. There were streaks of black eyepaint on the white pillowcase.

In the morning Dinah was downstairs early. She loaded the washing machine and fed Ape, promising that she would take him out for a proper walk later. Perhaps Milly would want to come, and they could take one of the paths that led through the woods beside the Franklin river. It was another white-skied day, but perceptibly colder than it had been. Bare fingers of branches were beginning to show through the burst of fall colour, and waves of burnt-out leaves accumulated beneath the trees.

The morning crept on, until Dinah had done all her usual chores and found herself some extra ones as well. When she looked out into Kendrick she saw that most of the driveways were empty; everyone had gone off about their Saturday morning business. There was no sound from upstairs. The silence of the house began to oppress her. She felt confined and then, with a sudden clap within her head, anxious for

Milly. Of course she couldn't be asleep all this time. Some-thing must be wrong.

She ran up the stairs two at a time and rapped on the closed door.

'Yeah.'

Milly was sitting on the bed, fully dressed. Clearly she had been staring vacantly out of the window. Dinah wondered for how long. She had preferred to sit alone in an empty spare room rather than come downstairs and seek Dinah's company.

The evaporation of her anxiety fuelled another spurt of anger, a stronger flame than last night's.

'Why didn't you come down? Don't you want any breakfast?'

Milly regarded her, judging the effects of her behaviour.

'What is there? Pizza?'

'Brown bloody rice and bananas, if that's what you want.'

'No thanks.'

'Milly, what's the matter? You must eat something. I don't want to force you into anything . . .'

'You couldn't. Don't bother to try.'

'. . . but you're here, and I'm responsible for you for this time, and it would make it pleasanter for us both if you were co-operative.' *I sound like the mother in some nineteen-fifties radio drama. We haven't even got a common language.*

There was no answer. Milly's eyes wandered back to the window. Dinah made a last attempt, breathing through the rising waves of her irritation.

'Come downstairs. Have some breakfast and then we'll go and buy tofu and mung beans. We can take Ape for a walk by the river. Or drive over to Northampton, there's a shop there . . .'

Milly leaned forward on the bed. One knee protruded through a hole in her black knitted leggings. Her chin jutted out as her gaze swerved back to Dinah.

'What do you *want?* Do you need some kind of a doll that

52

you can take out for walks and dress up in frocks and tip upside down to say *Mama*?'

Dinah's heart knocked in her chest, squeezing the breath against her ribs. 'Why are you so rude?'

'Is it rude to say what you think?'

'Yes. Don't you know that?'

She turned and left the room, aware that Milly was testing her for something, and that she was failing miserably.

It was another hour before Milly came downstairs. She skirted around Ape and made for the kitchen. She found the bread and cut herself two doorstep slices, then smeared them thickly with raspberry jelly. She wouldn't talk, although Dinah offered her the most neutral of openings. She turned on the television and sat in front of it, her eyes fixed on the screen as if to let them wander elsewhere would be to betray vulnerability. Dinah couldn't persuade her to leave the house, and Ape's demands for exercise were becoming impossible to ignore. In the end Dinah took the dog for a walk and left her.

It was a raw afternoon with a taste of fog in the air. Ape ploughed through the undergrowth beside the river path while Dinah shivered and stared into the grey-white rush of water. She was glad when the moment came to turn back towards Kendrick Street. There were plenty of logs on the back porch. If she lit the fire perhaps Milly might even enjoy something improbable like toasting marshmallows.

As soon as she came back into the house she sensed that Milly's mood was different.

She was waiting in the kitchen, holding back the knots of her hair with one hand so that her face was completely exposed. It was small, triangular, almost pretty under the disfiguring paint. The silver rings in her nose glinted.

'You were gone a long time.'

'Only an hour.'

'Seemed like longer.' Milly's eyes were very bright.

'Glad you missed me. Would you like some tea?' There was

something different about the kitchen, a detail that Dinah couldn't quite place.

'Nah. I thought I'd go out for a bit.'

'Out?'

'That's right. See some friends. You know? Be back later.'

'Milly, I can't let you do that. You're not old enough to go wandering off on your own in the dark. Wait. I'll drive you, if you're going to someone's house, if you'll tell me who so I can call the parents first . . .'

Milly grinned. 'No thanks. Don't need a chaperone. I can look after myself. Promise.'

'That's not the point. I promised Sandra I would look after you.'

Milly was demonstrating deafness. She had her satchel slung over her shoulder, was moving towards the door. Dinah scrambled after her, realising that the child would walk out. She caught hold of her arm and tried to pull her back. At the same time the detail that had nagged at her revealed itself. Matthew kept three bottles on a small wooden tray at the far end of the work surface, one of gin, one of whisky and one of vodka. The vodka bottle was missing.

'Have you been drinking?'

The shrug inflamed Dinah. Her grip on Milly tightened and the child began to struggle in her grasp. Her arms felt like sticks, but she was surprisingly strong.

'You can't keep me here.'

They were wrestling in earnest now, Dinah's hands clamped around Milly's wrists. It was absurd to fight with her, as well as misguided, but Dinah's sense of proportion deserted her in a tide of panic that burst out of some closed reservoir within herself. They lurched backwards, struggling against each other.

With Milly's weight falling on her the edge of the worktop dug into Dinah's side, winding her.

She would not be able to hold her much longer. Milly would break free; she would disappear. The knowledge was fearful and the fear came out of somewhere long ago, unacknowledged and more terrifying for it.

Dinah felt that she would choke. She realised that she was crying.

'That fucking hurts,' Milly spat at her, enraged. She disengaged one leg, drew it back and kicked Dinah square in the shin with her steel reinforced toecap.

Dinah yelped in pain and at the same time Milly ducked her head and bit hard into the back of Dinah's hand. Dinah jerked the bitten hand to her mouth and swung out with the other. She slapped Milly satisfyingly across one cheek, and was rewarded by a flash of astonishment and respect in her pale eyes before fury blotted out everything else.

'You hit me.'

'Milly, I'm sorry, I shouldn't have done that . . .'

Milly was out of her grasp and she darted away while Dinah hesitated. The kitchen door slammed and an instant later the front door swung and banged shut on its troublesome spring. Ape barked at the empty air in Milly's wake.

Dinah walked slowly across the hallway to the front door. It seemed to vibrate still with the force of the crash. It was dark outside, and Kendrick was deserted. Milly had vanished. I should run after her, Dinah thought. I should catch her and bring her back.

But she only checked the door, making sure that it was on the latch so that Milly could come in again when she was ready. Dinah couldn't chase after her now, for even if she caught up with her she would not be able to force her to come back. She had been clumsy enough for one day.

In the den, on a low table beside the dented sofa cushions, Dinah found the vodka bottle. The level in it, as far as she could remember, had hardly dropped at all. Bravado, Dinah thought. A child's bravado. She sat down and rested her head against the cushions. The back of her right hand showed an inflamed ring of crimson teethmarks.

Ape heaved himself on to the sofa beside her, and Dinah

twisted her fingers in his rough coat. She sat and waited for Milly to come back again.

As the time crept by Dinah dismembered their argument over and over again in her mind. She was shamed by the evidence that she had done everything wrong. She had let her own needs and anxieties bleed out into her dealings with Milly. Where she should have been detached she had been demanding. Instead of encountering a cool, dispassionate adult Milly had met a creature as unstable as herself.

With a shiver of fear, Dinah realised that the tight seals she had kept on the past were straining and threatening to give way. At home in England she had been able to contain herself with familiarity and routine. But in Franklin she was out of her place and adrift, and her awareness of this intensified with time rather than diminished.

Then Milly had come, and her age and her fury and fragility had all touched a rawness and longing in Dinah that was frightening, and always increasing, and now threatened to overwhelm her.

Dinah grew cold and stiff with sitting. She stood up and walked the length of the room and back, and the dog raised its head to look irritably at her. It was two, nearly three hours since Milly had run out of the house. The night was bitter, and she had been wearing only the usual layers of ragged woollens. Where had she gone? Was she outside in the darkness, wandering by herself, or was she in some dangerous warm place, shut in and at even greater risk?

She was only fourteen. A child, a little girl. Her responsibility, entrusted to her.

Dinah ran to the front door and jerked it open. Cold air met her, and the scent of woodsmoke, and the sight of the cosy curtained windows of her neighbours' houses. The wind carried the irregular hum of distant traffic.

She closed the door again, pressing the night away behind it. Denied images rose up before her eyes, making her roll her head in an effort to dispel them. None of her old methods of deflection would work any longer, because Milly had unlocked the sealed place.

Dinah ranged through the rooms of the house, looking for somewhere to hide and collect herself, but there was nowhere. The tidy defences of possessions and pictures and an ordered life looked irrelevant now. Guilt emerged from its lair as tangible as another human being until she thought that she could hear its breathing, smell the rankness of its sweat.

She could stay in the house no longer, she would have to get away from this foetid personification. She snatched a coat from its peg and pulled it on. She called to Ape and he came bounding eagerly towards her. The sight of him gave her an idea and she ran up the stairs to Milly's room. At first it looked bare of her minimal possessions, but then she saw a frayed and shapeless garment discarded on a chair. Dinah bore it downstairs, and gave it to Ape to sniff.

'Find her,' she ordered. 'Seek, there's the boy.'

When she opened the door for him he set off up Kendrick, tail waving like a plume. Dinah ran behind him.

The dog thought it was a good game. He ran in a diagonal line across Pleasant, and plunged into the dark area between two houses. Dead leaves crackled under Dinah's feet as she followed him. There were garage doors with basketball hoops, fences and paved yards and silent porches. Ape ran her until she was gasping for breath and then circled back to twist between her legs, panting and slobbering. She could have kicked him for his amiable stupidity. Milly was nowhere in these quiet streets, why should she be? The peaceful sub-urban darkness only emphasised her fears. But still she walked on, with the dog now scuffling at her side. She threaded up and down the neighbouring streets, peering at each house as her shadow reached ahead of her and then fell back again between the blue-white auras of the street lamps.

Dinah knew that she could walk all night and not have a hope of discovering where Milly might be.

A need to return home as urgent as the one that had driven her out took hold of her. She swung round and began to walk, faster and faster until she was running, into Kendrick and across the grass to the steps of her house. The door was still on the latch, as she had left it. She knew as soon as she stumbled inside that Milly had not returned.

It was after midnight.

Dinah picked up the phone and dialled the Parkeses' home number. The answering machine picked up, Ed's confident voice. If Milly was there she wouldn't answer. Dinah quickly hung up.

Whom to call? The Parkeses were staying at the Bel Air Hotel, Ed had told her that twice and Sandra once. Not yet. She couldn't call them yet.

The police? What to say, that a difficult teenager had banged out of the house to sulk for a few hours?

Matthew?

No, not Matt. Not Matt, most of all.

Dinah went into the kitchen and slowly, deliberately made herself a cup of tea. As an afterthought she tipped a measure of Scotch into it. She stood by the uncurtained window and stared out into the darkness of the yard as she drank the peaty tea. She began to see faces other than her own mirrored in the black glass.

At one a.m. she called Nancy Pinkham. Nancy answered the phone after two rings but her voice was thick and bewildered with sleep.

'I know I've woken you up,' Dinah said.

'I'll be right over,' Nancy answered, when she had explained.

Ten minutes later she was sitting in Dinah's kitchen in her blue terry robe. She drank the whisky that Dinah poured for her and rubbed her smeared eyes.

'Listen, don't you worry. Not yet, anyhow. I'm certain the kid will be back when she's ready, when she thinks she's done enough mischief. Don't you think?'

Dinah nodded, Nancy's prosaic common sense like a buoy to catch at in a riptide.

'Yes, I guess so. But I'm so scared something's happened to her, that it's my fault . . .'

'Sure you are. Who wouldn't be, with any imagination? But it isn't your fault, okay? The kid's a monster, how can you be responsible for that?'

'She isn't, it's not that . . .'

Nancy took her arm and the whisky bottle and drew them into the den.

'We'll just make ourselves comfortable here and wait for madam to get back.' She looked shrewdly at Dinah as they both sat down. 'I'm more worried about you than her.'

They drank some whisky. Nancy punched the television remote and found an old Clint Eastwood movie that had only just begun. They watched it to the end and then dozed a little in the grey light from the screen.

Dinah woke up with a shudder. The television light had been replaced by the beginnings of daylight, and Nancy was standing over her.

'She's back. Coming down the road, large as life.'

Dinah jumped up. Through the window she saw Milly swinging up the path to the porch steps. She looked no more dishevelled than usual.

'Where've you been? Do you know we've sat up all night, you thoughtless little tramp?'

It was Nancy who began shouting as soon as the door opened. Dinah had never seen her so angry. 'How d'you think Dinah felt? If you were mine, I can tell you, I'd cane your ass.'

Milly walked straight past her into the kitchen.

'Shit. I'll leave you to it,' Nancy muttered. 'If there's nothing else I can do?'

'Nothing. Thanks, Nancy. You're a good friend.'

'Do the same for me sometime. Although, Jesus, if Laura and Brooke turn out like her . . .'

Milly scowled in the kitchen when Dinah came wearily in.

59

'Go on, then.'

'Go on where?'

'Say your piece, like mother tightarse out there.'

The softness of relief was wrapping itself around Dinah. The kitchen and its everyday instruments looked sweet and wholesome in the strengthening light.

'I wasn't going to say anything. Only that I'm pleased you've come back.'

Milly suddenly smiled, the merry upward-slanting smile that transformed her face. Her shoulders dropped and her head lifted. 'Well, great. Yeah. Thanks.'

Dinah wanted to hug her, but remembered in time that Milly didn't like to be touched. She asked her instead if she was hungry.

'Starving.'

'There are some English muffins.'

'Why are they called English? They aren't *English*, are they, they're bloody American.'

Dinah toasted the muffins and spread jelly on them. She made rosehip tea and gave Milly a mug, and Milly wrapped her black-varnished fingers greedily around the warmth. Dinah noticed for the first time a clumsy tattooed flower in the vee between her thumb and forefinger.

'Did you go to friends?' she asked at length, when Milly had drunk two mugs of tea and eaten the muffins.

'What?'

'You said you were going to see some friends. Last night, before you went out.'

'I haven't got any friends here.'

She said it coolly without inviting sympathy but Dinah's heart still twisted for her.

'So where did you go?'

'I walked around a bit. Then I remembered some people Sandra and Ed know, across the other side of Main Street, they've got, like, this big barn thing at the side of their house. They keep all the garden furniture and stuff in it. The door wasn't locked so I just went in and slept on a kind of padded seat thing. It was fine. I can look after myself.'

'Yes, I suppose you can.'

Milly was studying her tattoo.

'I'm sorry about last night, right?'

'I'm sorry I slapped you. I shouldn't have done.'

Milly laughed. It was the first time Dinah had heard her laugh and it was as attractive as her smile.

'Actually that was kind of funny. It felt like we were two kids fighting. Let's have a look.'

Dinah realised that she meant the bite on her hand. Obligingly she held it out to show the red weal. Milly sighed.

'Maybe you should get a tetanus shot. You know, I asked Sandra if she could fix it for me to come here this weekend. After that time I met you I thought you were kind of okay, and I liked you. Only when I like someone I can't believe they could like me or anything because I'm so shitty, and then I have to be like, really as bad as I can be so they *won't* like me and then everything's sort of proved for me so that I don't have to *speculate*.'

It was the speculate that touched Dinah. With an effort to find the right neutral voice she said, 'I think I understand. But why were you so determined not to go to LA with your parents?'

'Because that's what they always *do*. Or what he does and she lets him do. He just announces that we're going somewhere, to suit him, and up and off we go. Franklin, Zermatt, London, back to bloody Franklin. For his writing. As if it's some kind of art, instead of crap paperbacks with swastikas on the front.'

Milly paused, trying to arrange her words. 'And it's like, that's how she needs it to be. She wants him to act that way so she can, I don't know, accommodate him. It's like a deal between them.'

Yes, Dinah thought. That's what it's like. We all have our different deals.

'Anyway, I didn't want to be taken like some parcel and left to sit in a hotel. I thought of asking to come here. Like I said. I do like you.'

And showing her liking, however grudgingly, was an added way of attacking Sandra. Milly was no fool.

'Thank you,' Dinah said. She would not make the mistake of offering clumsy reciprocal assurances just yet. The conversation was about what Milly thought and felt.

'Is there any more tea?'

'I can make some.'

While her back was turned Milly said, in a rush of words, as if she wanted to get it out while no one was looking at her,

'I'm adopted, you know. They couldn't have any kids of their own so they got me.'

Dinah moved carefully, not letting her surprise show. She put down the refilled teapot and took her place again opposite Milly at the table.

'I didn't know that.'

Sandra might have told her, she realised, that day in the café-bar. But somehow the as-yet unmade friendship had developed a flaw, like a pattern going awry. They had become suspicious instead of intimate.

She thought of Ed and Sandra and their castle in the woods, but a different perspective made them seem smaller, farther off, while new questions and associations hung between Milly and herself, pricking her, hooking into her skin.

'Yeah. They told me all that shit when I was a kid, they talked about it all the time in churchy voices, about how I'm special. They got me from the adoption services in London. Specially chosen, they wanted me so much, you know? I never believed a word of it. I don't think they do nowadays, either. How could they, seeing what they ended up with was me?'

The small pale face with the angry make-up mostly rubbed away by the night in a barn. The lower lip pushed out, simultaneously aggressive and tremulous. Eyes fixed on Dinah's face, greedy for attention and affection and reassurance, as well as routinely defiant. Another woman's child, her history compacted within her. God forgive me, Dinah thought.

'I had a daughter too.'

Milly gaped at her, silenced for once.

'She's fourteen, the same as you. Only I haven't seen her since she was a little baby. I gave her up for adoption.'

There was a long pause. Milly picked reflectively at the smaller of her nose rings, turning it in its reddened puncture. Dinah could almost follow her thoughts down through their faltering spirals. Finally she breathed the question,

'Are you saying, like, *I* could be your daughter?'

'No. I know you couldn't be.'

'How do you? Why did you have her adopted? Was she, kind of, somebody's she shouldn't have been?'

'No. She was Matthew's baby too.'

It had been a long time, such a very long time since Dinah had allowed herself the luxury of words to vent the pressure. Silence had contained everything like a cold crust over molten liquid. She felt the pressure increasing, cracking the crust and pushing words into her mouth. They were ready to spill out of her mouth now. It was wrong that it should be Milly to hear them, Milly with her own pressing needs. Wrong, but right also.

'Why, then?'

Dinah turned her head. Through the window she saw the Berkmanns driving off to their Sunday morning tennis game. Kendrick Street, Franklin, Massachusetts, coming alive once more.

'I'll tell you, if you like.'

'Yeah. I'd like. Make a change from going on about me.'

Awkwardly at first, then fast, Dinah began to talk.

Four

'When Matthew and I were first married we lived in a flat, a rented flat over a greengrocer's shop,' Dinah said.

How had he changed, since that time? What had brought them both from that time to this?

He was thinner in those days, of course, with coathanger shoulders and a limited wardrobe of jeans and frayed shirts invariably topped with a leather jacket. Laughing was how she remembered him; he put his head back and shoved his fists downwards in his pockets, and his jaw dropped open as he gave himself up to a startling eruption of noise. It made people look round in pubs, Matthew's laugh.

What had amused them so much, all that time ago?

Eccentricities; their own as much as other people's. The small comedies of ordinary life. Relief, after some threatened crisis.

There was one time when the two women in the flat upstairs let their bath overflow. The water came pouring through the ceiling, bringing a great scab of soaked plaster down with it on to Matthew and Dinah's bed. Matthew had been hauling at their sodden bedclothes and shouting in rage at the exposed wet-black laths and floorboards overhead, until he caught sight of his red face in the wardrobe mirror and the imprecations curdled in his throat.

'You pair of mad tarts,' he was yelling, 'you stupid snot-brained couple of cripples . . . don't you know how a *tap* works? You turn it bloody round and the wet stuff stops gushing out before it pisses down all over my bloody *bed* . . .'

Dinah was already laughing. Matthew choked on his fury and his fist punched weakly at the pillow he was holding, and then he crumpled backwards on to the mess of the sheets. Clods of plaster pasted themselves to his sweater as he rolled over, coughing and gasping for breath through the convulsions of laughter.

When they had recovered themselves a little they hauled the mattress off the bed and leaned it against the wall to dry. Then Matthew marched Dinah off to a hotel two streets away. It had seemed very grand because there were white towelling bathrobes and a mini-bar stocked with tiny bottles, and they knew it was way beyond anything they could rightfully afford.

'Don't even look in that mini-bar,' Matthew had ordered. 'See this?'

He had stuffed their overnight belongings into two Tesco carrier bags. From the heavier one he produced two bottles of Rioja.

In the swish mirrored bathroom they filled the bath with scented water and lay in it to drink the wine. Afterwards they went to bed, and watched the coupled reflections of themselves in more mirrors.

Dinah remembered that their conjoined skin looked very pale, young and unblemished, almost greenish in the thin light.

Later Matthew had managed to claim back from their insurers the cost of that night and the next in the hotel. That was like him: the initial bold manoeuvre followed by prudent consolidation.

Their world seemed a benign and sunny place in those days. The Stewards lived in the cramped flat on almost no money, and gazed ahead at an infinite vista of possibilities.

And since then, Dinah thought, between then and now, a narrowing and hardening had taken place. The view had been cut off, as if the two of them had walked into the wide mouth of a tunnel. Then the passage had slowly but steadily closed in, and darkened, until they reached this single point, the present.

The present, in which the past and its contracts were embedded so deeply that the scar tissue of normality had long ago closed over them. Dinah thought of the thin red line of a surgical incision, and the exposure of raw flesh beneath.

'Just two rooms, really,' she said, catching herself before the associations ran on and dried the voice in her throat. She would talk, just letting the words come out.

Milly was watching her, not scraping a knife or twisting her hair or picking at her nose-rings, but sitting still, listening.

It had been cramped and noisy, the flat. There was traffic in the street below, day and night. In the evenings when the greengrocer's shop closed, a metal shutter rolled down with a melancholy roar. The pavement outside the door was often a mess of cabbage stalks and soaking wisps of royal blue tissue paper in which satsumas or Golden Delicious apples had once nested. Sometimes the sad-looking wife of the Greek shopowner came out with a yard broom and swept up.

There was nowhere for Matthew to work in the evenings except at the same table where they had eaten their supper. They would clear away the dishes, and then he could spread out his papers. If he was concentrating particularly hard Dinah withdrew into the bedroom and sat on the bed, knees drawn up, to watch their temperamental black-and-white television or read a book.

When Dinah came out of the bedroom and found Matthew still working she would put her hands on the bony ridges of his shoulders and lean over to look at what he was doing. With her cheek resting against his head she thought, *We have everything, we can do whatever we want. Anything is possible.*

She loved him simply and entirely, and she knew that he loved her in the same way.

66

He would tell her, absently, 'I just want to do this.'

His Manchester accent was still noticeable in those days. It had almost gone now, unconsciously obliterated by years in the south, by years of association with people whose backgrounds were different from his. The flat vowels only came out when he was tired, or angry.

Dinah would nod, pat his shoulder and go on into the kitchen to make tea, leaving him to it. Matthew always worked hard, he had never been any different. He had the ability to concentrate when he wanted to, so that nothing could intrude upon him.

He had worked his steady way through school, the comprehensive in Salford, doing his homework at the kitchen table in his parents' semi, oblivious to his surroundings, much as he worked now while Dinah watched television in their bedroom. Then there was a first-class degree in chemistry from Manchester University, followed by postgraduate research. After his doctorate he had spent three years at the Laboratory of Molecular Biology in Cambridge, working on DNA sequencing under Sanger's direction. Dinah didn't meet him until he came to London, but she felt that she knew the eager, absorbed Matthew of those days as intimately as any of the later versions. He often talked about Cambridge as the most stimulating time of his working life. She could imagine how fervently he had worked, excited by sharing his ideas in a place where even the refectory was equipped with blackboards for the scribbling of spur-of-the-moment formulae.

After Cambridge there had been University College, London. Matthew and Dinah had met in his first week there, introduced at an unpromising party by a cousin of his who worked at Dinah's ad agency.

With a heavy teaching load as well as his own research Matthew worked like no one Dinah had ever met before. She was accustomed to her own business, where in the seventies work often meant lunch. Within a short time Matthew was heading his own research team at UCL.

67

But it would be a mistake, an underestimate, to assume that Matthew achieved his successes simply through application. Matthew never wasted effort, and he never lost sight of his main objectives in a fog of detail. He was capable of looking beyond the known horizon, making imaginative conceptual leaps that linked facts to bold theories in beautiful arcs of conjecture. As a research scientist it was his imagination that made him special. Dinah loved him for that imaginative power, and for his intellectual boldness, and his single-mindedness. Matthew never let anything stand in his way.

When they married, within a year of their first meeting, Dinah was working as a very junior copywriter. Always, from the time of their first date, the differences in their working lives were part of the currency of laughter between them. Matthew would try to explain his latest data, his search for non-random associations that might yield the beginning of a pattern and then the solution to some biochemical conundrum, and in turn Dinah would regale him with her creative team's current struggle to devise an arresting sanpro or lager campaign. It amused them to pretend incomprehension of one another's business because this arbitrary distance only intensified their closeness. They were certain that they fitted one another exactly.

It was Dinah's earnings from lager and tampon ads that enabled them to buy their first house; she earned more money in those days than Matthew did.

They agreed that they needed a bigger space than the flat over the greengrocer's, and it did not take long for them to find what they could afford, just. The two-up and two-down house stood in the middle of a red brick terrace in Finsbury Park, not far from the Arsenal ground. On Saturday afternoons they could hear the huge, single-throated bass howl of the crowd bursting and subsiding like the voice of some beast in its lair. Afterwards the streets at either end of their little road would fill up with red rivers of supporters chanting their way home. Matthew and Dinah both liked the flavour this proximity gave to the drab area. When Manchester United were away to Arsenal, Matthew would go to the game himself.

During the rest of the week the house and the street were quiet. Their neighbours were either old people who had lived there for a long time, and reminisced about the Blitz and sheltering in the Underground and piano singsongs in the pubs, or else they were young couples like themselves, busy with daytime jobs and evenings and weekends of house restoration.

Dinah and Matthew worked on their house too. They stripped off the woodchip paper to reveal the shaky plasterwork beneath, and sanded clotted gloss paint off doors and window frames. Matthew was surprisingly deft with a plane and saw. The dovetail joints he made dovetailed perfectly and the screwheads were countersunk. He worked in shirt-sleeves, whistling, and at times Dinah was surprised to recognise that he looked and sounded like his father at home in Salford.

Piece by piece, cupboards and shelves were constructed to hold their books and clothes and saucepans, walls were painted and secondhand or Habitat furniture was arranged in the rooms.

The house filled up with people. They seemed to have hundreds of friends in those days. Sometimes it took no more than a convivial evening in a pub or in someone else's house for someone new, part of the infinitely extended lattice of people who knew each other, to cross the casual boundary between acquaintanceship and friendship. Their tolerances were easy, elastic. They were alert, and curious, and they had time to spare for the meandering routes of developing intimacy.

Everyone gave and went to haphazard parties, where unrelated bottles of cheap wine stood in corners and the rooms were filled with dope smoke. There were spaghetti dinners, after which people slept the night on cushions, and hectic weekends in unheated houses in the country, and cheap holidays in Italy or Greece. And in all this time, wherever they were, Matthew and Dinah knew without even talking about it that it was their partnership that provided the foundation for their enjoyment. It was simple. Everything else, the exuberant friendships and diversions and pleasures, sprang from this fertile ground.

To Dinah, Matthew was part of her. To their friends, everyone else who knew him, he was funny and charming but he was also slightly detached. His cold brain kept him separate. But for Dinah he was entirely present, and it gave her a luxurious satisfaction to think that only she knew him entirely. She knew his ambition and his anger as well as his tenderness. She understood him and admired him and she felt that they moved in unison, animating one another.

Dinah conveyed to Milly only the barest outline of all this.

How could recollected and now misplaced happiness be relevant at this distance to anyone but those who had shared it?

It was the next interval that was significant and this was never discussed. Not with Matthew – and if not Matthew, then with whom else?

The surprising answer seemed to be with this farouche teenager who lounged at the table opposite her.

The kitchen was sunlit now, and the light gilded the counter-tops and a paper-plumed message board and the silver arch of mixer taps.

'Yeah?' Milly prompted.

The Stewards did not decide to have a baby, exactly. They were not yet organised enough for that.

It merely happened that Dinah became pregnant.

They were disconcerted, and then pleased. They were not quite the first of their married friends to do it. At some of the parties and dinners now there were Moses baskets parked in upstairs rooms.

70

'Without even trying,' Matthew said when they announced the news. 'Bang, just like that.'

'*Bang* bang,' Dinah added.

'Another genius in the making,' their friends laughed. 'Chairman of J. Walter Thompson or Nobel laureate?'

Matthew raised his eyebrows. 'Since when have the two been mutually exclusive?'

The weeks passed and Dinah thought more and more about the curl of cells developing inside her. From books, she charted its progress, the budding of fingers and toes from formless knobs, the unfurling of ears, eyelids, lips. In her imagination she could see it as clearly as if the walls of muscle and tissue that obscured the baby were transparent membranes. And this internal preoccupation was not, could not be, shared with Matthew. It was her own secret, and the secrecy meant that it was faintly – very faintly – tinged with shame.

It was a quiescent foetus, making discernible kicks only rarely. But sometimes Dinah seized Matthew's hand and placed it on her belly, so that he could discover the unmistakable pressure of a tiny foot nudging beneath the stretched layers of skin and muscle.

'There,' Dinah would say, her face radiant. 'Did you feel?'

'Yes,' Matthew wonderingly said, the first time. 'I did feel it. Squirming in there.'

The rest of the baby was folded around that extended foot, only centimetres out of their grasp.

Dinah saw Matthew's amazed comprehension that their baby was a reality, not a theory, and in his eyes the sudden leap of awe and love that followed his recognition. She leaned forward to him, so that her mouth touched his.

'I love you,' she said. It seemed incredible that there should be so much happiness. Superstitious, she knocked on wood.

The Stewards went to natural-childbirth classes. After the sessions they laughed a lot about the other couples, from the hippy pair who dragged in their own patchwork-covered beanbag on which to practise panting, to the embarrassed husband who was speechless until a discussion of how to anchor restraining straps in a Volkswagen Passat brought him out in a sudden glow of animation. But for all the comedy, the Stewards were determined that they would have a natural birth. Their baby would have as perfect a start as it was possible to give.

Dinah remembered the last three weeks as a golden time. It was September, and the weather was flawless. The sun slanted at a lower angle, softening the summer's tired perspectives and revealing the crisped margins of the leaves. The mildewed purplish asters in the Stewards' neglected garden were draped with spiders' webs that shone with intricate dew in the early mornings. Dinah was no longer working, and she moved heavily through the house, opening and closing drawers, listening to the unfamiliar sleepy wash of mid-afternoon radio. The rooms were filled with sweet, soft autumnal light.

Matthew spent as much time as possible at home with her. They rested on the bed and he lay with his head against her belly, trying to hear the baby's heartbeat. Dinah's fingers wound idly in his hair.

'Do you think it's indecent to feel so happy?' she asked him.

'There's no indecency in happiness,' he answered at once.

Matthew was always sure of what was right, even in abstract matters. His certainty created an opposing tentativeness within her but it also reassured her, as it was meant to do.

Whenever she fell asleep Dinah dreamed wildly. They were overpopulated dreams filled with half-recognised threatening faces, and voices with familiar cadences that seemed very close to the surface skin of consciousness. Once or twice she woke up, blinking and looking around for these faces that seemed too familiar to be allowed to slip back into the subconscious underworld.

*

72

She went into labour early one morning. Matthew brought her tea in bed and she sipped it while they timed the first mild contractions.

'What is this? No one told me it was going to hurt,' she tried to laugh when they grew less mild.

Matthew drove her to the hospital, exactly as they had planned.

The labour room had green-painted walls and a white-faced clock with beetling black numerals that swam in and out of focus with the wringing contractions.

Matthew and Dinah tried to sing the special song they had fixed on in the classes, and panted with the remnants of the breathing exercises. But Dinah realised with rising panic that she was sweating and gasping, and all the time the pain was rolling over her and shaking her in its grip, instead of allowing itself to be ridden, as she had been encouraged to believe would happen. This was not part of their plan. The certainties were being whipped away.

A Chinese midwife examined her.

'Quite a rong way to go yet,' she announced.

'How long?'

'You are onry five centimetres.'

The pains threatened to consume her. They came inexorably, the blessed intervals in between growing shorter and shorter. She was being turned inside out, that was what was happening. She thought of a pink rubber kitchen glove, and tried to say something witty about it. She could smell the cheesy, nappy interior of the glove as if it were being held over her mouth and nose, and nausea swelled with the next contraction. Matthew and the midwife stared uncomprehendingly at her. She was trying to be stalwart and funny but she could not even make herself understood. She kicked against the pain, lost her footing and was swept away by it. She began a cry that turned into a scream.

The midwife peered down at her, her fingers around Dinah's wrist. Her face looked a long way away. There was a connection here, a link. Yes, dreams. She had dreamed this, the faces looking down at her.

'Now, we don't want to hear any of that,' the midwife admonished. 'What about the rady next doh?'

Matthew sat by her side, holding her hand and stroking her hair. She felt weakly angry with him, for sitting so comfortably with his concern on display. He was patting and stroking away on the periphery, whilst she was being pulled inside out. It was not fair.

'I want something,' Dinah said to the midwife, when she could speak again. 'An epidural.'

Matthew leaned forward. His face loomed. 'Are you sure?' he asked gently.

This was only what they had agreed beforehand. Dinah had told him to make sure she didn't waver, that the nurses didn't talk her into analgesia she didn't really want.

'Yes.' She couldn't do it without. 'I can't.'

Dinah saw Matthew's face. He was disappointed. They had planned to give birth with breathing and singing, and she had let him down, and the baby.

An anaesthetist arrived and pushed and prodded agonisingly at her to set up the epidural. At last the anaesthetic took effect and the pain faded grudgingly away, leaving her numb and exhausted.

Matthew resumed his position beside her, holding her hand loosely in his.

'I'm sorry,' Dinah said.

'I love you,' he told her. 'I felt so useless, seeing you in pain. It doesn't matter how we do this, only that we do it right. Yes?'

'Yes.'

His love and sympathy comforted her, but she couldn't forget the shadow of disappointment.

It was late in the evening before the baby was ready to be born. It was difficult for Dinah to push because she could not feel the contractions. The Chinese midwife had gone off

74

duty and now there was an older, more motherly woman. She put her hands on Dinah's belly and Matthew watched the monitor.

'Ready,' they kept telling her, 'here it comes, one, two, now *push.*'

'It's like trying to stir a pea-soup fog with a tennis racket,' Dinah protested.

The baby was delivered at ten minutes to midnight, a girl.

Matthew wiped Dinah's face and kissed her mouth. She saw that he was crying. The midwife gave them their daughter wrapped in a paper blanket and Dinah held her. The baby's tiny face was streaked with blood and mucus.

'Is she all right?'

'She's beautiful, dear.'

Dinah was dazed and exultant. Matthew shaded his eyes, resting his forehead in his hands. His own tears shocked him.

'I have never seen anything like that,' he said. 'I had no idea. And yet, every one of us arrives in the same way.'

'It's always a miracle,' the midwife said.

The new parents' heads bent over the green-wrapped infant. Wonderingly they touched her clenched fists, the wet, black head.

'May I take her now, to weigh her and clean her up for you?'

With capable hands a nurse lifted the baby out of Dinah's arms.

Matthew went to telephone Dinah's mother and his parents. The nurses made Dinah comfortable and brought her a cup of tea. The delivery room door opened and closed as people came in and out. The baby was crying, a small weak cry, and there was a young woman paediatrician in a white coat examining her with her back turned to the room. Dinah could see her conferring with the midwife.

After a few moments the doctor came and stood at the foot of the bed. Dinah was still balancing her cup of tea. The doctor smiled at her. She was wearing a little make-up, neat pearl studs in her ears, and her hair was held back with a velvet band.

'Have you thought of a name yet?'

'Sarah. I think we're going to call her Sarah.'

'That's nice.'

'Is she all right?'

'She seems very healthy.'

The cautious words snagged a thread of anxiety in Dinah's head.

The post-natal ward was dim and quiet when Dinah was wheeled upstairs at last. They put her in a cubicle off the main ward. Matthew had gone home and the baby was in the nursery with the other newborns, but Dinah did not sleep. She lay back against the pillows with her eyes open, listening to the squeak of footsteps in the corridors outside.

In the morning she held the baby again, lifting the wrapped package out of the hospital crib and holding her in the crook of her arm to inspect her. The red puckered face was inscrutable and the eyelids were folded tight shut against her intrusive regard.

From a distance, the nurses watched Dinah watching her baby.

The first bouquets of flowers arrived, crackling in cellophane and looped with pink florist's ribbon. A student nurse arranged them for her, and set the cards on the bedside locker. Later in the morning Matthew came. He took Sarah and awkwardly held her. Dinah was quiet, and he thought it was natural after the long labour. They were sitting like this in silence when a doctor came to see them, another paediatrician. She was older, more senior than the one who had examined Sarah the night before. She closed a door behind her, screening Dinah's cubicle from the rest of the mothers.

'May I have a word with you both?' she asked kindly, taking a place opposite Matthew.

They waited for a moment, within earshot but isolated from the business of the ward.

'Is something wrong?' It was Matthew who spoke. Dinah was looking nowhere. The flowered curtains at the window blurred before her eyes.

'We are a little concerned. We would like to do some tests on the baby.'

'Tests for what?'

'For Down's syndrome.'

'*Dinah?*'

Matthew's chair creaked as he swung to face her. He wanted Dinah to contradict what the doctor was saying, to deny this for him. He was still holding Sarah, clutching her against him now.

Dinah whispered, 'I knew there was something.'

The words came out of her on an exhaled breath. Matthew's shock seemed a greater weight than her own fear. His distress gathered itself, a threat poised somewhere close to her head.

'What *something?*'

'Just . . . the shape of her head. Her eyes. She seems . . . closed.'

Dinah could not articulate it any more clearly than that. There was only the conviction that Sarah was sealed up, a package quite unlike the other babies in the ward. They were their own mysteries now but time and intimacy would unravel them. Dinah knew that Sarah was not like them.

The doctor stood up, moved to stand in front of Matthew.

'May I?' she asked.

She reached gently inside Sarah's blanket wrapping. The baby's tiny red arm was exposed.

'Look.'

With her fingers she uncurled the tiny flower of Sarah's fist to expose the minute palm. The flesh was divided by a single deep crease.

'This is called the simian line. It is an almost certain indication. There is this fold of skin that she has over the eyes,

77

the shape and size of her head and ears, and the degree of hypotonia. Taken together, I'm afraid that the signs are unmistakable.

'We would like to take some blood, to do a chromosome test. It will take five days for us to get the results. People with Down's syndrome have an extra chromosome, as you probably know . . .'

'I do know that you shouldn't make any assumptions until you've done the tests and have the evidence to show us.' Matthew's voice was loud and made harsh by shock.

'Of course. But all the signs are there, Mr, I beg your pardon, *Dr* Steward. I have never seen a case in which these signs are present and trisomy has not been confirmed by the chromosome test.'

Matthew's face was white. There was a twist at his mouth, a distortion that Dinah had never seen before.

'Last night we were told she was healthy.'

'Oh, we think she is. Don't mistake me. About fifty per cent of these children are born with congenital defects, most usually of the heart. But as far as we can tell at this early stage, your daughter is free from any such problem.'

'Except for the problem itself.'

'The condition. Yes, that's so.'

Words, Dinah thought wildly. All these words conjured up and laid end to end to describe her baby.

She was waiting for Matthew to turn to her again so that they could meet this together. All night and through the long morning she had kept the queasy fears at bay with the thought of their unity, and she shivered with longing for it now. But Matthew did not look at her. He was staring down at the baby in his arms. He was rocking her but it was not a comforting motion. It was more as if his body was vibrating, as if his arms jerked with sharp urges that he could barely suppress.

Dinah wanted to hold them both, her husband and her child, drawing them in against the reassuring rhythm of her own heart, but she could not reach. Matthew sat apart

78

from her in the hospital armchair, his arms mechanically jerking, his head bent. She knew that his mind was working, flashing ahead of hers. For the first time, she perceived this as a threat.

'What will the tests reveal?'

Matthew was a scientist. Results, data. This was his language.

The doctor looked uneasy. Matthew's manner was too challenging. Distress she would deal with more sympathetically.

'Not much more than I have told you now, I'm afraid.'

'There are different grades of this disability, I think?'

'This condition . . . Down's children form a small population of their own. They are different from the general population, but they also differ individually.'

The paediatrician was comfortable on her own ground, even fluent. Matthew watched her, assessing.

Dinah thought, he is right. To seek to know, at once, however difficult the knowledge. Her own instinct was to shrink, to avoid asking and so to make a precarious refuge. Intense love for Matthew wound with her sadness, and the twin threads of old love and new responsibility twisted her viscera like another birth-pain.

'The spread of IQ is quite wide, but this only becomes apparent with natural development, as it does with a normal child. There are sometimes hearing and more often sight problems associated with the condition. But there is a good possibility that your daughter will be able to go to an ordinary school, live a life within . . .'

'No.'

Matthew stood up. The wooden arm of the chair clattered against the radiator and he almost stumbled. He laid Sarah down in the crib and his empty hands hung at his sides as he stood upright.

'No,' he repeated. 'Not ordinary, not normal. How could that be?'

He did come to Dinah then. He stood beside the bed and

rested one hand on her shoulder while the other stroked her hair. She had longed for this comfort but now she found that she could not connect with it. There was only an awareness, like a premonition, that the alignment was unnatural. She did not want to be with Matthew but separate from their baby.

'I know how difficult this is,' the doctor began. 'I do want to reassure you both . . .'

'Thank you,' Matthew said.

'Mrs Steward . . .'

He interrupted her. 'May my wife and I have some time alone together now?'

'Oh yes, of course. Later, when you are ready, there is information . . . And anything you need to . . .'

'Thank you.'

The doctor went, the tail of her white coat flicking behind her.

When the cubicle door clicked shut Dinah levered herself upright and swung her legs off the bed. The after-effects of the anaesthetic made her limbs shaky but she lifted Sarah out of the crib. The baby made no sound, seemingly unaffected by or unaware of being passed to and fro. Holding her tightly Dinah sank back on to the edge of the bed.

Now that she looked at her with clear eyes, the features were unmistakable.

The midwives, nurses, must all have seen it at once. The paediatrician last night, that was why she had hurried into the delivery room.

'She is *here*,' Dinah said. She meant that Sarah was herself, an individual, whatever her capabilities might turn out to be.

She was crying, not wanting to but unable to stop it. A tear fell like a cliché on the baby's blanket.

'Look. She's beautiful . . .'

Matthew had not moved. Stiffly, he lowered his hand. He did not look, even though she had asked him to.

'Down's,' he repeated, unbelieving.

Dinah remembered the shadow of disappointment his

face had betrayed in the labour room. Only the first intimation of failure, it seemed now. She held on to Sarah, making an inarticulate contact, *Somehow, we will, together, you, your father and me* . . .

'What shall we do?' Matthew asked. She did not think that she had ever heard him articulate such a question.

'Whatever we have to do.' The avowal of strength made her feel stronger. 'Sit down here.'

To her relief he came, the familiarity of him easing beside her. The metal bedframe squeaked under his weight, setting up reverberations of memory that did not quite surface now, here. They made a family, as they had done last night in the minutes after the delivery. Some of the exultation that she had felt then flicked in Dinah again, and seemed to flow out and illuminate the nodding heads of pink roses and white carnations in their hospital vases.

Matthew said, 'I don't know how even to begin to interpret this. All the things I expected of a child, of our child . . .'

Dinah's premature confidence faded. She understood that Matthew was not connecting to the baby and herself, wherever he might sit, or whatever unconscious associations might stir within her.

'We'll have help, we can't expect to . . .'

'I don't want medical euphemisms and social workers' jargon. None of that will alter the reality.'

Harsh. That was so harsh, but it was also the man he was.

'She is my baby too,' Dinah said.

'Yours, and mine.'

There it was again, the *disappointment*. Matthew had expected other than this.

Dinah thought that the two of them had been engaged in the construction of some intricate pyramid, all through their time together, fitting the blocks sweetly in place so that the structure grew and grew between them, increasing in dimensions and solidity, and now . . .

She tried to imagine how it must be for Matthew. The

geometry had failed him and the structure was thrown all off balance. Some of the blocks were falling, hurled aside . . .

They did not talk any more, then. Afterwards, Dinah wondered if it would have been different if they could have done. She might have deflected his intentions before they were fully formed. But now a nurse tapped on the cubicle door.

'Mrs Steward? Your mother is here.'

Dinah's mother had promised last night that she would come down by train from Northamptonshire to see her daughter and granddaughter.

'I need to talk to you,' Matthew said urgently. He made a clumsy gesture with his arm, trying to keep everything else at bay. 'Dinah, we have to understand each other first, before anything . . .'

But now here was Eleanor in a smart tweed suit with a velvet collar. She carried a bunch of chrysanthemums and a parcel no doubt containing a hand-knitted bonnet and matinée jacket. Her mouth was tucked in at the corners, always a sign of anxiety. At the sight of her mother Dinah felt like a child again, wishing for Eleanor's comfort and for her vanished ability to put all wrongs right.

Eleanor said in a rush, 'I saw the sister, she told me . . .'

'Look, Mum, here she is.' Dinah held up Sarah in her arms.

Eleanor laid her offerings aside. 'Ahh, the little thing. The little dear, let me see her . . .'

A flood of relief washed through Dinah. Her mother had come. Here was a connection, at last. Eleanor took the baby.

'Oh darling, are they sure? She looks so lovely, so pretty.'

'See. See her hands, look? And her eyes, and her head here.'

Dinah's fingers touched the same places as the doctor's had done and her mother's reached out too, echoing the gesture, stroking Sarah's small head. The women murmured to each other, excluding Matthew.

'She looks like you, when you were tiny. I remember so well, when they gave you to me to hold, the first time.'

There were tears in Eleanor's eyes.

'What does it mean? What do the doctors say? That sister was kind but she couldn't tell me much.'

'Mummy, I don't know. She has Down's syndrome. We only just saw the doctor ourselves . . .'

'I came at the wrong time.'

'No, no, I want you here.'

Dinah was exhausted. Her mother held the baby and with her free hand she stroked Dinah's hair.

'It's all right, darling, it's all right. She is beautiful.'

A thread drew tight between the three of them.

Yes, Dinah thought.

A movement made them look up. Matthew had been watching them, sitting with his hands awkwardly empty in his lap. Now he stood up again.

'Isn't she, Matthew?' Eleanor asked.

His face was frightening to both of them. It was all knobs and protuberances of bone as if the flesh had shrunk away from the skull beneath.

'Don't,' he said. And then his voice grew louder until he was shouting. 'Don't look at her, not like that. It isn't the right thing to do, don't you understand?'

While they stared at him he reached down and took Sarah out of Eleanor's hands. He swung the baby out of their reach, and she gave a thin short cry that trailed away almost at once.

Matthew hoisted the baby against his shoulder and pushed out of the door.

Eleanor made to pursue him and Dinah held on to her.

'No, wait, leave him. He won't . . . he needs . . .' She couldn't finish. Her instinct was to defend him, but she couldn't define what he needed. Eleanor broke away and marched to the door. Matthew had already disappeared into the web of corridors.

'I'm going to call the nurse,' Eleanor said. She pressed the call button by the bed. When a nurse put her head round the door Eleanor murmured to her while Dinah lay with her head against the pillows, too weary to intervene.

'They'll find him,' Eleanor said when the nurse withdrew.

The two women sat together.

'It's harder for Matt,' Dinah whispered.

'He should be helping you,' Eleanor retorted. Her first consideration was Dinah, now and always.

'I know what he's feeling,' Dinah lied. The reality was that she did not know, and she was afraid of what the truth might be. She had seen his disappointment, and glimpsed the implacability behind it. 'I know what he needs. Some time, just a bit of time, that's all.'

And she had always understood the necessity to shield her husband and her mother from one another. They were separated by too many barriers, of age and class and experience, ever to have grown close. It was her role to soothe and protect, Dinah wearily reflected, not Eleanor's any longer. They had changed places.

'Sit here by me,' she begged her mother. 'Hold me.'

Eleanor put her arm around Dinah's shoulder, and Dinah rested her cheek against the smooth tweed of her jacket.

'I'm here,' Eleanor murmured, as she had done when Dinah was a little girl waking up from a bad dream. They sat quietly.

Dinah's eyes were fixed on the door, waiting and watching for Matthew and the baby.

After about half an hour Matthew came back again. He looked beaten.

Dinah sat up. 'Where is she?'

'She's all right,' Matt said at once, taking her hand. 'They've taken her to the nursery. They want to run some tests.'

Eleanor murmured, 'I think I had better go. I'll be back tomorrow, darling.'

'They may let us go home tomorrow afternoon,' Dinah said.

Matthew's fingers tightened warningly on hers.

Eleanor hesitated, looking at the two of them. 'Listen. Everyone will say this to you, I might as well be the first. She is a beautiful little thing. These babies are special. They can bring great delight.'

Matthew gazed coldly back. 'How do you know? You didn't have one, did you? You had Dinah.'

Eleanor had her coat on. Dinah said quickly, 'I'll call you in the morning, Mummy. Thank you for coming. Don't worry too much.'

'I do,' Eleanor said. 'I am your mother.'

After she had gone Dinah asked Matthew,

'Where did you go?'

'Nowhere. I just walked around. Sat down with her, to try to think. Then a nurse and a porter tracked me down and took her away. Very kindly but firmly.'

'And what did you think?'

He could not reassure her. She could almost hear the cold reckoning within him, the machinery of it functioning smoothly beneath the blur of his pain and shock.

'I love you. You know I do, and you know I don't ever want anything to change that.'

'I know.'

She waited.

'I didn't expect this. It . . . defies reason.'

His disappointment, again. And was *reason* the only principle that might guide them?

He would not say any more, not yet.

'The paediatrician wants to talk to us again,' Dinah wearily told him.

Matthew submitted himself. There was a long interview with the doctor. He asked questions mechanically and the facts accumulated in a sullen log-jam.

After the doctor there was a midwife with Sarah. The baby was proving difficult to feed: her muscle tone was very poor and she could not latch on effectively. Dinah struggled, awkwardly manipulating her nipple at the baby's mouth. The

85

effort made beads of sweat break out around her hairline, and still the baby would not connect.

'There's plenty of time. I'll take her back to the nursery, love, and try her with a bottle solution just for now,' the midwife soothed.

Dinah lay weakly against the pillows, her face turned aside. There were tears at the back of her eyes again.

'I want to do it, to feed her.'

'I know you do.'

Matthew encouraged her to eat some hospital dinner off the tray, and finished her leavings himself. He telephoned the friends who were close to them, explaining what had happened, and conveyed their various sympathies to Dinah.

'I told them that you are wonderful,' he said.

It was a long day, seemingly stretching on and on, drawing out the thread of their suffering into the thinnest filament.

It was dark outside and an angled lamp shone over Dinah's bed. The staff had left them alone at last. Dinah lay with her eyes closed.

'Are you awake?' Matt asked.

After a minute she stirred.

'Yes. I want to sleep but I can't.'

'Tomorrow I'll take you home. You'll be able to sleep in our bed, with me.'

You, he said. He did not, would not mention the baby.

'Matt?'

'I'm here.'

'Go on, then. Say it.'

She braced herself. She heard him take a breath before he began.

'My darling, I'm sorry for this. I wish it could be different. But I can't take this baby home and love her.

'I don't want to compromise every day. I don't want only to celebrate partial victories, small things achieved against great odds.

'I know what it makes me, and I'm ashamed of it. It's as if

86

there's a piece of me, compassion and humility, that's missing. I wish it were different, I wish I were someone else, but I also know that what I'm telling you is the simple truth. If I try to ignore it, it will only make it worse. If I pretend to feel otherwise it will be more damaging in the end for the three of us.

'You and I have been perfect together. I can't dismantle that, even let it be threatened.

'I can't take her, Dinah. I'm so sorry. But I can't.'

A silence bled between them.

She had feared that this was what was coming, of course, but still Dinah was stricken by it. She asked the question through stiff lips.

'What do you want to do?'

'I want to place her with a family who will love her in the way that I can't.'

'And if I don't want to give our child away? To bundle her off into obscurity like some dark secret?'

She spoke harshly and Matthew accepted it. There was no reason for him to be spared. The ground between them had shifted. Unwillingly, in a matter of hours, it seemed they had become unacknowledged adversaries.

'I am not making a secret of her. I am trying to confront this thing that has happened to us and to understand what it will mean.'

'We can love her, Matt. She'll become part of us, and we'll be proud of whatever it is she can do.'

Such limited horizons, such small and painful triumphs compared with what might have been?

He did not say the words, but they both heard them.

'What if I tell you that I will keep her whether you want her or not?'

She could do that. Dinah knew that she could.

He told her the truth as he saw it, as it reproached him.

'I believe that her disability will come between us.'

There. The fact of his belief, as cold and deadly and pointed as a blade, slid silently between them.

87

That was her choice, Dinah understood. Her husband or her child. How bald and tragic and unthinkable a choice.

'Say something,' Matthew pleaded with her when the silence seeped too long between them.

'What do you want me to say? That I can easily choose, that we'll let her go or that I'll love her and care for her alone? That I don't need you, that I don't bleed for her? I only gave birth to her twenty-four hours ago. That isn't a very long motherhood, is it?'

'Please, don't . . .' Matthew's fists pressed into his eye sockets, blinding him. 'There will be other children for us, the children we . . .'

'*Don't say that.* Don't you dare ever to say that again, to promise other babies who will be the image of perfection when this one . . . Oh, *God.*'

He took her in his arms then, and let her cry. She did not resist him.

After Matthew had gone home that night – she told him to go, and he went obediently – Dinah lay in the circle of light made by the angled lamp. She was dry-eyed now and exhausted but weariness lent her thoughts a sharp-edged, crystalline hardness. Was this how Matthew always thought, she wondered, with harsh reason and clarity unsoftened by the infinite shades of uncertainty?

In the small hours of the morning she left her bed and went to the nursery where Sarah was quietly lying in her crib next to the nurses' station. Dinah unpeeled her covers and looked at her tiny crimson hands and feet with their odd, deep creases.

A young nurse came by.

'She's settling quite well,' she told her. 'She's a lovely little thing, really.'

'Oh, fuck,' Milly breathed, when Dinah stopped talking at last. 'It's like, I just don't know what to say.'

'If you don't, it's the first time since we met.'

'Shit, what does that mean? Are you angry with me now?'

'Milly, what do you think? When I've just told you things I have never told anyone else.'

'Okay, I know. I'm sorry. So what did you do?'

Dinah turned up her hands, showing their emptiness.

'You know what I did.'

'Right.'

Milly put her own hands, black-varnished nails and blue amateur tattoo at the base of one thumb, into hers. They clasped each other.

'You know,' Milly said, 'when I was little and Sandra and Ed talked to me about how I was adopted, you know how sane and understanding and stuff they like to be? Well, when I'd listened to all that, I used to tell myself that my real mother must be some famous person. Or some genius who went mad, whatever crap. I don't believe that any more, or even bother fantasising about it. It's probably some dead ordinary sordid story. But, you know. I wish you could be her.'

Dinah held her hand. She felt calm now. All the tumult had receded, leaving her with a single clear note of certainty.

She knew what she must do.

'Thank you. Thank you, Milly. I think that's about the best thing anyone has ever said to me.'

Five

'And then what?' Milly asked.

It was like telling a story, and that made it easier.

Milly had eaten breakfast, a concoction of her own made from oats heaped with brown sugar, and Dinah had had scrambled eggs. She was surprised by how hungry she felt.

'A chain of things happened. One led on to the next, in a sequence that was logical but at the same time seemed quite mad. Doctors, counsellors, all the professionals came to see us. It was just as painful for Matthew as it was for me, but from the beginning he was certain of what we should do. You see, he knew he couldn't accept Sarah. He was sure, and I wasn't sure of anything except that I loved him.'

Dinah bent her head. 'In the end it was his voice that was heard. As if it was his voice that spoke for both of us.'

She shaded her eyes with one hand, conscious of Milly intently listening.

'Only that sounds as if I blame Matthew for what we did. I don't. The only blame – the only judgement – I can direct anywhere is against myself. I should have shouted, I should have fought to keep her if I knew it was right. But I didn't. I didn't *know* what was going to happen, in the way Matthew seemed to. I only understood I had to make a choice. Husband or child.'

Bitterly Dinah repeated the words. *Husband or child.*

90

Or maybe, she thought, that only seemed to be the choice she was forced to make. If she had been braver or more cruelly determined she could have kept Sarah. Maybe in the end Matthew would have accepted her and grown to love her, just as he loved Jack and Merlin.

Or maybe the daily abrasion of Sarah's presence would have separated them anyway, just in a different way from how they were separate now.

Dinah never would know. The uncertainty was part of the damage she must live with.

'We never took her home. Sarah was fostered straight from the hospital.'

Milly thought about this.

'You let her go. Gave her *away*,' she said, as if a light of understanding had suddenly clicked on within her.

Dinah looked up again. She made herself meet Milly's gaze.

'Yes. It was a wrong thing, a weak and wicked thing to do. There hasn't been a day of my life since when I haven't judged myself for it.'

It had been so long since Dinah had admitted her guilt. So many layers of varnish had been applied over the truth, without ever successfully obliterating it. It was for the silence that she blamed Matthew. The failure to acknowledge damage done. He had turned his face away, implacable, trapping her into silence, and she had permitted it. That was their contract. They had their own version of the marriage agreement, just as Ed and Sandra had theirs. And the Pinkhams, and the Kerrigans, and everyone else.

'I'm glad I told you,' Dinah said, after a moment. It was true. The room seemed warmer, the daylight softer and brighter.

'I don't think it was wicked,' Milly said wonderingly. 'Because it was you, because it was what you thought you had to do.'

She jerked her hand to her mouth and gnawed at the

ragged flesh around her thumbnail. The primitive tattoo paled and stretched with the thin skin.

'Was it like that for my mother as well? I always thought before, how *could* she?'

It was hearing the other half of a story that might have been her own that held Milly transfixed. She sat so still, as if to move might be to run the risk of missing some detail of it.

'I was *hers*. Why did she have to give me to someone else?'

Dinah was suffused with tenderness and sympathy for her. She began to see the roots of some of Milly's anger, against Sandra and Ed and the world itself.

'She must have felt the same loss and grief.'

'She didn't have to give me away. *I* wasn't defective.'

'There might have been all kinds of other reasons why she couldn't keep you.'

Milly wouldn't look at her now. Dinah knew that there were tears in her eyes that she would want to hide.

Angrily Milly burst out, 'Oh, yeah. She was very young, not married. Her boyfriend, my *father*, had left her. Ed and Sandra told me that, and how she wanted the best for me. Or is that just an invention, the kind of happy crappy gloss they like to put on things to make me feel better about everything?'

Dinah told her, 'How could she not have wanted the best for you? Doesn't the fact that she gave you up for adoption mean that she did, when she knew she couldn't give it to you herself?'

'You think? Or perhaps it was just easier for her to get on with her life without some snotty baby.'

'Neither way would have been easy, Milly.'

Milly sighed. 'You make it sound so reasonable. Go on telling me about your baby. It makes what my mother did seem less weird, knowing you did it as well.'

Dinah accepted the rebuke.

'Sarah was fostered, to begin with, by a very experienced couple. They had had other foster-children. They knew what to do, and they did it very well.'

Malcolm and Pauline Green lived in a part of London Dinah had never visited before. Malcolm was a machine operator in a factory producing household chemicals, and they lived in a neat house with its windows blinded by net curtains. The Greens had one child of their own, a daughter in her early teens.

The second meeting between the two families and the social worker took place in the Greens' home. Dinah had wanted that, although it was not usual. Sarah lay asleep under hand-knitted blankets in an old-fashioned coach-built pram.

Dinah could still see that room as clearly as if she carried a snapshot of it in her purse. There was a tiled fireplace with polished brass knicknacks set in niches, many framed photographs of children, a three-piece suite with velvety covering and a carpet patterned with leaves. She remembered the leaves now, as the trees in Franklin began to shed their prodigal colourings.

She sat on the Greens' sofa with a teacup on her lap, listening to Pauline talking about foster-parenting and all the time knowing that she was handing over her child into a world quite different from the one she would have known with her real parents. Not better or worse, she would not have presumed to make that judgement. But remote, and therefore much harder to understand.

Afterwards, when Matthew drove her away, she had to resist the impulse to pull at his arm to make him turn back again. He seemed rigid, drawn apart from her, and she remembered the look of his hands on the wheel. They were too big for his wrists, weighty and bone-knuckled and tightly clenched.

'It's for the best,' Matthew kept saying, then and in the time afterwards, as if repeating it could direct Dinah into belief.

Dinah wept, helpless and unrelieving tears, all the way back to the little house by the football ground.

'I wonder if my mother cried for me,' Milly said.

93

'Yes,' Dinah told her. 'And she will have worried and wondered about you almost every day of your life.'

'Phhhht.'

It was a little sound of disbelief, accompanied by the characteristic shrug, and it betrayed longing and a sadness that affected Dinah directly. She stood up and went round the table to Milly, and she put an arm around her shoulders and held her head against her.

'I know you don't like to be touched,' she forestalled, and for a moment Milly did not pull away.

In the months after the fostering, Dinah made permitted visits to the Greens and Sarah. Her counsellor and social worker advised her about the continuing contact, but Dinah felt that each of them was engaged in some elaborate charade designed to suggest that there was still some element of choice concerning Sarah's future. Whilst all the time Dinah knew the truth, that the choice had already been made, and each visit was an infinitely painful reminder of her own guilt and cowardice and inadequacy.

Sarah flourished in Pauline's care. And at the same time Dinah's strength of will faltered and declined. Each visit made Sarah less her own, more Pauline's child.

After the first time, she always made the trip alone. Matthew never offered to accompany her, and she never made more than a token suggestion that he should. Sarah's existence was laid to rest between them, the absence of acknowledgement its only marker.

All through this time, Dinah tried to see her husband afresh, and it puzzled her that however she might try she could not detect any change in him. He was still the ambitious, clear-sighted man she had fallen in love with. The difference was that they had become solicitous for one another, tender and observant, as if there had been some grave illness in the past, now never spoken of. And day by day, the silence placed another sliver of space between them.

When the time came for a visit, Dinah would drive alone

to the Greens' house. Pauline would be waiting for her in the front room, with Sarah dressed in the pink babyclothes her foster-mother favoured. Pauline would tell Dinah about what Sarah had been doing, the progress she had made and how the paediatrician had been pleased with her after her last tests.

Dinah would lean forward on the velvet sofa edge, listening greedily and at the same time painfully trying to disconnect the tumult of longing she felt from the reality of this padded pink baby, who reserved her fuzzy, gummy smiles for another woman.

Dinah was never able to warm her respect for Pauline Green into liking. She sensed from the outset that Pauline felt quite differently about Sarah from the other children she had fostered. Pauline was possessive of this baby, and she was quick to defend her and assert her own importance in her life. She deluged Sarah with love, leaving Dinah to wonder at and envy the ready accessibility of that love when she and Matthew could not get in touch with their own. And she could never escape the knowledge that Pauline must judge her harshly for having given up Sarah.

The hurtful formality of the visits never softened into mutual understanding. Dinah would drive away again after an hour, her eyes stinging with tears.

But she would not let herself cry, because this new version of her life had been constructed on denying the reason for her grief.

The last visit Dinah made was when Sarah was a little more than twelve months old.

Eleanor was staying with her, and at Dinah's suggestion her mother drove her across London in her car. Dinah no longer felt that she could bear the pain of visiting alone, but now the weight of Eleanor's concern pressed into her, increasing the pain. Eleanor had never complained of it, but Sarah was also her granddaughter, and they should have been pushing her in the park together, instead of negotiating the traffic on the way to see her in some other woman's care.

When they reached the house Pauline showed them into the front room.

To their amazement Sarah was sitting upright within a rampart of cushions. Her button features shone with happiness and wonder at this new achievement. Dinah saw in that moment that she was not a baby to be passed from hand to hand but an individual, with her own joys and triumphs. The eyes of that separate person searched for Pauline after her momentary absence, and widened with delight when they found her.

It was Eleanor who knelt on the rug to baby-talk to Sarah, and who listened to Pauline's proud recital of her latest achievements. It was Eleanor who swung her up, with Pauline's nodded permission, and walked her in her arms the few steps across the room and back again.

'They say up the hospital she may not walk until she's three. But we think different, Sarah, don't we?' Pauline said loudly.

Dinah could hardly speak a word. She sat on the velvet sofa, watching her mother and her daughter and Pauline, and her clenched fists lay stiff in her lap.

Afterwards, when the visit was over, Eleanor turned the car around and began to drive back the way they had come. She was a cautious driver, sitting hunched up against the steering wheel and peering suspiciously at whatever lay ahead. Her husband had always done the driving in their life together. It took an effort for her to remove one hand from the wheel and place it over Dinah's.

'What do you want to do?' Eleanor asked her.

Dinah gazed through the blots of rain starring the nearside window. London looked grey and greasy, as hopeless and colourless and extinguished as she felt herself.

The answer was always the same. 'Nothing. There is nothing to be done. Each time I see her she is less ours, more theirs. I can't take her back. I can't take her back to Matthew, and there isn't anywhere I want to go without him.'

The line of Eleanor's pale pink-lipsticked mouth tightened, but she made no criticism of her son-in-law. From the first week that Dinah had known him, Eleanor had recognised that setting herself against Matthew would be to set herself against Dinah too.

There was a silence between them.

'Then you must let her go,' Eleanor said at last. 'You must accept what letting her go truly means. Otherwise you'll destroy yourself.'

Dinah echoed the words. 'Let her go? But she's yours, too. Don't you care about her?'

'I care most of all about you. Sarah is safe and happy where she is. Let that be enough. You must do it.'

Dinah closed her eyes, shutting out the weary view.

'I know,' she whispered.

Dinah did cry, after that time.

She held it in for a day until Eleanor had gone home again, pretending to her mother a resigned acceptance. Then she crept upstairs like an animal in distress and lay in her bed for a week. Matthew nursed her with tender concern, and the saving explanation they offered each other was that she was suffering from a bad dose of flu.

A year later, the Greens applied to adopt Sarah.

Dinah knew that this last step was not only logical but inevitable.

There was another session of counselling, and the professionals were encouraged to note that Mrs Steward now seemed more certain of her motives and intentions in giving up her child. The papers were prepared with the full consent of all parties. They were formally signed, and the adoption went through without any complications.

Some time after that, Dinah heard that the Greens had moved to Thetford, in Norfolk, where Malcolm had found a better job. Their new address imprinted itself on Dinah's memory, but she never made another attempt to see Sarah or to contact Pauline and Malcolm.

Her life with Matthew appeared to resume its pattern, and the layers of varnish were steadily applied to cover the wide-open wound.

The Stewards sold their terraced house near the Arsenal football ground, and bought three labourers' cottages, semi-derelict but ripe for conversion, in a village just outside London. Sheldon was an attractive village, still almost rural, and the people who lived there felt a strong sense of community.

In her spare time from work Dinah immersed herself in supervising the rebuilding and decorating of the new house. She was drawn into local life, devoting yet more energy to amateur dramatics and village hall fundraising and conservation projects, and she made new friends amongst the Sheldon people. The Stewards were a popular addition to the community, although Matthew had less time to devote to village life than Dinah did. He was teaching as well as pursuing his own research into engineered proteins, and he worked long, long hours in the labs and lecture rooms.

As the weeks and months after the move went by, Dinah and Matthew found that they saw less and less of their friends from the casual, easygoing days before Sarah was born. The distance from London, their tiredness from commuting, and their involvement with building work and new friendships provided good reason.

But yet, it was also as if they had separately decided that this part of their history should be snipped away, leaving no evidence to remind them of what had really happened.

The new arrangement of her life suited Dinah well enough.

She still enjoyed her work, the teasing and juggling with words and images, although some of the competitive edge that had made her so good at it had softened away.

She liked Sheldon because it contained no painful memories, and in her unadmitted distress she felt supported and confirmed by the unspectacular rituals of village life. Helping to raise funds for a new stage for the village hall was no great contribution to the world, but Dinah thought that she might as well do that much since there was nothing else she wanted to do or believed herself capable of doing.

She knew that Matthew loved her as much as he had ever done, but she also understood that now there was a deeper, darker dimension to his love that contained guilt and discomfort.

For herself, she was partly able to believe that he was still her best friend and true partner. For most of the time she could look at him and think, yes, I understand him, I know why we had to do what we did, and I love him.

And then there were other times. She knew that Matt was rigid, and ruthless in the pursuit of what he wanted and believed in, and that his selfishness was in equal proportion to his brilliance. Her admiration for him had faded with her recognition of his fallibility.

Her own weakness was no mystery to her, but the reality of Matt's was shocking. She would remind herself, *This is what I chose. How can I not love Matthew? I owe that much at least to Sarah* . . .

There was not a day when she did not think of her.

Dinah never told Matt any of this. Her suppression of her thoughts and her imaginings of Sarah became another facet of the silence that lay like a blade between them.

If Matt and Dinah knew that they laughed at life and at themselves much less than they used to do, their explanation would have been that the world was a serious place, and that they were grown up now.

Then, four years after Sarah's birth, Dinah at last allowed herself to become pregnant again. For a long time the idea of another child had been both fearful and a reward that she did not deserve. But the years slowly separated her from Sarah, and her fear and her sense of unworthiness diminished as her longing for another baby grew. Dinah's memory of Sarah and her guilt remained as sharp as they had ever been, but now there seemed also to be space to look beyond them. It was what Matt wanted.

This time, nothing was left to chance. She submitted to the tests for foetal abnormality, moving in Matthew's white-lit clinical domain instead of her own messy, hormonal, female one.

The baby she was carrying was a boy, and normal.

It was a straightforward pregnancy but Dinah felt that it was the tests and the attendant medical technicians who were responsible for this new child, not her body at all. There was none of the wondering fascination that had absorbed her the first time.

Jack was born on the due date, quickly and easily. Out of his crumpled, tomato-red face Dinah saw his father's eyes staring up at her.

When she brought him home to Sheldon, Dinah found that she was drawn into an inner village world populated by young mothers and small children. There was a crèche and a playgroup, an exercise group and a babysitting circle. Although she continued to do freelance work when she could manage it, Dinah found that a substantial portion of her time was spent sitting in her own or another woman's kitchen, exchanging the small currency of mutual support while the babies and toddlers slept and played around them.

Dinah discovered that she possessed all the usual maternal skills. The company of the other young mothers assured her that what she was doing was normal and natural, even admirable. It was just that the very rightness and normality of so much motherhood made it harder for her to place the existence and absence of Sarah.

None of her new friends knew that she had already had a baby.

The secret perpetuated itself, frozen between Matt and herself, and the chill that came off it was like a cold wind blowing over open water on a summer's day.

Two years later, making an entrance that was an almost exact replica of his brother's, Merlin was born. The boys looked alike, taking after both sides of the family, but in their temperament and in their precocity they resembled their father.

Matthew was a good father. As Dinah would have predicted, he was adept at amusing and stimulating his children with potato clocks and magnets and kites, but he was also tender and patient with their demands. He was fiercely proud of the two of them. Jack and Merlin were always the first of their peers to reach new milestones. They balanced wooden blocks and placed coloured cups in size sequence and recognised letters and distinguished colours. Jack could read at three and a half.

They were the children Matthew wanted. Dinah told herself in her moments of secret bitterness that they were the children he was certain he deserved.

And Sarah, with her gummy smile for Pauline, Sarah never could have been, never would be.

Dinah kept the memory of her like an intimate wound that fatally drew the touch and then deflected it with pain.

The Stewards lived in Sheldon for ten years.

The boys began and remained effortlessly at the top of their school classes. They were physically on the small side, short-sighted and uninterested in competitive sports, but they were popular enough for their quick-wittedness and originality, and for their skill at computer games. If they were bored or understimulated they became difficult, but Dinah and Matthew learnt that early on. The house filled up with games and music and computers and a library of books.

During the week, Matthew was almost never at home. Professional success and the recognition that came with it began to carry him forward at gathering speed. He was made head of his research group, and under his direction the team investigated the design and synthesis of enzymes in relation to insulin receptors. There were informed whispers that Steward's team at UCL might be on to something new and significant. Matthew began to travel to conferences to deliver

101

papers, and to publish his findings in the science journals. His name was increasingly mentioned amongst those of the coming men.

Dinah was proud of his achievements. She compensated herself for his lengthening absences with her children and her work, with local friendships, and with the small affairs of Sheldon. She began to see that life had mapped itself out and that she was patiently following the prescribed route without looking much at the country that stretched on either side of it. The memory of Sarah was embedded within her, dark and rubbed smooth by her constant referral to it, but never brought out into the light of day.

By the end of his time at UCL Matthew was growing increasingly tense and tired. He was overstretched by the weight of administration, by the unending battle to keep his projects funded, and by the declining morale of his team in the face of disappearing grants and diminishing research facilities. Dinah couldn't understand the concepts of his real work, but she could and did listen to his anxieties about the management of the department and its useful future.

She could not know for certain, but she suspected that the greatest of Matthew's talents as a scientist, his ability to make free and bold imaginative leaps into the realms of pure conjecture and then to motivate more pedestrian talents to prove the theories to him, might be being eroded by lack of money, lack of thinking time, and lack of support.

'Is it time to move on?' she asked him, late one night when they had shared a bottle of wine and her feet rested in Matthew's lap where he absently massaged them.

'Maybe,' he said. Dinah thought that might perhaps mean Cambridge again, or even a chair at Manchester or some other redbrick university.

'Maybe,' Matthew repeated.

In the early spring of the year Jack was ten, Matthew went to Stamford to deliver an important lecture at an international conference.

At the reception afterwards he was informally approached

by the Dean of School from the University of Massachusetts at Franklin.

'It's a great offer,' Matthew told Dinah. 'They want me to go over there and set up a new department for them. Listen, I get an absolute guarantee of all the funding I need for the first three years. After that I'll have to pursue my own, but then I should have at least a couple of good projects fully running. I get sixty thousand square feet of lab space, and twenty or so personnel. I can take one or two of the key people from here with me, so I won't lose Sean Rader to anyone else. I recruit six or eight post-docs to begin with, get the graduate students and technicians I need, and I can name the game. No interference from governing body, anyone else. They just want an international calibre department doing high-profile research. What do you think they're offering to pay me to give it to them?'

He told her the figure, and Dinah whistled.

'Not bad, eh? Franklin isn't first rate. It's not MIT or Harvard, but it's not some obscure little school either.'

Dinah waited. The old Matt was looking at her. She should have felt happy to see him but what she did feel was a selfish flicker of fear that her steady, contained world would be knocked aside, and a premonition that the disturbance would uncover her sad scar in some way that would affect them all.

'I want it,' Matthew said. His face burned with the fire of renewed ambition.

'Then you must go for it,' Dinah told him.

Six months later they were in Franklin, and a matter of weeks after that they were installed in the house on Kendrick.

And now Matt had his department and his devoted team, misanthropic Sean Rader and gnomic Jon Liu and the pretty woman PhD and all the rest, and the work had begun to sing for them. Their aim was to re-engineer the peptide molecule – insulin – so that it could be taken orally. No more injections for sufferers from diabetes, just a pill or a spoonful to swallow. They were getting closer, Matt would say, non-committally.

Everyone was pleased with him.

It was good work. Nobel work, murmured those who were in the know.

When Dinah stopped talking Milly waited a moment or two, to see if she was going to say anything else. They both looked out of the window again, at the Saturday apple-pie wholesomeness of Kendrick Street. A Kerrigan child flipped past on rollerblades and Milly breathed hard through her nose.

'When I think of home there are all these fakey images of church bells and cricket matches and long shadows on mown grass. Like in a tourist board ad,' Dinah said.

'Shit. And I think of London, piss-wet doorways and the smell of takeaway curry and Inverness Street market, and hanging out in Camden doing, like, what you want. I love it. I love the way you can be, look like anyone, anything, and no one cares. No one stares at you the way they all do here. I've got mates in London, proper mates. I miss them like mad. They have this, like, really simple life. Somewhere to sleep, just enough to eat. That's all they need, and everything else is freedom. Caz, he's one of them, he could do anything, but he's just chosen to keep everything dead simple. Just to have a laugh, not to belong, not to have to keep up with everything like this.'

Milly gestured dismissively through the kitchen window at the orderliness of Kendrick Street and the entirety of Franklin beyond it. And by implication Ed and Sandra in the Hotel Bel Air.

Dinah smiled. 'Is that what you want? Is that what you think a simple life is?'

'It's how I'm going to live when I get away from Ed and Sandra. Not going to LA and being *tutored* and *gawped* at because of the way I look instead of just being able to be the way I *am*.'

'How much of the year do you get to spend in London?'

104

The shrug. 'Before I got expelled, all the term-times, at least. Yeah, I know. My own fault. Now I've got a fucking *tutor* and it just depends on what suits Ed.'

'Whereabouts in London do you live?'

Milly frowned. 'Hampstead.'

Dinah turned her head to hide her amusement. Milly's romantic dreams of Camden Town were spun from the silky fibre of extreme privilege.

Dinah said quickly, 'I think my dreams of home are fake because all I really miss is standing on the same ground as Sarah. I used to believe that if something happened to her I would somehow feel it, like a vibration in the earth. But being here, the last connection with her is gone. Milly?'

'Yeah.'

'I've never told anyone any of this.'

'Okay. I won't say anything. Who would I say it *to*?'

'I didn't mean that.'

The child's face grew opaque to fend off the unwelcome responsibility of adult secrets and strictures. Milly had her own secrets.

'So what's going to happen?'

'I'm going to go home. To look for her. Just to see her, that's all.'

Dinah expressed the intention aloud for the first time. It gave her a sense of triumph, just the uttering of it.

Obstacles reared up ahead of her but she thought around them, imagining Sarah's face, trying to mould an almost-woman's features on to the baby's she had last seen.

Milly nodded. 'It's what I'd want you to do if I was her.'

'Is it what you'd like for yourself?'

'I suppose. Yeah, I would. For my mother to come and find me. Only that can't happen, can it? So I'll have to go looking for her. Like, when the time comes. When I'm old enough. It's not that Ed and Sandra aren't right enough in their way. But it's kind of like what you said about the ground, feeling connected. There's someone out there who belongs to *me*.'

Dinah saw. The hair and the clothes and the snarling

disaffection and the sad centre were all explicable. Milly flopped the matted black ropes forward to hide her face.

'My *mother*, right? I just really want to hear why she gave me away.'

'How could you not want to know?'

Dinah spoke gently. Milly would find her birth mother, in time, in all probability. Pieces would fit together for her, whether they made the picture she wanted or not.

It was not the same with Sarah. Dinah could not gauge what Sarah might want.

'Right.' Milly stood up abruptly. The confidences had suddenly begun to bore and embarrass her. 'I'm going upstairs. To sleep, or something.'

Without looking back at Dinah she slouched away, giving Ape a wide berth as she passed him. Dinah let her go. She sat on at the kitchen table, gazing ahead of her, thinking.

Matthew and the boys came home again on Sunday evening. Not knowing exactly when to expect them back, Dinah had taken Milly to a movie. She felt secretly flattered that Milly had agreed to the outing at all, and accepted her sneering afterwards at the cringey loveyness of Tom Hanks and Meg Ryan and the 'awful, puke-making kid' as a necessary piece of face-saving.

The Toyota was parked beside the house when they returned.

'Hi,' Dinah called cheerfully as the front door shuddered open on its spring. Ape was barking. She felt Milly crowding behind her, glaring over her shoulder. It was a very long time since Friday evening, Dinah realised.

The three of them emerged from the kitchen together.

'Where've you been?'

It was Jack who said it, accusingly, but he spoke for them all.

'Just to the movies.'

You shouldn't have gone out. You should have been here, waiting for us. The unspoken words hung in the air. There was a second when they seemed ranged against each other, herself and Milly flushed from the cinema and darkness on one side, the boys and Matthew on the other.

'I've only been gone for two hours. Did you have a good time? Catch anything? Are you hungry?'

She went to Matt and he pecked her cheek.

'Hi. Hello there, Milly. We just wondered where you'd got to. It was so good. Remote, beautiful scenery, so quiet and peaceful. We had a great time, didn't we kids?'

Merlin hung with his arms around Dinah's waist and Jack pulled at her arm, both of them talking across each other. They wanted to repossess her. Their antennae were so sharp, self-preserving, sensing the tiny risk of her defection.

Milly crossed the hall and walked up the stairs, ignoring them. Dinah knew she wouldn't reappear. *Damn. And bugger,* she thought, with sudden savagery.

Matt said as soon as she was out of earshot, 'What's the matter with the girl? She never even said hello.'

'She's fine,' Dinah answered shortly.

She went through into the kitchen. There were four big silvery fish, their scales dimming and their eyes clouded, lying on wet newspaper on the kitchen table. Ape's front claws shredded the newspaper as he sniffed at them. Damp and muddy belongings were shed everywhere else.

'Lovely to have you back.'

Dinah began to gather up the clothes for washing.

'Oh, for Christ's sake,' Matthew muttered. When Dinah looked for him again she saw that he was sitting on the edge of an armchair in the den, utterly absorbed, scribbling on a notepad that belonged to Jack.

Later, after she had cooked the fish and loaded the washing machine and put away the boots and anoraks, Dinah went upstairs to see the boys in bed, Merlin first.

He was lying with the covers close up under his chin but as soon as she opened the door he flung his arms out to pull her down to him. Dinah settled alongside him. His hair was wet and he smelled of soap and toothpaste.

'Had a good clean-up, have you?'

'Dad didn't make us. Mum, I love you. I missed you.'

He wanted her reassurance and she offered it willingly. 'I missed you too. It was quiet without you. Didn't you enjoy yourself?'

'It was cold in bed, actually. Dad was thinking a lot.'

'Was he?' Dinah felt a skip of anxiety. 'It's what he does, you know.'

She hugged him, rubbing the damp base of his skull with her cupped hand.

'Go to sleep now. Everything's okay.' A necessary, temporary lie.

Next door in a litter of magazines and computer discs Jack was reading. The light from his angled bedside lamp reflected off his glasses. He put his book aside with a little show of reluctance. Dinah chatted lightly about the weekend and the movie, but then he cut her short.

'Mum, is everything all right?'

Two years older than Merlin and the antennae were already much more sensitive. And he was like Milly, wanting to be reassured and not willing to admit to the need for it. Dinah took hold of his hand, noting as she always did that the shape of it was the same as Matthew's.

'Why?'

'I wish you had come to the cabin with us.'

'It was a men's weekend, wasn't it?'

'Yes, I suppose. I'd have liked it better if you were there. Dad would, as well.'

The notion pleased her. She felt a surge of warmth in her veins, all the long muscles of her back and legs easing with the flow of it.

'Would he? I'll be there next time.'

'How long is *she* staying?'

'Jack. Don't be unfriendly. Until tomorrow evening, when Ed and Sandra get back from the coast.'

108

He was jealous; he had sensed some connection between herself and Milly that excluded him. And if he was jealous of Milly, how much more jealousy and incomprehension might there be for both of the boys to deal with over Sarah?

Dinah turned their joined hands over. Jack's quilt cover was printed with a map of the world, and their fists now rested on the island of Borneo.

'What do you think about making a trip home to England, to see Granny? Perhaps at Christmas.'

'Cool. Dad would come as well, wouldn't he?'

The question reflected his anxiety. The boys were afraid of what they did not understand.

It will be better for all of us to acknowledge the truth. Even at this late stage.

Dinah smiled and stood up. The long conversation with Milly had opened new channels and given her a feeling of sureness and optimism that had been missing for a long time.

'Oh yes. I should hope so.'

Jack regarded her. 'You look nice,' he said. 'Pretty.'

'Thank you. Time to go to sleep now, all right?'

Dinah kissed him goodnight.

On her way downstairs she was humming, still smiling. They would find a way together. Matt would listen and she would be able to make him understand why she couldn't deny the truth any longer.

He wasn't in the den, where she had left him. The living room was empty and so, except for Ape's rebarbative presence, was the kitchen. Dinah retraced her steps and found Matthew at the far end of their bedroom, sitting with his back to the door at the desk he used for doing serious work. Jack's notepad was open beside him and his shoulders were hunched forward.

She was standing right beside him before he looked up.

'Everyone asleep?'

'Soon will be.'

Dinah had tapped on Milly's door. The response was firm.

'Goodnight, okay?' Dinah was thinking that Milly's assurance had been right, she could look after herself. She was impressed and admiring in equal parts.

'Good. That's good.'

Matt was still scribbling, multiplying chains of formulae. At times in the past Dinah had thought of these spidery markings as code, impenetrable messages that contained some part of her husband she would never be able to read.

She waited now for him to stop and look at her. When he did not she moved deliberately in the space behind him, moving a jacket from the back of a chair and placing it on a hanger, carrying a sheaf of magazines from one place to another and then turning back the covers on the bed, brushing the undersheet smooth with the brisk flat of her hand.

She could feel the heat-waves of irritation emanating from him. But she had spent too many years tiptoeing away from Matthew's sacred concentration. He had all week to concentrate, and the ranks of post-docs and grad students and technicians to revere him for it. Her contribution had become redundant.

'Merlin said you were thinking a lot, up in Vermont.'

Matthew sighed. Then he pushed the sheet of work away from him and clicked the nose of lead back into his propelling pencil.

By the time he swung round in his chair to look at her he had recomposed his face.

'We were out there on the lake, yesterday afternoon. Late on, and the light was fading. The trees had already gone black and there was that pale phosphorescent green in the sky. The boys were getting cold. I stood up carefully, to edge over into the stern and start up the outboard.'

The boat had rocked and set up a series of little ripples that radiated away and changed the colour of the water surface. Mirror grey to oily green-black. As if something innocuous had been peeled back to reveal a threatening underside.

'I was suddenly afraid of falling in.'

In fact he had been frozen with fear in mid-movement. His knees locked as he realised how it would be if the boat tipped over and the three of them fell in. Then the business of rational thought took over. The boys were wearing life-jackets, they would all have a nasty, cold plunge and an uncomfortable trip back to the cabin. But they wouldn't drown. There was no real danger.

The fear sluiced away again as quickly as it had come, and it was as if it left a vacuum behind it. And into that space came an idea. One minute there was terror, then nothing, and immediately after it a perfectly clear-cut possible solution to the problem that had preoccupied him for weeks.

Matt leaned forward with his hands clasped between his knees.

'Ah . . . I suddenly thought of a way of fitting the particular peptide we are dealing with into an active site on the molecule to enable us to synthesise it more readily . . .'

His face furrowed with the effort of translating his abstruse ideas into language Dinah might begin to understand. Ignorance of one another's business no longer seemed to emphasise their closeness in everything else.

'It came so quickly that I was still staring into the water, half-crouching, the boat rocking underneath us. But I knew I had something. It was . . . quite exciting.'

He looked boyish again, as he had done in the thick of the frisbee game. *Quite exciting* was an odd understatement. But then Dinah understood that he was wary of her. He didn't want to emphasise the importance of his work or his commitment to it because he knew that she was out of sympathy with it.

How long had he felt this way?

It saddened her to think that it was the instant of terror that had given him his idea, whereas once he had made his conjectures out of passion and happiness and confidence.

Matt was fearful too. He walked as narrow a path as she did, controlling himself with work and responsibility and the wary tenderness that had taken the place of love.

Dinah put out her hand to touch his head, and then cupped the hard curve of his skull, as she had done with Merlin.

'I'm afraid I got pretty absorbed with the idea after that. I wanted to think and the boys needed me to play cards or something. I was kind of short with them.'

She knew how it would have been. When he was absorbed in something Matt had to be reminded to eat and keep himself warm and clean. Usually she was there to make up the shortcomings.

'They seem to have enjoyed themselves anyway.'

'Mm. I'm not going to be sure of anything until I can get to the lab and have Sean look at the model on the computer. But I'm sure there's something here.'

'Good. That's good news.'

Matthew unclasped his hands and rested them on her hips. There was something in the way he touched her that was not quite direct, as if he were handling a shop-window mannequin. Dinah looked past him at the scribbled formulae. Code. Connecting and conveying him elsewhere, excluding her. She had never felt jealous of his work before, but she did now. Buried associations nibbled somewhere beneath the surface of what she knew, bothering her with a sense of imperfect understanding.

'Are you coming to bed?' she asked him.

'Yeah, I guess so. I can't do anything else tonight.'

He would have liked to go to the labs now.

Dinah imagined him impatiently walking the rubber-floored corridors, flipping on the lights to beam ahead of him. There was a notice on the door of the computer room. 'This equipment must be kept cool. If you are cold, wear a coat.' Once she had been shown inside. On the big square screens were red and blue and green and yellow strands caught in a complex blue lattice, modelled protein atoms in the amino acid chain, like fish suspended in a net. The technicians manipulated the fish and the nets, twisting and drawing them through the depths of black computer seas.

112

Dinah had stood for a while, watching over the shoulder of a girl in a UMass football jersey. Then Matt had come back and led her away.

When they were in bed in the dark she slid her hand over his upper arm and down over the discernible collar of flesh around his waist. There was a need to feel connected to him. She stroked him and waited. After a moment he responded. On her face she felt the warm exhaled air of his inaudible sigh as he ran his fingers over her skin, outer thigh and inner thigh, and then between her legs.

He was being obliging. Following the success of a thousand previous occasions. Only indirectly now, as if he were handling someone who was not quite herself, or as if the image of someone else hovered between them.

He remained limp in the palm of her hand.

Was there someone?

Dinah kept still. He had time, and opportunity. He was so often away. There were the lectures and conferences and all the hours in the lab. But the possibility had never occurred to her before. How naïve. Or had their failures of communication merely corroded her trust?

'I'm sorry,' Matthew whispered. 'Tired, I guess.'

'Doesn't matter.' She put the suspicion aside with an effort of will. They laced their arms around each other and lay with their faces a centimetre apart.

Dinah thought of explaining about Milly, and the conduits that their talk had opened up.

Home, searching, Sarah. Truth for the boys, and for themselves at last.

The words formed in her head only to be discarded.

Not now, but she would find a way to get what she wanted.

Matthew and she had made a mistake, and the one essential was to put it right.

The polite silence could not endure any longer and she would not allow it to.

If she was mad and dangerous – why then, so she was. But

Dinah did not think that was the case. She thought she was right.

'Goodnight,' Matthew said. He turned a little away from her, preparing for sleep.

She echoed the word, releasing him.

Six

It was the day before Thanksgiving, and the building was almost deserted. Matthew had been to a two-day conference in Washington and on the way home he had found the flights and airports crammed with holiday travellers. Dinah was expecting him home by the early evening, but he had driven straight from the airport to the lab.

He unlocked his office and put his flight bag and briefcase on the floor beside his desk. His secretary had gone but she had left his letters in neat stacks on the blotter, with a row of coloured Post-it messages beside them. Matthew picked up an offprint of a journal article that Jon Liu had left for him, and glanced at the abstract. It was a preliminary report of some findings by the team at Cal Tech who were working in the same field as his own, but even so he couldn't properly focus on the figures. He was straining his ears for the sound of a door closing or a radio playing, anything that would tell him that there was someone else still at work.

After a moment he dropped the offprint on to the heaped papers on his desk. He took off his suit jacket and hung it over the back of his chair, then went out into the silent corridor. There was no one to be seen. Sean Rader's door was open, but the light was off and his ancient donkey jacket was missing from its hook. Matthew had no idea where he might be spending Thanksgiving. Sean had no family, and no interests beyond his work.

The computer room was locked, but the set of double doors beyond it was hooked open. Matthew saw it with a quick beat of satisfaction, but he put his hands in his pockets and made himself walk slowly, as if he were thoughtfully checking his domain before heading home for his family holiday.

The lab corridor was also empty, but now he was sure that there was someone else about. He could hear what he had been straining his ears for, the cheerful bass thump of radio rock music.

The light in the lab was bright. The brilliance thickened the late afternoon into premature darkness beyond the dusty glass and the cacti and overgrown spider plants ranged on the high window-sills.

Matt always liked this time for working, when the world outside receded and the benches and stools and sinks and familiar equipment composed themselves into a creaking, dust-scented inner universe.

Kathrin was at the other end of the room with her back to him. Her red knitted coat hung in a tangle at the end of the bench, as if she had pulled it off in a hurry to get to work. Her small dark head was bent over a rack of test-tubes and there was a battered transistor radio wedged between the reagent bottles on the shelf above her. She had told him that she liked to have the local rock station playing because it helped her to concentrate.

Matt stood in the doorway. Pleasure at the sight of her loosened his limbs. He hesitated for a moment, enjoying the privilege of watching her unobserved. She made small neat movements with the glass pipette in her fingers, bestowing a single drop of colourless liquid on each tube in turn. Her absorption in the task stirred a sense of intimacy within Matthew that was more potent than his physical desire for her.

116

He was almost sorry when she sensed his eyes on her and turned her head. Dark hair briefly fanned around her face.

'Hi.'

She jumped and a quick flush of blood coloured her cheeks.

'You startled me.' She was smiling. He knew at once that his appearance out of the holiday silence was welcome to her.

'I didn't mean to.'

He crossed the lab to her side. Kathrin emptied the pipette carefully into the beaker at her elbow.

'Nearly done, this lot,' she murmured. She hooked a strand of hair behind her ear. She was small-boned and her hands seemed tiny and fragile.

Matthew looked at the numbers on the labels. Kathrin was making a series of tests involving minute chemical variations on the newest batch of re-engineered insulin. The idea he had had on the lake in Vermont was already having an effect.

'It looks good,' Kathrin said. 'Really good. I wanted to run these through before I went . . .'

She glanced up at him, silently acknowledging that there was a much more significant reason for her to be late in the labs when everyone else had gone on holiday.

Matthew hesitated. He was eager to see the latest results and his eagerness was fired by Kathrin's excited absorption in what she had been doing. His sense of the inevitability of their connection grew stronger. She was here, part of his thinking, as close to him as anyone could be.

'I was afraid you would already have gone,' he whispered.

Her face changed again, now coolly acknowledging that Matthew's words took them beyond the boundaries of a neutral exchange about work.

Kathrin had been waiting for this moment. She put the pipette tidily aside.

'I'm not going home. All the way to Fort Worth and my mom's got my brother and his family there. I'm quite happy just to be here, getting on with this. Look at the readings . . .'

She put a print-out into his hands. Matthew ran his eye down the columns of figures.

He thought, *yes.*

The beat of triumph was like a fist pushing his ribcage upwards and outwards. It was going to work. For the first time he knew with certainty that they were going to get their result. How soon, whether it would be before Korner's team at Cal Tech, that would be the question now . . .

When he looked down at her again, Kathrin's black eyes were shining under the dark curve of her eyelashes. Her smooth olive skin stretched over her cheekbones. Matthew's pleasure in the new results and in her closeness felt like a warm spoon dipping into honey, into a hollow somewhere within himself, a place that had not been reached into in a long time.

He cut off the thin-voiced alternative commentary that ran in his head. He cupped his hands on either side of her face and turned her mouth up to his. And she edged closer to him as he kissed her so that he felt the faint remembered pressure of her bird-bones against his thighs and his chest.

There had been only one other time, although in the interval since that night Matthew had imagined countless variations. Once or twice he had caught sight of her across the corridor or sitting in the dining commons with Jon and Fraser and the other post-docs and found himself unable to believe that these vivid encounters were only the product of his middle-aged imagination. Kathrin seemed always to know when he was watching her. She never made any tactless show that might incriminate either of them, but she tilted her head in faint acknowledgement, turning her lips inward in the ghost of a smile before she looked away.

The silky threads of her hair spilled between Matt's fingers as he kissed her now. He forgot the lab, and the reality of harsh lights and benches and chemical smells, and the radio drive-time banter that wormed into his head, and lost himself again in Kathrin.

118

The first time had been after a dinner, one of the convivial evenings Matt's team often shared after a good week's work. Matthew took a pride in these joint celebrations, like the frisbee games. They were indications that they all worked well together. At the end of a noisy evening in a pizza restaurant Matthew found himself with two passengers in the Toyota. One of them was Jon Liu and the other was Kathrin Pang.

Matt and Kathrin had seen Jon home together; Jon was socially excitable and had a notoriously weak head for alcohol. Together they hoisted him into bed, and left him snoring.

'I'll drive you home,' Matt offered when they stood on the path outside Jon's house.

'It's a bit of a way out of town.'

'No matter.'

She had twiddled with the radio knobs as he drove, and then settled back with a sigh of satisfaction having found what she wanted to listen to. Rock music. He twisted his head to glance at her, and was struck by her smallness. The car seat seemed almost to swallow her up.

Kathrin lived in a frame house in a settlement out on the Northampton road. Matthew turned into the driveway and the Camry's headlamps briefly lit up the peeling paintwork of the front door.

'Come in?'

He peered through the windshield. There were trees behind the house, and an area of rough grass surrounding it. Kathrin seemed too young to be living in this isolated place.

'Just for a minute.'

The business of putting Jon to bed had created an intimacy between them that now seemed ready to swell into something more. Matthew was aware that he had drunk a good deal of wine. He should not have been driving, he knew that, and he had the half-formed thought that black coffee would be welcome.

He followed her into the house and half stumbled over the

step. There was a scent of joss-sticks and girls' perfume in the close hallway.

'This way.'

Kathrin turned on the light.

Her room reminded him of a student's in a hall of residence. There was a desk in an alcove and an angled lamp, and the walls on the three sides of the alcove were papered with art postcards and snapshots. He glanced quickly, half guiltily, but the few articles of clothing draped over the back of an armchair were innocent outer wear. A low divan bed, neat under a quilt, occupied the length of one wall. Kathrin took a disc from a rack and slipped it into the player.

Matthew stood uneasily. This was an innocent place, reminiscent of other rooms that held fragments of his own history, and it was therefore exciting and faintly disturbing.

'I should go. Really, it's late.'

'Won't you have a last drink?'

She left the room and came back again with wineglasses, a bottle. She was talking, explaining that her room-mate was in New York for the weekend, that she was looking for somewhere to live closer to the department, that her old car was about to expire. She sat down on her patchwork-covered bed, leaning with her head on her hand and her knees drawn up.

The conversation separated itself, becoming something they continued between them whilst all the time there was another exchange of unspoken language. Kathrin leant forward, refilled his glass, her cuff riding up to reveal a thin gold chain around her wrist.

Matthew had no idea how long they had been talking.

Her body made a neat series of curves. Matthew knew that he would not evade the moment that was approaching soon, almost now, when he had taken another mouthful of wine, when she stood up to post another disc into the player.

It was Kathrin who made the move. She put down her glass and came to him, leaning down over him so that she seemed momentarily huge, blotting out the light.

'I wanted you to come back here tonight.'

'Did you?'

She swayed forward, closer, fingers on his shoulders and hips tilted forward. Then she quickly sat down, straddling him, locking her arms around his neck.

Her face swam out of focus. She kissed him, and he lifted his hands to centre her, spanning her narrow ribcage, holding her where he wanted her to be. She rocked gently against him.

And after that there was the expected sequence of events, familiar and yet entirely unfamiliar.

Thinking back, Matthew could not determine any point when he could have extricated himself, even if he had wanted to.

The scent of her and the remembered texture of her skin stayed with him in the days afterwards. He did not feel awkward about her as he had imagined he would do – he found instead that he went looking for her in the labs, making up reasons for calling into the office she shared with two other post-docs.

In these public places Kathrin did not give any sign that she expected anything from him. But he knew she was waiting. That was why she was still at work on the night before Thanksgiving when everyone else had gone home to their families. And in acknowledgement of that – he now admitted to himself – he had come here to find her.

Her fingers explored his face, as if she were trying to memorise the contours.

'I hoped you'd come. I thought you would,' she smiled at him and Matthew wondered briefly if he were so predictable.

'Shall we go home?' she whispered.

He had not intended to, he did not know exactly what he had planned once he had seen her, but still he found himself following the tail-lights of her VW out of Franklin to the frame house and the innocent bedroom. The room-mate was away again.

'I can't stay long,' Matthew said, sitting on the quilt.

121

Kathrin undid his tie and the cuff buttons of the pale blue starchy conference shirt.

'Anxious?'

She was teasing him a little, even as she undid his zipper and bent her head.

I won't do this again, Matthew thought.

It was late, and Dinah and the boys were waiting for him. This girl was a colleague, and he was falling into an intimacy with her that was based on a false premise.

And yet.

Dinah was angry, and her anger had begun to rub patches of hard indifference in him. It was often easier to be apart from her, to be at the labs or travelling, or somewhere between the two.

It was a long time since they had done anything like this together.

Matthew's hand cupped the back of Kathrin's smooth head. He came quickly, into her mouth, thrilled and ashamed of himself.

Kathrin sat back on her heels, resting her hands on his thighs. She looked up at him triumphantly.

'I love you,' she said.

He said dazedly, 'No, you don't. You don't know me, anything about what I'm really like.'

'I do. I know what you can do, what you're capable of. Your ideas, the way you direct them. Do you think I'm just acting out a cliché, falling in love with the boss? Professor? Is that what you think?'

'Of course not.'

'Good. Because I know what I feel and need. I'm not stupid.'

'You certainly are not.'

It was true. She was a clever scientist, capable and accurate in her methods, if a little plodding. She was also, he thought now, just a little frightening.

'Lie down here with me.'

She held out her arms and drew him down to her. He

made himself comfortable, holding her against him. Five minutes, he thought. Kathrin was pliant as soon as she got what she wanted. She sighed with pleasure and he breathed in the scent of her, letting his apprehensiveness break up and drift away. He might have dozed, but they talked instead about the new molecule and the difficulties of synthesising sufficient quantities of it. It was stimulating to be physically so close and all the time to have her follow his thinking as well.

He missed that with Dinah, whereas once their ignorance of each other's work had only emphasised their intimacy in everything else.

After a little while, Matthew felt himself harden again in Kathrin's hand.

She hoisted herself on top of him. Her spine arched as he drove into her and her throat and small breasts and flat stomach made an arc above him.

'You are beautiful,' Matt said truthfully.

But there was something in her abandonment to him that reawakened his anxiety, as well as his pleasure.

After she came she lay on top of him, frogwise, her open mouth hot against his neck. Matthew eased his wrist to one side, so that he could look at his watch.

Very late.

Gently he murmured to her, 'I have to go home now.'

'*Now?*'

She sat up again. Her submissiveness vanished.

'I'm afraid so. I was supposed to be back and I haven't even called to say . . .'

'What about me?'

He wanted to reassure her and to make his defection less brutal. He stroked her cheek with his fingertips.

'I wish I didn't have to.'

'You don't.'

'Kathrin, you know who I am. You told me earlier, you know how I think. Therefore you must also know the obvious things. I am married, I am a father.'

Tears came into her eyes. Matthew thought, *This is trouble.*

'What about me? It's Thanksgiving, and I'm going to be here all alone.'

'You have friends, plenty of people in Franklin.'

Tears were visible on her cheeks, but she kept her voice steady. 'I love *you*. What about this, didn't it mean anything to you?'

'Yes, it did.' It was the truth, and she could not help but be convinced by it. 'But I still have to go home now.'

Matthew got up and dragged on his clothes while Kathrin stared mutely from the tangle of quilt. He felt suddenly very tired. When he was ready to leave she scrambled up and wrapped herself in a kimono, and followed him to the door.

'When can we see each other again?' she asked.

'On Monday, in the department.'

'I mean like this.' Her finger touched the lapel of his crumpled suit jacket.

'I don't know. If I've hurt you, Kathrin, or misled you, I'm truly sorry. I don't *know* anything else, for sure.'

He left her, and backed the Toyota away from the little house. The road back to Franklin was almost empty of traffic. Everyone else had already reached their destination.

Matthew drove without seeing anything. He was angry with himself, and distaste made his mouth sour. At the back of his head, a pulse beat out a nagging reminder, *trouble.*

Dinah was sitting at the kitchen table reading. She had lately started wearing glasses, and the lenses seemed to shield her eyes from him. There was a single place laid at the opposite end of the table, with a covered plate to one side of it.

Matthew leant down and kissed the top of her head, but she made no response. 'I'm sorry I'm so late. Where are the boys?'

'In bed, of course. Hours ago. What kept you?'

'I ran into a guy from Dartmouth, stopped to have a beer with him. Then there was a delay on the flight.'

'I called Logan. They said it was on time.'

'I told you, I met someone and got a later flight.'

'Ah.'

'And then there was hideous traffic across Boston.'

'Why didn't you call?'

'Didn't really get the chance. Is this for me?' He took the cover off the dish and pinched a cold potato between his finger and thumb.

'Who else might it be for? I'm not expecting anyone. You may be, of course.'

'Di, don't be like this.'

'Don't you be, then.'

She stood up. As she moved away, breaking out of the circle of light over the table, Matthew looked at her as if he were catching sight of her for the first time. In his head there was a laughing, vivid-faced girl. This older Dinah who had slid into her place wore the same striking face but it had grown thinner, and she moved wearily, without the springing energy she had once possessed. Her mass of dark hair was pulled into a careless knot and her expression was exhausted and sad, her lips colourless and nipped into a thin line.

Beneath his diaphragm Matthew felt the nagging burn of remorse. He put his arms around her waist, but she held herself rigid.

'Let's try to have a good weekend,' he coaxed.

'Do you remember that we're going to the Parkeses?'

'Yes, I remember.' There would be an overabundance of elaborate food and drink and the expectation that everyone would enjoy themselves in direct proportion.

'Fine,' Dinah said. She moved away from him, gathering up her book. 'I'm going up to bed, now I know you haven't had a crash on the freeway or a heart attack or something.'

Was that what she wanted?

Matthew sat down at the table and ate the remains of dinner, tasting none of it.

'Come on in,' Ed called to them. He put his arm round

Matthew's shoulder and drew him into the crowd. The big room was hot, full of people laughing and talking.

Dinah saw the boys edge away to join the Berkmann children at the pool table. There was no sign of Milly anywhere, but Sandra was in the kitchen. There was a rich mix of cooking smells, and she was basting an immense turkey. She introduced a large, white-haired woman to Dinah as Ed's mother.

'Thirty people for Thanksgiving,' Sandra said. 'Am I crazy?'

Mrs Parkes was folding napkins. 'We always had a big party in the old days, when Milton was alive. I used to do it all myself.'

'Can I help?' Dinah asked Sandra. They had not seen much of one another since the Parkeses' return from the coast. Milly had gone home, with her rucksack, and obviously under Sandra's direction had written Dinah a stilted letter of thanks for her hospitality. The contrast between the note and Milly's actual behaviour made Dinah smile. She had folded the sheet of paper and put it in the drawer of her writing desk.

'You could chop these.' Sandra passed her a handful of shallots.

A troop of small children swarmed through the kitchen, spreading candy wrappers.

'These are Richie's kids,' Rene Parkes beamed. 'Ed's younger brother, that is.'

'His third lot. The oldest two from his first wife are here as well. The boy's at Columbia and the girl's an assistant in publishing.' Sandra slammed the oven door shut on the bloated turkey and exchanged a glance with Dinah.

'Richie always loved children,' his mother chuckled. 'Where is Camilla, anyway? I've hardly seen her.'

'In her room. Leave her be for now. God, it's hot in here. I've got to have some fresh air. Bring your drink out on the deck with me, Dinah.'

They stepped out of the glass doors. It was a sharp, clear

126

day scented with woodsmoke. Sandra spread her hands on the rail as she looked down over the treetops, and the diamonds on her fingers refracted tiny rainbows in the sunlight.

'Are you all right?' Dinah asked her.

'Apart from it being Thanksgiving, d'you mean? No, not really. Milly's very difficult. She hardly speaks nowadays. Except to sneer at us. Times like now just make it worse, more apparent. Look at all this. Ed's mother, and her oldest friend. Richie and his third wife and kids, his *second* wife's sister and mother, believe it or not. The kids from the first wife. Ed's father's younger sister and her son the dentist. Have you met him?'

'Not yet. And that's just family. You've got the Berkmanns and us and who else?' Dinah laughed. 'You can't really blame Milly. *I'd* want to hide in my room . . .'

'It's not so funny.'

'I know. I'm sorry.'

Sandra turned, folding her arms tightly across the apron that covered her cashmere tunic. Her face had a yellowish tinge that made her look older and exhausted. Dinah saw how unhappy she was. She wondered about the particular terms of the Parkeses' contract.

'I'm sorry . . .' she began again, but Sandra cut her short.

'Milly likes you,' she said. It came out as an accusation. Sandra drew a corner of her mouth between her teeth and began again.

'After that weekend she told me you talked to her like no one else ever does. It isn't that I don't try to talk, to understand her. God knows, I want to badly enough. But she doesn't want to hear anything that comes from me, or from Ed. What *did* you say to her?'

Dinah moved back a little. All her instincts were against talking about this now, with the intrusive backdrop of relatives and children behind them. Her fear was that Sandra might unknowingly come too close to her own secret, that it was too near to the surface of her own thoughts. She was turning over and over in her mind the intention she had formed to go home, to find Sarah. There was no question now that she would do it. Only when, and how.

Dinah hesitated. 'I . . . talked mostly about myself. And Milly listened.'

Sandra knew that she was being deflected again.

She asked harshly, 'Did she tell you that she's adopted?'

'Yes.'

Sandra's fingers dug more deeply into her crossed arms. It was cold out on the deck.

'And so you think I've done everything wrong?'

The aggressiveness of her tone overlaying jealousy and uncertainty made Dinah say too quickly,

'No, not at all. It wasn't an easy weekend, but I think Milly is admirable in many ways. I also think she is rather remarkable.'

'*You* think she's remarkable?'

Sandra's anger and bitterness were clear to see. Dinah understood that she was painfully vulnerable where Milly was concerned. She resented even the tentative friendship Dinah had begun with her.

'Yes, I do,' Dinah said gently. She did not want to give Sandra any cause for jealousy, but she also wanted to speak up for Milly.

Sandra turned aside and stared down over the relief map of trees.

'I don't know what to do,' she shrugged, her anger fading into helplessness. Dinah reached out and covered Sandra's hand with hers. The diamonds on Sandra's fingers felt like small rocks.

The glass doors opened behind them and Ed emerged.

'Honey? When're we going to be ready to eat? People are getting kinda hungry in there.'

She closed her eyes for a second.

'Be right with you.'

Dinah said in a low voice, 'Just let her grow up a bit. Not that I know anything.'

'You're right. You don't. But thanks, anyway. Let's go and see to the bloody turkey, shall we?'

There seemed to be even more people swarming through the house. A long table filled the dining space. Rene and her friend were tweaking the elaborate napkin folds at each place setting and Richie's youngest child was howling in a high chair. Dinah could hear Max Berkmann's raised voice explaining to the Columbia sophomore that the best French burgundy he had ever tasted had been at the domaine itself, not far from Beaune. In the kitchen Maria Berkmann was setting out plates with Ed at her elbow piratically swishing a carving knife over a steel.

'I'm going to take the turkey out, let it rest while we eat the first course,' Sandra told him. 'Will you just get everybody to sit *down?*'

They were marshalled into their places. Four branched candlesticks with blazing candles were set down the length of the table. Max and Richie and the dentist had jocularly different ideas about the seating plan, until Ed came and rearranged everyone. The older children slithered into their places, covertly making faces at each other.

'So lovely to be together again,' Rene was singing. 'Where *is* Camilla?'

Sandra picked up the intercom and murmured into it.

There was too much noise and confusion for her to make one of her entrances. Dinah was watching out for her and she saw her hesitate at the top of the steps, then trail slowly down into the party. The only empty chair was at the far end of the table, near the opening into the kitchen, between Merlin and Richie's daughter who worked in publishing.

Milly was, unusually, not wearing her shredded black clothes although her hair was more fantastically matted and dead looking, by way of compensation. She was shrouded in a huge white T-shirt, on which stark black letters spelt out 'NO more slaughter'.

She carried her little rucksack, which she hung very carefully over the back of her chair before sitting down. She didn't look at anyone, although her publishing cousin shot her a warm smile and a 'Hi!' in greeting.

'So what's this, Milly?' Richie called down the table. He looked and sounded a good deal like his brother, only in a smaller and less luxurious edition. 'Anti-war protest today?'

'Yeah. Right.'

Milly's scorn for the question and for the table and the whole of this Thanksgiving was palpable and corrosive. Dinah felt it from where she sat, and she had to duck her head to hide her smile of amused sympathy.

'Let's eat,' Ed called. The focus of attention shifted with relief away from Milly to food and wine and general conversation. Dinah began to talk to Ed's surprisingly well-preserved aunt about her home in Connecticut. The candles quartered the table with sixteen golden points of light as the daylight faded outside. Dinah caught Matthew's eye just once. He gave her his smile that cut out everyone else, even the boys, reminding her of intimacy they had once enjoyed without enabling her to recall just how that intimacy had felt.

Ed was still talking, explaining some point to the top end of the table. Sandra had cleared the soup plates and now heaped dishes of vegetables and corn bread were passing the other way. The volume of noise was steadily rising. Yet somehow, there came a moment of relative quiet into which Milly said,

'I'll bring the turkey in for you.'

She stood up in her white T-shirt.

'It will be much too heavy,' Sandra said.

'I'd like to.'

'Let her do it,' Ed called across to them. Milly went round into the kitchen and after a moment reappeared with the great bronze shining bird borne ahead of her on an oval dish. There was a good-humoured anticipatory chorus of compliments and admiration.

'That one looks a real beauty,' Rene said.

Milly put the turkey down on a side table, where Ed's

sharpened carving knife lay ready and waiting. Sandra was busy with the vegetables, and Ed was finishing his anecdote.

Dinah saw Milly move unhurriedly to her bag slung on the back of her chair, and remove something from it.

It was a quart-sized can with a coloured label.

Milly put it on the side table next to the turkey dish and used the point of the carving knife to lever off the lid. Then she lifted the can to head height, as if she were offering a libation to some deity.

The conversation around the table faltered and faded away. All eyes turned to Milly.

Dinah heard Ed splutter, 'What are you *doing*?'

And in the same instant Milly's wrist tilted and there was a flash of something red, bright hard scarlet, much too bright for blood.

'Je-*sus*.'

Ed was out of his chair and so was his brother, but too late.

Milly had poured an entire can of scarlet paint, a viscous trail of flashing red antisauce, all over the Thanksgiving turkey. There was an antiphonal chorus of shock and dismay out of which Rene's voice squawked, 'Whatever has the girl done now?'

Milly dropped the can and turned her back on her handiwork, and her eyes searched for Dinah in the line of open-mouthed faces.

'Meat is murder,' Milly said. But so glibly that Dinah knew her act was far more one of naked defiance against Ed and Sandra and the familiar rite of Thanksgiving than any vegan protest.

Sandra dived at the dish and dabbed at it with kitchen paper. Blobs and dribbles of scarlet seemed to appear retroactively on the wall and furniture and now on her clothes. Yet Milly had managed to stay pure white, like some turkey-avenging angel.

Ed reached the side table and seized her arms. For a moment Dinah thought he intended to wrestle the child to the ground.

131

'You will come with me. Out of here. Right now.'

He propelled her up the steps and beyond the balcony, out of sight. Milly went willingly, without a backward glance.

The women clustered around Sandra.

'No good,' somebody said. The kitchen paper was taken out of Sandra's hands.

'I'm afraid you're right,' she agreed. Her face was hard and bright.

Almost everyone had left the table. There was a mêlée of paint-wipers and helpers to remove the ruined turkey. It took Ed to come back and restore some order.

'Milly just asked me to apologise to everyone,' he called from the balcony, and then as he descended the stairs, 'She does feel kind of strongly about animal rights. Not that that gives her any right to do what she did. Now, Sandy, what have we got?'

There was chestnut stuffing and sweet potatoes and gravy, and cranberry sauce and mounds of vegetables with excellent pumpkin pie to follow, and that was what they ate. A meal that Milly would have approved of, Dinah thought. Surprise and gastronomic disappointment and a kind of gloomy relish gave the talk an added edge, and sent the wine down freely. Ed and Sandra became heroically cheerful and even more hospitable, and everyone understood that the turkey-and-paint Thanksgiving would some day pass into family mythology. Not yet, but eventually.

When Dinah looked at Matthew she suddenly recognised that he was creased with contained laughter that answered her own. But I *do* remember, she thought, and her anger with him eased a little.

In the car on the way home Jack asked, 'What would you have done if I'd done that?'

'Oh, thrown you out with the garbage, I expect.'

'Rolled you off the roof.'

'Put you in the blender and made *purée* of you,' Merlin shouted in triumph.

They were reciting a family mantra. When Merlin was born

Jack had been so jealous that the three of them had spent hours devising the worst things that could be done to the new baby. When Matt came up with the purée suggestion Jack had finally protested. 'Oh no, that's *cruel.*'

'No, I mean really. What would you have done?'

'I would have been very, very angry with you,' Dinah said simply.

'Yeah,' Jack breathed. 'I can imagine.'

I love them both so much, Dinah was thinking. The Toyota rolled smoothly back towards Franklin. Her love for the boys felt concrete for an instant, a solid smooth shape lodged within her, hampering her breathing, but the love was also all wrapped around and rubbed with the irritations of proximity and familiarity. They made her angry and impatient too, just as Matt did. And all the time her closed-off love and longing for Sarah was sharp and separate, denied its outlet, unhealed beneath the scar.

I have to find her, Dinah repeated to herself. Whatever it will mean.

Matthew lifted his hand off the wheel and reached for hers. When he laced their fingers together she felt the warmth of him, and let her hand lie instead of withdrawing it.

Perhaps after all we could look for her together, she thought. Perhaps I can make him understand why I need it so much.

The next afternoon the boys went out to play somewhere at the cul-de-sac end of Kendrick with an assortment of children. It was a raw afternoon with a thin mist hovering at the margins of the river and woods, and Matt and Dinah preferred to sit inside by the fire. Dinah had her book and Matt his papers and journals. Ape lay on the rug between them with his belly luxuriously exposed to the warmth.

'This is okay,' Matt sighed, stretching his legs. 'Thanksgiving has its good points.'

A log fell into the hearth in a shower of red sparks, making Dinah jump. She felt uncomfortable with this show of domestic calm whilst the twists of discord were temporarily frozen beneath the surface. The sentences and paragraphs she was trying to read skidded away from the point of her attention and she forced herself over and over again to backtrack and reread. She must talk to Matt about the trip to England. This evening, perhaps. When the boys were asleep.

She had given up trying to read and gone into the kitchen to make tea when the telephone rang.

A woman's voice announced itself as Dr Kathrin Pang, and asked for Professor Steward.

'Matt? It's for you. Dr Pang.'

A sheaf of manuscript pages slid from his lap and fanned across the floor as he picked up. The doors were all open. Dinah did not try to overhear, she could not have avoided doing so. She remembered now, Kathrin Pang was the little dark oriental-looking post-doc. The frisbee game. She had seen her playing frisbee that day with all the others, she had stumbled on the bank and then raced after them, anxious not to be left behind.

Matthew answered. 'Yes?'

'I wanted to talk to you.'

It was Kathrin's voice, there was no mistake although his first wild hope had been that he had somehow misheard.

'Yes?' he repeated.

'I'm in the lab. I'm here all alone. I spent yesterday alone too.'

Matthew transferred the receiver to his other hand, an inch or two further away from Dinah. The house around him became a giant shell, a listening ear to pick up and amplify this whispering until it roared around them all.

'Is there a problem?'

'Only that you aren't here. Come down now, say you have to work or something.'

'It isn't very convenient at the moment.'

'You didn't have convenience in mind on Wednesday evening. I want to *see* you. Is that wrong? I'm only asking for a little piece of your time. Or I could come to you, if you'd rather. I can drive over to your house now, would that be better?'

'No.'

She was teasing him and threatening him both together. She wasn't crazy, there was no refuge for him in that. Kathrin was sane, and sure of what she wanted.

'What, then?'

Matthew could not make his mind work. He had seen this trouble coming and still it had caught him unprepared.

'Wait, listen. Um. I'll come in as soon as I can. Leave it as it is until then, and I will try to sort it out.'

Did he sound as though there was some urgent problem with the computer? In his own ears his voice was reedy and desperate.

'I'll be here. I'm sorry, okay? I just had to call you.'

Matthew bent down and gathered up the scattered pages. When he straightened up Dinah was standing in the doorway.

'So that's who it is.'

Of course she knew.

'What do you mean?'

He began the obligatory denial wearily, without any appetite for it.

'Matt, don't lie. Why should you think I don't see anything? How long has it been?'

He held up his hand, fending off her anger and grief. He felt as if he had been doing so for a long time.

'I have to go to the lab for an hour.'

'Yes, I see. Will you be coming back?'

'Of course I will.'

She stood aside to let him pass, drawing herself and even the loose folds of her clothes away as if to avoid contamination.

'Dinah . . .'

'Just go.'

He went outside and got into the Toyota. In the rear view mirror before he turned into Pleasant Street he caught a glimpse of Merlin riding someone else's bicycle at speed through a complicated coke-can slalom course.

Dinah walked through the house, entering each room as if taking an inventory of everything she had shared with Matthew. Her heart was thumping uncomfortably but she did not feel deeply shocked. The sight and sound of Matthew on the telephone to his Dr Pang only confirmed what she had known already, down in some denied compartment locked within herself.

In Jack's room she made a neat pile of the floppy disks that lay scattered on his desk. Merlin still had babyish soft toys on his windowseat, a felt-antlered moose and a grinning dinosaur. In the big bedroom she picked up and folded clothes that had been left lying on a chair, and scooped a necklace and bracelet from the day before into the box where she kept her jewellery. Otherwise everything was tidy, the bed made, the wicker lid of the linen basket in place.

She had a sense of a logical conclusion reached at last. It was the saddest conclusion, but there was no denying its inevitability.

If it was the truth that she and Matthew had failed one another – and she did not yet know that for sure, but it seemed that they had – then it was vital not to fail elsewhere. She must make everything right for Jack and Merlin, and that making right meant going back to the beginning, to Sarah, and unpicking all the mistakes that she had made since then.

Dinah said aloud, 'Sarah.'

Her name fell strangely in the warm room, well-furnished with all the things that Matthew and she had chosen together.

She had known ever since the weekend of Milly's visit that she must search for Sarah, but she had put off choosing the day and announcing her decision because it seemed to mean a choice between Matthew and everything else.

And now the choice was made for her. Matthew was

unfaithful. Her own lack of surprise at the discovery was more shocking than the truth itself, but she no longer felt that his needs weighted the scale against her own.

The boys came in, hungry and muddy.

Jack looked at her and said, 'Mum, what's wrong?'

Even Jack had lately taken to calling her *Mom*, but anxiety made him reach further back.

'Nothing's wrong. Dad's gone to the lab. Come here to me. Are you ready for some supper now?'

Dinah held them against her, too tightly, with the pressure of love bursting in her chest. She saw that they twisted their heads, trying in confusion to see her face.

She let them go and reassured them as neutrally as she could, trying to make up the shortfall with dry clothes and hot food. She did not yet know what she would tell them.

When Matthew found her, Kathrin was working at her bench with her radio playing, just as she had been two days earlier.

At first she was apologetic, and then angry with him, and then she wept. He stood with his arms around her while she cried, bitterly aware of his own helplessness and futility.

'Didn't you understand?' Kathrin sobbed. 'I love you and I thought you knew. I thought you felt something the same, only you were too loyal to say so.'

'No,' Matthew said sadly. He wondered what kind of messages he had unwittingly given to this girl to make her think that. 'You are lovely, but I should have been able to resist what happened. I'm sorry that I didn't, and I'm sorry all this has hurt you so much. But you see, I love Dinah, my family . . . I don't want to risk losing them.'

How pathetic it sounded, Matthew thought. How self-interested. And was it true, even? There was Dinah, shrinking away in order that he didn't brush against her as he passed. Angry. And his own determination, containment. Work, labs and late hours, his team, an alternative family.

'I'm sorry,' he repeated.

137

At length, Kathrin turned away from him. 'What about all this?' she asked. She meant the bench, glassware, print-outs. Her importance in this hierarchy, at least.

Matt felt a whisper of relief, and then optimism that surprised him.

'There is always this, work to do. Good work. Look, we're nearly there.'

It was true. Another two, three weeks. There would be months of clinical tests to be done, but they had almost perfected the new insulin in its raw form. Before Christmas. It might be before Christmas. Matthew felt the old pressure of ambitious longing beneath his ribs.

'Nearly,' Kathrin echoed. She rubbed her eyes and nose savagely with the back of her hand.

Matthew drove the familiar route home again. He had been out for nearly two hours.

Dinah and the boys were playing cards. As soon as Jack saw his father he folded his hand.

'Dad?'

'I'm back. I'm sorry I had to go out.' Dinah did not look at him. 'Listen, both of you. I want to talk to your mother. Will you go and watch TV or something for half an hour?'

They looked at one another, and then at Matthew and Dinah.

'Just half an hour,' Dinah smiled at them.

They went without protest, moving close together as if in mutual support.

Matthew circled around the table. He wanted to take Dinah's hand, but he also wanted to shout at her. He made himself speak slowly.

'I'm going to tell you the truth. Please believe me. It happened twice, and I regret it very much. Kathrin's a good colleague and a useful scientist, but I don't feel any more for her than that. I've just tried to explain that to her.'

'Was she very upset?'

'Yes. But that's for me to accept, isn't it?'

138

Dinah nodded, almost absently. He wondered if she was even properly listening.

'I've booked a flight to London,' she said. 'For Monday.'

'Dinah.'

'Let's not argue about it. I want to do it, and I will do it.' There was a pause. She did look at him now, a full gaze of assessment. 'Of course, you could come too.'

'To England? On some wild chase for Sarah?'

He hardly ever said her name. To hear it from him was almost a triumph. Dinah nodded again.

Matthew shouted at her, 'I can't. I can't leave the work now, I can't abandon everything just at the moment when we're about to . . .'

'Then don't.' Her coldness was absolute. 'I'll go. And the boys will come with me.'

'Dinah . . .'

'*With me*,' she repeated. He had never seen this steely certainty in her before.

'And if, when, you find her? What will happen then?'

Dinah breathed out slowly. 'I don't know,' she said truthfully. 'But I will have found her, won't I?'

Seven

Dinah sat on the edge of her mother's bed, holding her hand. She had come in to say goodnight.

They had watched the ten o'clock news together and now Eleanor was leaning back against her pillows in a pale cream bedjacket. Even in bed Eleanor managed to look elegant. Her spectacles in a needlepoint case lay beside her book on the bedside table, next to a framed photograph of her husband in uniform. There was another photograph of Dinah and Matthew with the boys, much younger, taken in the Hertfordshire garden.

Everything in the bedroom was polished, ordered, easily contained in the limited space. The rest of the bungalow was just the same, organised to suit a solitary routine. Eleanor's life had redefined itself on a small scale. Dinah knew that her mother was happy to have her and the children here, but she was also aware of the noise and mess and disturbance they caused.

'I love you and the boys staying with me,' Eleanor said suddenly, apparently reading Dinah's thoughts. 'Why do you have to go so soon?'

'I told you why,' Dinah answered.

Eleanor had listened to her explanation. She had not tried to dissuade Dinah from beginning the search, but neither had she attempted to conceal her own misgivings.

'But where *exactly* are you going? Isn't it a mistake, darling, after all this time? What have you told the boys?'

Dinah shook her head. 'I only want to know that she's well. Happy, even. Is that a mistake? Just to want to see her face? I'm going to Thetford, to the last address. Jack and Merlin think we're taking a holiday trip. It isn't that I don't want to see you, you know that.'

Eleanor's hand was thin and blue-veined although her nails were as immaculately manicured as they had always been. One of Dinah's earliest memories was of being ill with measles and her mother bringing her a doll, and her red-painted nails had been so bold and glossy in the coloured net of the doll's skirts. The varnish was pale silvery pink now. There were the same rings on her fingers, although seeming looser and larger than they had once been.

'I do know that, darling. Can you tell me what's the trouble between you and Matthew?'

It was the first time since her daughter's marriage that Eleanor had sensed a distance between Dinah and Matthew. She had always believed that the crisis of Sarah had brought them closer together, but now she doubted her own judgement.

Dinah turned her head a little. The oval mirror of the old-fashioned dressing table reflected them both. As a child she had often thought that her mother's face offered a perfect, finished version of her own undefined features. She remembered pressing her nose against the firm ridge of Eleanor's, enjoying their physical resemblance and the way that it confirmed their connection for the world to see.

I know whose little girl you are, people would say.

Far away in Franklin, Dinah had begun to be afraid that distance had broken the link. Now she understood that the change was simply a reversal. Her own face had become the defined version – how recently? – the planes and angles of it announcing age and experience. And Eleanor's had shrunk, the flesh loosening and the bones losing their definition as if she were the child, as if childhood were reclaiming her. They were assuming one another's roles.

Dinah was filled with love and tenderness for her mother, but on the other side, where there should have been the counterweight of her own daughter growing, there was only windy space.

The broken link was there, between herself and Sarah. With Eleanor it held firm. What could she tell her now, about the cold division between herself and Matthew?

'Matt believes that what we did when we gave her up was final. Right or wrong, it's in the past. Only I can't leave it there. She appears in my head, every day, in a thousand different shapes. Reproaching me, confronting me. I'm afraid of what I might find, and at the same time sick with longing for it.

'The only answer I can give myself is just to see her. Once I understood that, I couldn't dismiss it. I won't hurt anyone, Sarah or her parents. I'm just afraid that if I don't . . .' Dinah spread her hands apart, surprised by their steadiness, with all the eagerness and fear within her '. . . If I don't, something will break. Only Matt can't comprehend it. Won't, perhaps. And it causes such pain between us.'

Dinah said nothing about Kathrin Pang. She didn't want her mother to know that about Matthew.

Eleanor put her arms around her. She smelled of old lady rather than Arpège, of woolly folds and face powder and indoors. Mother-daughter, Dinah thought, as she let herself be held. The balance of mother to child swinging between them, and her own adult need childishly raw in the transaction. Not quite assuaged by mothering Merlin and Jack. However much she loved them. Shameful, perhaps, but true.

'I think so often about that day, the last time we went to see her. There she was, sitting up in all those cushions, smiling with the joy of it. I've always been afraid I might have influenced your decision. I told you to let her go, didn't I?'

Dinah rested her head against her mother's shoulder.

'No. You didn't influence me. I did it myself. It must have

been almost as hard for you as it was for me. To give up your only grandchild?'

In all the intervening years they had almost never talked about it. The burial had been so determined and the varnish so thickly applied.

'You were my first thought.'

'And now?'

'The same.'

Without warning, Dinah began to cry. Eleanor let her, holding her and waiting until the weeping finished.

'I think I do understand what you want,' Eleanor said at length. 'But will you promise me that you'll be careful?'

Dinah sat up. 'Yes. No. What does careful mean?'

It was her mother who glanced sidelong at their joined reflection now. She sighed. 'I don't even know. It's what mothers say. Don't be hurt, don't make yourself vulnerable where I can't defend you.'

'Don't make me cry any more. Do you disapprove very much? Matt thinks I'm mad, dangerous. I can't talk to him any more.'

Eleanor shook her head. 'I'm sorry to hear that. It isn't that I disapprove, Dinah, only that I'm afraid of whatever pain it might cause. But if you want to see her so badly, if that's what it really means, and all it means, then you must do it. How can you help yourself?'

'Thank you,' Dinah said.

In the morning, Eleanor waved them off.

'Have a lovely trip, darlings. Lots of bracing walks. Norfolk is very flat, Merlin. You won't have to do any uphill.'

'I know that, Granny.'

She smiled in the doorway as the car pulled away, bright-faced for her grandsons.

Dinah negotiated the suburban avenues of Eastbourne in the unfamiliar rental Cavalier, uncertain of the manual shift. There were already Christmas trees in many of the wide picture windows, and outdoor lights strung in some of the

143

bare-branched cherries and acers along the roadside. She did not feel comfortable with these reminders of approaching celebrations and she was glad when the outskirts of the town dropped behind her.

The countryside seemed miniature in scale, a little landscape of brown-patched fields and humped hedges threaded with lanes, domestic and tender and familiar. The near contours of unambitious hills and thin copses standing out against the pewter sky were wonderfully intricate and varied after the huge forested breadths of country surrounding Franklin.

Dinah's spirits lifted. She was happy to be home, driving through this intelligible landscape. It was a relief not to have to remember to decode the signals of a different culture. Being without Matt was strange, but the very fact of taking this action for herself made her feel stronger than she had done for months. Even the thought of Kathrin Pang was less disturbing than it had been. Perhaps what Matthew had tried to insist, that she meant nothing to him, was even true.

Dinah put the speculation to one side. She was on her way to find Sarah, that was what mattered now. There was an instant pressure of excitement and apprehension within her that diminished the importance of everything else.

The boys were insulated by their Walkman headsets, their faces turned in opposite directions as they watched the scenery. Dinah sang her own song as she drove steadily north-eastwards.

They stopped at lunchtime at a roadside Little Chef, and the boys complained that the burgers as well as the fries were horrible compared with the ones back in Franklin. Merlin almost said 'back home', but stopped himself before Jack could pounce on him. There was confusion in his face. Dinah tried to joke it away, covering his hand with hers at the same time. She was not sure now that it would not be better to tell them what this hasty visit to England really meant. She had only said that she wanted to see Granny, and thought it would be a good idea for the three of them to take a little

144

holiday at the same time. Matt had explained that he was too busy at the lab, right now, to think of coming with them.

They finished their unappetising meal and Dinah decided that she would say nothing until they reached Thetford. Until she had discovered what was to be found there. Otherwise, she reasoned, it would be like telling them that they had a sister and in the next breath saying that they did not, because she could not be found.

They reached Thetford in the middle of the afternoon.

Dinah found their hotel and booked them into it. As the daylight drained away outside they sat on one of the green candlewick-covered beds and looked out at a car park and the blank rear of a supermarket.

'What are we going to do now?' Jack asked, mutinously.

'Let's go out and have tea,' Dinah suggested.

Derby Road, number eleven Derby Road. She had held the address in her head for so long. How far was it from here?

There was no cosy tea-shop to be found. The only option was a steamy cafe with smeared mirrors and melamine-topped tables, and a couple of pinball machines in the corner. A middle-aged woman came out from behind the high counter to bring them thick cups of tea and sugary doughnuts. They were the only customers.

'Quiet today, for Thetford,' the woman said to Dinah. The boys wolfed their doughnuts and then asked for change to play the machines.

While they were occupied Dinah chatted to the waitress.

'Are you local?' she asked.

'Lived here nine years. Came from Norwich originally.'

'Do you know where Derby Road is, by any chance?'

The condensation on the mirrors seemed to freeze, the clicking and ringing from the pinball machines to disperse into a silent vacuum. The woman leaned with one hand on the tabletop.

'Oh yes, Derby Road's just down here. Straight on past the crossing there, and it's, let's see, second on the left.'

145

She paused, inquisitively, waiting for Dinah to tell her why she wanted to know.

'Thank you. Jack? Merlin? Are you ready to go?'

'I haven't finished.'

'I want another game.'

She gave them a pound coin each and smiled hopefully at the waitress. Her voice clogged in her throat.

'Will they be all right here for five minutes?'

She could look at the house, at least.

The woman shrugged, disappointed. 'Yeah, I suppose.'

'Don't wander off, either of you. I'll be back in a minute.'

Dinah slipped out. The street was quiet, greasy with damp. There was a cold mist of drizzle in the air that blurred coloured haloes around the Christmas lights in the window of a hardware shop. A jagged star-shape of fluorescent card stuck on the top of a screwdriver set read 'Ideal Gift'.

The orange globes of the pelican crossing winked in the murk. Dinah hurried towards them. A hundred yards beyond she found Derby Road.

It was an ordinary residential street. The houses were semi-detached, with a single pointed central gable bisected by different decorative finishes. There was a bay window on each side, a recessed porch beneath a rounded arch.

Dinah walked along the left-hand pavement, counting. One and two, three and four . . .

Number eleven had a little Christmas tree in the window, and the window itself was outlined with a string of lights that flashed on and off in sequence.

She paused at the wrought-iron gate. Then, without giving herself any longer to think about it, she walked up the front path and rang the doorbell.

If Sarah were to open the door. Eleanor's face. Her own. Or a face nothing like either of theirs, a reproach or a blank . . .

The door was opened by a woman in her late twenties. She had fair hair and she was wearing shellsuit pants and fluffy slippers. There was the noise of children playing.

Dinah managed to say, 'I'm sorry. I think I've come to the wrong house.'

The woman glanced beyond her and then seeing that she did not look threatening asked helpfully, 'Who did you want? I know nearly everyone along here.'

'The Greens,' Dinah blurted out, having come too far now to be evasive. 'Pauline.'

'Oh dear, this is the right house but they've gone. We bought the place off them three years ago. Four, it'll be in the spring.'

'Do you . . . have you got a forwarding address?'

'Well, the thing was that they were going into a rented place until they got straight again. He lost his job, you see, so they had to sell up. They went to Cromer, she was going to work in an old folks' home. I did have an address for forwarding the mail and all, but there hasn't been any for a good long while. Except for the odd circular and that.'

'Could you . . . can you remember the address?'

The woman stared into the middle distance, puckering her face to indicate concentration. A second or two later she sighed.

'No. No, it's completely gone. I'm really sorry.'

'Did you have it written down anywhere?'

The woman had lost interest now. A child was crying somewhere in the house.

'I must have done, but God knows where. It's kids, they get into everything. I'm sorry, but I'll have to go and see to her now.'

Dinah knew that she would get no more than this fragment. Nearly four years ago the Greens had taken Sarah to a rented house in Cromer.

'Might your husband remember?'

'Ha. You wouldn't ask if you knew him.' The door was closing.

Dinah thanked her as pleasantly as she could. She retraced her steps through the drizzle to the cafe.

Jack and Merlin were sitting at the table waiting for her. Their pinball money had run out.

'Where have you *been*?' Their alarm expressed itself as anger with her. The waitress was wiping tables, listening.

'Just having a walk around. Are you ready to go now?'

Outside Jack took hold of her. 'Mum, are you all right?'

She put her arms around their shoulders as they walked, drawing them against her sides. She felt raw with guilt and disappointment.

'Yes, of course I am.'

The hotel's dark threadbare decor and atmosphere of old cooking depressed them all.

Dinah promised, 'We'll go somewhere else tomorrow. What about to the sea?'

Later she lay in bed listening through the papery partitioning to the rush of water in adjoining rooms and the wheezy rise and fall of the lift. There were occasional bursts of laughter or shouting from the car park. She thought of Milly, who had been first sullen and then angry at the idea of Dinah abandoning her to come to England. But in the end Milly had wished her good luck. Dinah's search had become identified with her own. If Dinah found what she was looking for then so might she.

'I think I know someone who might be able to help you,' Dinah had promised her just as she was leaving. 'A woman friend of mine, a solicitor who specialises in family law and adoptions. I could ask Lavinia where you should start. But I think you should talk to Sandra and Ed seriously about it first.'

'Yeah,' Milly had said. 'But you will ask what's-her-name, your friend, won't you?'

Milly was sitting at the big table in the dining space of the Franklin house. Her tutor, a gentle-mannered liberal arts grad, had spent the morning with her and left her with plenty of work to do. Books and papers were spread out on either side of her.

Milly picked at the rings in her nose. She scraped her chair back, deliberately making an ugly noise in the silent house. She wandered to the nearest window and leant her face against the glass. Snow had recently fallen, and the disturbingly altered light reflected through the house.

She thought of something Ed always said to visitors, in the genial version of his voice. *All the glass is so important. It lets every change in the seasons right into the house. When there's snow on the ground it's magnificent.*

Milly's shoulders twitched with sour impatience. She hated snow.

The house was so quiet.

Sandra was in her study writing letters, and Ed was working in his. Milly knew that he would be sitting in front of the computer. His big head and broad back would be massively outlined by the whitish glow from the screen. It occurred to her as she thought about him that she had no idea where the image had come from. Ed was never to be disturbed at work. His work was sacred.

The silence grew oppressive. Milly turned away from the window. She picked up her workbook, and then slapped it back on the table. The noise was feeble. All around her surfaces glowed or seductively absorbed the blue light. Everything was orderly, cherished, expensive. There was a crystal bowl on the sideboard, occupying the space where she had placed the Thanksgiving turkey before anointing it with paint. The bowl radiated little hard points of light. Milly slipped across the floor and cupped her hands around the swelling curves of it. She lifted it gently to eye level, and then let it drop on to the slate floor.

The ringing crash brought Sandra flying out of her study.

'Sorry,' Milly murmured. 'Accident.'

Little shards of shattered crystal glinted on the floor for yards around her. Sandra's fingers fluttered, the diamonds echoing the broken glass.

'Get a brush, Milly.'

Ed's bulk emerged from his study.

149

'Jesus Christ. Sandra, what's this?'

'An accident,' Sandra soothed. 'It can't be helped.'

Milly looked her father in the eye before he could force her to do it by twisting up her chin. They had barely spoken to each other since the bout of screaming after the turkey episode.

'Sorry,' Milly repeated flatly.

'Go on back to work. There's nothing to worry about, Milly and I will clear this up. Go on, Ed.'

She's afraid of him, Milly thought, with a bleak shudder of disgust. Not because he's a bully, although he is one, but because she thinks he's got all the power. As if everything about him is important and nothing about her.

I'm never going to end up like that. Never.

After Ed had gone they cleared up the broken glass together. Sandra wrapped the splinters in newspaper and placed it carefully aside from the ordinary trash.

'Did you smash it on purpose?' she asked.

'Yes.'

'Milly. Why?'

The shrug. 'Bored. Stupid. Shit. It was so quiet. *I* don't know why. I said I was sorry.'

Sandra came alongside and tried to hold her in her arms. Her hands patted Milly's shoulders, trying to stroke an explanation or a recognisable edge of reason out of her. Milly stood unresisting. She felt a stale confusion of pity and exasperation and impatience towards her mother.

'Sandra?'

'Yes, darling?' The response was eager.

'I want to try and find out about my real mother.'

Sandra's hands dropped to her sides. 'Did Dinah Steward suggest that to you?'

'What do you mean? Why don't you like Dinah? She's my friend. Anyway she didn't. I just want to do it. For *myself*.'

'I see. And what about the people who have been your parents? What about us?'

'Everything *is* about you. Well. About him.'

Sandra sighed. This was familiar ground. The more privileged Milly's life became, the more she resented it and the success that provided it for her.

Milly asked angrily, 'Didn't you want your own babies, instead of having to put up with me?'

'It isn't putting up. We love you very much, both of us.'

It was Ed who had been unable to father a child. Sandra had never told Milly so. 'It just never happened,' she said vaguely. 'We agreed that adoption was best. And so you came to us.'

When they had learned the news about his sperm count Ed had been furiously opposed to Sandra undergoing artificial insemination. And she had understood that to adopt an unrelated child would help to blur Ed's failure for him. He did not accept inadequacy bravely.

'Why didn't you get another baby? Aren't there supposed to be brothers and sisters?'

'We had everything we wanted in you, darling.'

It was what Sandra always said.

In fact Ed had refused to consider any more children. He preferred the matter to be closed. Except, Sandra sometimes thought, that Milly herself was a constant reminder of the truth that no amount of bullish behaviour could alter. And yet he loved his daughter, and masked his sadness at her rebellions with his own rage and anger.

Milly snatched herself away and slouched to the other corner of the room. The questions and the emollient answers never changed, and never produced the raw edge of truth she thought she wanted. Through the tall window she saw that it was starting to snow again.

Sandra was on the verge of tears. Milly knew it and kept her back turned to her.

'Why are you always so angry with us?'

Milly bit the inside of her cheeks. 'I feel. Fucking. Rejected.'

'But we haven't rejected you. How can you say that?'

The snowflakes were tiny grey specks floating against the weighty sky.

'Never mind. *Shit.* It doesn't matter,' Milly spat. 'And no, I won't go and see anyone to *talk out* the anger, before you even suggest it, right?'

She walked away from Sandra. She told herself that there was Dinah.

Dinah and the boys found a hotel overlooking the promenade and pier at Cromer. It was a huge, gaunt, redbrick building with a north view of the corrugated gunmetal sea and a smell of salt and damp in all the rooms. They were almost the only guests.

Dinah grandly took a corner suite. The two bedrooms were connected by a small room containing a wooden-armed sofa and two chairs, and a big old television set. There was a three-bar electric fire mounted on one wall, and a burn-scarred nylon rug laid obliquely in the middle of the floor. The boys liked the view and opened the salt-fogged windows to let in the sound of the sea. Cold air poured in, carrying the rhythmic grinding of waves breaking on the shingle.

They spent the afternoon exploring the pier and the tiny amusement arcade and the shops in the town centre behind the hotel. A penetrating wind whipped straight off the sea and there were few people about in the soaking streets, but the Christmas decorations and jingling music relayed from loudspeakers gave the shopping centre a thin illusion of festive prosperity. Dinah felt a surge of affection for the place. She had never been here before but she knew the mild introversion and resolute lack of expectation and patient Englishness of it all as if it had been familiar to her all her life.

She recognised how much she had missed England. And how in some way the half-denied longing had connected with Sarah, and heightened that other sense of loss.

As they wandered through the small streets Dinah looked eagerly at each corner and turning. Sarah must be familiar with these places. Perhaps the girl behind the till in W H Smith's would know her by sight, perhaps she borrowed books from the new library or waited sometimes at the bus-stop opposite Boots.

The boys complained that they were cold, and bored.

'This is kind of a dump, isn't it?' Jack scowled.

Dinah took them back to the hotel via the Post Office, where she collected a copy of the electoral register.

While the boys watched *Neighbours* she sat on her bed beside the telephone. There was no Malcolm or Pauline Green listed on the register, but there were two M. Greens in the telephone directory. Dinah dialled both numbers. One was a repair garage, and an irritable-sounding mechanic informed her that old Mr Green was now retired and the business was run by his son Richard. The second subscriber was Margaret Green.

There were several old people's homes listed. Dinah rang each one, but none of them had a nurse or auxiliary worker called Pauline Green, nor could anyone remember having had one.

She had already drawn a blank by the time the *Neighbours* theme tune re-insinuated itself into her head.

'What shall we *do*?' Jack asked, coming into the bedroom to find her. 'I wish I was at home.'

The next day was a Saturday and Dinah took them swimming at the big modern pool further up the coast road, and then to a butterfly farm. Both boys responded obediently to these entertainments, but without much enthusiasm. They were beginning to be suspicious of this pointless and cheerless holiday, and anxiety made them irritable. In the afternoon they insisted on telephoning Matthew at home in Kendrick Street.

Dinah listened sadly to their eager questions about what he was doing, and about Ape and the Kerrigan boys. This was not what she had planned, to cut them off from home and security. Their sense of isolation made it a bad time to introduce either the idea or the reality of a lost sister.

It was becoming clear that she had made a mistake in whisking them away to England. She was jeopardising the balance of the existing family, maybe even committing the deliberate sabotage of which Matthew had accused her. And she had not found Sarah.

'Mom? Dad wants to talk to you.' Merlin was holding out the receiver.

'Hello Matt.'

'Hi.'

His voice was warm, the sound of it almost made her smile until she remembered how they had parted. Dinah was so used to thinking of Matthew as her best friend that it shocked her to realise that he might not be any longer. She had manœuvred them out of their friendship, it was not Matt's doing. She had brought their children here and had made no discovery, and she could not even be sure that Sarah would want to be found. Milly and Sarah were not the same.

But still she clung to her intention. She could not give it up.

'Fine. We're all fine. Yes, it's wet and very cold. We've been sightseeing a bit, the boys aren't very keen. What have you been doing?'

'Work. We're at a kind of crucial stage.'

Dinah thought again of Doctor Pang. She imagined Matthew in the Toyota, driving across town at night to wherever she lived, across empty intersections and under strings of traffic lights and finally turning into some dark road and parking by the house where she was waiting for him.

'Have you found her?' Matthew asked.

'No. Not a trace. They've gone.'

Dinah listened to the space between them.

'How are the boys dealing with all this?'

'Stoically.'

'When are you going to bring them home?'

154

There was no avoiding this. She had taken a gamble, and lost.

'In a couple of days.'

'Good. Let me say goodnight to them now, will you?'

After he had gone, Jack asked her, in a tight voice that betrayed his concern, 'What is happening with you and Dad?'

Both boys stared at her while she groped for what to say.

'Adults don't always agree about everything all the time, even married people. Perhaps married people particularly. Sometimes the disagreements are small, about holidays or work. Sometimes they are bigger, about responsibility or truth or history.' She hoped that large vague concepts would be dull enough to deflect their sharper questions.

'What are yours?'

'Just disagreements. I hope we can solve them.'

'Are you going to get divorced?'

'No.'

She said what she hoped, not what she feared.

'When are we going home, then?'

'How about the day after tomorrow, or Tuesday, if I can fix the flights?'

Their faces dissolved into identical smiles of relief and satisfaction.

'Great.'

If she had one more day, Dinah thought, she could obtain a list of all the local special schools and youth centres. Sarah must have gone to school somewhere while the Greens lived in Cromer. Someone would remember her. And she would be able to pursue all those avenues from Franklin as well as from anywhere else.

The boys did not want to go out into the cold again, and so she left them watching more television while she went out to walk on the beach. She needed to think. It seemed that Matthew had become the question, whilst the importance of finding Sarah was the remaining certainty.

Dinah walked along the tideline with the foam-laced sea fretting on one side of her and the sea wall rising on the other. Beyond the sea wall the houses and hotels reared with their lighted windows and bunched curtains and Vacancy signs. The wind blew against her back, almost bowling her along, and she could not distinguish whether the water soaking her hair was rain or spray.

It was exhilarating to be out in the last of the afternoon light. Dinah walked fast with her head up, over the debris of the highwater mark.

There was only one other person in sight.

The man wore a long dark coat. He was coming from the opposite direction but following exactly the same path, striding over the litter of wrack and shards of plastic bottle and glimmering bone-white chunks of polystyrene.

Dinah felt a moment's uneasiness. She hesitated, half-forming the impulse to turn aside and make for the shelter of the wall.

The man broke his stride only a few yards ahead of her. He was bare-headed, greying, very tall. There was something incongruous about him, perhaps the coat he wore instead of oilskins or a waxed jacket.

'Good afternoon,' he said.

Dinah nodded a greeting.

'We are the only brave souls in Cromer. Or the only crazy ones.'

'Either way, it's good to be out.'

The man smiled. 'Enjoy your walk,' he said pleasantly.

He passed her by, and Dinah walked on without looking round. When she finally turned back towards the hotel there was no sign of him. She was the only person on the beach, and it was almost dark.

Jack and Merlin were especially tractable that evening. They were bright and charming over dinner and they went to bed without complaint, both of them locking their arms around her neck with noticeable affection before they settled down.

156

'I'm looking forward to it being Christmas,' Merlin said. 'Dad told me the snow's already real deep. The Kerrigans have decorated their outside Christmas tree.'

Dinah hugged him, rubbing the tuft of hair at the back of his head.

'We really are going home, aren't we?' Jack asked. When he took off his glasses his face looked round and defenceless.

'Yes, we are.'

She could promise them that much, Dinah thought sadly.

The cramped room between the two bedrooms was bleak and the window rattled in its warped frame. Dinah rejected the option of sitting there contemplating loneliness and defeat. She went down to the hotel bar instead to buy herself a nightcap.

Dinah was sitting with her whisky and the morose barman had gone back to his job of sluicing glasses through greasy water before she noticed the man at the other end of the bar. He had half a pint of beer and a folded newspaper in front of him. There was a handful of other people sitting at tables near the gas-log fire.

'Hello again,' Dinah said.

'Did you walk far?' he asked her. There was a husky, faintly unused note in his voice. It made Dinah suspect that he did not talk much.

'No, only to the end of the beach. Not such a brave soul.'

The phrase had stuck in her mind.

'You're not local.' It was a statement, not a question.

'I'm here for two or three days with my children. Just a short holiday.'

The man's eyebrows made amused circumflexes. He was hollow-cheeked and the length of his hair made him look faintly unkempt. But his face was mobile and the tentative quality of his voice was attractive.

'Do you live here?'

'In Redemption Street.'

Dinah remembered the name, and the double row of tiny three-windowed terraced houses whose front steps led directly on to the street. She had wondered if Malcolm and Pauline might have rented one of these houses.

'May I buy you a drink?'

Dinah realised that her glass was empty. The man's offer was polite, even formal, but she said hastily,

'No, no, I'll get it. Would you like one?'

'I only take half a pint. Thank you.'

She wondered if this was out of financial constraint, or for some other reason. There was something in the man's face that suggested current asceticism and past excesses.

'I saw the street when I was out walking,' she said, while the barman sluggishly refilled her glass. 'I wondered how it got the name?'

'There is a story. Where the street now stands there was once a witch's house. She was a powerful witch, who could infect people with the plague and cure it at will. She could blight the crops and maim children and poison live-stock and predict the future, and the people lived in terror of her. No one ever went within half a mile of her or her house.

'Then one day an itinerant friar rode by. He was hungry, and his mule needed water. He asked the witch to give him what he needed, and she responded with potions and poison. The friar ate his fill from what she offered, and wat-ered his mule, and instead of falling under her evil spell they were refreshed and invigorated and ready to continue their journey.

'The friar humbly thanked the witch for her generous hospitality, and blessed her. And the witch was so overcome by his goodness that she repented of her wicked ways and confessed her sins to the friar. Thereafter she became a holy woman, and devoted the rest of her days to prayer and good works. She was always known as Mother Redemption.'

Dinah had edged closer to the man, in order to hear more clearly, cupping her chin in her hand as she leant on the bar. She liked the way he told the story.

'Hmm,' she said, and the man laughed.

'That's the legend. I take no responsibility for it.' He held out his hand and Dinah shook it. Clean, well shaped, no rings. 'Francis Ingram.'

'Dinah Steward. Do you know all the local legends?'

'Some. I'm an archivist, part-time historian. I do some writing, a little journalism.'

As he talked, Dinah had the impression of a life lived apart, of choices willingly dispensed with. Francis Ingram did not drink much because he did not have the money, whatever other reasons there might also be. She found that she warmed to him, losing her wariness.

'And you?'

'Oh, I'm a wife and mother. We live in the States at the moment, my husband's job is there. We've been visiting my mother, and now we . . . I'm looking up some old friends.'

Francis raised his eyebrows. This is where we began, Dinah remembered. He was appraising her. She also realised that she did not mind at all.

Then he looked at his watch. It was a cheap one on a peeling strap.

'I have to go,' Francis said.

'I . . . of course. I enjoyed our talk.'

We are both lonely. The brief meetings of lonely people in bars in rainwashed towns. The deflections and sidesteps and hasty movings on. The commandments of fear and pride and decorum. Dinah recognised that her own solitude was only a pinprick, one of Matthew's molecules, in the infinitely wide and varied expanse of other solitudes. And she found that she was strengthened by her understanding of this, not defeated or even threatened by it. Francis Ingram was looking at her.

He said slowly, 'Would you like to come and have something to eat with me? At Redemption Street? Perhaps tomorrow evening?'

'It would have to be tomorrow. We're going back to London the day after, and then flying home to Boston.'

'Eight o'clock,' Francis said. 'Number twenty.'

He did not expect that she would refuse, nor did Dinah consider it. It seemed that simple.

The house was at one end of the narrow street. The door was painted some dark colour, and the curtains at the downstairs window were drawn so that not a chink of light escaped.

She had told the boys exactly what had happened. Francis was an interesting man, a historian who knew a lot about the area. His house was only a few hundred yards away, and one of the hotel chambermaids had agreed to babysit.

'Do you have to go?' demanded Jack.

'Why not?' Dinah smiled in the face of their disapproval.

Dinah hesitated before pressing the white plastic bellpush. She was about to walk alone into the house of a man she barely knew. But she was certain, even knowing him so little, that there was no violence in Francis Ingram.

She rang the bell.

Francis's front door opened straight into his living room. Over his shoulder she saw walls lined with books, a round table laid for two with a clean white cloth, an open fire crackling with driftwood, and an extra chair that clearly didn't belong there drawn up on the opposite side of the hearth to the single armchair.

'Come in,' Francis said, holding the door wide open. 'You'll have to forgive the impromptu arrangements, I don't have many guests.'

Dinah stepped inside. On closer inspection she saw that the simple furniture was tired, with the look of having been salvaged from elsewhere, but the room itself was warm and there was a smell of cooking. All the space on the white-painted walls not occupied by bookshelves was covered with pen-and-ink drawings. There was the beach, and the pier, and Redemption Street itself. Some were cheaply framed, but most of them were just pinned to the plaster.

'Did you do these?'

'Yes. I started about four years ago. I used to look at things and wish I could draw. Then I thought I might as well try as

160

go on wishing. There's no technique, as you can see. I enjoy doing it.'

'They're good,' Dinah said.

The drawings were energetic, full of bold lines. Some were no more than scribbles, others were intricately detailed. Several showed views of wintry fields and woodland. Dinah wondered if Francis sat on a field gate to draw, wrapped up in his long black coat.

'Would you like a glass of wine?'

There was a bottle standing in the warmth to one side of the hearth.

'Yes please.'

He drew the cork and poured the wine. They raised their glasses to each other and smiled. Dinah felt happiness warming her face.

'Are you hungry?'

Francis hovered in the doorway that led through to his tiny kitchen. Dinah could see open shelves with a few plates and cups and two saucepans. There was another table, oil-cloth-covered. She remembered that his voice had sounded unused when she first heard it; he was unaccustomed to there being anyone else in this place with him and he was anxious about the arrangements.

'Not just yet. Shall we finish this drink first?'

Francis had barely touched his glass. Dinah turned to look at the nearest shelves. There were Dickens, Scott, Spenser, and three thick volumes entitled *The Paston Letters*. Francis pointed to the letters.

'Those are interesting, have you read them?'

Dinah shook her head and he took down one of the books and gave it to her. She would have settled in the temporary chair, but he directed her to his own. She began to read, and Francis went into the kitchen. She heard the thump of the oven door and then a spoon clinking in earthenware. The rich smell intensified and she realised that she had under-estimated her hunger.

The letters were printed in tiny type and the language

was archaic. Dinah laid the book aside as soon as Francis reappeared.

'I'm not much of a historian.'

'The Paston family lived quite near here. The letters date from the fifteenth century, probably the same period as Mother Redemption. They are very domestic, but they also describe a violent, anarchic time.'

'Like now.'

Dinah was suddenly, tangentially thinking of Milly.

'In a way. Although I don't see much violence or anarchy at first hand.'

Francis's gesture took in the tiny house and Redemption Street and the closed-up, patient seaside town and acknowledged his withdrawal from what lay beyond them.

'Why are you here?'

Dinah felt that even in so short a time they had covered enough ground for her to ask this without being intrusive or impertinent.

Francis considered. 'It's a long story. I'll tell you, if you really want to hear. Shall we eat at the same time?'

He brought a covered dish to the table, and potatoes baked in foil. The dish contained a casserole of rabbit with winter vegetables. Dinah wondered if there were poachers' pockets inside the long black coat. Francis filled her plate, and poured more wine for her. His first glass was still barely touched and she was already on her third.

Dinah said, 'Go on.'

'I used to be a teacher. A history teacher. I was married to Alison and we had two daughters. We lived in the west country, not far from Taunton. I was an alcoholic.'

Yes, Dinah thought. Present self-denial, past excess. The marks showed in his face, but those lines were also relaxed by tolerance and humour and by a kind of calm acceptance.

'In the end I lost my job. Not through doing anything outrageous. I was never a flamboyant drunk. But by a long, slow and humiliating process of small incompetences and deceits and failures. I liked teaching and I loved history and I

162

enjoyed the schoolkids, but I liked drinking much better. The steady serious business of getting blind, starting every day as soon as the day began. To begin with I was good at all the lies and concealments that go with being drunk. Then I got less good because I cared less, and in the end there was no real pretence at all.

'Once I was out of work it was harder to drink. Alison and the girls were always watching me. There was no money, either. Alison got a job and we managed for a while.

'I tried to dry out two or three times, but I never wanted to do it quite seriously enough. There were a couple of years of intervals when we'd all start thinking everything would work out, and the girls would be happy and Alison started smiling, and then I'd drink again. Up and down, raising their hopes and knocking them over again.

'In the end Alison left me. She went to live with one of my colleagues. He taught French. I did want to get sober then, to get her back. I stopped drinking but Alison was gone. Who could blame her? She divorced me and married him, and they took Jess and Amy and went to live in France. The girls are fifteen and sixteen now. I haven't seen them for a year.'

Dinah put down her knife and fork. Francis gestured to the dish and she nodded. He gave her another spoonful.

'You have a good listening ear,' he said.

Dinah was afraid that was not the same thing as needing to hear. She wanted to hear other stories, and at this moment Francis's especially, to knit them up alongside her own. To listen and compare, to experience compassion, and to soften her own loneliness and guilt by so doing. She knew it was an impulse less simply generous than the one Francis gave her credit for.

'And so you came here?'

'Eventually. We sold our house, and divided the proceeds. Alison was kind, even though she could easily not have been. I wandered about for a year or so, thinking about going back on the bottle, never doing it. I came here, as far east and away from home as I could go, ending up with my back to the sea. I bought this house, unpacked my books, began drawing. I do odd jobs, a little writing. I read a lot, I don't talk to many people. I'm enjoying talking to you.'

There was a small shiver of intimacy beginning to flicker between them like a tiny electrical charge.

Dinah became intensely aware of Francis's physical presence across the table from her, the reddish glow from the fire outlining his hair and shoulders. She looked down at her hands and saw Eleanor's in the shape of the nails and the whorls of skin at the knuckles, then hid them in her lap.

'Are you unhappy?'

Francis was amused.

'No. And not happy either, before you ask that. It is possible to achieve a state of suspension somewhere between the two. There are a hundred small satisfactions to distinguish in almost every day.'

In the quiet firelight with her hunger satisfied and the wind and the sea outside Dinah could imagine what the pleasures were.

'But they don't total up to happiness. Nor is there any reason why they should. We make ourselves unhappy with the belief that we each have a right to happiness. Contentment might be a more realistic aim.

'Look at this.' Francis indicated his house. 'I'm lonely, but I find I'm content to live alone. There are bad times when I miss my children, and when I long for the sweetness, the refuge of a woman. As an escape from the unremitting self. But then the self is certain, and there is security in that. There are moments of intense joy. And long stretches of balance, of absence of pain. That may not sound very much to you.'

'It does.'

Dinah was moved. The red fireglow blurred at the periphery of her vision and she blinked to sharpen it. Francis was reaching to pour her some more wine but she shielded the mouth of the glass.

'I'd better not drink any more.'

'You don't look like a drunk to me. And I would know.'

They laughed, having becoming easy with each other.

Dinah was thinking that Francis's unexpectant calm was enviable. His difference from Matthew was striking. Matthew was busy and ambitious, and his attention was always focused on some goal whose significance was partly beyond her. Matthew selected and judged and discarded, chewing up obstacles in his onward drive.

It occurred to Dinah that as well as grieving for Sarah she might also be exhausted by the relentless forward progress of the Steward family. Matthew always had a new goal to aim for, beyond Cambridge and beyond London, and now in Franklin. Before too long, no doubt, he would have yet another in view. Her energy and optimism had gradually been channelled into supporting him, and setting him free from the mundane demands of family and home.

There had been nothing left over for herself, Dinah realised. Until now, this minute. To come to England, to search for Sarah against Matthew's wishes, that was to set herself free. And to be here, alone, with Francis Ingram, that was also to be free.

Francis noticed her expression.

'I think it's my turn now. Why are you here?'

Dinah told him about Franklin and Matt's research and Kendrick Street, and her sense of displacement from the village and the niches of work and friendship, and from England itself. She tried to use the estrangement to explain her urgent need to find old friends with whom she had lost touch, Pauline and Malcolm Green. She told Francis that the Greens had two children, an elder daughter in her late twenties, and a younger one, with Down's syndrome.

He listened intently, but without interrupting. Dinah said as little as she could about Sarah. She was so used to keeping this secret that she could not admit it, even in this isolated place to a stranger who had confided in her. Then she was startled by the thought itself. Francis seemed so far from being a stranger.

'They moved here four years ago?' he asked.

'Four years this spring.'

He shook his head.

'I don't know them, and I know most of the locals by sight. Are you sure they came here?'

'It's the only lead I have.'

'There are enquiries you could make about the younger girl.'

Dinah nodded. Tomorrow morning, Monday, she would make a list of the local authority special schools and youth groups.

'I know. I've thought of that.'

'Could I help in some way?'

It was late, Dinah realised. They had been talking for a long time. The fire had faded because Francis had not interrupted her by moving to put on another sawn piece of driftwood.

'Keep a look-out for them,' she smiled. She was buttoning the jacket that she had undone a little in the warmth. She saw the tightening of the muscles in his cheek that was the only indication of disappointment, and felt an answering faint anxiety.

'Thank you for a wonderful dinner, and for the wine, and the talk.'

The words sounded inadequate. Francis's wine was still barely touched in his glass. What would he do with it, she wondered, after she had gone? He was admirable, she thought, as well as likeable.

'I'll walk you back to the hotel,' he said.

After he had put on the black coat and helped Dinah on with hers he leant across and unpinned one of the pen and ink drawings from the wall beside the table. She had noticed it while they were eating, a view of the beach and the sea wall and the huddle of houses rising above from almost the point where they had met.

'May I give you this?'

She took it, and looked at it for a long silent moment

166

before rolling it into a neat cylinder and sliding it into her inner pocket for safety.

'Thank you. I wish I had something to give you in exchange.'

'You have given me something.'

They walked the two hundred yards to the sea front and into the wind without saying anything more. They did not touch, not even the sleeves of their coats.

At the door of the hotel Francis asked diffidently, 'May I write to you?'

Dinah hesitated. And then she took out of her bag one of her postcards printed with her name and the address of Kendrick Street. She folded it in two and gave it to him. Francis put it in an inner pocket, mirroring her safe-keeping of the drawing.

'Thank you.'

He did touch her then, his fingertip briefly on her cheek.

'Goodnight.'

They both turned, as quickly as they could, and lost sight of each other.

Lying in her bed with the sound of the sea in the room, Dinah threaded her way back through the evening. She had made a friend and for a reckless few moments she had balanced on the brink of something more.

In London, from the airport hotel, Dinah telephoned Eleanor.

'I haven't found her, but I haven't given up hope either. It was so exciting and strange, kind of close-making, to be where she had been, even recently. I may still be able to trace her.'

The list of possible leads was rolled inside Francis's drawing.

'Are you all right, Dinah? You sound different.'

'Do I?'

'Keyed-up. Happier.'

'A bit of both.'

'Are you going home to put things right with Matthew?'

There was the dark side, out of reach, now seeming uncharitable where it had once been plain, the reassuring topography of marriage grown alien by slow inches.

'I don't know. I don't know what will happen. I only know that I have to pursue this or lose myself.'

'I'm worried for all of you. But listen, darling. You can count on me for anything. I love you.'

Eleanor in her cream bedjacket with her library book beside her. Conventional, careful, but still reaching out for Dinah where she had not ventured herself. The old mother-daughter link. *Oh, Sarah.*

'I love you too.'

'Call me.'

'I will, I promise I will.'

The boys were asleep, primed for home and Matthew. Tomorrow.

'Goodnight.'

'Goodnight Mummy.'

Eight

It was just two days before Christmas and there were paper stars and lanterns hanging above the benches in the lab. Matthew could see them through the open door of the stuffy conference room where he was working with Sean Rader and Jon Liu and two technicians. They had eaten bagels for lunch and the wrappers lay on the table with empty paper cups and Coke cans. Matthew was giving instructions for running a new series of isolated fat cell tests. He spoke quickly and the technicians made obedient notes.

The chain of successes already achieved weighed pleasantly behind all of them.

The computer program designed by Sean had run through myriad chemical sequences until the first and best breakthrough had come, the discovery of the exact fit between insulin and the receptors on the cell surface. After that, it had been Matthew's aim to design a protein, a peptide that would bind with the insulin receptors to mirror the action of the naturally occurring peptide in the human body. He had made several attempts, twisting the coloured atoms of three-dimensional protein structures in his mind's eye and in black computer space, until the solution had suddenly delivered itself to him in the boat up on the lake in Vermont.

Since then they had been working even harder and faster as the momentum built up and propelled them onwards.

Kathrin and the other biochemists set to work to synthesise the molecule that Matt had designed, and the first batch of peptide was now ready for testing. They would use radio-active tracers to monitor the action of the engineered molecule on the fat cells, and record the insulin-like effect achieved against the performance of real insulin. It was only the first step in a long series of tests that would unwind ahead of them, but it was a crucial one. Anticipation brought everyone in the team in early, and kept them in the labs until late. They were held together by the glue of mutual effort and the prospect of imminent reward, and that was how Matt had always liked it.

'Okay guys,' Matt smiled, aiming an empty paper cup at the trash basket and hitting it dead centre. 'Let's get on and do it.'

'What about tonight?' asked Don, the younger of the technicians.

'You get tonight off, special seasonal dispensation. Eight-thirty, Pantucci's.'

It was the night of the department's Christmas party, to be held in the same pizza restaurant from which Matt had taken Jon and Kathrin home. The powerful associations clustered around the name and the place made Matthew glance uncertainly at Jon, sure that he must also be aware of them. But Jon was gathering up his notes, joking with the others about staying off the beer this time and being fit for Christmas. The boys went back to their benches and Jon and Sean hurried away too, Sean calling over his shoulder that he would catch Matt later. Matt was left sitting alone.

He felt the tide of purpose ebbing away. He could motivate the rest of them, but the inner drive had momentarily and frighteningly deserted him.

He closed his eyes for a second, pinching the band of gristle above the bridge of his nose. He could no longer quite grasp the importance of all this, the urgent expenditure of effort and intellect, whereas it had once seemed so defined and immediate. If he and Jon and the others did not manage to design and synthesise an orally ingestible insulin, well then, their competitors at Cal Tech or Dartmouth or Cambridge would do so within a matter of months.

That this no longer seemed the greatest threat made Matthew feel exposed, as if some invisible hand had twitched away the layers of insulation that protected him.

He opened his eyes and stood up abruptly, knocking the chair sideways so that he had to catch it before it fell. He shuffled his papers into a sheaf and marched out into the lab. There were several people at work. The radio was playing Christmas jingles and someone was whistling. Kathrin was standing at the far end of the room in her white lab-coat. She was rinsing flasks at one of the sinks, her smooth head bent, apparently intent on the task. Matthew knew that she would not look round.

Since the fatal Sunday afternoon when she had telephoned him at home and Dinah had guessed the truth, Matthew had miserably done his best to avoid Kathrin. While Dinah and the boys were in England he had made sure that he was never alone in the department, always busy with and protected by Sean and the others. He had been careful to screen all the calls he received at home before he answered them. He felt despicable, but he stuck to his intentions.

Then Dinah came home again, without having found Sarah. She did not talk much about the collapse of her hopes, or say what she intended to do now. She seemed contained within herself, and almost content with this detachment, like an ascetic with an unvarying, plain diet. Matthew could not find it in himself to offer sympathy, nor did Dinah ask for it. They had begun to live together separately, neither of them confiding their needs or fears, in a state of mute and weary truce that denied friendship and no longer even recalled the warmth they had once taken for granted.

At about the same time Matt became aware that it was not he who was avoiding Kathrin, but vice versa.

She slipped away whenever he joined a group in the lab,

and when she was positively obliged to see and speak to him she kept her face turned away. There were no more sidelong glances. Matthew found himself studying the line of her jaw and the exquisite intricate folds of her ear with the wing of glossy hair tucked behind it, and feeling the disappointment with him that radiated from her. He was stricken in response with a sense of loss and longing so severe that it made him feel ill.

He tried for two days to tell himself and the world that he was ill, and Sean Rader remarked that he had never known him have so much as a headache before. But the pretence, and the idleness that went with it, only made Matthew feel worse and he forced himself to return to work and the intense pursuit of what had begun to seem almost irrelevant.

He stood and watched Kathrin as she worked. Running water splashed in the sink, over her fingers and the glassware and bounced in rainbow droplets from the stiff-bristled wire brush. She did not turn round.

Matthew went to his office and opened a file of financial projections. The insulin project was not the only research occupying his team, and there were new directions that he must find and suggest to all these eager young people for whom he was responsible. Their funding was secure for the time being, but the moment would come when he would have to apply for and justify further grant aid. There was plenty to be done. Matt bent his head and tried to concentrate on the figures dancing in his folder.

At six o'clock he left for home.

'See you at the party, Prof,' his secretary called cheerfully after him.

Kendrick Street was diamond-white and still under a thin layer of fresh snow. Matthew sat in the car for a moment, looking at the black trees frosted with ice and the powder coating the roofs and porches. He let the particular snow-silence seep into him, realising how tired he was. He could easily have drifted into sleep.

He made himself run the few paces from the car to the

porch steps. His breath puffed in a brave cloud ahead of him. The house, when he opened the door, was scented with popcorn and fir branches and woodsmoke.

'Hi, I'm here.'

The Christmas tree he had brought home was set up in one corner of the hallway. Dinah and the boys had decorated it while he was out.

Merlin and Jack appeared at the top of the stairs and then hurtled down to him.

'Dad, Dad, *Dad*.' They swung on his arms and pulled at his hands.

'D'you like the tree?'

'Looks great. Where's Mum?'

'In the bath. She's going out. Why are *you* going as well? We've got to have Heidi.'

Heidi was the teenage sitter who lived in the next street.

'You'll have a great time. She'll let you watch unsuitable videos, she always does. And I've got to go to the department Christmas party, so think of some jokes for me to tell while I go upstairs to see your mother.'

The bathroom door was closed but not locked. Before he opened it, Matthew heard Dinah humming. She was lying in a loose meringue of bubbles with her hair pinned up on top of her head. Matthew edged in and sat down on the edge of the lavatory seat. The scented steam and the confined space and Dinah's hair reminded him suddenly of the bathroom in the old flat above the greengrocer's shop. There had been some crisis to do with bathwater, and they had had to spend the night in a hotel. He had made love to his wife in front of a tall mirror. He remembered their reflections, her pale legs wound around him.

'Are you coming this evening?' Matt asked.

Some of his colleagues were bringing their partners, but Dinah had refused the original invitation as if he had been crazy to extend it. Now he wanted her to come, as security and insurance and a proclamation of who and what he was, and he was also afraid of it.

She turned her head but did not quite look at him.

'Of course not. I told you. It's eggnog at the Pinkhams'.'

'Aren't you taking the boys?'

'Nope. It's a grown-up evening. For once.'

'Ah. Right.'

Matthew went through into the bedroom. Dinah's red dress, the best one, that left her shoulders bare, was laid out on the bed. He took off his shirt and put on a clean blue one that Kathrin had once admired. Dinah emerged from the bathroom, wrapped in a towel. She unpinned her hair and sat down to massage lotion into her legs.

The scent was one that Matthew liked, sharp with a suggestion of eau-de-Cologne. He finished buttoning his shirt and stood with his hands loosely hanging, watching her. Her spine and thighs and wrists and ankles made planes and curves that held and absorbed the light. She was utterly familiar and yet he felt that she contained some kernel that was unknown to him. Matthew took a step towards her. He was thinking about the boys downstairs, about the bedcover lightly wrinkled under the weight of her hips, the way that her hair would fall back as he lowered himself above her. And yet, in the car as he drove home he had been dreaming with painful, sharp regret of Kathrin and her tiny hands and busy mouth.

He hesitated, and in that second Dinah looked up at him. Her eyes were clear and they seemed to read his confusion without difficulty or forgiveness. There was still a small pool of white lotion held in the cup of her hand.

Matthew turned aside. Lately they had barely touched each other. When he looked again, Dinah's head was bent once more and she was smoothing lotion into her skin with calm unhurried strokes.

Pain buckled and compressed itself beneath Matthew's diaphragm. He sat down on the opposite side of the bed from Dinah, conscious of the counter-wrinkles made by his own weight and the unconnected space between them.

'I want to talk to you,' he said. 'I want to tell you what really happened with Kathrin and me.'

Dinah's response shocked him. She flung the bottle of lotion aside. It hit the wall and spilt a thin trail over the skirting board.

'I don't want to hear,' Dinah cried. 'Why should I let you force the details on me when I can't bear to hear them? It hurts me less to leave it blank. I don't want to be made to remember what you both did, and where and when. Why should I listen to it to make you feel better?'

'I'm sorry. I wasn't thinking of it as a comfort for myself.'

Dinah stood up. She was shaking, but she retrieved the bottle and screwed on the cap, and mopped up the spilled lotion with a tissue from the box on her dressing table. Matthew watched her. He was thinking that she must believe the end was coming, and did not want his unnecessary confessions to distort any more of her memories.

She began to put on her clothes, with her back turned to him, while Matthew sat immobile and silent. When she came to her dress she slipped it over her head and wriggled to settle the fabric smoothly over her hips. The long zipper at the back gaped open.

'Could you?' she asked coolly.

He did up the zipper and frowned over the tiny hook and eye at the top. He had performed a similar small service so many times, before all the parties and dinners and the joint celebrations that marked the years, and he and Dinah had gone out together dressed up and ready to take on the world. It was extraordinary, unthinkable that they had now come to the point of presenting separate faces to the same world.

Matthew kissed her bare shoulder.

'Won't you come with me tonight?'

Dinah walked away. She stood in front of the mirror to put *diamanté* earrings in her ears, tipping her head and deftly slipping the butterfly on to each metal post in turn.

'To sit smiling and talking to Sean Rader while your girlfriend looks on?'

'She isn't my girlfriend. I'm trying to tell you.'

'And I told you I didn't want to hear. I'm going to Todd and Nancy's.'

She put on her shoes now, red suede to match her dress. The high heels made her look tall. Dinah did indeed have an inner kernel that he didn't know, Matt thought, or had not known until just now. And the meat hidden within it was her anger with him. He was going to say so, to try to provoke a real response from her when he heard the boys running upstairs. They elbowed into the bedroom, jostling each other.

'We thought of a joke for you.'

'*I* thought of it, in fact, Merlin.'

Dinah was sitting down now, contemplating her face in the mirror, the peeled wand of her mascara in one hand.

'Let's hear it, then,' Matthew said.

'It's about a duck who went into a chemist's shop to buy some *condoms*.'

'Oh, really?'

'And the chemist man said, "Certainly Mr Duck, are you paying cash or shall I put it on your bill?".'

Jack threw himself backwards on the bed, laughing and kicking. Merlin laughed too, less certainly.

Matthew said to him, 'What d'you think, Mer? Is it a good one for the guys in the lab?'

'I don't know if I understand it properly,' he confessed.

'You know what a condom is, dummy,' Jack mocked him.

'Of course I do. It's the bit about the bill.'

'Like a bill you pay, right? And also it's a beak. He'd have it, like, *quaaack*.'

Merlin's face lightened. The boys began to mime ducks gagged with condoms. Matthew turned to look at Dinah's reflection in the mirror. She seemed to have painted out her real expression with cosmetics. The doorbell rang and the boys ran away again to let the sitter in.

'It's Christmas,' Matt said.

'I know.'

Dinah was wondering what Francis did to celebrate Christmas in Redemption Street. The drawing he had given her was in her desk, laid flat between two sheets of blank paper. She thought of Sarah too, and tried to imagine what she might be doing and thinking at this instant. 'I know,' she repeated, guiltily catching herself and realising that Matt was staring at her uncomprehendingly. She picked up her coat and bag, then went to him and touched his arm.

'Enjoy the party,' she said. 'I'll talk to Heidi on my way out.'

From what she could glimpse through the windows, the Pinkhams' house was already full of people. Dinah stamped the little ruff of fresh snow off her suede shoes and rang the bell.

There was a log fire in the big room, and a decorated tree, and a mixed crowd of neighbours and medics. Todd gave her a drink and George Kuznik kissed her on both cheeks. He was wearing a pink shirt and a red tartan bow tie, and his good humour touched Dinah and made her remember how much she liked him.

'You look sensational,' George told her. He made a show of protest after they had talked a little and one of Todd's colleagues came by and demanded to be introduced to the lady in red.

It was odd to be without Matthew. But this is how it would be, Dinah thought. She would go to parties and talk to people, come and go and be part of a pattern that would contain work and friendships, and yet she would still be separate, not half of the blurred composite of a couple. After so long.

There was a conversation with Francis running in her head.

Is this how you feel? Or not even this much connection? Is this what you prefer? You said you sometimes missed the refuge of someone else, a woman . . .

In the days since she had come back to Franklin the dialogue had become part of her consciousness. Francis and the simplicity of his existence stood for clarity and containment. Measured against Francis's life her own was full of confusion, but still she thought she had come a little way. She was strengthened by her determination. Dinah had written letters to the local authorities in Norfolk, and to all the other organisations who might have some knowledge of Sarah or the Greens. Each letter that she sent off felt like a link forged.

Somewhere, Dinah knew, at the invisible end of one of those links, Sarah was sitting beside a Christmas tree. She would find her. Soon, she was certain of it.

Dinah talked and joked her way through the cross-currents of the party. She attracted attention, and she accepted it.

She might not fully belong here, but neither was she as isolated as she had imagined. It was Matthew's fierce involvement with his work and his people that had given her the sense of standing on the margins of their joint existence. Alone, she stood on her own ground.

It was almost the end of the evening before she had a chance to talk to Nancy. They sat down on a sofa away from the music.

'Was it okay?' Nancy demanded. 'Did everyone have a good time? Did you?' She was wearing a black dress a shade too tight for her that exposed the tops of her breasts. Heat and exertion had damped her cottony hair so that fronds of it stuck to her shiny cheeks. 'Honest, I have hardly even had time for a drink. Where's your glass? Whoops. Little spill, never mind. Won't show on these cushions.'

'I had a great time.'

Todd was dancing with a good-looking blonde and they watched him for a minute. He did not have a natural sense of rhythm and his knees and elbows jerked out at angles. Nancy grinned. She eased off her shoes and tucked her legs beneath her, turning sideways to Dinah to exclude the rest of the room. She examined her with her head on one side.

'I've been meaning to say. You look nice tonight. Very

pretty. In fact you've been looking good ever since you got back from England.'

'Why, thank you.'

'Listen, don't fend me off with that Brit reserve stuff. Are we friends?'

'Of course we are.'

Dinah did not know whether they were or not.

There had been the promise of a friendship with Sandra Parkes, rooted in the similarity of their backgrounds and their mutual exile. But Sandra's hostile jealousy and Dinah's mistrust had not been tranquillised by shared memories of Sooty and Sweep or knowing all the words of every verse of 'All Things Bright and Beautiful'. Dinah regretted that Sandra and she were wary and suspicious of each other now.

Dinah knew how much less she had in common with Nancy, yet it was comfortable to sit on one side with her while the party sailed on past them. The sofa itself felt like a boat, rocking a little. That was the drink, and it was Christmas, as Matt had felt the need to remind her. Dinah sighed and rested her head on the cushions.

'Of course we are,' she repeated.

'Come on, then. Let's hear it. You go away looking like you had hot wires pulling you every which way and you come back happy. You haven't looked happy in months.'

'Haven't I?'

'No. Not happy. Not at all, nohow. Is it Matt?'

'What?'

'Shit. Okay, I'm prying. It's nothing to do with me. Forget it.'

That was what she had done, Dinah thought. Tried to forget. Dealt with Matt and Doctor Pang in the way she had painfully learnt, by pinching down on the truth and obliterating it. Nancy was watching her with real concern in her face. There was a sudden reassurance for Dinah in sensing the plain connection between them, a rooted female sympathy that had a value beyond the measures of friendship.

For too long Dinah had drawn away from other women, denying herself the comfort of honest communication because she did not believe she deserved it.

'Nancy, you're not prying. I'll tell you what's happening. Matthew is seeing a woman in his department. I've met her a couple of times. She's a post-doc, half-Asian. Tiny, beautiful. Clever and also kind of submissive.'

Part of the story. Only a small piece, but like a fragment of a puzzle that linked two bigger portions. Such a relief to tell it.

Nancy bit her perfect teeth together, whistled through them.

'Oh, how original. Someone who works for him. Great lord and master, behold thy handjob. Handmaid. Is that where he is tonight?'

'Kind of. It's the Christmas party.'

'Wow. Beer and frisbee.'

They looked at each other and laughed. 'Something like that. Is it funny? I don't know what I think. I've tried not to think.'

'No, it's not very funny. It's sad and he's an asshole. You're a great couple with great kids. A real family.'

Careful, watch the words. Not so close as to rub away the protective layers, even tonight, even with Nancy.

Milly was different. In Dinah's mind Milly had long ago become half-identified with Sarah, and lately her fantasies were inhabited by a hybrid daughter who seemed sometimes to be more real than Jack or Merlin. It was easy to talk to Milly, essential to talk to her . . .

'I think Matt and I used to be a great couple, only we faded. Make sure it doesn't happen to you and Todd.'

'Forget me and Todd. Is it serious, this affair he's having?'

'I don't know. Maybe. He wants something that he doesn't get from me, isn't that what they say?'

'What happened in England?'

What happened was that she had allowed herself the luxury of friendship with Francis. His confession had matched her unmade one. She had felt almost equal, but had kept her own guilt preserved beneath the varnish.

'I saw my mother, went to look for some old friends I've lost touch with. I didn't find them, though.'

'And what else? Come on, I can see it in your face.'

'What is this? The Inquisition? I met a man, someone interesting to talk to. A chance encounter, an evening's talk, no more than that.'

'A*ha.*' Nancy triumphant.

'Nothing more than that, truly.'

'Listen.' Nancy put her hand on Dinah's arm. 'I'm with you, okay? In the end there's no way Matthew's going to go for some little girl in preference to you. He's a fool maybe, but so are most of them, and Matt's not the biggest. You've got his boys, and all your life. I've seen the way you look at each other. Everything'll be okay. And I'm glad you came back from England with something, whatever it is. You just look like your perspectives have changed. Could be that's just what you need.'

'Perhaps. Thanks, Nancy. You're a good friend.' Dinah meant it. The evening had made her feel surprisingly happy, for all the dislocation of its beginning.

There were more than twenty of them, and so that meant two separate tables in Pantucci's.

Matthew had seen Kathrin hanging back to make sure that she found a place on the other table, and at the last minute she had slid into a chair between two of the graduate students. He could just see her from where he sat at the head of his table. She was wearing a tight little blue velvet jacket he had never seen before, and a clip in her hair made up of a row of silvery stars.

The meal seemed to go on for hours.

He heard himself carrying on a series of conversations, catching up on the trailing ends of other people's remarks and tacking on his own, asking questions about skiing trips and heartily talking about next year's programme. All the time a series of images played and replayed themselves in his head. There was Dinah bare-shouldered in her red dress, and Kathrin in her student bedroom with art posters on the wall behind her, and the mirror reflections in the long-ago hotel room, and his boys laughing and pretending to be ducks. He tried to dispel the images and concentrate on the faces around him, but he could not. They were all out of focus except for Kathrin's.

Everyone except Matt changed places with each course, according to some complicated scheme devised by the secretaries. Only Kathrin never came any closer to him. The noise level rose steadily. A plate of some creamy pudding that he did not want was placed in front of Matthew, then eventually it was taken away again. Sean Rader materialised in the seat next to him. He was hand-rolling an emaciated cigarette out of an Old Holborn tin. Sean clung tenaciously to his old habits.

'You okay?'

The cigarette was alight now and Sean squinted as he dragged hard on it.

'What? Yes, sure. What're you doing for Christmas?'

'You fucking asked me that an hour ago, and I told you then.'

They had worked together for a long time. Sean cultivated his abrasive manner and his Liverpool accent as a form of defence, mainly against women.

'Sorry. It's so noisy in here.'

'Matt. You look like shit.'

'Thanks.'

'Not the job, is it?'

Matthew frowned at him. Sean was intensely loyal, and single-mindedly brilliant at what he did. He had followed Matthew out to New England without question or hesitation. It would be the job that he would think of and worry about first and last, and it was disorientating for Matthew to realise that he no longer felt exactly the same.

'Of course not. We're right on course, you know that.'

'Yeah. Well. Something else?'

In all the years they had known each other they had never talked about what they felt or feared, beyond the level of a joke or a shrug. Matthew was only briefly tempted now. He could not discuss anything with Sean here. Nor could he think of anyone or anywhere else that he might try. Dinah had always been his audience and adviser, but now it seemed that even that had been only a partial conjunction. For years they had left unsaid more than they had revealed to one another. Across the room he caught sight of Kathrin's silver stars.

'Nothing else. Nothing serious, anyway.'

Sean thoughtfully detached a whisker of tobacco from his lower lip.

'Watch yourself then, mate.' He had picked up his Old Holborn tin and slipped it into his pocket.

The evening wound on. Matthew drank some more beer and joined in a game of Buzz, and was eliminated in the first round. Everyone was laughing and shouting. He had always enjoyed these evenings but now he felt himself on the outside of the team he had picked and directed. He tried to think of the work itself and of the steady ambition that had connected him to it and therefore to all these people, and he realised that some thread had snapped. The jumpy adrenalin-fuelled determination was no longer there.

I am so tired, Matthew thought. It is only because I am tired.

And then without warning another thought came. Would anything have been different now if we had kept Sarah?

Only everything.

He stood up. Another game was in progress. Jon Liu was lying between two chairs, his head supported by one and his heels by the other. His back was rigid and his face contorted with the effort of staying horizontal.

Everyone else was counting off the seconds, shouting in a chorus, *Fifteen, sixteen . . .*

Matthew saw Kathrin sitting to one side with her chin

183

cupped in her hand. He took the chair next to her, with his back to the players. She turned at last and looked full at him.

'I'm sorry,' he said. And then, 'I seem always to be apologising to you. Must sound like a dreary repetitive litany. How are you?'

He wanted to reach out and touch her. To do something simple like stroke her hair, following with his fingertips the curve of it inwards to the line of her jaw.

'Why do you want to know?'

Her eyes were as dark as plums. The convex double bow of her mouth looked crimped with pain.

'Because I do. Because I know I hurt you. Because you are avoiding me.'

Kathrin's eyes did not flicker.

'What exactly do you want?' she asked him.

There was a roar behind them. Someone had collapsed between the two chairs.

'I don't know.'

It was comforting to admit it, even though it also made him ashamed of his helplessness. In all his life Matthew had very rarely admitted that he did not know anything, and now he wished that he could tell Kathrin more. He would have liked to lie down beside her in the dark and talk until his head was empty. How long since he had done that with Dinah?

Kathrin leaned forward an inch. He remembered her perfume. Points of bone at the base of her throat. Pale sallow skin taut over her hips.

'Come home with me tonight.'

Patchwork quilt on her bed. Shreds of his own history already contained in the room.

'I can't.'

She drew back again, her mouth indrawn at the corners.

'I'm flying to Texas tomorrow, to join my family for Christmas. Ten days' leave.'

Ten days without seeing her, even with her face averted.

'I'll miss you,' Matthew said awkwardly. This was the truth,

184

although even as he said it he wished it was not. He had the sense of following a route with paths leading in different directions, and of taking a series of significant but unmarked turnings.

Kathrin smiled then. All the curves and ellipses of her face widened with delight and happiness.

'Good,' she whispered.

They were calling her to play the chair game.

'You'll be good at this, Kathy,' someone shouted.

Matthew reached home before Dinah. He paid the sitter and walked to the end of the block with her, to see her safely home. As he passed the Pinkhams' on the way back, he thought of looking in, but he recrossed the street to his own house without doing so. Fine, light snow had begun to fall again.

It felt odd to be alone in the house with the boys and without Dinah. Unease made him go upstairs to check on them.

They were both asleep, although Jack turned over and opened his eyes, murmuring something urgent and unintelligible. Matthew bent over to try to catch the effluent of his dream but there was only a brief gasp of exhaled breath. Matthew fought the sudden impulse to gather the child up out of his covers and squeeze him in his arms, as if that could keep him safe. Instead, he picked up Jack's spectacles which had fallen by the bedside, patiently folded the arms, and replaced them on the table.

Downstairs, Ape was waiting, his tail thumping gently on the floor. The dog followed him into the den and bounded on to the sofa beside him. They settled down together to watch the end of the sitter's late movie.

It was one-thirty when Dinah came home. Matthew heard her outside, calling goodnight to the Kuzniks and laughing at something that George said in return.

He waited for her to look into the room, but she did not. He went out into the kitchen and found her tidying away the remains of Heidi's supper. The perspectives of the house shifted again for Matthew. Dinah was here. There was a knot of anger in him, and fear, connected with the possibility that she might not always be.

She stopped, with a square of pink kitchen sponge in her hand. She was bright-eyed, a little flushed. Matthew knew just how much she had had to drink, which was exactly the right amount. Dinah did not like to lose control. She was careful, watchful of herself, as if – he understood now – she was frightened of what might otherwise be unleashed.

'Good party?' Dinah asked.

'Yes, in the way these things are. I didn't enjoy it much.'

'I'm sorry.'

She returned to her task, wiping crumbs from the counter-top with smooth sweeps that reminded him of the lotion earlier. Her older and fiercer anger with him seemed tangible to Matthew, like some rock wall ugly with jagged fissures that he could not scale or sidestep.

'And the Pinkhams'?'

'I had a good time. There were some nice people from the hospital.'

'And faithful George, of course.'

'Matt, don't demean yourself. I'm going up to bed now.'

When he followed her up he found her already in bed, lying on her back in the dark. He undressed and lay down beside her, and the inches between them had become unknown terrain, with their topographical markings all eroded.

I won't, Matthew thought. I won't let this blind space exist between us, as if by a mere effort of will he could bridge it. He was conscious of the angles and recesses of their bedroom enclosing them, the drawers and shelves and closets with their contents like the index to a complicated history, and of the snow falling outside. He lifted his hand, and reached out for Dinah. His fingers met the arc of her ribcage, the deckle-edge of bone prominent under the smooth flesh between her waist and her breast. She had grown thinner. He stroked

186

her skin lightly, feeling the slow rise and fall of her breathing. He rolled on to his side, facing her, his hand travelling over her belly.

'Are you awake?'

He knew that she was.

'Yes.'

Neither an invitation nor a rebuff. His hand dipped between her legs, and he splayed his fingers from the knuckle to invite their parting. The resistance to him made her seem a stranger, for all her familiar scent and texture. Disconcerted, Matthew heaved himself closer, and his uncertainty made him clumsy.

He lay half on top of her. His hand made an awkward movement, a scrape more than a caress, over her breast. His partial erection had already collapsed.

'This is me,' she said harshly. 'Dinah. Are you confusing me with her?'

Matt rolled away from her again. He put up his arm to shield himself, partly from the awful recognition that he was confused on some deep level by Dinah's foreignness, by the way that even her flesh was dissolving, as if he was subconsciously and horribly willing her to be Kathrin. And he also shrank from the first real hammer-blow of unhappiness. Incoherently he thought, *This is what it will be like. This is what we have done.*

'No. How could I confuse you? We have been married for fifteen years. I went to bed with Kathrin twice, I . . .'

He was going to make her listen, to knit together the truth and what he wished to be true to make a bandage for both of them. But Dinah prevented it. Her hand shot out and found his wrist and for a second her fingers were like a claw on him. And then she flung his arm away from her.

'Don't,' she commanded.

There was a silence, compounded by isolation and the snow steadily thickening outside.

At last Dinah said, 'Perhaps we should think about separating.'

187

'I see,' Matthew said. He was wondering how they had come so frighteningly far, at such bewildering speed. How far back was it that they had gone wrong? He wanted to go back to try to find the signposts, to acknowledge them at least. And he remembered the feeling he had had earlier, with Kathrin, of taking important turnings that were somehow unmarked.

'I need to think,' he said dully.

He sat up, and moved his legs over the side of the bed. He groped for and found the folds of his bathrobe.

'Where are you going?'

There was a sharp note of fear in Dinah's voice.

Yes, he thought with a touch of cruelty, you should be afraid as well as me.

'Downstairs. I can't sleep now.'

He left the room and padded down to the kitchen. Ape emerged from his place and stood with his tongue affectionately lolling. Matthew pushed him aside and took out the whisky bottle and a glass. He poured himself a measure and then slopped another two fingers on top. The Kerrigans had left their outside Christmas lights on, and he could see red and blue reflections of them in the window glass blurred by snow. Matthew tasted the whisky, sourish on his tongue. He leant forward so that his face touched the cold glass.

If we had kept Sarah, he thought.

But that was a speculation that could meet with no conclusion, because they had not done so.

Upstairs, Dinah turned over with her back to Matthew's side of the bed. She had tried the words, flinging them down, and instead of rejecting them outright he had taken them in.

She closed her eyes. She tried to will herself into the temporary solution of sleep.

Nine

Dinah and Milly were out walking Ape in the woods bordering the river at the nearest point to Kendrick Street. Milly and her parents had just returned to Franklin from their Christmas break in Switzerland. It was the end of January and there had been a slight thaw followed by penetrating cold, so the earth was hard and treacherously icy beneath the dead blanket of the latest snow. The trees were black, with only the windward sides of the boles crusted with powder and ice. On either side of the woodland path the ground was a featureless expanse of rounded hummocks and bluish hollows. Ape slithered ahead, tracked by the marks of his own circular progress, his panting breath clouding the air like a small steam engine.

Dinah was exhilarated by the cold and the graphic purity of the winter woodland, but Milly was less happy. She had only agreed to the walk because it offered the opportunity of an hour of Dinah's undivided attention. She wore a knitted hat pulled down over her ears, and a long thin worm of a scarf wound around her neck and chin. She walked slowly, stopping whenever Ape crossed the path ahead of them to preserve as wide a margin between them as possible.

'Winter. It always seems to be winter,' she complained. 'I hate the cold, and wind that makes your eyes water, and always shivering inside your clothes.'

'Aren't you wearing enough to keep you warm?' Dinah asked, but Milly only shrugged. However many layers of clothes she wore the New England cold scythed through them and her flesh as well, and penetrated into the marrow of her bones.

Dinah noticed that Milly was even thinner, and her face was a small colourless triangle in the coils of ratty wool. Her eyes were less defiantly painted and her clothes were more like just clothes, pulled on anyhow for decency's sake, rather than the old calculated anti-dress. Perhaps isolation and her long absence from London and her friends were taking their toll, and Milly was slowly losing her appetite for the battle with Ed and Sandra. Dinah wanted to reassure her that she was not necessarily wrong or even particularly unusual, only temporarily out of her place. Time and the possibility of adult choices would probably solve almost everything for her.

Dinah controlled a smile at the thought of what Milly would say if she suggested as much. She contented herself with linking an arm through Milly's, keeping off some of the wind as they walked on.

'Look,' Dinah pointed.

There was a ski-trail below them, running alongside the river. A group of cross-country skiers approached from the opposite direction. They wore baby-bright clothes and jaunty little packs on their backs, and they were swinging vigorously along the trail in a co-ordinated line. 'Dumb,' Milly said.

Milly was right, Dinah thought. They did look comically like marionettes.

'Don't you ski in Zermatt?'

'Not if I can help it. I'm crap at it.'

Dinah smiled at the honesty. Milly would not want to fall over and risk looking vulnerable, and so would dismiss the abilities of others with scorn and derision.

'I've never even tried.'

'Ed loves it. He goes off every day with all the stuff, avalanche gear and thermal earmuffs and flasks and one of his fifteen pairs of skis. This dumb Swiss guy comes for him and they macho off together.'

'Dumb?' Dinah glanced sideways at Milly's profile and saw a scowl and a dull patch of colour. Milly was blushing.

'Yeah. You know. Pathetic.'

The handsome ski-guide. Dinah was enchanted by this evidence of her normality.

'Oh, yes. I see. What about Sandra?'

'Outfits. Fur parkas and dinky mittens and big zips.'

Dinah nodded.

'What do you do?'

'Not much. Listen to music. Wait for it to be time to go somewhere else. Like back here.'

'I'm glad you're back.'

'Did you miss me?'

'Very much.'

It had not been the happiest of Christmases, although they had tried to preserve the appearances for Jack and Merlin's sakes. Matthew had gone back to work as soon as it was over and immersed himself in the newest phase of his research. They had not discussed the possibility of a separation again, although they were both aware of it like a chasm over which they trod the daily precarious bridge. Dinah waited for the authorities in Norfolk to respond to her letters. There had been no positive news as yet.

Dinah was very glad to see Milly, both for herself and for the hybrid-daughter that she now partly represented in Dinah's obsessive imaginings.

In her objective moments Dinah thought that Sandra was probably right to be resentful and suspicious of her relationship with Milly. They had too many needs between them, needs that mirrored each other, reflecting back without properly matching or meeting. They couldn't be mother and daughter to one another, but the much deeper longings that made them dream of it could not be unlocked either. Not yet, Dinah thought.

She was bitterly aware of being caught between adult and

191

childish imperatives, between dark and light, truth and secrecy. Her secrets and desires made her unable to be a real friend, either to Milly or to Sandra.

The realisation made her feel cold, as the snow and icy wind had not.

They had almost completed the circuit of their walk. The path led over a wooden footbridge across the river, and through the thinning trees to the cul-de-sac end of Kendrick. Milly stopped on the slimy planks of the bridge and stared down into the ice-grey water breaking over the rocks.

'What's going to happen, do you think?' she asked in a flat voice.

Dinah heard her aimlessness and disaffection and unfocused longing, and ached for her and Sarah together. Only Milly had nothing really to fear. She tried to reassure her, in the very words she had rejected earlier.

'Everything will be all right. You'll grow up, that's what'll happen.'

Milly laughed harshly. 'Oh, great. I can get some outfits like Sandra's.'

'Don't be so tough on her,' Dinah bit back.

Milly looked surprised. 'Sorry. I thought you were on my side.'

'I am, Milly. But I'm a parent as well, aren't I?'

They were walking up Kendrick now. It was almost the time of day for Jack and Merlin to come back from school. Dinah saw that the flap of the mailbox was down. The usual thick pile of circulars and catalogues and polywrapped journals protruded from the open mouth, almost all of it for Matt, as usual. Dinah gathered the mail in under her arm and hurried Milly into the house. Automatically she put water on to boil for tea and slotted bread into the toaster. When she had a free hand she flipped through the stack of mail.

Buried in the middle of it was a plain white envelope, hand-addressed to her in black ink. Dinah knew at a glance, before she even saw the stamp or the postmark, that the letter was from Francis.

She took two slices of toast out of the toaster and handed them on a plate to Milly. She put the jar of strawberry jam on the kitchen table at her elbow, and placed a mug of the hot juice drink that Milly favoured beside it. Then she took a clean knife and carefully slit open the white envelope. There was a single folded sheet of paper, the same paper that he used for his drawings.

Francis wrote just as he talked. She could hear his voice.

I have found your friends and their two daughters. They are living up on the coast, near Blakeney. This is the address.

Dinah stared at it. Her hands were shaking.

The letter was quite short. Francis apologised if it had been presumptuous of him to continue the search on her behalf. He said that it had been very easy for him to find the Greens because he was close at hand. He hoped that she was well and happy, and added that he often thought of her.

That was all.

34 Church Walk, Wivenham, Norfolk. The letter was dated only four days earlier.

'What is it?' Milly asked curiously. When Dinah did not answer at once she repeated, 'What's happened?'

Dinah sat down at the table, carefully refolding the letter along its creases.

Her first reaction was relief, a great wash of it like bright light flooding through her. Sarah was alive, safe with Pauline. One of her deepest fears had been that she might not be.

She looked up, saw Milly staring at her. She realised that she was smiling, a silly, wide smile that almost split her face.

'I know where Sarah is. Someone has found her for me.'

Milly put down her toast, fiddled with the knife that had been lying on her plate.

'Right. God. That's so, like, weird. What will you do?'

'Go to England and see her.'

To her credit, Milly did her best to be pleased.

It was good news, she said. Dinah must feel very happy

now, and it was wonderful that she had found what she wanted after so long. But her face contradicted her words. It was much easier to see what Milly felt without her obscuring layers of make-up. She ran out of positive things to say and sat for an instant staring unseeingly ahead of her.

'I wish my mother would find me,' she blurted on a swallowed breath. She hid her face in her hands.

Dinah bent over her, holding her shoulders.

'You will find her,' she promised. 'When the time is right. You will know the answers. They might not be the ones you want to hear, but you will have the answers to your questions.'

Blindly Milly stood up and flung herself at Dinah. In Dinah's arms she began to sob. Dinah closed her eyes as she held her. She tried to see Sarah alone, instead of the hybrid daughter who was a confusion of the two of them with her own longing, and who must be put aside now the reality was only a measurable distance away.

Sarah, Sarah.

'You won't forget about me, will you?' Milly wept. 'Now you've found her.'

Dinah stroked her hair, twisting her fingers through the matted plaits and feeling the smallness of the skull beneath. Milly seemed so young, younger even than Merlin.

'I won't ever forget about you.'

'I wish you could be her. I wish I was the daughter you've found.'

'We can't be those things. But we can be others.'

She was relieved, and at the same time afraid, concerned for this child who was another woman's daughter and filled with swelling excitement for her own. The pressure of it tightened against the plates of her skull and within the cage of her ribs. There were only airports and roads, days and hours, separating her from her daughter now. Negotiable obstacles. Easily imagined and overcome.

34 Church Walk, Wivenham, Norfolk. Mr and Mrs Malcolm Green, and two daughters.

Dinah hid her face against Milly's hair.

They heard Merlin and Jack outside on the porch, shouting across to the Kerrigans. School was out.

'Shit.' Milly jerked her head up. Her tears had left a wet
patch on Dinah's shoulder. 'Why are they here?'

Dinah gave her a handful of tissues and rubbed her own
eyes.

'Could be because they live here.'

The boys surged in to the kitchen.

Merlin made straight for the food but Jack eyed his mother
and Milly.

'What's happening?'

'We've been for a long cold walk,' Dinah said. 'Did you
have a good day?' Milly ignored them all, drawing a curtain
of hair over her smeared face. She picked sullenly at the
crusts of toast on her plate.

'Jamie Weisner got sent home for bad behaviour,' Merlin
announced. Jack hesitated, looking jealously at Milly, but in
the end he took his plate and cup and followed Merlin off to
watch TV.

Shortly afterwards Sandra came by to pick up Milly. She
came into the kitchen in her cashmere coat, shedding scarves and a pair of cream leather gloves that looked soft
enough to melt in the kitchen's heat. She had been to the
hairdresser's.

'Have you had a nice time?' she asked Dinah and Milly.
She accepted the cup of tea that Dinah handed her, but
would not take off her coat. Dinah tried to take the exact
measure of her ambivalence. Sandra was eager for Milly to
have a friend in Franklin, because friends were natural and
desirable. But for the friend to be Dinah, in what Sandra
perceived as her secure motherliness, only peeled away the
skin of desirability to reveal the vulnerable flesh of anxiety
shivering beneath it.

Dinah sighed inwardly. She could not think of a solution
to this conundrum. She told Sandra about the walk and the
cold and the skiers. Milly walked away, deliberately insulating
herself within the chatter of afternoon television. She did

not like seeing her mother and Dinah together. It was much easier to have them apart, opposing.

'How does she seem, to you?' Sandra asked, looking away. She wanted to know, but she did not want to have to ask Dinah.

'She seems all right. A bit subdued, perhaps.'

'She's been talking about tracing her birth mother, again.'

Sandra had suggested to Dinah that she had sown the idea in Milly's mind, and Dinah had denied it. The idea had been there already. Dinah had simply given her the chance to explore it.

'What did you say to her?'

'That she'll have to wait until she's older.'

With her fingertips Dinah eased away the smile from the corners of her mouth. 'That's more or less what I told her, too.'

'It's easy for you,' Sandra angrily turned on her. 'Your children are yours. You don't have all the confusion and history of adoption to deal with. It's easy.'

'If you say so,' Dinah answered.

They faced each other. Dinah was aware of the little tick-tick of possibility and counter-possibility, the avenues of admission and concealment leading away from this moment's intersection. She could offer Sandra her confidence, or not. They could understand one another, or fail to do so.

And she said nothing. The habit of suppression was ingrained, and with it the belief that she did not deserve sympathy or the comfort of another woman's understanding.

'Is something wrong?' Sandra asked, after a moment.

Dinah was looking at the envelope containing Francis's letter. It lay on the worktop, amongst the breadcrumbs and the rings of juice left by the children's cups. There was a single droplet of strawberry jam gleaming like a jewel on the flap. She reached out for it with the tip of her finger, and then licked off the jam's sweetness. She could see Francis's room in Redemption Street in every detail. The thought of him brought her comfort. Francis had somehow unstopped her voice. She had been able to talk, in Redemption Street.

'No, nothing is wrong.' With an effort of will she asked, 'Where's Ed today?'

'In New York. Seeing his publishers. How's Matthew?'

'He's fine. Just back from a conference in Florida.'

They met each other's eyes this time, half-smilingly, wryly acknowledging what was acceptable to acknowledge, that men did what they did.

Sandra gathered up her scarves and gloves. 'Thanks for the tea. And for having Milly over.'

'It was a pleasure,' Dinah said coolly.

'See you,' Milly muttered at the door, not looking at Dinah. Dinah could only watch her go and wave to the tail end of Ed's Porsche shimmying up Kendrick.

This evening there was her own family to consider. The question of what to say to the boys, and when. Dinah thought of the alternative moves she might make, like openings in a chess game.

She went through the routine of preparing a meal, listened to the boys, and wished for Matthew to come home. She wanted him to hear that Sarah was found. She planned how she would tell him and allowed herself to imagine that by some miracle he might be happy about it.

Matthew came home a little later than usual, with a pile of work to do. The boys went upstairs with him to talk over the day while he changed, as they always did. Dinah set the table for dinner, laying out four of everything. She lingered foolishly over the fifth plate, glass, spoon.

'Are you ready to eat?' she asked when Matt came down again.

'Please. I've got a lot to do afterwards.'

They were polite to each other, as had become their habit.

It was an ordinary family meal. Dinah thought that surely her face or her voice must give away her feelings, but Matt did not notice anything.

As soon as he had finished eating he cleared the table

and then took his briefcase into the den. Dinah loaded the dishwasher and followed Merlin and Jack upstairs. She went through the motions of opening closets and drawers and laying out what they would both need for tomorrow. All these mundane activities had acquired a different colouring. The business of preparing food and sorting clothes seemed to have expanded to take account of Sarah, who was no longer imaginary but real, rooted in a real place. Dinah also felt the beginnings of anxious impatience. If the Greens were to up and move again, without warning, would she be able to find them once more?

Dinah bundled clothes into heaps, pointlessly hurrying.

When she went in to say goodnight to Jack he took hold of her hand and made her sit on the edge of his bed. Dinah controlled her eagerness to go downstairs to talk to Matthew.

Did Pauline Green sit like this to talk to Sarah before she settled down to sleep?

'What did you do today?' Jack asked.

'Nothing very exciting. I told you I went for a long walk with Milly.'

He was turning something in his head, unsure of what he wanted to ask.

'Mum, don't you like living in Franklin?'

'I like it because you and Merlin and Daddy are here, of course. It's important because of Daddy's work. We've talked about all the good points often enough, Jack, haven't we? Different people and customs and landscapes and weather. New things to see and learn about. But on the other hand I do miss England.'

'That's kind of what I feel as well. Half and half. Is that all?'

'Yes, Jack.'

He knew that there was something awry but he accepted her reassurance with a kind of resignation. He was becoming used to half-answers and evasions.

'What about Milly? What was she crying about today?'

He was asking not out of sympathy but suspicion.

'Jack. I know you don't like her particularly, but Milly

doesn't have a very easy time. She's in a battle with her mother and father and in a way with herself as well.'

'She's all right, I don't mind her that much. They're a weird family. I like our family.'

Jack was lying on his back. His hair fell away from his face, showing the shape of his forehead. He looked like Matt.

'So do I,' Dinah said. She leant across and kissed him.

This was not the time to tell the boys. Not yet, before she had made the discoveries about Sarah for herself.

Jack sighed, and settled himself under the covers. 'Good-night,' he said finally, dismissing her.

Dinah went downstairs. Matthew was working and did not look up.

She went into the kitchen and poured herself a drink. She would wait half an hour, until the children were asleep. She sat at the kitchen table, turning her glass round and round in her fingers until the minutes had passed.

'Matt?'

'Yes.' He was busy, scribbling a note on a pad.

'Can we talk?'

There was an almost audible sigh.

'Yes, of course.'

He put his work aside. Now he did look up at her.

'Matt, I had a letter today from someone I met while I was in Cromer.'

She waited and saw his eyes sharpen with attention.

'He made some enquiries and he has found the Greens. They live in Wivenham, on the north Norfolk coast.'

There was a silence. Then Matthew picked up his pen and tapped it on his thumbnail, as if to compress the tobacco in a cigarette before he lit it. He had not smoked for twelve years, since before Jack was born.

'I see.'

Dinah waited again, disbelieving, and then could no longer contain the swell of her animosity.

'Is that all? *I see?* As if someone's just explained some small theoretical principle to you?' Her voice was harsh and much too loud.

Matthew sat back, putting the pen aside. His empty hands curled loosely, helpless-looking.

In a flat voice he asked, 'What else am I to say?'

'Oh, say that you're pleased. Say that you're happy to know that our child, *our child*, is alive and safe, that she is growing up with people who care for her.'

'Dinah. We knew that already.'

'We did not.' She was shouting. 'We knew nothing. We'd let her go and that was all.'

'That was the decision we made. Everything that came after it was natural and inevitable.'

Dinah couldn't even see his face any longer. There was a sickening coloured blur in front of her that made her rock on her feet. She was panting for breath.

'It wasn't my decision. It was yours. I didn't make it. Nothing since then has been natural or inevitable, it's been full of hurt. Every day has been. I wanted to keep her but she wasn't good enough for you. You made me *choose*, Matt. It was you or her.'

With utter amazement she listened to the words spilling out of her. She had thought them so often and kept them pinched within her head, and now they had escaped. She was shouting, as if she had gone mad. Her mouth felt skewed and her tongue swollen as if her involuntary muscles no longer controlled them.

Matt was very quiet.

'This is the root of everything, isn't it? Your anger with me, because you think I made you give up our child.'

'I am angry, yes. Are you surprised by that? Shocked?'

The simple acknowledgement of her anger ignited a reservoir of it within her. Dinah shakily wiped her mouth with the back of her hand. She wanted to hit out, but she bit into her clenched fist instead, hurting herself so that she almost yelped.

'Neither. I don't believe you have any reason to be angry.

In pain, perhaps. I can understand that. You could have kept her if you had insisted. But you had your doubts too. And so you let me carry the burden of the decision because it was easier for you.'

This was how it seemed to Matthew, looking backwards down the long tunnel of time to the day after Sarah's birth. He had done what needed to be done for Dinah as well as himself.

'No. Oh no, no. That wasn't how it was.'

'Do you wish you had chosen differently? If the choice was what you said it was?'

He was so disdainfully cold and matter-of-fact. A scientist setting out the facts as he saw them, and as if there were no other way of seeing those facts.

'Yes.' Dinah spat. 'I wish I had.'

'I see.' Again. 'And so what do you intend to do now?'

'I'm going back to England again. To see her, because I have to see her. After that I don't know.'

'What about the boys? We do have two other children. What about your responsibility to them? If you had made the other choice, you wouldn't have them at all.'

'I love them. You know I do.'

Dinah was crying. The tears and the weakness they suggested enraged her, but she couldn't stop them coming.

'I do know that.'

She went to him and took hold of Matthew by the wrist, digging her fingers into his flesh.

'Come with me this time. We know where she is, we can go straight to her. It isn't a wild goose chase any more. Come with me just to see her,' she begged.

'No. I told you before.'

She let go of his arm, stepped back from him.

'Then I'll go alone. I can't take Jack and Merlin with me. You'll have to look after them. Do what I do for them. Why not? They're your children. The ones you wanted.'

'Of course I'll take care of them.'

Dinah nodded.

'I don't care what you think, Matt. I don't even care if going to see her is the right thing or the wrong thing. I just know that it is the only thing. Essential. Irrevocable.'

'For you. What about the rest of us? Pauline Green? Sarah herself?'

Hotly Dinah said, 'I won't hurt Sarah. I won't hurt Pauline either. I know I don't have any right to go to her and ask for anything. And I have thought of you, and the boys, for fourteen years.'

'Who is this person who helpfully found her for you?'

She turned away. 'Just someone I met.'

After Dinah had gone back upstairs Matthew sat gazing at his papers.

In the place of columns of figures he saw a face, slanted eyes with the epicanthic fold of skin, flattened cheekbones and protruding lower lip and tongue characteristic of Down's syndrome. But the features also took on a different dimension, and became Sarah's.

'When are you going?'

'Tomorrow evening,' Dinah told Milly.

'But . . . *tomorrow?*'

'I don't want to delay it. Milly, are you okay?'

'I want to come with you.'

'I can't take you to England. Ed and Sandra wouldn't want me to, apart from all the other reasons.'

'They wouldn't care.'

'They do care. You know that. If they didn't, there would be other problems, but not the ones you have. They love you.'

'Fuck. Everything. I hate it here. I hate being so lonely.' She screwed up her face and began to wheedle. 'Dinah, you're the only friend I've got, don't go off again and leave me behind. You promised.'

'I didn't promise you that. Listen, here's the address and number of the hotel I'll be staying at, up in Norfolk. You can call me, I'll call you. We can talk just like we're talking now.'

'Will you tell me about her? I want to hear what happens. What it's like.'

'Yes. I'll tell you.'

'What about your friend, the one who knows all about adoptions?'

'Lavinia Jackson.'

'Her. Will you talk to her about me?'

'Milly, I'll try to.'

'I'm just taking a short trip to England, that's all. To see Granny again, and some other people. I'll call you every evening, when you get in from school. You can tell me everything that's happening.'

'How long will you be gone?'

Jack and Merlin looked at her with their father's eyes. They were suspicious of her explanations, resentful of her abandoning them.

'I'm not quite sure. It won't be very long.'

'*What* other people?' Merlin asked.

'No one you know, Mer. And I also need some time to myself. Everyone does, once in a while.'

'Time to yourself even from us?'

How insistent and continual were the demands of children, present and absent. There was no slipping out of these bonds.

'Even from you, darling.'

'Mom, you will come back soon?'

'I don't want you to *go*.'

There were tears in Merlin's eyes, and Jack furiously stared at her. Dinah pulled them against her, fighting her impulse to give in, to stay, to be silent. No. She could not. That would not work any more, even if it had worked for so long.

'I love you both so much.' She bent her head over them. Their skulls were hard, under the childish floss of hair, bruising her mouth.

The car came to take Dinah to the airport. Nancy and Dee waved her off, with the boys between them. It had been arranged that they would take turns to look after Jack and Merlin after school, until Matthew came home from the lab.

Twenty-four hours later Dinah was in Norfolk.

There was no sign of spring under the rain-heavy sky, although closer to London there had been daffodils in the gardens and pink early-flowering cherries in bloom. Up here the hedges were still winter-black, and the fields colourless and wind-scoured.

Beyond Norwich the minor roads were slow and greasy with rain. Dinah drove steadily, blinking away her sleepiness and the beginnings of jet lag. She had intended to take the Cromer road to her hotel and a bath and a night's rest, but instead she found herself heading irrevocably farther east and north, towards Wivenham.

She felt as if she were driving to meet a lover. It was a Saturday and the traffic was heavy. The winding roads and heavy lorries were obstacles in her path, but no obstacle was insurmountable.

It was mid-afternoon when she came to the coast. There was a thin line ahead of her at the horizon and a glimpse of seal-grey water and tide-bitten marshland. Dinah fumbled for the unfamiliar controls and wound down the driver's window. At once a gust of salt air flooded into the car.

There was an old signpost at a junction. Wivenham was only two miles away.

Dinah pulled in to the side of the road and stopped in a field gateway. When she stepped outside the car the wind caught her full in the face. It took her breath away and held her pinned for an instant against the car's side, but there was none of the New England bone-chill in it. There was underlying warmth in this wind, from the marsh mud and sheltered creeks where sea birds waded in white flocks. Dinah had been travelling for twenty-four hours, but she did not feel even the faintest suggestion of tiredness now. She found that she was buoyed up by a strange exhilaration.

To collect herself before driving the last tiny leg of the

journey she climbed the five-barred gate and perched on the top. She could see the sea ahead, and across the fields away to her left the high flint tower of a church. She pulled her coat closer around her and listened to the cries of gulls over the wind. Once, when the wind dropped a little, she thought she could just hear the sound of the church bells.

Several cars passed her. The road led to Wivenham and no further, but it was busy this afternoon with shoppers and weekenders.

Here was where Sarah lived.

Now that she was so close to her Dinah could not quite think of what she might see or feel. To try to imagine it was too intense and she drew back from the impulse. Instead she tried to picture the street and the house, the ordinary details that might surround this extraordinary reality of her daughter.

Dinah sat on the gate for a long time, until she realised that she was chilled by the insistent wind. She jumped down and ducked back into the car. She ran the engine until the heater gave out a dusty, plastic heat and she stopped shivering. Then she put the car into gear and slowly drove the last two miles into the village.

Wivenham was a small place. There was one main street that led down to the quay. The tide was out in the wide estuary, exposing banks of mud and a few moored sailing dinghies tipped on their keels. There was a Co-op store and a handful of small shops, a pub and some terraces of tiny flint-faced cottages. The church stood back from the main street, down an unmade road lined with bare trees. A line of cars was parked under the spiky branches. At the far end a lich-gate led into the graveyard.

34 Church Walk. Near here.

The church bells were ringing, she had not misheard from her seat on the gate. Perhaps the ringers were practising for Sunday.

Dinah left the car to one side of the main street. She put on her coat and buttoned it up to the neck and tied a scarf around her head. She walked slowly down to the quay and back, checking the names of the small side streets. She could have gone straight to the church, but it was important to eliminate the least likely corners first. Now that she was here she was cool and methodical, except that on the quayside she found that she was panting for breath and her fists were clenched in the pockets of her coat.

She uncurled her fingers and made herself breathe evenly before turning back to retrace her steps to the church.

There were plenty of people in the street, pensioners and housewives with babies in buggies, and groups of children. Dinah looked quickly at the children but they were all much younger than Sarah. As she passed the butcher's shop a woman came out, cheerfully calling something over her shoulder to the man in the shop. Her height and colouring made Dinah stop short and pretend to look in the window of a yacht chandler's, until she realised that the woman's resemblance was to Pauline as she had been fourteen years ago.

No one looked at Dinah herself. She was entirely inconspicuous in her plain coat and headscarf.

She reached the other end of the main street and turned back again, strolling past the shops on the other side of the road. Then she turned into the walk leading to the church. The bells had stopped ringing while she was down on the quay.

The lich-gate had been erected in 1919 as a war memorial. Dinah lingered to read the names on the stone tablet and then opened the gate into the churchyard. It was neatly kept, with tidy grass around the old stones as well as the newer marble fenders with their gleaming chippings. There were spring flowers with their petals browned by the wind in several of the marble vases.

When she reached the church porch Dinah realised that she was not alone in the graveyard. There was a group of small children swinging their legs on top of one of the old table tombstones, and a hardy-looking trio of old ladies sheltering from the wind in the lee of the porch. A man was setting up a tripod with his back turned to the jeering children. A photographer.

It was a Saturday wedding, not bell-ringing practice. Through the inner doors, Dinah could hear the hymn-singing.

And beyond the far set of gates the wedding cars were parked, two shiny black old Daimlers with white ribbons. The drivers were leaning against the bonnet of the front one, smoking and talking.

Now that she could see past the church, she realised that there was a second half to the village. A jumble of post-war housing extended away from the sea. Dinah walked in front of the waiting cars, nodding to the drivers as she passed. The first turning she came to was Church Walk. It was a small estate of sixties semis with neat squares of gardens in front and cared-for elderly cars on the hard standing beside the rose bushes.

Dinah's throat was tight and her fingernails dug into the palms of her hands. For all the times she had imagined it, knowing that it would look approximately like this, its ordinariness was surprising.

She hesitated at the end of the road. She wanted to stop and think and take this much in. This was the road where Sarah lived. But she knew that she would be more noticeable if she loitered here than if she walked on, another woman in early middle-age going about her Saturday business. There were people hurrying past her, all of whom seemed to know each other and where they were going. Dinah walked on, trying to make her steps even, counting the house numbers off in her head without looking at the doors.

Number thirty-four stood on a bend. It looked the same as all the other houses, with net curtains at the windows and pruned shrubs in the garden. Only Dinah had the impression that this house was busy today. There were several cars parked directly in front and some crates and boxes stacked on the step. Dinah kept walking, hardly daring to turn her head. Which room, which window was Sarah's?

There was no one visible behind the nets.

Did the boxes mean something significant, a move or some other unguessable threat?

She hesitated for a second or two and then she had passed the house and it was impossible to look back.

A woman came along the pavement towards her. She had seen Dinah lingering.

'Not a bad day for them, after all,' the woman said heartily.

'Not bad,' Dinah agreed, uncomprehendingly.

She saw to her relief that Church Walk was U-shaped. She could reach the road to the church without passing by the house again.

The bells began to ring once more, starting up one by one and then following each other into the celebratory peal. The wedding service was over. Dinah wandered back to the church gates to catch a glimpse of the bride, glad that there was something else on which to focus her attention.

A younger man was waiting beside the camera tripod. The photographer himself had gone, presumably into the church to take pictures of the couple signing the register. The knot of onlookers had grown and the chauffeurs had put out their cigarettes. Dinah stood a little to one side, watching, for no other reason than that she could not think exactly what to do next.

The organ music reached a crescendo as the church doors opened. The bride and groom came up the aisle and out into the porch with the photographer backward-stepping ahead of them. The bride was a pretty brunette made radiant by the day, and her new husband was a red-faced young man who looked as if his shirt collar might be too tight. In the dimness of the church's interior Dinah caught a glimpse of turquoise bridesmaid dresses.

Wedding guests in pastel hats and best suits began to stream out of the church in the wake of the bride and groom. The women held on to the brims of their hats and fumbled with boxes of confetti and the men gathered in dark groups to joke away their awkwardness. All these social manœuvres held Dinah's attention for a moment, and then she turned to look at the photographer posing the wedding group.

One of the men being directed into place was Malcolm Green.

His hair was grey and his face much heavier, but there was no mistaking him.

Faces and images clicked in Dinah's head faster than she could register them.

The bride was not just any dark-haired young woman sacrificially swathed in white net.

Jennifer. Pauline's daughter. Last glimpsed as a lumpy thirteen-year-old.

Three bridesmaids. Two little girls with puff-sleeved dresses and posies of white and yellow freesias, and one older.

Plump in folds of shiny turquoise satin. A bigger posy for the senior bridesmaid, ribboned, held firmly in two hands centre front. *Hold your bouquet like this, remember.* Under a circlet of daisies, sensibly short-cut hair, the same colour as Dinah's. And her face in profile. Flushed with excitement, bright-eyed, a broad and delighted smile. Eagerly watching the others to see that she was doing the right thing. Edging into position at the photographer's command.

Dinah had stopped breathing. Even her heart seemed stilled.

No palely static imaginary child or hybrid daughter. Just herself. Laughing, proud and pleased. Her sister's chief bridesmaid. Facing forward now. Chin lifted. The characteristic features that Dinah had over-imagined clearly visible, but other features too. Family resemblances. Merlin. Matt. Even herself.

And she was also lovely. Sarah was beautiful.

The frozen moment dissolved, and amazingly ticked on into the next. The photographer's assistant moved forward and fussily repositioned the group.

Dinah gasped for breath. She was full of wonder.

This was her child, but she was much more than that. There were all the big and small realities of an unknown life woven around her. Realities she could not guess at yet.

Sarah was standing forty feet away. Not a secret or an absence or a fearful loss but a young woman, solid, round-faced under a flower crown, lit up with the pleasure of the day.

Dinah imagined running forward. Taking her hand. Hugging her. But she did none of these things. Instead her eyes travelled reluctantly along the group, across a line of unfamiliar faces broadly smiling for the lens. Next to the groom, her new son-in-law, was Pauline. Navy and yellow two-piece, a yellow hat with the brim braided in navy. Stouter than she had been, with creases in the skin around her eyes. Otherwise not much changed. From beneath the brim of her wedding hat she was staring straight at Dinah.

Pauline had seen her and recognised her. Her expression was hostile but there was no surprise in it.

Dinah moved a little to one side behind the other onlookers. She stood on the grass with one hand on a corner of a raised tomb to support herself. She was a trespasser here, but she could not have moved away, even if she had not been afraid of making herself more conspicuous by doing so. She felt crumbled lichen and pitted stone under her fingers and her eyes turned greedily back to Sarah. She was fluffing out the folds of her dress and then craning her head forward for her mother's nod of approval.

The photographer was satisfied by the time the bride's lips had begun to turn blue with cold. The wedding party was discharged and little storms of cheering and confetti broke over them as the bride and groom went hand in hand towards the ribboned car. Sarah made a dash after her sister and pulled at the folds of her veil, and Jennifer smiled at her and passed her bouquet to her husband so that her other hand was free to take Sarah's. Dinah saw that there were paper snowflakes of confetti caught in her hair.

The smaller bridesmaids followed on, and Malcolm and Pauline paired up with the couple who were evidently the groom's parents. Pauline did not look in Dinah's direction again.

The cars rolled away and the guests streamed off towards their own vehicles, cheerfully anticipating warmth and drink and food. Within minutes, Dinah was the only person left in the churchyard. The wind drove the confetti into whirls and eddies and an old man came round the corner with a broom and a sack.

'Vicar don't like it,' he complained to Dinah as he swept up. 'But all of 'em do it just the same.'

She walked slowly away, back through the lich-gate and under the trees to the main street. She couldn't think yet, could do no more than replay the images in her head. They composed themselves like photographs in an album with Sarah's face spotlit in the centre.

The hotel in Cromer was as empty as it had been before Christmas.

The last light of the afternoon was fading as Dinah unpacked her bags in a room overlooking the sea. She lay down on the bed and closed her eyes. She was tired but there was no question that she could sleep now. She could only see Sarah with her smile bursting with pride and the stars of confetti in her hair. It kept coming back to Dinah that she had been so lucky to arrive on this day, and to see this moment after all the others she had missed. The misfortune was that Pauline had been so quick, as if she had all the time been expecting Dinah, fearing her appearance. If she could have chosen to be invisible to spare her, Dinah would have done so.

But she could not regret having been at the church.

No one could take the pictures away from her now.

She lay still for as long as she could. Then she got up and took a shower, changed her clothes, and walked through the early darkness to Redemption Street.

She had not given Francis any warning. She had not even replied to his letter; there had been no time. But when he opened the door to her it was as if they had a long standing arrangement to meet at that moment.

'Come in,' he said simply.

The room was exactly as plain and welcoming as she remembered it. The fire was lit but there was only one chair beside it. The table was covered with paper and drawing materials.

'It's good to see you. Come and sit here. Are you cold?'

'No, not at all.'

'I'm afraid there isn't any wine . . .'

'Francis, I'm sorry, I should have brought some. But I'd rather have a cup of tea.'

'Tea it is.'

'I've only just arrived. This morning. I drove straight from Heathrow to . . . to Wivenham.'

'Let me make the tea first.'

While he was in the kitchen, Dinah sat looking into the fire. To be here made her feel calmer. She was weary and pulled in different directions by all the conflicts of her feelings but she also realised that she was happy. It was a plain and satisfying happiness of a kind that she had not experienced for a long time.

I was right to come, she thought. Whatever happens, I was right to come.

Francis brought the tea and she drank it gratefully, realising that she had had nothing since breakfast on the plane. He did not press her to talk until she was ready; one of Francis's abilities was to make silence as comfortable as conversation.

He sat on the stone hearth, leaning back against the chimney breast and looking into the fire. His hands hung loosely between his bent knees in worn jeans. He also had the gift of stillness.

'Thank you for finding the Greens for me.'

'It wasn't difficult. A matter of asking a few questions. I was afraid that you might think it was an interference. After I had posted the letter I wished I could grab it back again.'

Even the thought was excrutiating. 'Thank God you didn't.'

He looked at her then, and Dinah met his eyes.

'The Greens are more than just family friends,' she said.

'I think I understood that.'

'I didn't tell you the story, even though you told me yours. The younger child is my daughter.'

'I see.'

It was easy to tell him. It was like putting down a heavy weight. Dinah's happiness ballooned and swung up, out and away from her, filling the room, colouring Francis with its light. She looked at him, and pleasure that he was here to share this moment, that he had made it possible, almost swept her away.

Francis stood up and lightly touched her shoulder.

'Let me give you something to eat. You must be hungry.'

Dinah was suddenly ravenous.

There was thick vegetable soup and chunks of bread. Dinah ate, and talked and talked. She told him everything, from the beginning with Matt. Francis fed her and listened with unwavering attention and without interruption.

'I can't describe what it was like to see her today,' Dinah said at last. The end of the story left her inarticulate, reliving the wonder of the moment. 'In a turquoise blue satin dress with a daisy crown on her head. She looked like . . .' her throat tightened. A spasm of relief and astonishment and longing passed through her and she closed her eyes and bowed her head as she whispered,

'*She looked like a queen.*'

Francis watched her face.

'She must have done,' he said, at last. 'I can see it in you.'

They sat facing each other for a little while. Each of them was thinking that the other looked familiar, loved but unsurprising, like an old friend. And then Francis stood up and came around the table to Dinah's chair. He took her hand

and helped her to her feet, and he wrapped his arms around her and held her against him.

Dinah rested her head on his shoulder, neither resisting nor yielding.

It was comforting to be held. His warmth and support soothed her. She was very tired now, and also contented.

'Thank you for what you did,' she murmured. He had to bend his head to catch the words.

He lifted his hand, awkwardly, and stroked her hair.

'I'm very tired,' Dinah said. She thought she could fall asleep just standing here with her head against Francis's shoulder and his hand stroking her hair.

'I'll walk you home.'

The wind was still blowing, stinging and reeking of salt.

At the hotel doors, Francis leaned down and kissed her on the mouth. He raised one arm as he turned and walked quickly away.

'Goodnight,' Dinah whispered after him.

She went to bed and slept a deep, dreamless and refreshing sleep.

Ten

'Let me talk to the boys first.'

Dinah was sitting on the unmade hotel bed in Cromer with her shoulder hunched to hold the receiver at her ear. It was eight in the morning in Franklin. Three thousand miles away Matthew called to their children.

'Jack? Merlin? Come and talk on the phone to Mummy.'

They came at once, running, their feet thumping on the stairs of the house on Kendrick. Matt held out the receiver to them.

'Mummy? Mom? Why didn't you call yesterday?'

'I didn't get a chance, darling.'

'We called the airport anyway to make sure your flight got in safely.'

'Of course it did. I'm in the hotel now and I can see the sea, just like from our other room. What did you do yesterday?'

'Uh, Dad took us bowling and to a movie.'

Merlin was pushing, demanding his turn. Matt tried to hold him back until Jack had finished.

'Mum?' Merlin won the tussle anyway. 'What are you doing?'

'Talking to you.'

'I can't believe how far away you are.'

Distance had never troubled him when Matt rang from conferences on the other side of the world.

'But we can talk as if I'm right beside you.'

'How does it work? How do the sound waves get from me to you?'

'Um, do you know, I'm not quite sure? Something to do with vibrations. Ask Daddy. After I've talked to him.'

Merlin wouldn't let her go until she had promised to call him the next day.

'I promise, I promise,' Dinah said.

'I miss you, Mum.'

'I miss you, too.'

Matthew took the receiver back. He heard the last words as he lifted it to his ear.

'Tell me what's happening?' he asked. The words pulled a thread of intimacy between them, somehow connecting the moment with all the years of confiding in one another.

'I saw her.'

Matthew had known this was what she would say, but he was still amazed. His expectation had been that he would feel nothing, and instead an ungainly confusion of fear and joy and apprehension sprang up in him. He was silenced by the rush of it.

'She was a bridesmaid. At her sister's wedding.'

Dinah told him what she had seen. The bare words were inadequate but Matthew sat unblinking, absorbing them. The picture delivered itself to him, entire and ineradicable. There was the Norfolk flint church with its square tower and the windswept churchyard, and the wedding party's finery, and the child in her blue dress.

'She looked so proud, Matt. And complete.'

Complete.

It was odd that Dinah should use the word, Matthew thought, and yet it gave him what he had been afraid and also needful of hearing.

Sarah had been something awkward and unfinished, wrapped up and bundled away. He had been able to pursue other challenges and had solved them all, but this one evaded him because at the very beginning he had denied himself the possibility of solving it. He had registered it as insoluble. The internal image of Sarah that he carried with him was of something raw, and fearful for being unknown. He had been unable to picture her face or summon up her voice. Some of that fearfulness had been trapped between Dinah and himself, and he had obliterated it with work. Yet now he had to learn that Sarah had achieved completion without them. Without him.

The thought was infinitely sad.

'Matthew?'

'What does she look like?' He meant who. Whose eyes, and hair.

'She looks like herself.'

'Yes. I suppose so. What are you going to do now?'

'I'm going to go and see her.'

'Be careful.'

'Matt, we have been careful. It hasn't answered anything.'

After she had rung off, breaking the connection, Matthew went downstairs to make himself a cup of coffee.

In Dinah's absence the kitchen was already looking dishevelled, and therefore unwelcoming. While the coffee brewed he gathered up dirty plates and cups and swept up the crumbs the boys had left, knowing that he would have to repeat the process later. The task annoyed him and so did the banality of missing Dinah in just this way, as the presiding spirit of the house. He loaded an armful of the boys' clothes into the washing machine and slammed the door. With brisk activity he was just able to contain the queasy swell of his anxiety about Sarah's proximity and the sadness that threatened him.

Once the kitchen was approximately tidy Matthew sat down to drink his coffee. Unheralded, the memories swept back over him.

Dinah's hospital cubicle, himself holding Sarah in her white wrapping. Tiny puckered face, asleep, inscrutable. The doctor coming to see them, sitting down on the other side of Dinah. The baby's hand held out for him to see, an accusation.

It was as clear as this morning, and he thought he had forgotten it all.

Eleanor had come, with an armful of flowers.

It was not forgotten. He had only closed it away, blocking the light so it could not illuminate any of these memories.

The two women sitting together, heads bent over the baby.

Dinah looked like her mother; sometimes, and in a certain light, the resemblance was close. It seemed to him as though the act of giving birth had taken Dinah across some female threshold that he had not foreseen, that her face was much more than merely like her mother's, it had become almost the same face.

Only there was the dislocation in front of him. The break in the orderly progression from mother to daughter was brutal. This poor baby would not, never could replicate Dinah in the way that Dinah resembled her mother. And it was Dinah he loved, with a fierce and jealous love that could torture him now as it had eased him before.

Dinah and her mother should not be leaning over the baby like this, their faces reflecting, drinking her in.

The two women were murmuring to each other, words of explanation and reassurance. He knew that bonds were forming, alarming bonds which should not be allowed to tighten because they would only have to be severed again.

The coolness of self-discipline deserted him. Matthew's heart heaved in his chest, bringing a sour wash of saliva into his mouth as he heard himself shouting.

'Don't. Don't look at her, not like that. It isn't the right thing to do, don't you understand?'

He lurched towards the women and his hands descended, huge in his own eyes, fleshy scoops knobbed with bone. He snatched the baby in two hands and lifted her up out of their reach. She began a cry of protest.

He had no idea what he intended to do.

He pushed the door open, hearing Eleanor calling out behind him. With the baby in her blanket hoisted against his shoulder, he half-ran down the corridor. He felt over-sized, his legs bizarrely elongated as he overtook dressing-gowned women shuffling and open-mouthed nurses.

The corridor was long, running the length of the Victorian hospital to a patch of window at the far end. There were blue and white signs, wheelchairs parked against a wall, stone stairways and trolleys loaded with metal jugs. No one tried to stop him. The baby's head wobbled and he cupped it in one hand.

There was a lift on his right. The hand-written sign beside it read *Porters only*, but the doors were open and it was empty. Matthew swerved inside and jabbed at the single button with his elbow. The doors rolled to and the lift sank downwards. The baby was weakly crying and he tried to comfort it with rocking as they descended.

When he emerged, he saw that they were on the ground floor at one side of the hospital's casualty department. Rows of red plastic chairs, sparsely occupied for once, stretched ahead of him. There was an air of resigned patience, the expectation of long stretches of inactivity.

A place to think, Matthew told himself. He could sit quietly here and no one would notice him.

As soon as he took a seat in the middle of the sea of chairs, the baby stopped crying. He stole a look at her. Under the black hair he could see that her scalp was still scabbed with dried blood. Uncertainly he put his fingers to the soft dip on the top of her skull, where a determined pulse beat.

His breath steadied. He tried to tell himself, *My child, my daughter.* But there was no warming. All he could see were the characteristic features of her condition. A series of images unscrolled, of his child at different ages, never to win prizes as he and Dinah had done, never to play dangerously, or dare independence, or marry and reproduce. Always to be sheltered, to be allowed for.

'Do you need any help? Have you registered?'

A nurse had stopped at the end of the row of chairs. He was not as inconspicuous as he had thought.

'I'm waiting for my wife.'

'Oh, I see.'

She passed on her way. Matthew looked about him. There was a broken-faced old derelict dozing in a corner, his mouth quivering with his rattling breaths. A blank-eyed boy in a running vest stared at nothing, and a workman supported his hand wrapped in a bloodstained bandage in the crook of his other arm. As the time crept by, these people's faces printed themselves in his mind. He thought he would always recall them, how they had sat, the sounds and smells of this waiting area.

As he sat there in his red chair nursing the child, the first waves of shock subsided. From the pain of his feelings, deliberately and clinically, he made himself tease out the logical threads of reaction and intention.

This was a child in his arms, of course.

But she could not be Dinah's, and his. He did not want to compromise, every day, to celebrate only small and partial victories. He did not have the love within him, any capacity for the kind selfless love that he had observed in others. It was their great good fortune that Dinah and he had achieved a kind of perfection. He could not dismantle that, or even jeopardise it by admitting this imperfect child.

Could not...

There were hurrying footsteps approaching him from behind him. Automatically Matthew turned around. He saw a nurse and a porter, and it was obvious that they were looking for him. The porter came round to one side and the nurse to the other. She was smiling as if he were dangerous.

The nurse reached out. 'Shall I take her for you, Mr Steward?'

The porter nudged closer to him. Matthew could smell stale sweat in the folds of his overall.

'They've been hunting high and low for you, they have.'

220

'She's quite safe,' he said.

'Of course she is.'

They took Sarah from him. More than fourteen years later Matthew remembered exactly what it was he felt. It was relief.

Matt rested his head in his hands. His coffee had gone cold beside him. He waited until the waves of memory receded a little, with the sense of being newly washed ashore in some place that he did not quite recognise. The kitchen was quiet, gently humming with its own machinery. The mixer tap rhythmically dripped into a bowl.

He would have liked to go to the lab. The sense of order and control that work would offer tempted him strongly, as always. But he wasn't sure he could either leave Jack and Merlin alone or ask the Pinkhams or Kerrigans to look after them. He dismissed the possibility and decided that it would in any case be better for the three of them to spend the day together, like yesterday. Yesterday had gone pretty well, except that they could hardly go bowling and see a movie all over again.

Matthew had spent plenty of time with his sons and without Dinah, but it had been on fishing or skiing or camping trips where he was the leader and the boys his busy lieutenants. Almost none of it had been concerned with the expendable, humdrum hours of ordinary life. Ordinariness and normality meant Dinah being there.

If she were no longer here, what would that mean?

The prospect was fearful, and the experience of fear made Matthew angry. He was angry with Dinah for initiating the sequence of events that had led to this point. It was unreasonable, the unravelling of their successful life and the destruction that followed on. They owed it to one another to be reasonable. Reason was the fundamental on which everything else was based. It had informed the decision about Sarah in the first place.

'Dad? What's happening?'

Jack stood in the doorway. It was nine o'clock in the morning and the day was waiting to be filled. The time was long.

'Hi, Jack. What about a bike ride this morning? We could go over to Bear Ridge.'

'Oh. Okay, I guess.' He turned away without much enthusiasm.

It was a fine day, blue-skied with a pine-resin suggestion of spring in the air. The boys obediently followed Matthew on the new mountain bikes that they had been given for Christmas, but they were subdued, and vetoed his suggestion that they might extend the circuit. They completed the shorter ride and stopped off at Burger King on Main Street on the way back across town. Nancy Pinkham, with Laura and Brooke in the back of her station wagon, pipped her horn at them as she drove by. It was still barely one p.m. when they reached home.

'I'm going to spend an hour doing some work,' Matt said.

He had a paper to prepare, and if he couldn't get into the lab for a look at the fat cell assay preparations, he might at least do something else that would be useful. If he thought about his work he could block off the memories, and the thoughts of Sarah, and his anxiety for Dinah.

'Do you two want to go and play outside for a while?'

'Okay,' the boys agreed. They drifted away and left him.

Matthew wasn't sure how long he had been absorbed in his work when he heard feet drumming on the porch and urgent thumping at the locked front door. The boys had gone out by the yard. He ran down the hallway and saw Jack peering through the screen.

'Dad? Quick. Merlin's hurt himself.'

'Where?'

'Foot. He jumped on something.'

'Where is he?'

They ran out of the house and down the steps.

'Behind old Mr Dershowitz's.'

Matthew raced with Jack pounding ahead of him. Merlin was lying awkwardly on his side, small in the middle of a rough piece of ground. There was a big tree beyond him with low overhanging branches. When Matthew knelt down he saw there was rusting metal amongst the dead leaves.

Merlin was crying.

'Let me look.'

Matthew's mouth dried. Merlin's sneaker was impaled on a thick spike. The metal looked as if it might have been part of a fence post from which the wood had rotted away. The point had come through the rubber sole of the sneaker and out at one side of the canvas upper.

'It's all right, you're all right. Hold still, darling. I'll have to undo the laces.' He could see no blood.

'It hurts,' Merlin moaned. His face was white. Jack knelt at his other side, looking to his father for rescue.

Matthew unlaced the shoe and slid his finger under the tongue. There was blood here. He saw now that the murderous spike protruded from a cement block buried in the leaves. He eased the heel of the shoe with his other hand, watching Merlin's face. The wince was anticipatory, not reactive. Matthew unthreaded the lace from the eyelets and opened the shoe wide. Then he quickly twisted and pulled the foot free. Merlin screamed and Matthew held him tight.

'It's all right.'

He bent over to examine the wound, hiding Merlin's view of it. The sock was torn and soaked in blood, but the wound was not deep. The spike had gashed the side of his foot, but nothing worse. Matthew breathed in relief.

'Your sneaker's had it, I'm afraid. But your foot will live to walk another day.'

As he spoke he lifted Merlin up and hoisted him over one shoulder.

'It's a long time since I've had to carry you home.'

They walked slowly back up Kendrick.

Jack said miserably, 'Mummy doesn't let us play down there.'

'So why were you?'

'The tree's got good branches for jumping out of.'

223

'Just because she isn't here, Jack, it doesn't mean you can do all the things you aren't allowed.'

George Kuznik was arriving back from golf. Matthew called a reassuring answer to his alarmed question, and carried Merlin into the house. He sat him down in an armchair and bathed his foot with diluted antiseptic, and let him examine the extent of the damage. Both boys looked pale and unhappy. Someone tapped on the front door, and Jack went to answer it. He came back with Todd Pinkham in his Sunday sweater and cords.

'Hi. George said there'd been an accident.' He knelt down by Merlin's chair. 'How're you doing, guy?'

'Thanks, Todd. Good of you. It's not too serious,' Matt told him.

'Hm. Uhuh. Yeah. I guess you'll live, Merlin. You want to look where you're jumping next time. Could have been right through your foot, you know.'

Merlin nodded, his lips pale and compressed.

'You'll need to take him over to the emergency room for an anti-tet shot, Matt, unless he's had one recently?'

Matthew thought, and shook his head. 'I don't know if he has or not.'

'It's always the women who remember these things. Won't hurt to get another, anyway.' Todd made a boxer's feint at Jack. 'How about you come over and watch some TV while your daddy drives Merlin to the hospital?'

Jack shook his head. 'No thanks,' he said clearly. 'I'll go with them.'

The drive to the hospital and back and the wait for the shot and the dressing took almost two hours. By the time they reached home again it was time to make supper. Hunger and tiredness and relief that the foot was not as bad as it could have been made Matthew tetchy. He threw together a meal and Jack laid the three places.

They sat down at the table, but the boys only picked at their food.

When he looked across at Merlin, Matthew saw that his

224

eyes were red and his face was streaked with fresh tears. He suppressed a sigh of irritation.

'What's up, son? Is the foot hurting?'

'I miss Mummy.'

'Mer*lin*,' Jack hissed at him.

'Well I do.'

'Crying won't help, baby.'

'That'll do, Jack,' Matt rebuked him, too sharply. Jack turned on him. His eyes were bright and round and hard behind the lenses of his glasses.

'Merlin knows what I mean. And I wish Mummy was here as well.'

They faced each other across the congealing plates. Matthew was taken aback by the way his children immediately drew together in their hostility to him. He was going to say something soothing and neutral but Jack jabbed sharply at the bridge of his glasses with a forefinger and demanded,

'What's happening? Nothing's been right lately. Why has Mummy gone away?'

Merlin nodded and sniffed beside him.

'Are you going to get divorced?'

'No, no of course . . .'

'*Are* you?' Jack's voice and manner were aggressive, but his quivering mouth betrayed him. 'Why do you think you don't have to tell us the truth just because we're kids?'

'I don't think that,' Matthew said humbly. He wondered what the truth might be.

Jack began to shout. 'I hate not being told things. I hate being shushed, and you both looking angry and silent and then yelling downstairs. I'd rather know what's really happening than be pretended to like a dumb baby.'

'Me too,' Merlin said.

With his head bowed, Matthew spread his hands on the table. There was something sticky bedded in the grain of the wood.

'Sometimes the world doesn't seem any more explicable

to adults than it does to children. I'd like to be able to tell you what the truth is but I don't think I know it.'

Both boys were crying now, Jack angrily with his mouth pulled square and tears running down his face. A strand of determination snagged and then caught in Matthew's mind. There was a truth that he could tell them. He had not intended to say this now, had not even considered it, but as soon as he thought of it he was convinced that he should not put it off.

He left his seat and put his arms around them, feeling the rigidity of their shoulders.

'Listen. Hey. Come on. Come and sit down with me so I can talk to you.'

He led them, one on either side, to the sofa in the den and sat down still with his arms around their shoulders. Merlin cuddled against him with his bandaged foot on a cushion but Jack remained stiff, staring straight ahead.

'There's something important I want you to hear. It's about something that Dinah and I did a long time ago, but it still has an effect now. It's why Mummy is away, and it's why you feel nothing has been right lately.'

He didn't try to plan the words and phrases in advance. Slowly Jack's head turned so that he could see Matt's face.

'A long time ago, long before you were born, Jack, even before we lived in our house in Sheldon, Dinah was pregnant.'

The boys listened wide-eyed, concentrating, without moving or interrupting.

'Have you ever heard of Down's syndrome?'

'No,' Merlin said. Jack said, 'I think I have. Sort of.'

'The baby had it. She was a little girl called Sarah. The paediatrician, the baby specialist, came to tell us the day after she was born.'

His children nestled against him now, these children, round-eyed and solemn with the importance of the moment.

Matthew told the story straight, exactly as it unwound in his memory.

226

At the end he said, 'It will be fifteen years ago this September that she was born.'

'So she was our sister. An *older* sister,' Jack said wonderingly.

'Yes.'

They were busy assimilating the facts. Evaluating what he had told them and relating it to themselves, and no doubt judging him and Dinah too. How we underestimate our children, Matthew thought.

'What does the Down thing mean actually?' Merlin asked.

As plainly as he could, Matt told them.

Jack asked, '*Why* did you give her to be adopted?'

Matthew heard a shade of righteousness in his voice. Jack was ready to be indignant on behalf of the sister he had only heard about half an hour before.

He tried to answer honestly, 'Because we were afraid,' and then corrected himself. 'Because I was afraid.'

Jack nodded. He was also capable of recognising the truth when he heard it. 'Are you afraid now?'

'No.'

'Will we see her, now that Mummy has found her again?'

'Jack, she doesn't belong to us. She belongs to the mother and father who have taken care of her, all this time.'

When Matthew was seeing him into bed, Merlin asked, 'If I had had Down's as well, would you have had me adopted too?'

He was ready for the question.

'No, we wouldn't. You know how we work in the labs? We make discoveries by trying to prove our ideas; first comes the theory of what we think is right, and then we run experiments that will prove or disprove the theory. I told you Sean Rader and I have designed something called a d-deca-peptide that I think will mirror the effect of insulin on the surface of the human cell?'

Merlin nodded happily. He loved to hear Matthew talk

about his work. The words had a proud significance when he repeated them afterwards, *pipette, centrifuge, dilution.*

'We've made up batches of the molecule, and now we're going to test the effect of it on some irradiated fat cells taken from male rats. If I am right, we'll have a big breakthrough in the treatment of diabetes. And if I'm wrong we'll have to start all over again to solve the problem of insulin in a different way.

'The point is, we work by learning from our mistakes as well as from our successes. To make a mistake is painful, but we should only have to make it once.'

'You mean you found out it was a mistake to have the baby adopted by someone else and you wouldn't have done it with Jack or me?'

'I didn't think it was wrong when we did it. I learnt, I am learning, from what happened afterwards, that it probably was. Two of the things that happened later were you and Jack, who made me understand that people are themselves regardless of what they can do.'

'Is this what you say to Mummy?'

'No. I should, shouldn't I?'

'Is it why you quarrel with each other?'

'Partly.'

'Will you be able to make it all right now?'

'I hope so,' Matthew said. He gave his voice conviction. 'I want to, very much.'

'You know, you could have done it the other way round and tried the experiment by keeping Sarah.'

'Yes, you're quite right. Life and science aren't quite the same. You can't put real life aside and start again, so my comparison isn't really a very good one after all.'

Merlin put his arms up and Matthew kissed him goodnight.

'Have I given you too much to think about?' he asked.

'It's quite a lot. But I'd rather know, like Jack said. Is she happy, do you think?'

'Yes. Dinah said she looked proud of herself. And complete.'

'That's good, isn't it?'

'Yes, Merlin.'

'Does she miss us?'

'No. Because she doesn't know us.'

Downstairs again Matthew noticed through the chilly eye of the washing machine that the clothes inside were still dry and dirty. It seemed a very long time since the morning.

He found the detergent and put it in the slot, and switched the machine to what he hoped was the right programme. If the boys couldn't have the clothes they wanted for school tomorrow then at least they should be done for Tuesday.

After her visit to Francis, Dinah waited alone until Monday afternoon. She passed the intervening time in painful slices, by walking on the beach and wandering distractedly through the underpopulated shops in the town centre. She felt lonely and excited and more than a little crazy, and wondered if people in the streets and in the hotel's sepulchral lounge might be covertly staring at her.

When the afternoon came – she had reasoned with herself that she could not decently go sooner, but should not leave it any longer, as if it might be some trivial errand – she drove back again to Wivenham.

Dinah drove past the house in Church Walk once.

She could see no signs of life. The clean net curtains were pulled tight, and there was no car drawn up alongside the rose bushes. That was good, in a way. Malcolm must be out at work.

Dinah parked her own car at the far end of the walk, facing into the main road. Then she walked slowly back along the pavement towards Pauline's house. At the low wooden gate she hesitated for a second or two. And then, decisively, she undid the catch and felt the splintered wood under her fingers as the gate swung open. The path was concreted, cracked in a ragged transverse line.

Dinah lifted her eyes and saw the doorbell, the tongue of opaque glass in the door itself. She was breathless now, no longer imagining or rehearsing challenge and response. She let the momentum of her determination carry her to the doorstep. Her hand was already raised to the bell, but the door swung open to forestall her.

Pauline stood framed against a sliver of the hallway. There were steep stairs, a wood and brass barometer hanging on the wall. She must have been watching the quiet road from behind the veil of net curtain. Waiting for Dinah, knowing that she would come.

Now that she saw her face unshadowed by the brim of the wedding hat, Dinah saw that Pauline did look much older. Her trimly permed hair had lost its colour and there were new folds of flesh around her small jaw and under her eyes. She was much plumper than she had once been, and the increased weight made her seem shorter. She had to look up at Dinah. Her small round eyes were hard.

Dinah waited on the step. Pauline held the door, the gap not wide enough to be inviting. Her face was stiff with hostility, and underlying the hostility there was fear, and anger.

'Could I come in?' Dinah asked at last.

There was a pause.

'You can't stop out there, I suppose,' Pauline said.

Dinah followed her into the house, relieved to escape the unseen eyes of the road.

There was a living room to the right of the hallway.

Immediately Pauline showed her in, the familiarity of it closed around Dinah. She had never been there before but the layout, the furniture, even the scent of it flooded back to her. The afternoon light swam palely through the folds of net. Everything was tidy, well dusted. Stiff-fringed cushions were placed exactly in the corners of a green sofa. She could hear her heart thudding in the swathed silence.

'Sit down, then,' Pauline said.

'Thank you.'

Dinah sat on the corner of the sofa. The carpet was brown

and cream, patterned in loose swirls. In front of the stone fireplace there was a cream-coloured rug, in the shape of a half-moon. Pauline stood on the rug with her feet planted together. Dinah stared down, and then lifted her head. Pauline's hands were folded tightly. They were slightly chapped, businesslike hands, with red knuckles. Dinah remembered.

'You'd better have a cup of tea.'

'Thank you,' Dinah repeated.

Pauline turned and left her, and she ventured a more detailed examination of the room.

It was so similar, it might have been the same one, where she and Eleanor had left Sarah for the last time. She had been sitting up in a ring of cushions, smiling at Pauline with pride and pleasure. And Dinah had crept home afterwards like someone sick or wounded. Home to Matthew, who had tenderly looked after her as if she were ill, and they had never discussed why. Never, never . . .

Dinah closed her eyes. She pressed her knuckles into her mouth and pinched the skin in the hollows of her cheeks.

It was the visits she remembered, to Sarah and the Greens while they were still her foster-parents. Not the day of leaving her behind in the hospital. She had felt too shocked and bewildered then. Sarah had been the package that she could not unwrap, seemingly belonging more to the nurses and paediatricians than to Matthew and herself. But each of the visits to the foster home was a sharp and separate pain. At each one she had seen Sarah unfold, the slow and uneven process made to seem rapid by the lapses of time.

Then the last visit. Suddenly Sarah was no longer a baby but a child who looked round in anxiety when Pauline left the room, and beamed with delight when she returned. Dinah had understood that it was already too late. Sarah was not on loan to the nurses or to Pauline. She belonged elsewhere, to another woman. That was what she had done, for Matt.

She opened her eyes and looked at the room again.

In that moment her eagerness and anticipation peeled

away and she felt as desolate as she had done fourteen years ago. She had done wrong to come here. She had no rights, and no business to inflict the damage and uncertainty of her own needs upon Pauline Green.

But she could not help herself.

Dinah stared wildly around her. She was afraid of herself, and of what she might do, having done this much already.

An upright piano stood against the wall opposite the bay window. There was the sofa and two matching easy chairs, a shiny coffee table, low bookshelves built in the fireplace alcoves. Fleshy-leaved plants stood in china saucers on top of the shelves. There was a big television set in the corner with framed photographs arranged on top of the cabinet. Dinah left her seat to look greedily at them. There was Jennifer with her fiancé, now husband, their faces turned to the camera at identical angles. Her hands were clasped awkwardly to show off the ring on her fourth finger. The engagement picture. No wedding photographs yet, of course. And in a gilt frame, Sarah. She was on a swing, poised at the split-second height of the backwards arc. Her hair was a blur but her face was pin-sharp, eyes wide, tongue between her teeth, and mouth stretched in a great beam of delight. Perhaps seven or eight years old.

Quickly Dinah put the picture down and turned away.

She was at the other side of the room looking at the music on the piano when Pauline came back with a tray.

'I'm sorry,' Dinah blurted out. 'I'm so sorry to have come. I know what you must think. I just . . . I just wanted to see her.'

'Well then, you've seen her,' Pauline said flatly. Louder, she added, 'She loves music. Really loves it. Pop, classics, the old songs, anything. Jenny can play, so we have a good singsong now and again.'

At Christmas, birthdays, celebrations.

'David, that's Jenny's new husband, he bought her a Walkman for her bridesmaid's present. We thought a locket or a bracelet or something, but she would have a Walkman and so that's what she got.'

Dinah went back to the corner of the sofa. She took the cup that Pauline handed to her. A silence that matched the pallid light seeped through the room. She felt out of place here, somehow given away by her clothes and expensively casual shoes and bag, although she had dressed as neutrally as she could. The proper words of reassurance and apology deserted her. And on her side Pauline was firing out these details deliberately to emphasise the tightness of the circle from which Dinah was excluded. Dinah knew it and through the wash of her guilt came the involuntary swell of jealousy.

They drank their tea. Pauline sat stiffly, her face turned aside. She did not look directly at Dinah even when she demanded with renewed bitterness,

'Why did you have to turn up on Saturday, of all the days you could have chosen?'

The bitterness was justified. Dinah accepted it.

'I didn't know. Pauline, believe me, I didn't choose. It just happened. I'm sorry. I'm sorry you had to see me there on Jennifer's wedding day.'

'Did you think I wouldn't see you? That I've forgotten what you look like?' The flick of Pauline's glance took in Dinah's clothes and shoes as well as her face.

'I didn't think at all. I just stopped to see the bride. And then I saw Malcolm, and you, and . . . there Sarah was.' Dinah could not suppress the truth. The words came out of her, as if from another person. 'But I'm glad I did, just the same. I'm so glad I saw her. She looked . . .'

Dinah stopped herself, glanced down. She would not, could not cry here, in front of Pauline.

Pauline's face tightened further.

'But you must have been hunting for us. Why have you come? What do you want?'

'Just to see her.'

There was a clock somewhere loudly ticking. Dinah stared

at the brown and cream carpet, at the stitching of Pauline's house shoes, concentrating on keeping her eyes dry and wide open to hold back the tears.

'What does that mean?'

'Just that.' She lifted her head, met Pauline's stare. Of course Pauline was suspicious and aggressive. Would she not feel the same way herself?

'Just to see her, to know that she's all right. I haven't come for anything more threatening than that. How could I? What right do I have, after . . . after what I did, and what you have done for her?'

Pauline sat, considering.

'How did you find us?'

'It wasn't all that difficult. I went to Thetford and then to Cromer. Following links in a chain.'

'And why come now? After so long?'

Because I couldn't not come. It is as plain, as unvarnished as that. I couldn't help myself, or stop myself.

'I . . . happened to be back in England, on a visit. We live in the States now. We have two children. Boys.'

'Are they normal?' Pauline pushed the word out, delivering it like a cherrystone into a spoon.

'Yes.'

'And that's not enough?'

'Pauline, I know – no, that's not right – I can *guess* some of the things you must think, and feel, about me and my coming back here. I'm not surprised by that. I don't deserve that you should think any differently.

'But neither has there been a day since I last saw you when I haven't thought about her, wondered about what she is doing, imagined her face and her voice. I had to see her to fix those things for myself. Nothing more.'

But even as Dinah heard herself delivering the last words, she knew with a shiver of fear that they were not the truth – or only a sliver of it, a crescent of moon with the remainder obscured. Desperation lent her momentary cunning.

234

The other woman put her cup aside. She tilted her head, pointedly considering. At length she said,

'Well. The bus brings her back from school at half three every afternoon.'

Exactly as Dinah had calculated it would.

'May I stay to see her today?'

There was another pause. She might be hostile and fearful, but Pauline was also relishing this exercise of power. Humbly, Dinah waited.

'I can't say no, really. Not since you're already here, can I?'

'Thank you.'

'You can say you're a friend of mine from London. Sarah loves London, or the idea of it. She's only been two or three times, on outings with her school. Don't try to tell her anything else. I don't want her confused or upset, by you or anyone else.'

Dinah did not warm to Pauline any more than she had done years ago, but she felt a flash of delighted gratitude. In half an hour, Sarah would come through the door and she would be here to meet her. All her energy had been focused on this moment. She could not think beyond it yet.

'Of course. I understand.'

Pauline sat back in her chair. Some of the rigidity left her now that the boundaries had been drawn.

'Do you want some more tea?'

Dinah passed her cup. It was bizarre and also inevitable that the two of them should be pinned in this constriction of social behaviour, handing the best china back and forth. She suppressed a sudden need to laugh, and wondered how crazy she might really be.

'I'm sorry I appeared like that outside the church. I hope it didn't spoil the day for you.'

'It went off well enough.'

'Jennifer looked lovely.' Although in truth Dinah could not recall how she had looked. 'And so did Sarah.'

'We're very proud of her.'

'You must be,' Dinah whispered.

'We haven't got the photographs yet, of course.'

'No.'

Pauline unbent a little further. She glanced to one side and then said quickly, 'There are all the other photos here. In the albums. Would you like to see? While we're waiting for her to get back?'

'Oh, yes. Please . . .' She wanted it more than anything she could think of.

Pauline knelt at the bottom shelf in the alcove and lifted out a pile of thick-spined books bound in red and green mock leather. They were the kind of albums that held a sheaf of clear plastic envelopes to contain the pictures. She placed one in Dinah's lap and then came to perch on the sofa beside her.

'You won't recognise anyone except the family, of course.'

Dinah opened it. Her hands were shaking.

They were like any family pictures, taken with a cheap camera by an inexpert photographer. Red faces and wide smiles around tables, pink eyes, blurred gardens and beaches and inexplicable landscapes. Only, in the middle of most of them there was Sarah, in swimsuits or party dresses or snow-suits or fancy dress outfits. Holding hands, waving, sitting on the back of a seaside donkey. Paddling and laughing and asleep and blowing out the candles on a birthday cake.

Dinah stared down at the pictures, a miser counting treasure beyond her dreams, trying to print each one in her mind so she could come back to it in her own time.

'There she is in the infants' play. They did Postman Pat that year. She went to the primary here, until she started falling too far behind.'

The plastic wallets flipped over.

'That's her at Skegness, with our link family. Jan and Stephen, and their three. They take her for weekends some-times. It gives Malcolm and me a bit of a break.'

'That's her school, on an outing.'

A minibus, a group of children and adults in front. Some

236

of the other children in wheelchairs, their heads tipped on one side.

A hundred questions boiled within Dinah but she only nodded.

The snapshots were so ordinary, and so astounding. Dinah felt as if the whole missing story of Sarah's childhood were being opened for her, like a tantalising secret that she had to unfathom and memorise in an instant before it could be shut up and locked away from her again.

There came a whole series of Sarah in a hard hat and an anorak, astride a stolid pony.

'There. She does riding for the disabled. I made sure she got on to that.'

The pride in Pauline's voice. A mixture of love and satisfaction and triumph. Sarah did these things; Sarah had grown from the baby in a smocked pink dress to an almost-adult, under Pauline's care, with Pauline's help and devotion. They had achieved this much, slowly passed all these milestones.

That's what this cinema-flicker through the photographs was intended to demonstrate to Dinah. Pauline was not afraid or angry now. She was relishing the moment, safe and secure in having all the cards firm in her hands. Perhaps Pauline had even imagined doing just this, some day, as she slipped the latest pictures into their plastic sheaths. Showing off the triumphs to the other mother who had failed Sarah and allowed Pauline her success.

Numbly, Dinah accepted this too. It was enough for now to see the history here, haphazardly captured in the drained tints of over-exposure and the half-mad red-eyed blaze of a score of frozen celebrations.

She took each album hungrily as Pauline handed it to her. The last one was only half-full. The final snap was of Sarah in leggings and a shiny blue top. Her hands were held up and out in front of her. She looked as if she might be dancing.

'Not that she's always easy,' Pauline said. 'Far from it. She's got a mind of her own, she has.' She took the pile of albums from Dinah's side and replaced them on the bottom shelf.

Dinah followed them with her eyes, longing to take them back again. She had an instant's vision of seizing and hiding them, running away with the red and green covers sticky against her breast.

She stammered out the uncalculated sum of all her questions.

'Tell me. What's she like?'

'Like? Well. She's like these children are, you know. And she is also just like herself. She's lovely.'

Of course.

There was a sound outside. Pauline half stood, peering over the sill into the road.

'You can see for yourself. She's here.'

Dinah sat very still.

'I always go to the front door to meet her. She likes me to open it before she gets to the gate.'

From outside there came a confused sound of voices calling goodbyes, and then a bus engine noisily revving. Dinah looked, saw a blue local authority minibus, and two or three passengers. A man waved from the driver's seat. The gate was swinging on its hinges.

Dinah heard the front door slam shut. There was a kind of roaring tightness within her ears and chest as if Sarah's arrival in the house had altered the ambient pressure.

She could hear her voice, loud, the words not distinguishable, spilling out some news to Pauline. Pauline said,

'That's nice, isn't it? And we've got a friend for tea. Come and say hello to her.'

Dinah waited, motionless, even the breath frozen in her throat.

Eleven

A second later, Sarah was there.

She came into the room with Pauline's arm round her shoulders. Dressed in stonewash jeans, and a padded jacket made of some shiny dark pink material.

Pauline said, 'This is Dinah. Say hello to her.'

Sarah was smiling eagerly, her cheeks plumped out and her eyelids creasing upwards. Her tongue protruded between small, uneven teeth.

No one would have mistaken her for a normal teenager.

She moved forward awkwardly, in a kind of lunge, with her hands folded like small fins in front of her stomach.

All these impressions formed for Dinah in a clear sequence, placing a sharper, crueller focus on the image she retained from Saturday. And yet even in that split second further realisations crowded in on her. Sarah had fine, clear skin and her hair – exactly the same shade as Dinah's own – was thick and shiny. Her eyes, behind pink-framed spectacles, looked like Merlin's, but as if they were formed from soft clay and then pressed upwards and outwards.

'Dyah? Hel-*lo*.'

She took hold of Dinah's arm, peering close into her face and saying something in a loud voice, half a dozen blurred syllables that Dinah could not interpret.

Denied an immediate response, Sarah repeated the words, louder still.

Dinah realised with shame that she did not know what to do because she had no experience of handicap. She wanted to connect, longed to do so, but was afraid of doing it somehow wrong. She looked over Sarah's shoulder, to Pauline.

Pauline was smiling too, a knowing smile that thinned the corners of her mouth.

'She's telling you she's got a new Walkman. You have got a Walkman, Sarah, haven't you? Who gave it to you?'

'*Da*-id.'

'That's right, David did. For being a bridesmaid, wasn't it?'

Sarah was hauling at Dinah's arm now, and pointing at the door. She was solidly built and strong.

'She wants to show you,' Pauline said. 'Go with her, if you like.'

'I'd like to see it,' Dinah told Sarah. Her reward was another smile coupled with an appraising sidelong glance of startling acuity.

Sarah's bedroom was at the front of the house, overlooking the road. There was an array of cuddly toys on shelves, stacks of tapes and books, pink curtains and bedcover and cushions. It was the room of a child much younger than Sarah's real age, although there were posters of Keanu Reeves and Take That stuck to the walls between the puppy and kitten pictures. A ginger cat lay curled up on the quilt.

'*Mi*cah,' Sarah pointed.

'He's yours, is he? He's a beauty.'

'Arthur.'

Her words were becoming easier for Dinah to distinguish.

'Hello, Arthur.'

Sarah picked up a yellow Walkman. She fumbled for a minute, peering at the controls. Dinah began a movement that said *Let me*, but forced her fingers down to her sides again. Sarah unwound the headset for herself and pressed the earpieces in place. She began to hum, wagging her head and swaying to the music that was turned up loud enough for Dinah to hear.

Dinah looked around her, at the hairbrush on the dressing table, the sea shells and ornaments and innocent clutter. She was thinking of the countless times she had tried to imagine this room. The details of it in reality were not so different from the imaginings – what was different, so much so as to take her breath away, was the essence of Sarah herself. As Dinah had realised as soon as she set eyes on her in her bridesmaid's dress, Sarah was not a condition or a set of characteristics or an empty container that held no more than the projected desires and defaults of those around her. Sarah was Sarah, as Dinah had failed to create her in her imagination.

Now that she was here, her presence filled the house.

Sarah took off the headset and held the earpiece to Dinah's ear. The assault of tinny noise made Dinah exclaim, and set Sarah off into a peal of delighted laughter.

Disturbed, the cat sprang off the bed and walked away, tail erect.

Pauline was calling from downstairs.

'My *mum*,' Sarah explained.

Dinah followed her down again. In the living room Sarah put her arms around Pauline and rested her head on her shoulder, crooning, 'My mum, *my* mum.'

'Don't be so soft,' Pauline remonstrated. But her glance at Dinah said, *You see? What else should you expect?*

'Come on. Are you going to watch your programme now?'

Sarah detached herself and made for the television. Once it was on she settled herself on the sofa with evident pleasure. There were two biscuits laid ready for her on a plate.

'She'd watch TV all night if I let her. But she knows that it's just an hour of children's programmes and then it goes off. After that we do something together, or she helps me with the tea.'

Dinah nodded, accepting these crumbs of information.

We do something together.

Sarah's eyes had been fixed on a cartoon, but now she turned to Dinah and imperiously extended her hand. 'Watch too.'

Dinah sat down beside her. Sarah wriggled closer, happily settling herself.

'Another friend,' Pauline remarked. Dinah heard the unspoken rider, that Sarah was open and affectionate to everyone, that Dinah was not to allow herself even the hope of special recognition. 'I'll go and make a start on the tea, then.'

Sarah watched her cartoon and covertly, greedily, Dinah watched her. There were biscuit crumbs caught in the faint dark fuzz on her top lip. Her mouth hung open a little as she followed the squeaks and dives of the cartoon, and she pushed her glasses back up the soft bump of her nose.

Dinah found herself thinking suddenly of Milly. Milly was so intent on fighting and squirming her way out of childhood, was so foxy and furious that it was difficult to remember that she was still only a child. It seemed extraordinary now that she had become yoked with Sarah in Dinah's imaginings. Sarah was making little grunts of encouragement at the screen. It came to Dinah that this was much more like how watching television had been with Jack and Merlin when they were smaller. They had once had exactly the same capacity for short-lived but utterly rapt absorption.

The loss of those early versions of her boys struck Dinah with a sudden pang. Jack and Merlin were selective in their enthusiasms now, and knowing, and ready with their dismissals.

The impression that Sarah was still as they had once been touched Dinah deeply, tapping a spring of maternal intimacy and tenderness that washed all through her. It was as though her little children had been handed back to her. She could not stop herself from reaching out and putting her arm around Sarah's shoulder, drawing the child close.

The solidity of Sarah's body, padded with heavy flesh, was startling.

Under her fingers, Dinah felt the deep channel where her bra strap dug into the skin. This was not Dinah's little child, nor anyone else's. Within the wraps of her handicap, Sarah was almost a woman, as much so as Milly.

Dinah was troubled by the same sense of her being a package, for ever sealed, that had come to her immediately after Sarah's birth. She gently withdrew her arm and Sarah half turned, unworried.

'Gooh,' she confided, pointing to the screen.

'It is good, isn't it? Funny.'

She stayed still after that, making do with studying her daughter's rapt profile and the set of her head and the small ear protruding between two thick hanks of hair. Memorising all these details as she had stored up the photographs, to return to when she needed them.

Just as the programme was ending someone came up the path to the front door and they heard a key turn in the lock.

Sarah scrambled up and when Malcolm came in she ran full at him and buried her face in his overalls. He swayed on his feet, rocking her from side to side in what was evidently a special ritual between them.

'Dad, Dad,' she crowed softly.

'How's my girl, then?'

'Dad girl.'

It was plain that Sarah adored him.

Dinah's guilt bit into her again. It was true that she had no right to make this intrusion, trailing her own imperative need, into the simple life of another family. A sense of dislocation crystallised around finding herself alone and a stranger here, in this small neat house, thousands of miles from Matt and her boys. She missed Merlin and Jack. Not their younger selves but the solid insistence of their present tense.

She missed Matthew too. The two months since Thanksgiving and her discovery about Doctor Pang had sheared them apart. Without Matt to balance her she was unweighted, dangerously veering from fear to euphoria. The room shifted giddily around her.

Why am I here? Why am I so destructive?

Dinah's gaze fixed on Sarah. Here was the riddle and the answer. Now that it was over, the absence of her and the absence of knowledge felt like a hole gouged in Dinah's torso. She had bled internally for fourteen years. Dinah clenched her hands into fists, breathing, controlling herself.

Malcolm partially detached himself from Sarah and awkwardly shook hands with Dinah. Pauline had come in in an apron. She must have forewarned him because he betrayed no surprise at the sight of Dinah, although he looked sidelong at his wife for guidance. Malcolm had never been an articulate man.

Dinah spoke in a rush. 'I told Pauline, I'm sorry to appear from nowhere like this, Malcolm. I had no idea that Saturday was Jenny's wedding day. I'm just back in England for . . . for a short time. We live in the States now.'

'Are you stopping for tea with us?' Malcolm asked, looking again at Pauline before hastily adding, 'You're more than welcome, of course.'

'No, no,' Dinah said. 'I must get back now.'

Pauline and Malcolm stood close together with Sarah. Making a tableau, consciously or otherwise.

'Would you like another cup of tea before you go?' Pauline asked.

'No. Thank you. I won't stay any longer.'

Relief was plain in the Greens' faces. Sarah's attention was drifting back to the television, although her cheeks were still flushed with the pleasure of Malcolm's arrival.

'Sarah, say goodbye.'

She swung round at once. There was another surprising flash of a look, half masked by the spectacles, before she lowered her head and charged at Dinah. She threw her arms around her and noisily kissed her cheek.

'Cheers,' Sarah beamed.

Dinah was rocked on her feet. She kept her balance but

she had to fight to stop herself seizing Sarah in return. Now the moment of parting had arrived she wanted to hold her and keep her and never let her go. The shock of longing and the effort of restraint made her tremble. Sarah was already retreating to Malcolm.

'Goodbye,' Dinah murmured. The impossibility of the word screamed a refrain in her head.

But there was nothing for her to do except follow Pauline. They came out into the hallway, and Pauline closed the door behind them.

'You see?' Pauline asked. There were a dozen shades to the question, all of them fading into full stops. Dinah pushed back the finality.

'May I come again? To see her another afternoon before I . . . before I go back to the States?'

Before what happens next, whatever that might be. Dinah felt herself spinning faster, on the very edge of control, out of the magnetic field of habit and loyalty and reason.

Pauline answered precisely, 'I don't think so.'

Beyond pride, Dinah begged, 'Please. Just to spend some time with her. To get to know her a little.'

They were in opposition, of course, in spite of the tea and the photograph albums. Pauline would not welcome Dinah another time. Why should she?

'No. I don't want that. I don't know how you can even come asking, after I've done everything for her. Years of fighting for her, getting her what we could. What did you do? You see the way she is.'

'Yes. She's wonderful.'

'She's ours.'

The front door was open. Somehow Dinah found herself out on the cracked concrete path. She sensed the eyes of the other houses upon her.

'Can I at least keep in touch, now that I know where you are?'

Pauline opened the gate.

'I can't promise you'll get any answers.' She was growing firmer as Dinah was propelled further from the house.

Dinah took a breath. She wanted to cry out, *She is my child too. As much as Jack and Merlin are.*

But that was no claim. Pauline was also a mother. She knew the joy of it, and the counterweight of terrible fears, and the implacable need to protect and shield and the steady chafe of responsibility. The only difference between them, a hair's-breadth and a mile-wide gulf, was that Pauline had been Sarah's mother and Dinah had made a different choice. One child amongst so many mothers and children.

Their eyes met. Dinah thought of Sandra and Milly, and was touched with sadness that Sandra and she had not after all become friends.

'I understand,' Dinah said.

The gate latch clinked shut after she had passed through. Dinah walked away, past Malcolm's green Avenger parked at the kerb, towards her own car waiting at the end of the quiet street.

She drove back again to Cromer.

The sun had come out in the late afternoon and now it was setting far away on her right hand, behind thin bars of green and gunmetal cloud.

The desperation at leaving Sarah behind suddenly receded. Dinah now felt an extraordinary beat of mad happiness, almost exultation.

The real Sarah had slipped squarely into the painful daughter-shaped void that had shadowed her for so long. She did not need to make any more dreams and fantasies out of Milly, out of memories of her own adolescence, out of fears of what Sarah might be. She had seen the pictures, a snapshot collage of a happy childhood. She had talked to her, felt the warmth of her skin and the weight of her affection.

As she had told Matt, Sarah was complete.

That was what Pauline and Malcolm had helped her to achieve. The truth was not to be denied or diminished.

246

Dinah also knew that her longing for Sarah was something else, fierce and separate. She had spent so long denying it, and now it possessed her. Merely to acknowledge it made her happy. And even in her light-headed state Dinah recognised that the longing was nothing to do with the Greens; that she would either have to find a way to contain it or exorcise it for herself.

There were flocks of birds settling in the wind-carved trees between the road and the sea.

Dinah sang fitfully to herself as she drove, fragments and tail-ends of songs that came into her head, and where the words eluded her she hummed to stitch up the tune until it ran into another.

She left the car in the lot behind the hotel. She thought of going up to the silent room overlooking the sea, and then deliberately turned in the opposite direction. She crossed the road and slipped in through the doors of Tesco just as they were closing for the night. She threaded rapidly up and down the aisles and loaded her basket with whatever she could find that seemed remotely celebratory – a punnet of pinched-looking strawberries, a bottle of champagne, French cheeses nested in a brown plastic basket. She added the makings of a simple meal, and with her purchases in two plastic carrier bags she crossed the street at the front of the store and walked quickly down Redemption Street.

Francis opened the door again. Behind him she saw fire-light, the table piled with books and papers.

Dinah held up the bags. She felt suddenly uncertain of her welcome.

'It's my turn to cook for you. If you'll let me.'

'If?'

His face reassured her. She was welcome here, and always would be. The idea pleased her.

'I was just writing something.' He indicated the spread of papers.

'Finish what you were doing. I'll do this, shall I?' She meant the food.

Francis let her pass into the kitchen. Dinah went on through into the bathroom beyond. It was whitewashed, cold, spartan, with water dripping in the cistern. Francis's shaving brush and soap stood on the tiled window-sill. Dinah ran cold water into the basin, then leant forward and splashed her face with it. The chill made her gasp but she shook the drops out of her hair and straightened up to look in the plain square of mirror screwed to the wall.

She was not quite recognisable to herself. Her face seemed paler and her eyes wilder than the familiar versions, while her mouth was bigger, and threatened to move in unpredictable directions.

Dinah hid this other face behind a threadbare white towel and then went back into the kitchen.

She unpacked her purchases and laid them out on the oilcloth, looked around for knives and a chopping board and suitable pans.

She had been absorbed in her cooking when she became aware that Francis was leaning in the doorway watching her. At once she let her hands drop, laughing apologetically.

'I didn't mean to come in and take over.'

'I like it. I like to see you doing the things that you must do at home.'

Dinah nodded. There was an acknowledgement between them of her life behind and away from this present point in Francis's kitchen.

'You look different,' he said.

'Do I?'

He moved a little to one side, into the kitchen, touching the corner of the old stove and the handle of the saucepan she had placed there.

'I could say something conventional. Pay you a compliment. I can remember how it's done.'

'Don't,' Dinah said. She stared down at her hands, resting flat on the table. The oilcloth was blue and white gingham, tiny checks, faded with time. Little ruffs of carrot peelings and trimmed fennel lay scattered over it.

'Don't say anything at all?'

'I don't deserve compliments.' There was a flicker of anxiety. She was not afraid of Francis, but of hurting him. She turned to see him better and his closeness startled her. He reached out and held her wrist, catching her before she could withdraw.

'You do. You're very beautiful. And you amaze me. Just by being here.'

'I'm not amazing or even pretty. But I am here.'

The luxury of being with Francis astonished her. There was a simplicity in it that was entirely opposite to the confusion that swirled everywhere else. In this calm place it seemed natural that she should be both elated and distressed by her discovery of Sarah, that she should be angry with Matthew and shocked by his unfaithfulness and yet still love him. She could understand why she had abandoned Jack and Merlin to chase to England, into another home, with her pain and her questions.

She could talk to Francis, and he listened. There was no need here to suppress the past or the present.

Dinah knew that she had already made a choice, before even being fully aware of it. She had come here to Francis, instead of telephoning Matthew. She had put Matthew on one side of a tiny divide, and Francis and herself on the other.

Was that how it had begun for Matt, with Doctor Pang? A small choice, made without thinking. She understood that now, and all the balance of her hurt with Matthew minutely shifted.

Uncertainty and confusion smoked in Dinah's head again, unwelcome in Francis's quiet house. She struggled to dismiss them.

'What happened today?' he asked her.

She slipped her hand away from his and opened the door of the heavy old fridge. It was almost empty except for her bottle of champagne. When she took it out she noticed its incongruity but Francis only smiled.

'I'll deal with the Widow for you, shall I?'

Expertly he twisted off the foil and eased out the cork. He poured froth into two glasses.

Dinah checked her food. Chicken was simmering in a pot.

'Can we sit by the fire?'

'Of course.' He carried both their glasses through, and indicated the one armchair beside the fire for Dinah. When she sat down he settled himself on the floor and leant back against the chair arm. His face was half turned away, the visible planes of it coloured by the fire. She reached out carefully and touched his hair. It was thin and soft and clean.

'I met my daughter today.'

There was no more secret, she thought. She could say, I met her. She is well and happy.

The driftwood logs in the grate fell and briefly flared. With the tips of her fingers Dinah stroked Francis's head, follow-ing the smooth curve of bone down to the ridge of his ear. To make this small connection seemed natural, reflecting the ease between them.

He did not sprawl closer or move away but sat still, unaffec-tedly accepting her touch. It made Dinah think of watching Sarah, and touching her, and for a moment it was Sarah who was real and close to her, and Francis the recollection.

'What did you feel?'

Dinah moved her hand, lifted her glass and drank from it.

'I felt the greatest relief. A dozen, a hundred other things too, jealousy and loneliness and loss and regret. And all of those belong to me, are inside me, and I can absorb them because I have to. It is what I deserve.

'But before today there was also the blackest sense of having failed her. She was handed over into oblivion for not matching our notion of perfection. Matthew and I never spoke of her, and I started to think that all our lives had just become a way of avoiding the truth.

'And then I saw her and now I know our failure affects us

and not Sarah at all. I, we . . . Matt and I and her brothers . . .
have lost someone remarkable. Not the other way round. On
the way home in the car I *sang* because I was so happy. Do
you think that's terrible?'

'No, I don't think it's terrible. Tell me about her.'

The solace of talk. Matthew had not offered her that.

If only he had, Dinah thought. If we had made that choice,
at least.

She let her head fall back against the musty cloth of Francis's armchair. Turning her glass in her fingers, watching the
bubbles rise, she told him about the child she had met.

Francis listened to her. He said nothing, but she knew
that he was absorbing everything. Afterwards he poured her
more champagne, leaving aside his own untouched glass.

'Do you think I did wrong to go there to see her?' Dinah
asked.

'No. I think you did what you couldn't help. The question
is more about what you have to do next.'

'I know that.'

All her attention for so long had been fixed on reaching
this point, and now there was the necessity to move beyond it.

'Dinah, you are so occupied with blaming yourself. What
about the benefits of having made such a hard decision?
Were there none?'

'Of course there are.' They were easy to enumerate: Jack
and Merlin themselves and their untroubled childhood,
home life and Matt's success. 'But it has been harder to
celebrate those.'

'I understand.'

He turned full-face towards her and she saw the lines
around his eyes and bisecting his cheeks. Dinah had assumed
that Francis must be about fifty; now it occurred to her that
he could be as much as ten years younger.

'Yes. How much do you think about your daughters?'

'Every day. In all the phases of every day, and about Alison
too. I forfeited the right to them in a more damaging way
than you ever did. I try to remember when we were all happy,

when they were very little, and the odd few times that came between the binges, so that the damaged and dirty parts don't wipe out everything. Otherwise,' he moved abruptly, twisting away from her and standing up, 'otherwise how could there be a way to go on?'

Dinah looked around the little room, at the pen-and-ink drawings and the books on makeshift shelves and the drift-wood stacked in a basket beside the hearth. It seemed a haven to her. Francis had said when they first met that no one had an automatic right to happiness; that contentment was a more realistic aim. She was filled with admiration that he had after all achieved this much.

'You have found a way. You said there were small satisfactions in every day.'

'I did. And there are.'

She stood up too, facing him in the small space in front of the fire. 'Many people would envy the way you live.'

Francis smiled. 'I don't think it would suit everyone. It wouldn't suit you, Dinah.'

The logs shifted in the grate, sending out a powdery jet of sparks.

'No,' she agreed.

Francis was half a head taller than she was, almost the same height as Matthew. He was wearing a colourless sweater unravelling around the neck, and underneath it a shirt squared in tiny checks that frayed away from the points of the collar. Dinah saw all this in minute detail, and the pulse beating under the angle of his jaw.

There was a weightless instant before he kissed her, moving his hand up to the nape of her neck to hold her near to him.

It was Dinah who stepped backwards. Anxiety on his behalf, not her own, shivered once more. She stumbled and kicked over Francis's glass. A patch of froth spread and then darkened into a stain on the rug.

'I'm sorry.' She moved to remedy the damage.

'Leave it,' he ordered. 'Don't move.'

They stood still, looking at each other.

'I'm glad you're here,' Francis said.

They were both suddenly smiling.

'Let me pour you some more,' she offered.

He shook his head, and Dinah saw the effort of will.

'I can't. Champagne more than anything else. I never liked beer very much so I can take half a pint of that. The odd sip or two of wine. But not champagne or whisky or vodka. Because if I started I wouldn't be able to stop.'

'I'm so sorry. It was thoughtless. I wish I hadn't brought it.'

'You drink it, and let me enjoy looking at you.' He picked up his empty glass and clinked it against her full one. 'What is the toast?'

'To Sarah's health and happiness.'

'To Sarah.'

He took her in his arms, and combed her hair back with his fingers so that he could see her face more clearly. Dinah let herself be held. She was surprised by the warmth and ease of it.

'Shall we eat your dinner now or later?' Francis murmured.

'Oh now, I should think, wouldn't you?'

They were amused by the shared awareness that there was time to make their discoveries.

Francis cleared the table of his books and laid out plates and cutlery, and they sat down to eat.

'Not nearly as good as your rabbit,' Dinah judged.

'Can't you imagine how this tastes to me? I don't remember the last time anyone cooked food and presented it to me, like this, and then sat across the table the way you are doing now.'

He said it coolly, without a trace of self-pity, but Dinah heard the echo of his solitude. He had ended up here, she remembered him saying, washed up with his back to the sea. But Francis was neither weak nor defeated. She was intrigued by his ingrown strength that was entirely opposite to Matt's ambition and drive and determination. She did not think after all that Francis was vulnerable.

They sat for a long time after the meal was finished. They told each other about their lives and histories, simple details and uncalculated confessions. They also laughed a good deal. Dinah let herself forget her uncertainties and fears, although the day's disturbing elation remained with her.

Their talk wound on, binding them together.

Dinah thought, this is what I have missed, with Matt. The certainty that I could say whatever I liked to him and that he would hear me. Matt and I have spent too long being careful with one another, and examining our words before uttering them in case something pierced too deep. Did Matt talk like this, easily, in long swings of recollection and confession, to his Doctor Pang?

Perhaps he did, she thought. If it was so, she understood his need better now.

When the driftwood logs had burned down to a heap of ash, Francis stood up belatedly to attend to the fire. It was late, and neither of them had noticed the time passing.

He stood with his back to the fire, his shoulders a little hunched.

'Would you like me to walk you to the hotel?'

Dinah had finished the champagne. She knew that she should thank him for the evening, and perhaps regretfully kiss him goodnight, and then let him walk her through the cold wind to the hotel door. That would be proper, and rational, and it would also be to unwind the intimacy that had knitted between them. Unpinned by the warmth and the talk and the release of her painful confusion, it was not what she wanted to do.

And yet she was also vividly conscious of her body and bones and skin, the physical definition of herself that she would be obliged to hand over, and the truth that she was not young any more, and that no one except Matthew had touched her like this for almost twenty years.

And she wanted Francis to touch her.

254

Choice, Dinah thought. To stay or to go, to connect or to deny the wish for connection.

It must be the same for Francis.

Francis's usual stillness seemed to have intensified. He was like a statue, frozen. She put out her hand to him and was surprised when she touched it by the warmth of his skin.

'I would like to stay,' she said. 'But only for tonight. I can't . . . offer you anything more. I don't want you to misunderstand.'

He said fiercely, 'Please stay.'

He held her close to him so that she caught the unfamiliar scent of his skin. Dinah closed her eyes. The small room had grown very familiar. Even back in Franklin it had seemed close at hand, waiting for her to step back into it. It was safe here.

'Come with me,' Francis whispered.

The stairs led upwards from a door next to the kitchen. They were steep and the air smelt cold and damp after the warmth beside the fire. Francis led the way, holding her hand, and Dinah stumbled after him.

Francis turned on a lamp and drew the plain cotton curtains. The bedroom overlooking Redemption Street was exactly the same shape and size as the living room below. There was a brass-framed bed, tidily made, a bare pine chest of drawers and another set of bookshelves. It was cold here too, so that Dinah half expected to see her breath clouding in front of her. The room reminded her of cottages by the sea rented for childhood holidays, so much so that she could almost hear the rumble of her parents' voices rising up to her from downstairs. The association made her laugh and she stopped herself, unwilling to risk hurting Francis.

He put his hands on her shoulders, looking down into her face.

'It is funny, I know.'

'I didn't mean that this is funny. I suppose I mean all the associations and histories behind us both. I was thinking of my parents. The way that at our age you can't come fresh to sex, taking it just for what it is, the way you can when you're young. Everything we do now refers back to something else, to someone else.'

'I know that.' He undid the top button of her shirt. 'Does it matter, if what you want is here and now?'

'No, it doesn't matter,' Dinah answered.

'Lie down with me.'

They lay down, facing each other, their mouths an inch apart. Dinah studied his face. The tiny movements of his expression seemed close to the surface, barely covered by the thin layer of skin. She kissed the corner of his mouth and then opened her own to him.

He undid the rest of the buttons and released her breast into his hand. Touching him in return she felt the long bones of his arms, ribs and the hard crest of hipbone before her fingers moved inwards.

Clothes became an encumbrance. They sat up, panting a little, and fumbled to remove them. The pallor of Francis's skin seemed to bleed into the dark behind him. Dinah felt her own whiteness, and the exposed vulnerability of her flesh, suddenly and noticeably too soft and loose on her bones. She had forgotten age and time, and now the recollection swooped in again, making her body seem a stranger's. She made a half-movement to cover herself but he caught her hand.

'No,' Francis whispered. 'I want to see you.'

She sat up straight again, offering herself. Francis drew in a breath.

'Dinah.'

She shivered involuntarily at the note in his voice. It was a long time since she had felt wanted in just this way. Her thoughts flicked to Matthew and his Doctor Pang, and she forced them away. Not now. Here and now. This was her choosing, to take this moment with Francis, and he with her.

'You're cold. Here.'

He drew back the covers and they slid beneath them. Heat warmed the sheets as they held each other. Francis's hand

256

moved over her belly and down between her thighs. They explored each other under the shelter of the covers, unsurely at first, putting their separate histories behind them.

Francis's mouth moved against hers. 'It has been a very long time. And drunks don't make the most magnificent lovers.'

His uncertainty touched Dinah and sprang some erotic trigger within her. She wanted him more urgently than she had done before.

Sex was a paradox, as always. She forgot her own uncertainty, her awareness that she was no longer young, Francis's ravaged face.

'Now,' she commanded.

It was just the same act, Dinah thought when it was over.

The same, for all the differences of place and person. For Matthew and his post-doc, for herself and Francis and Ed and Sandra Parkes and the Pinkhams. The possibility of human intimacy and the scale of it, both universal and also contained here in one hour in Francis's tiny bare bedroom, seemed miraculous and intricate and at the same time luminously simple.

Dinah thought of Matt and the first time they had made love.

It had been in her flat, a cramped third-floor attic room-and-a-half in Notting Hill. It was at the height of her plants-and-baskets decorating phase and there had been wicker and swathes of tumbling greenery everywhere.

'All this bloody foliage,' Matt had complained as he pushed it aside to steer her to bed. 'Doesn't it give you hay fever or nettle rash?'

Some time later he had kicked over a weeping fig and showered the sheets with soil. As they rolled in it he had uttered some male crack to do with earthy behaviour that made her laugh a good deal, and at the same time realise with a shock of delight how much she liked this man.

He had hardly left after that night, and not long afterwards they had moved into the flat over the greengrocer's together. It was not much bigger than the old one on Notting Hill, but much more convenient for Matthew's lab. And between then and now stretched all their time together, and the steps and side-steps that had brought them to this. Almost to the point of separation.

They had made mistakes, but the responsibility for them was equal. She did not want their marriage to end. How had it taken her until now, in another man's bed, to realise as much?

Or perhaps, Dinah thought, there was a beginning in an end.

'Are you comfortable?' Francis whispered. They lay in each other's arms with the sound of the sea just audible through the layers of night silence.

'Yes,' Dinah said truthfully. She was more comfortable than she had been for a long time.

On Tuesday morning, when she woke up, the bed was empty. There was thin grey light coming through the cotton curtains, and her discarded clothes had been folded and placed on a chair. A slightly incongruous digital clock on the bedside table informed her that it was nine-fifteen. There was the sound of traffic now, not the sea.

She sat up and heard Francis moving downstairs. A moment later there was the sound of his steps on the stairs. He came in with a blue and white striped mug of tea.

'Thank you.' She smiled at him. He was already dressed and shaved, giving the impression of having being up for some time. 'Have I overslept?'

'No. It was nice to be downstairs thinking of you still asleep up here.'

He opened the curtains and Dinah saw a thin slice of pale grey cloud.

'It's going to be a fine day. When the sun breaks through this mist. I wondered . . .'

He hesitated.

'Yes?'

'If you would like to come for a walk with me. There's a good one that goes south along the sea wall and then turns inland across country and circles back again. It takes all day, but we could stop in a pub for lunch or buy a picnic.'

Dinah thought. Today she must telephone Matthew, and talk to her children. She must make decisions about the future. But she swung away from the responsibility because everything that must be done was knotted up with Sarah. Her closeness tempted Dinah like a drug, all the tangle of longing and guilt surrounding her tightened rather than unpicked by a single meeting.

'I'd like to come for a walk,' Dinah said slowly.

Francis sat down on the edge of the bed, and took the mug out of her hand.

'Thank you for last night,' he said.

Dinah saw that his face looked softened, rubbed out. She began to fear that he might after all want and need more than she could offer him. In her unbalanced state perhaps the simplicity had only existed in her imagination. Perhaps Matt had felt the same, and once his affair had begun he had only wanted to extricate himself . . .

Dinah looked into his eyes.

'It was wonderful,' she said truthfully. 'But it can't happen again. Twice begins to be hurtful.'

Francis bent his head. But then he lifted it again, smiling at her.

'I know. Let's go for our walk, shall we?'

Later, she went back to the hotel to change her clothes and put on walking shoes. She hurried, and within a few minutes was on her way back to meet Francis.

Dinah did not look and so did not see that there was a telephone message folded in her slot of the old-fashioned wooden rack behind the reception desk.

In Franklin on Monday morning Matthew answered the

phone. He was giving Jack and Merlin their breakfast, and wondering where to find another pair of shoes for Merlin to wear that wouldn't hurt his foot and thinking about the proper fat cell assay that Kathrin and the others were to begin running that week. The entire team had been waiting for this moment. He did not have much time or the patience to listen to Sandra Parkes.

'No, we haven't seen her.' He knew he sounded short, but already it was too late to pretend concern that he didn't feel.

'No, nor heard. I wouldn't expect her to show up here in any case, Sandra. She knows Dinah's in England.'

He sighed, looking at his watch and buttering toast as he hunched the receiver to his ear.

'She's done it before, hasn't she? I wouldn't worry. She'll be off with her friends somewhere and she'll turn up when she's good and ready.'

He handed the toast to Jack across the counter top and raised his eyebrows at him in a mime of impatience.

'Yep. Yep, of course I will, Sandra. Call me tonight and let me know, okay? Sure. Don't worry. 'Bye now.'

He hung up and took a gulp of coffee.

'Who was that?' Jack asked. 'As if I couldn't guess.'

'You're right. Milly has done another vanishing act, out all day yesterday and didn't come home last night.'

Merlin didn't look up from his Cheerios.

'Nothing'll happen to Camilla-and-custard. She's made of iron and steel. It's what she does to other people they ought to worry about. She's invincible herself.'

'Hey, good word. And I think you're right. Look at the *time*, will you? We're all going to be late and I have to be at the lab. Let's get going, both of you.'

The three of them were in almost exactly the same positions when Sandra rang again that evening. They were eating microwaved pizza and the boys had begun to talk wistfully about Dinah's cooking.

'When is she coming back?' Merlin was asking. One or

other of them asked him the same question a dozen times a day.

Matt reached from his chair to the phone.

'Sandra. Yep, hi. Really? I'm sorry. No, not a sign. But she wouldn't come here, I'm certain. Not without expecting to see Dinah.'

He waved a hand to silence the boys across the table.

'What? Oh Sandy, look. It's – what? – it's nearly midnight in the UK. I can't call her now, she'll be asleep.'

The boys could almost hear the yipping of the frantic voice at the other end.

'We-ell, if you really want . . . Okay. Put Ed on.'

Matthew listened more seriously.

'Sure thing. If you think she might have been in touch with Dinah. You never know, of course. Look, I'll call her right now and get straight back to you.'

Jack and Merlin sat expectantly. 'Can I talk to Mom as well? Please?'

Matthew found the number and dialled it, and spoke to the night porter in the Cromer hotel. Then there was a lengthy pause.

'Thank you. Could you leave a message to say that her husband telephoned?'

He hung up. Jack and Merlin stared at him.

'Where's Mom?'

'I told you. She's gone to see Sarah.'

'What's the time there? Can she stay up so late with Down's syndrome?'

'You're so lame, Mer. What difference does that make?'

'Quiet, both of you.' Matthew was dialling the Parkeses' number. 'Ed? I'm sorry, Dinah isn't in her room right now. I'll call her again in the morning. No trouble. No, don't worry. I'm sure Milly's fine. Goodnight.'

'Is Mom okay?' Merlin demanded.

'Yes, of course she is. She's just not in her room at the moment. Probably having a nightcap in the bar. We'll talk to her tomorrow. Come on, the two of you. Help me clear these plates.'

'I wish she was here,' Merlin said. 'I wish she hadn't gone to England to look for Sarah. She belongs here with us, doesn't she?'

'Of course she does,' Matthew reassured him. But absently, unconvincingly, because his thoughts were elsewhere. Dinah was not in her room at midnight. The spectre of jealous anxiety stirred within him until he thought, *I can't blame her.*

If she was all right, if she was safe, that was all that mattered.

Twelve

Matthew swung the Toyota into the faculty car park. He was late, on the very day when he would have wanted to be in the lab as early as possible. But once he had switched off the engine, instead of leaping out of the car he sat motionless with his hands braced on the wheel, staring out at the line of trees between the science blocks and the main campus. He could just see the spire of the college chapel beyond.

There had been no answer from Dinah's room this morning. The hotel receptionist told him that his first message was still in her pigeonhole. She could not remember having seen Mrs Steward since yesterday morning.

'Ask her to call me as soon as she comes in, would you?' Matt said neutrally.

He had not wanted to make any more of her absence for the boys' sake, although their sensitive antennae had already picked up too much. They were unnaturally quiet on the way to school.

Matthew called the Parkeses and told them he hadn't reached Dinah. There was no news of Milly either. He had driven the familiar route to the campus.

Now the tiny metallic clinks and creaks of the cooling car were obliterated by the roar of a VW Beetle skidding into the car park. A bunch of students poured out of it and sloped away, leaving their car occupying a faculty member's space.

Matt had no views on student parking infringements but the sudden noise cutting into the silence stirred his concern into full spate. He found that he was gripping the steering wheel still tighter and staring unseeingly at the needle point of the spire.

Dinah did not disappear.

She always telephoned and gave notice of being late.

She did what was expected, always, in her rational way. She was either at home, or within reach. He depended on that, and so did the boys. And the fact that she had never caused him to wonder before made this vanishing all the more alarming.

It was to do with Sarah. It must be. Matthew felt anxiety knocking in his chest. He did not relish the unknown when he couldn't leap to bridge it with formulae and figures.

Someone tapped on the rear window of the Toyota. Matthew had been so lost in thought that he almost cried out in surprise. In the driver's mirror he saw Jon Liu peering in. He wound down the window, collecting himself with difficulty.

'You okay?' Jon asked.

'Sure.'

It was twenty to ten, and Matt was almost always in his office by nine. He reached for his briefcase and eased himself out of the car. The two men crossed the tarmac in the direction of the biochemistry building.

'Could all happen today,' Jon said, stating the obvious as he sometimes did in his nervous way.

'Yep.'

There was a perceptible air of tension in the department, noticeable to Matt as soon as he walked in. On days like this, when crucial results might come, he would drink in the atmosphere, revelling in the excitement his work generated. Orally-ingestible insulin. It was a covetable prize, and he had been working towards it for years. Only today he scented the adrenalin working in his team but could not connect with it himself. He felt a flash of anger with Dinah. This was what he had worked for, and if it were to come he deserved the pleasure of the result. Yet anxiety for Dinah obliterated his anticipation. Matt was amazed to recognise how much stronger the one was than the other.

If anything happened to Dinah. If he should *lose* her. The thought froze him. The promise of a successful assay dwindled into meaninglessness. He could not even recall that it had meant anything to him.

'Hello Prof,' one of the PhD students called as he passed. Matt only nodded.

In his office he found Sean Rader waiting. Matt put down his briefcase and slung his jacket over the back of the chair.

'Everything ready?' he asked vaguely.

'Nah. Thought we might put it off for a couple of days,' Sean grinned. 'Either that or start without you.'

'I'm here now. Let's go.'

'Okay boss.'

The lab was packed with people. Matt automatically searched for and then saw Kathrin's dark head. The radio was playing rock music but someone reached up and turned it off as soon as he came in. Two technicians were waiting by the counter with racks of dozens of test-tubes half-filled with opalescent fluid.

'Morning, everyone,' Matt said.

There was a low murmur of response.

'Let's see what we've got, then.'

He stood at the front of the big group with his hands in his pockets. The other technicians and students and post-docs and senior scientists crowded in behind him, positioning themselves with a view of the LED display above the big counting machine.

One technician began to slot test-tubes into the machine conveyor. The room fell silent.

Months of work had led up to this moment.

The contents of the test-tubes were fat cells extracted from the epididymal pads of male rats and then elaborately prepared in a buffer for the addition of the significant reagents

– some with insulin, and the experimental tubes with varying quantities of Matt's engineered molecule. Then glucose had been added in a mildly radioactive form. The test would show by counting the little flashes of light how much glucose remained and how much had been converted into lipid.

The numbers on the LED would indicate clearly whether the new molecule did or did not perform its delicate task.

The first test-tube on the conveyor reached the counter. There was a click and sharp hiss of hydraulics as the tube was plunged into a lead container to exclude external radiation from the count. Digits flashed lazily on the display and after the two-minute counting time stabilised at 40, forty counts per minute. Nobody moved. The first ten tubes were for base line readings, containing neither insulin nor the experimental material. The conveyor shuttled busily, doing its job while Matt and the others were reduced to waiting and watching.

Kathrin was at the end of the line. She had done hours of measuring and pipetting to prepare the cells for assay. Now she handed the next rack, labelled *11–20*, to the technician for loading. Insulin in carefully calibrated concentrations would provide a standard curve against which to measure their results. She didn't look at Matthew as the hiss and clunk of machinery continued.

Little green numbers flickered and stopped. Higher and higher with each increasing dose of insulin. The fat cells were working well.

Sean took his Old Holborn tin out of the pocket of his leather jacket and longingly rubbed his thumb over the lid. There was no smoking in the labs.

The rack marked *21–30* looked identical to its predecessors, and the others waiting on the bench. It contained the new molecule in the first experimental dilution. The conveyor swept it towards its destination.

Matthew thought, I'll call again at lunchtime. Six p.m. in England. If I can't reach her then, I shall have to decide what to do. The press of people behind him was inching closer to the counter as they craned to see. He heard Sean next to him suck in a breath as if dragging deeply on a roll-up.

Test-tube 21 sank into the lead cylinder.

There was a weightless, silent, frozen instant.

The counter clicked and the digits flashed into a wild, greenish blur. The numbers leapt, seemingly towards infinity. More than 15,000.

There was a great, united roar of triumph.

'Wait,' somebody called out.

22 sank out of sight and produced the same result.

Another roar went up. Sean threw his tin in the air and caught it in a raised fist, like a salute.

'Fuckin' A,' he murmured.

23 and 24 repeated the trick.

Everyone was shouting now. There were smiles like melon slices everywhere, and half a dozen hands clapped Matthew on the back. He looked aside and saw Kathrin exchange a jubilant high five with one of the students.

'It looks like a good one,' Jon Liu said. He shook Matt solemnly by the hand. There was a chorus of laughter and cheering.

'We're not home yet,' Matt answered. He was still watching the numbers as the test-tubes rattled through. It was strange. He felt that he couldn't quite claim his own triumph.

'What do you want?' Sean exclaimed in disbelief. 'Written authentication from the Almighty?'

People from the back of the group were jostling forward to get a closer look at the numbers. Euphoria made everyone talk and laugh more loudly than normal. Two or three passers-by who did not work for Matt had already put their heads round the doors. The news would travel fast.

The newest PhD student punched the arm of the person next to him.

'Yeah, man,' he grinned. 'We'll be able to say we were on Steward's Nobel team back in the '90s.'

Matt rubbed his jaw, making a smile emerge. The results were good. As the tubes continued their merry shuttle there was no doubting that. The team deserved his thanks. He held up his hand.

'Listen, all of you. This looks great, and I'm delighted. No one can predict how the stuff'll hold up in clinical trials, of course . . .' Affectionate groans and exclamations almost drowned him out, '. . . but you've done a fine job to get us this far. All of you. Well done, and thank you.'

Matt shook hands with each of them, saying an individual word to everybody.

He was affected by their elated pride, and aware as he always was at these times of belonging to a group that was more than the sum of the individual elements. Yet he also felt apart from them. It came to him again that he had identified his research team as his family, and that it had been a mistaken identification. He was pierced by a fresh, sharp stab of fear that something had happened to Dinah.

Kathrin's hand when he shook it felt light and dry, like a fallen leaf. He asked her to bring a print-out of the data across to his office when the assay was complete.

Matthew went back to his desk. There was a series of calls to make and receive, and visits from colleagues on other teams. Accepting their congratulations, he acknowledged to himself that it was well done, but the success no longer filled and coloured all perspectives in the way it would once have done.

The morning passed without leaving him a spare moment.

Sean put his head round the door to tell him that there was a proposal to go off campus for a celebratory lunch at Pantucci's, and everyone hoped that Matt would preside.

'I'll try and get there. I've got an urgent call to make to England first.'

At one o'clock, six p.m. UK time, he dialled the Cromer number again. She must be there now, he thought.

What would he do if she were not?

The now-familiar singsong voice of the hotel receptionist answered and he asked for Dinah once again.

'Hold on please,' the woman said. He heard the tone

ringing through in Dinah's room. Seven, eight, nine, ten double burrs.

'I'm sorry, caller, there's no answer from her room.'

'I called and left a message last night. Did she get it?'

'One moment please.' After a moment she told him, 'There are still messages here for Mrs Steward.'

'Has anybody else seen her in the last two days?'

'One moment.'

There was the sound of a mumbled consultation. 'I don't think anyone has, but she hasn't checked out. And Mrs Steward has a visitor. Waiting for her in the lounge here.'

Matthew tried to think. Whom to call now. Eleanor? The police? Friends in Sheldon? The second part of the receptionist's information sank in slowly.

'A visitor? Who is it?'

'A young woman.'

There was a knock on Matt's door and Kathrin appeared without waiting for his invitation to come in. She was holding the print-out he had asked for. Matt angrily covered the mouthpiece with his hand.

'Could you come back later? I'm tied up now.'

Her face contracted into a dark little mask. But she withdrew obediently.

'Oh, wait a minute . . . Mr Steward?'

'Hello? I'm here.'

'I can see your wife now. She's just coming up the steps. If you'd like to hold on . . .'

'Thank you,' Matt said. He leaned back in his swivel chair, suddenly aware that his shirt was damp across the back and under the arms.

Dinah was pleasantly tired. Her legs and feet ached, and she was looking forward to a cup of tea and a hot bath, followed by a drink and a good dinner.

Francis and she had walked for eighteen miles, stopped halfway for a pub lunch of cheese and pickles and beer, and talked all the while. For Dinah, talking so freely was like drinking pure water after a long thirst.

The sun shone on the crinkled flint-coloured sea, and when they turned inland it slid overhead and westwards over the huge fields where flocks of gulls swooped after crawling tractors. Francis knew the country well, and the local legends relating to ancient isolated cottages and tiny hills crowned with stunted trees. She let herself take him and the scenery and the sunshine as they offered themselves, for now, for today. She fended off for a few more hours the necessity to pick decisions out of the vicious knot of everything else.

When they reached Cromer again in the late afternoon, Francis asked, 'This evening?'

She told him gently, 'I need to call and talk to Matt and the boys. And I must also do some thinking.'

His company had given her more concentrated happiness than she had known in a long time; the night and day that they had spent together seemed now like a brief interval of peace out of a bewildering war. But it was a finite time, begun and ended.

'It was just a day. You knew that, didn't you?'

He nodded.

'The happiest day I can remember,' he said.

He wanted more, Dinah understood, but he would not try to make her change her mind. He only touched her cheek and then stepped back.

'Goodnight,' he said. And then walked briskly away down Redemption Street. A tall man in a long black coat. A lonely man who had learned to be more adept at concealing his needs than even Dinah herself.

Dinah circled round to the front of the hotel. A cold wind springing off the sea chivvied her up the steps and in through the old-fashioned revolving door.

'Mrs Steward? Mrs Steward?' the receptionist called to her across the polish-scented lobby. 'Call for you.'

She went and picked up the phone to one side of the desk. As she lifted it she saw the sheaf of messages in her room slot.

'Yes? Matt. Is everything all right?'

'More or less. I called you yesterday morning and last night.'

Dinah felt breathless, caught out. Images of the day and night she had just spent marched through her head, the glow abruptly fading. She was guilty now as much as Matt, and shamed by the idea that even unconsciously she had needed to repay his betrayal with her own.

No. She had been drawn to Francis for himself, not as a childish tit-for-tat. Her jealous resentment of Matthew and Kathrin Pang shifted again, lifting a little.

'Matt, are you there? I . . . I've only just come in. I didn't see the messages.' There were more than two.

'Where were you?'

A second of silence ticked between them. Dinah thought, this is how he had done it too. By omission and evasion. Her anger with him dwindled and silently died away.

'Seeing Sarah. Matt, she's amazing. I sat with her and watched . . .'

Brutally, Matthew cut her short. 'Sandra phoned. Milly went missing on Sunday morning. She hasn't been seen since.'

Dinah saw the receptionist's face. Then something made her turn round and follow the woman's eyes across the lobby.

Under a transparent plastic sign engraved in green capitals with the word LOUNGE stood Milly. Her hair was teased into a black dome and her eyes and mouth made black slashes in her white face. Her clothes looked as if she had camped out in them for a week, but the effect was as calculated and extreme as it had been the first time Dinah saw her. In the dimness of the provincial hotel her strangeness was electrifying.

'She's here.'

'*There?*'

'I've just seen her. You'll have to give me ten minutes, Matt. Wait there and I'll call you back.'

Dazedly, Dinah replaced the receiver.

'Visitor for you, Mrs Steward,' the receptionist intoned unnecessarily. 'She *would* wait.'

Dinah went to her. Milly was fiercely smiling with her black mouth closed, in a way that Dinah understood kept everything within her.

'Are you all right?'

'Yeah. Never better.'

'Come with me.'

There was a kitbag and a supermarket plastic carrier on the nearest chair in the lounge. Dinah picked them up and Milly obediently followed. As they passed the desk Dinah said, 'My friend will be staying here with me. She will need a single room near mine. And please could you send up a big pot of tea for two and some sandwiches. No butter, any filling will do except meat, fish, cheese or egg.'

'Certainly Mrs Steward.'

They went upstairs to the safety of Dinah's room.

'I phoned. From Heathrow and my friends' place in London. You weren't here. So I just came anyway.' Milly was accusatory.

'Wait, wait a minute. Start from the beginning.'

Milly had left Franklin on Sunday morning while Ed was playing golf and Sandra was at her health spa. She had taken her passport, and a pile of money from the store of cash that Ed always kept in the house. She had travelled by taxi and train to the airport at Boston, and bought herself a standby ticket on the first available American Airways flight to Heathrow. From Heathrow, on Monday morning, she had gone by tube to friends living in Camden Town.

'Who? Who are these friends?'

'I told you about them, my mates. I stayed at Caz's place, it was okay.' Milly jerked her dome of hair. 'It's a good set-up. He lets people, like, come and stay if they need somewhere. I had a good time.'

Milly's face wore the same expression of faintly shy defiance as it had when she had told Dinah about the ski instructor in Zermatt. Dinah understood why Milly was suddenly alive again, down to the black tips of her hair and nails. It was the reconnection to people and places she missed, and evidently to Caz in particular, whoever he might be.

'I see. And then what?'

'Well, it's obvious. You gave me the number and address of this place, didn't you?'

On Tuesday morning, unable to reach Dinah by telephone, she had taken a train from Liverpool Street to Norwich and hitchhiked the rest of the way to Cromer.

'Easy. The only problem was the last bit. I had to wait hours for a lift and then it was with some slimeball.'

Milly told the story triumphantly. Dinah was impressed, although she hid it from Milly. She picked up the room telephone and handed it across.

'Right. Call your mother now. Tell her you're safe, and with me.'

'I don't know who my mother is. I want to find her.'

'Don't you be a slimeball. Tell Sandra where you are, and properly, or I will turn you straight round and send you back to Boston.'

Milly dialled. The call was answered on the first ring; Matt had already spoken to the Parkeses.

'Yeah. I'm okay. I said, I'm *okay*. I just did, that's all. Look you don't have to do that. I don't *want* you to, and Dinah . . .'

Dinah went through into the bathroom and closed the door. She turned the water on full and washed her face. The new and eerily distorted reflection of herself looked back from the mirror. When she thought she had given Milly long enough to explain herself she went back into the bedroom. Milly was stretched full length on the bed.

'They're on their way to the bloody airport now. They'll be in the house in Hampstead tomorrow. You know, where we lived all the time when I was at school in London? Sandra wanted to speak to you but I said you'd gone out again.'

Of course Ed and Sandra were on their way. They moved effortlessly between their houses. It was only Milly, as con-

273

servative in her habits as any child, who found the constant flitting difficult to deal with.

'Milly . . .'

There was a knock at the door. It was the tea; stainless steel pot and water jug, and cucumber sandwiches arranged on a paper doily. Dinah sighed. She had no wish to speak to Sandra at this moment anyway.

'All right. Have something to eat, and tell me why you've chased me across the Atlantic to the Seaview Hotel, Cromer.'

Milly bit into a sandwich without inspecting the contents first. 'I told you. I want to start looking for my mum. If it's all right for you to hunt for and find your kid, why shouldn't I do the same?'

Matthew rested his chin in his hand. Sandra's incredulous *In Norfolk?* still rang in his ear. She sounded bewildered and hurt as well as angry, and he felt sorry for her.

The corridor outside had gone quiet. Everyone must have left for Pantucci's.

After a moment he rang through to the cubicle at the other end of the department that Kathrin shared with another post-doc.

'Yes?'

'I'm free now.'

A minute after that she appeared. The door opened a sliver, just wide enough to admit her. She was wearing jeans and a white top in some stretchy material with a deep scooped neck that showed the tiny wings of her collarbone. Her skin was pale, smooth olive against the curve of white fabric.

Matthew said again, 'I'm sorry.'

She placed the print-out in front of him. Then she walked round and sat on the edge of his desk, her fingers and knuckles folded and her straight arms supporting her. There was a fine bloom of silky hair on the nearest forearm, just out of his reach. She was very beautiful, but Matthew found himself looking at her with a kind of puzzlement. He knew

274

her but he also felt that he had no knowledge of her at all. Had they done all those things together, within the walls of her disconcertingly reminiscent room? She was a young girl, perched on his desk a foot or so away, but Dinah seemed closer, more real to him. Small prickles of apprehension and irritation ran under Matthew's skin like tiny electrical charges.

'There was a crisis. A young friend of ours had disappeared and I couldn't reach Dinah in England. I was . . . worried about her this morning, and then she called just when you came in.'

Kathrin's head had been bowed but now she tilted it up so she looked at the ceiling. Her short hair swung in a glossy black wing and she put her hooked fingertip up and raked it backwards from her forehead.

Matthew watched all this. Then she turned to look sidelong at him, catching her lip between her teeth in a display of wistful reflection.

'It isn't worth me hoping for anything, is it? Between us?'

'You and me?' Matthew repeated thickly, caught off guard for an instant.

'Yes. That it might really come to mean what I understood it to mean at the beginning.'

'You understood . . .'

'I told you that I loved you. It was the truth. And I thought from what you did, the way you *did* it, that you might love me. That there might be a time when we could be together.'

Oh God, Matthew thought. 'Kathrin . . .'

'But of course I was wrong. What you wanted was just a *fuck*, Professor, wasn't it?'

Coming from her bruised-plum mouth the words sounded shocking. Matthew sketched a despairing shape in the air with flat hands.

'No, it wasn't. It was you. Mind and soul as well as body. But I shouldn't have allowed myself even to think it, because I wasn't free to do so. Then or now. I'm sorry for what I did. I am more sorry than I can say for hurting you.'

Kathrin's eyes were fixed on the trees outside the window.

'I suppose,' she said, almost dreamily, 'I suppose what you did could be construed as harassment. Don't you think? A department head coming on to one of his team with no motive except sordid sexual gratification?'

Matt shifted in his chair. Kathrin was still expressionlessly looking out into the blue-white afternoon light.

'That's not quite how I remember it,' he said softly.

Kathrin pursed her lips. It was strange for the department to be so quiet, with no voices or whistling or footsteps squeaking on the rubber floors.

'You could claim whatever you wished,' Matthew added less gently. 'But I would have to say it began with you coming on to me. I wonder how much Jon would remember of the end of that evening?'

Kathrin grinned.

'Not much, I'd bet.' She stood up, straightening her shoulders and flipping her hair again. 'There are the print-out figures. I guess I should have said congratulations.'

'Thank you. Your work was a major contribution.'

To his surprise she held out her hand, straight wrist and fingers, like a man's. He shook it, feeling the contradictory fragility again. Dr Pang was no fallen leaf, after all. She understood that she would not get what she wanted, and delicately retaliated with a threat. Enough to make him feel uncomfortable, washed through with middle-aged guilt, his relief twinned with regret. Reluctantly, he had to admire her.

'I'm going over to Pantucci's to join the others,' she said.

'Tell them I'm sorry, I'm tied up. I've got family stuff to attend to. Get everyone a Coke on my tab and tell them to be back here at work by two p.m. sharp.'

Kathrin didn't smile at the weak humour.

'Goodbye,' she said seriously. She slipped out of the same narrow space and closed the door behind her.

Matthew slumped back in his chair, breathing a little heavily as if he had just run upstairs.

The outside direct line buzzed on his desk.

276

'Matt? It's me.'

'Oh, hi. What's happening? I spoke to Sandra. Poor woman.'

'Yes, I made Milly call her right back. She's next door now, in the bath. I hope she's got some clean clothes in this kitbag of hers.'

'What a monster the child is.'

'No, she isn't. She's just full of anger and contradictions and bravado. Jack and Merlin will probably be just the same when they get to her age.'

'Christ. I hope not.'

Fourteen. The understanding flickered between them.

'Tell me about her.'

Dinah did not want to, now, even though she had longed to hear Matt ask it. Sarah felt too close and her own response to what was happening was too raw to be aired over the hollow echoes of a transatlantic call.

'I saw her and sat with her, and she showed me her room and her things. She's amazing. But I can't talk now. Matt? You sound harassed or something.'

'We ran the fat cell tests this morning. Looks like it's good.'

'Matt! Why didn't you say? How wonderful. I'm pleased, I'm *so* pleased for you. You deserve everything. That means you've beaten Korner and Cal Tech to it, does it?'

'I think so. This far.'

She laughed with pleasure.

'Well done,' Dinah said. 'I'm proud of you.'

'Are you? I don't know that I'm so very proud of myself.'

There was another pause. The distance between Cromer and Franklin seemed to diminish, and then expand again. Dinah could hear Milly banging about in the bathroom. She would be out in a minute. There was nothing to say, and also too much.

'What are you going to do now?' Matthew asked. The question again. 'When will you be coming home?'

'I don't know. Not quite yet.'

All she did know was that there was still some urgent and

unsatisfied need connected with Sarah. It possessed her and unbalanced her. It made her reflection stare back crazily at her from the mirror.

'How are the boys?'

Matthew told her about Merlin's foot, quickly adding that it was not serious. He filled in the small domestic details so that she nodded, reassured and at the same time startled to realise how she had disconnected herself. The thought of home pulled at her, making the hotel room alien and the hours she had spent with Francis seem shameful in her memory. The acrid smoke of confusion filled Dinah's eyes and mouth again so that it was difficult to speak.

She managed to say, 'Give them my love. I'll call when I can to talk.'

Milly came out of the bathroom, pink and barefaced and with a white towel wrapped around her head.

'I'd better go. Wait, Matt? Well done again.'

'Thank you. I love you.'

'Yes,' Dinah said. 'I'll talk to you soon.'

Dinah and Milly ate dinner in the hotel dining room. There were little lamps with red shades on the tables, silver service by a pair of pensionable waitresses, and just-audible muzak. The food was almost comically bad. Milly stabbed at her plate of tinned carrots and vegetarian lasagne and then pushed it to one side. She lit a Marlboro with a flourish.

Dinah didn't remonstrate. Dinah had seen the waitresses raising their eyebrows at Milly's appearance and murmuring together by the servery door, and she felt most definitely on Milly's side. An atmosphere of complicity grew between them as they suffered the dinner. It was as if they were playing truant. They eyed each other through the red glow of the lamp as Milly blew out smoke.

Milly voiced the feeling. 'It's like I'm out on parole or something, being here with you. And like tomorrow I'm going to be back inside with Ed and Sandra in Gainsborough Gardens. Probably in handcuffs.'

278

Dinah laughed. 'It'll take handcuffs. Or you'll be turning up next in Ulan Bator or Port Stanley.'

'It's not funny.'

'Not even a bit? All right. You've proved something just by getting here. Let's talk about what you want to do.'

'Tell me about the kid first.'

'She's the same age as you, actually.'

Dinah described what had happened, as she had not been able to do for Matthew. Milly listened, rotating her cigarette in the glass ashtray to trim off the ash. At the end she said,

'Can I see her as well? I'd really like to.'

Dinah was surprised. She had expected jealousy thinly veiled by dismissiveness.

'I don't know. I don't even know how I can get to see her again myself. Although I want to. I have to.'

'There's always a way,' Milly said sagely. 'It must have been amazing, seeing her like that after all that time.'

'Amazing? Yes, it was.'

'Is she very, kind of, backward?'

'No. And yes.'

'Shit'.

Dinah laughed again. Milly was very endearing.

'Now it's your turn.'

Milly lit another cigarette although she had barely puffed on the last one.

'I told you. I'm like, there in Franklin with Sandra and Ed and all the usual shit, being tutored in stuff I don't give a fuck about and staring out the window at the *trees* the whole time. And wondering what's the matter with me, right? That's their thing, like, always "What's the matter with you, with this lovely life and all your privileges and we love you so much as well, so why can't you be, you know, *nice*?" So by now I'm wondering it as well, aren't I?

'And since you've left and come here I'm thinking about you too, you know? What you said about having to see the kid, and not knowing what'll happen once you've found her but still *needing* to find her? And feeling you can't go on keeping the secret about her and letting everything go on building on top of something that's all wrong to begin with? Wasn't that what you said?'

Milly paused in mid puff, frowning at Dinah.

'Yes, it was. Exactly that.'

'Right. So I start thinking, maybe what's the matter with you is the same with me. I want to run and get away and I don't know where or why, only that I want to. That I'll burst or go crazy or something if I don't?

'Did you ever see that really sad tiger in the zoo in London? I used to get taken there all the time when I was a little kid, by nannies and weird au pairs and people. The tiger used to pace up and down the same track, backwards and forwards all day. It used to make me want to cry because he wasn't in the jungle. And now I think shit, that's like *me*.

'So I decide maybe this time I do something real instead of going off and, like, hiding in a barn for a night or something pointless?

'I'm thinking, if I come here to you, you can really help me start looking for her. My real mother. Like you did with the kid, right? And that will be not endlessly walking up and down and keeping a secret any more but kind of coming out in the open, and it will make things better. I'll be able to deal with Ed and Sandra and all of that because we'll all know where we stand, right? Do you know what I'm saying? Like, otherwise I can go on going to them "I want to look for her," and they go, "What about us?" and "You're not old enough," and "Don't we give you everything you want?" They think me wanting to do it is just part of all the other stuff with me, instead of all the stuff being because of it, right?

'So if I do something, it will be, you know, a real step, wherever it takes me. Instead of going round and round with my mum and dad.'

It was the first time Dinah had ever heard her call them that, rather than Ed and Sandra.

She nodded. 'I think that's probably very astute of you.'

Milly sighed. 'God. That's the trouble with all of you. You use crap words like astute. What I want to know is, am I *right*, or what?'

'Milly, I don't think I know whether you are right or not. I don't know anything any more.'

There was a startled pause. Then Milly's face split into her transforming smile. She had realised something.

'You really don't, do you? And you won't just trot out what ought to be right, pretending you've known and believed it all along, either. That's amazing.'

'I don't know about amazing. It's honest.'

Milly was still smiling. 'As soon as I got the idea of coming here I couldn't let go of it. I kept adding a bit more to the plan. Like, polishing it. I knew exactly how I'd work it. I knew I had to do it. It was exciting.'

'I bet.'

Milly was a survivor, Dinah recognised. More than that – she was formidable. Some of her anger must be to do with Ed and Sandra's unwillingness to acknowledge her strength in the way that she wanted and deserved that they should.

'So,' Milly held up her clenched fists, pulling them apart as if to demonstrate no handcuffs, for now, 'I'm here. Will you help me find my mother?'

They looked at each other with the sense of playing truant again. They were both of them on the run.

Dinah said, 'I told you. The best person to ask about where to start is my friend Lavinia Jackson. I haven't had a chance to telephone her yet for you. I know I said I would.'

Lavinia had lived in Sheldon in the early days, and then had moved back into London after the break-up of her marriage. She was a lawyer specialising in fostering and adoption cases, and Dinah had sometimes thought that she might ask her for advice about tracing Sarah. But she had never made the request, out of the old sense that she did not deserve help or sympathy for what she had done.

'We'll do it,' Dinah said now.

Milly stood up. She came round the table and kissed Dinah

before enveloping her in a bear-hug. She smelt of hotel soap and cigarettes.

'When?'

'Tomorrow, if you like. But you must be ready to hear that you can't do anything without Ed and Sandra's help until you're eighteen.'

Milly let her go and stood back a step.

'Mm. But we can try, can't we? And also tomorrow we can go and see the kid again.'

'She's the same age as you,' Dinah automatically repeated. 'And I don't know that we can go there again. There isn't an open invitation. Rather the reverse.'

'Go on. We don't have to, you know, *go* there. Just take me over and show me the place. The town, whatever it is. Perhaps we'll just, like, see her. You want to show me, don't you?'

That was it. Dinah did want to. Wivenham drew her as if she were pulled towards it on a wire. She had wanted to tell Milly, and now she wanted to go there with her. As if Milly's presence would authenticate it all, for afterwards, when she was afraid that Sarah and the place that contained her might shimmer into unreality, like a mirage.

The hybrid daughter, now two individuals. The one somehow confirmed by the other.

Am I mad? Dinah wondered. Or am I extricating myself from a long madness? To which state of mind did Francis belong?

'We could go,' she heard herself say slowly, 'and have a walk. I don't want to hang around there like a threat. I'm not a threat to them, you know.'

Milly regarded her, her face blanked into innocence.

'Of course not.'

The day was decided.

In the morning, Dinah was woken by knocking at her door. It was very early, the light in the room was still thick and barely touched with grey. She sat upright, disorientated, and then struggled into her robe. When she opened the door she was amazed to find Milly, fully dressed and war-painted.

'What's wrong? What's happened?'

Her previous experience of Milly's habits had led her to assume that the day wouldn't start before noon.

Milly shrugged. 'I thought we had a plan.'

'What? What time is it? It isn't light yet.'

'Quarter to eight. There's this thick fog outside. And listen.'

Dinah groped the curtains open. The sea was invisible behind a wet, colourless curtain. And from somewhere close at hand, captured and distorted by the fog so she couldn't tell from which direction, came the mournful blare of a foghorn.

'Doesn't matter,' Milly said cheerfully. 'We can still go. We'll be invisible, won't we?'

The road looked entirely different with the view of fields and sea blanked out.

Dinah drove very slowly, her eyes on the shining wet tarmac a yard ahead. The murk was regularly penetrated by the yellow blur of oncoming vehicles. Only the road signs as they swam up gave Dinah any idea how far they had come. Distance and sound were eerily distorted. Her eyes began to sting with the effort of staring at the white road markings. Beside her, Milly twiddled and station-hopped across the bands of the car radio.

'How far now?' she asked at length.

'Four or five miles, I think. The Wivenham turning should be a couple of miles ahead.'

A big dark shape loomed up behind the next pair of fog lamps and resolved itself into a high-sided cattle truck. The driver perched up in his cab was hunched forward over the wheel. He flashed his lights twice at them. There was a little line of cars crawling at his tail. Dinah pulled to one side and misjudged the distance, bumping harmlessly into the verge before righting herself.

'What was he flashing for?' she muttered, made irritable by being unable to see.

The road was empty for a moment. It swung sharply to the right and Dinah crept round the bend on the crown of the road.

At once she braked, seeing the reason for the truck-driver's warning. A blue bus was stationary on the opposite side. It must have skidded sideways, and come to rest with its nose in a shallow ditch and its tail slewed into the road. Two other cars had drawn up behind it.

There was a small group of people on the bank. One of them, a child, was sitting oddly on the wet grass. Associations beyond the automatic leap of fear at the sight of an accident pricked within Dinah for a split second before she made the identification. Then she saw the county emblem and initials on the side of the vehicle. It was Sarah's school bus.

She wrenched the wheel and drove on to the opposite verge out of the oncoming traffic. She leapt out of the car and ran across the road towards the bus.

The driver in his navy anorak was standing at the roadside. He had lifted a wheelchair from its stowage place. The chrome handles and wheels glinted dully in the mist. She saw that his face was creased but not stricken. A small crisis, not a tragedy. But Dinah whirled past him to the point where she could see the disgorged passengers.

Dinah saw Sarah's pink jacket first. She was all right. Her fin-hands were passively folded in front of her and she was looking the other way, in the direction Dinah had come from. Her shoulders were hunched.

All the six children had been swept into a huddle on the bank by a young woman in a raincoat who was holding a boy firmly by the hand.

'Don't you dare run off, Paul,' she was telling him.

Two other motorists were standing by, both men in work-men's clothes.

'Is anyone hurt?' Dinah called.

At the sound of her voice, Sarah's head slowly turned in Dinah's direction.

'No, no, we're all right,' the woman answered. 'Stuck, that's all. Isn't it, Paul? Someone's gone for help.'

The driver placed the wheelchair on to the verge and unfolded it. One of the motorists lifted the child from the grass, her legs dangling like a puppet's. Dinah absorbed rather than saw and heard all of this. Her eyes were fixed on Sarah.

Sarah's face flowered into a smile.

She ran forwards, unsteady on the wet tussocky grass.

Dinah opened her arms.

'Hel-*lo*,' Sarah crooned.

Dinah caught her, held her. A torrent of amazement and relief and delight at this unexpected gift swept through Dinah, breaking down and carrying away with it the fragile resistance of her intentions.

Sarah was here. She had run into her arms.

'Hello darling,' she whispered with her lips against the thick hair. She felt the pink plastic arm of Sarah's spectacles against her cheek.

They were isolated in the fog. There were no visible landmarks, no past or future, even. Only this instant and the ring of faces, the men and the young woman, and the uncomprehending children.

'I know Sarah, I'm a family friend. I'm on my way to Wivenham now. I'll take her back with me.'

Dinah heard her own voice. Crisp and clear and authoritative.

'We're not really supposed . . .' the woman began to remonstrate.

'No. Really. I'll take her.'

She folded Sarah's solid arm under her own.

'Come on now, Sarah. I'll take you home in my car. Mind the road going across.'

They began to walk quickly, back towards the glowing lights of Dinah's car. Sarah trotted beside her obediently.

Dinah's shoulders were stiff with the expectation of restraining hands, at the very least voices shouting after them. But there was nothing.

They reached the car. Dinah opened the nearside rear door and caught sight of Milly's startled face.

She helped Sarah into the back seat. They fumbled together to secure the seatbelt. The sight of Sarah's short clumsy fingers printed itself in Dinah's head.

She scrambled back into the driver's seat.

'Right. Off we go.'

The car bumped off the verge and back into the road. As she accelerated, Dinah saw in the mirror the tableau of bus and passengers diminish and then disappear. No one was pursuing her. Billows of fog swam between them, and they were gone.

The whole episode had lasted no more than three or four minutes.

'Well,' Milly said. She shifted round in her seat and held out her hand. 'Hi, Sarah. I'm Milly.'

Sarah grasped the hand, turning it over to gaze in fascination at the black-varnished nails. Grinning hugely, she uttered a stream of excited syllables in which the word *bus* figured two or three times.

Milly nodded sympathetically. 'Yeah. Bit of a drama for a boring old Wednesday morning, I'd say. Better than finger-painting or whatever else you'd have been doing, isn't it?'

'Painting. Nice.'

'Right. Painting's okay.'

The fog seemed thicker than ever.

They were utterly isolated in the small security of the car. Dinah only half heard Milly chatting easily to Sarah. The shiny road unwound a yard at a time. She drove as if mesmerised.

'Hey,' Milly said.

Then she repeated it. 'Hey, Dinah?'

'What?'

Dinah's voice no longer sounded authoritative in her own ears. It was cracked and muffled.

'That was the turning. I saw the signpost. You missed it.'

'I know.'

It had been easy. The blood sang deafeningly in Dinah's head. She drove stiff-armed, eyes fixed forward. There was a long, long pause.

'We're not going to Wivenham, Dinah, are we?' Milly said wonderingly.

'No.'

'Where are we going?'

'Dyah,' Sarah called, clapping her hands together. 'Dyah.'

In Dinah's mind there was the map of Norfolk. She saw the road they were on curling westwards and then south beside the great scoured space of the Wash to King's Lynn. And then still south beyond that, to Ely, Cambridge, London.

'Away from here,' Dinah said in the same shocked voice. The words came out without any predetermination.

Milly rocked back in the passenger seat. She pushed her coils of hair away over her shoulder and then laughed uncertainly.

'Shit. It's a fucking kidnap.'

She was admiring, and more than a little awed.

Thirteen

'When did you decide to do this?' Milly asked.

'I didn't decide. I just did it.'

They were sitting, the three of them, in a Little Chef on the fenland road south of King's Lynn. To Dinah's wild eyes these banal surroundings of plastic cruets and tables and gingham checked curtains were utterly surreal.

When the waitress brought their order Sarah carefully fitted her mouth over the straw in her glass of Coca-cola and noisily blew. Air erupted between the ice cubes and she glanced up, soft-faced and blinking, as if anticipating a rebuke. Dinah understood that Pauline would tick her off for making rude noises through a straw.

She smiled at her instead. 'Is that good?' she asked, too eagerly. Sarah's round eyes grew opaque behind her thick lenses. Dinah couldn't read her expression. She didn't know how to talk to her. Yet in the welter of Dinah's confusion her child seemed the only fixed landmark. Dinah was amazed by the solidity of her presence. The ribbed pink cuff of her jacket, the dimpled backs of her pale knuckles, the shiny dribbles of Coke at the corners of her mouth, all seemed to glow with a kind of hyper-reality. Her rounded bulk and her knobbed features were already acquiring the patina of loved familiarity.

Everything else, the restaurant and the road and even Milly, seemed as insubstantial as the fog.

Dinah's coffee cup clattered in its saucer.

She looked down at her hands and saw that they were shaking.

They couldn't turn back now; that much was clear. Already, in the short distance they had driven, she seemed to have put a great gulf between Sarah and herself and Wivenham.

Pauline would be waiting in Church Walk. Dinah found that she could make the unwelcome imaginative leap all too easily; as if she had somehow become Pauline, she could follow the sequence of her feelings through the beginning of disquiet to anxiety to the full flowering of fear and anger.

The bus driver and attendant would describe Dinah, of course. Pauline would know who had taken Sarah. She would know by now, this minute. Perhaps in turn she could imagine the sequence of Dinah's actions. Longing, exultation, awed realisation.

I don't know what right you think you have, after I've done everything for her. That's what Pauline had said. Only Dinah didn't think she had any rights. What she wanted she would have to take by stealth or force.

What have I done?

Dinah said to Milly, 'I saw the turning and I didn't take it.'

She shook her head, remembering how her arms and neck and shoulders had gone rigid with the force of her intention.

'I didn't know it was going to happen. I promise you.' She laughed, shakily, the note cracking.

Milly grinned, but there was a new wary expression in her eyes.

'Are you scared?'

'Yes. As though I don't know myself any more.'

I wish Matt were here, she thought. And then chided herself for the wish. What she had done was her responsibility alone.

'It's safe by me, anyway. You're her mother, aren't you?'

Sarah stopped blowing down her straw.

289

'Mum,' she said. With a stubby forefinger she pushed her glasses back up the puttyish ridge of her nose. She scanned the empty tables around them, and peered at the teenage waitresses lounging by the till. Ominously, her mouth seemed to change shape.

Dinah and Milly glanced a warning at each other.

Quickly, Dinah took Sarah's hand and rubbed it between her own. She was reminded so much of Jack and Merlin when they were smaller. Sarah shuffled closer to her on the bench seat.

'So. What d'you fancy doing?' Milly leaned towards her and Sarah's face immediately lightened. She took her hand from Dinah's and patted Milly's dreadlocks.

'Ride,' Sarah said. 'In the car.'

'Hey. Good idea. And I tell you what. We could even make it a ride all the way to London.'

'London!'

Sarah's shout made the waitresses turn round. She stuck her tongue between her teeth and looked sheepish again.

'Yeah. Thought you'd like that idea.' And to Dinah Milly murmured, 'It's obvious, isn't it? We can't stick around here or they'll find us, and London'll swallow us up like a can of Special Brew. Specially where I'm thinking of going.'

'Wait . . .'

Milly roughly shook her arm. 'No, we can't wait. What's the matter? It's done, isn't it? You've got her. It's like we're on the run.'

Crazily, Dinah thought she could already hear the sirens. Pursuing feet running at her back. Behind them lay Wivenham and Cromer with a hotel room containing a few clothes. She had a car and her purse full of credit cards and the road to London.

Only of course it was Matthew's money. She had nothing of her own . . .

She stared back at Milly. 'You're right.'

'So, where to?'

'I don't know. A hotel, maybe. One of those places down the Cromwell Road.'

'You're being dumb, Dinah. We can't take her to any place like that. They'll know she's missing and people will be watching for her. In hotels and airports, everywhere.'

'They know I don't have her passport,' Dinah said, as if this pedantry would help her to maintain a fingerhold on reality. But Milly was right. She had a queasy vision of receptionists and waiters peering at Sarah and whispering about her connection to '*snatched Down's Teenager*'. Where could they go, then? To friends? Back to Sheldon? To Eleanor?

Childish longing for her mother quivered within Dinah. If she could just reverse their roles again, be a child and be forgiven. Could she take Sarah to her grandmother, to a safe place?

The bungalow in Eastbourne and the beginning of this quest seemed remote in place and time. Be careful, Eleanor had warned her, before Christmas. I'm afraid of whatever pain this might cause.

No. Eleanor would say that she must return Sarah to Pauline. Nor could Dinah ask anyone else to take even partial responsibility for what she had done. All her connections to the outside world were fraying. She felt naked, dizzy, exposed. But she also wanted to keep Sarah. Longing for it was like a birth-pain, twisting inside her until it stopped her breath. Dinah gasped and tried to blink back the tears in her eyes.

'Well?' Milly coldly persisted.

'I don't know, I can't think.'

'Listen. We can go to Camden Town. To Caz's place. He'll let us stay there.'

'Will he?' Dinah was uncertain, but part of her seized giddily on the suggestion. It was a solution where no other presented itself.

'Yeah. No problem.'

'All right. All right then, that's what we'll do.'

They began to laugh, although Dinah's laughter contained the same cracked rising note that had made Milly look hard at her. Sarah obligingly joined in, her eyes shiny and opaque behind her glasses.

They ran across the car park, one on either side of Sarah, with their hands linked as if she were a toddler and they could swing her through the air in an exultant somersault.

On the road they sang. Milly stabbed at the buttons of the radio to find music and Sarah sat in the back and clapped her hands. She followed the beat with evident pleasure.

And as they drove, the fog lifted.

One minute there was the same dense cloud rolling over the car and then it thinned, and the light turned lemon yellow and opened up in front of them as if offering some ethereal highway. A second later there was a glimpse of fields and pylons veiled in a summer morning's thin mist, and then even that was gone. There was an ice-blue sky and hedges and sparse traffic, and a view all the way south towards Cambridge.

Sarah grew drowsy. Watching her in the driver's mirror, Dinah saw her round eyelids droop and her mouth fall wider open.

I'll care for you, she silently promised. *I will learn how. I can do that, can't I?*

But when they reached London, Sarah revived again. She pressed her face against the back window and shouted out at the sight of shops and queues of red buses and, when they reached Camden, at a man dressed in a top hat and Union Jack waistcoat riding a unicycle.

'Funny man,' she called. 'Hel-*lo.*'

'Wacky city,' Milly smiled at her.

Milly gave Dinah surprisingly cogent directions through the one-way systems and clogged streets. Their goal was in the hinterland between Camden and Chalk Farm, down at the far end of a sooty street above the main lines sweeping out of Euston. There was a tall gaunt building in shiny red brick, once a small block of mansion flats.

'This is it,' Milly pointed.

On the steps outside there were two boys sitting smoking, a heap of collapsing cardboard boxes, part of a bicycle and a thin black dog tied to the railings with a piece of string. A refrigerator with a television set crookedly balanced on top rested at the foot of the steps. The pavement was littered with tinfoil take-away cartons and scraps of food and more boxes.

'Here?' Dinah wondered.

Milly leapt out of the car. She kicked a food carton aside, walking in a wide circle around the mangy dog, and crossed to the steps. One of the boys ignored her but the other looked up and crazily grinned. His face was grey with dirt. Milly disappeared into the mansions. Dinah understood that she and Sarah were to wait in the car.

She peered upwards at the grimed windows. Over the arch of the door in blackened art nouveau lettering were the words *Fortinbras Mansions.*

Two or three minutes passed before Milly reappeared and beckoned.

'Let's go and see what there is, shall we?' Dinah said to Sarah. She locked the car very carefully behind them.

'Hey,' called the boy with the grin. 'I'll watch yer nice car for yer. Only cost yer a quid.'

'It's safe as it is, thank you.'

'Suit yerself,' he answered equably.

'C'mon,' Milly ordered. 'Caz is waiting.'

They followed her into Fortinbras Mansions. There was an unpleasantly distinctive smell made up of smoke and rotting vegetable matter and curry. The floor of the hallway was piled with more boxes and bulging rubbish bags and the spaces in between were silted over with circulars and flyers and newspaper freesheets. The stairs were bare with some of the boards missing, but the massive Victorian, turned mahogany newel posts were still in place. On the wall some-

293

one had spray-painted the words 'The air is free – for now'. There was much more graffiti, mostly elaborate tags and initials.

'Up here,' Milly ordered. They climbed the stairs in her wake. As they ascended the mess diminished. The top-floor landing was bare but clean.

A door stood open. The smell here was of burning joss. Dinah saw draped Indian-print bedspreads and dingy cushions and bulbs dimmed with handkerchief shades.

Caz was standing in the middle of his domain. He was a young black man of about twenty dressed in army surplus trousers and a greasy waistcoat. He had hair exactly like Milly's – or, as Dinah realised with a flash of comprehension, Milly had hair exactly like his. He put his arm round Milly and Milly came closer to blushing with pleasure than Dinah would ever have thought possible.

'These your mates, are they?'

'Yeah, Dinah and Sarah.'

Caz coolly examined them. He was naturally authoritative, and Dinah could also see that he was extremely good-looking. His glance flicked over Dinah's bag and jacket, and then slid to Sarah.

'They're all right,' Caz pronounced. 'You can all stop here if you want.'

Dinah could see through the connecting doors that the top-floor apartment was large. The rooms were shabby and cluttered with makeshift furniture, but the place looked ordinary enough, rather like a neglected student flat. It was the downstairs part that was disconcerting.

'Is this a squat?' Dinah asked. She heard Milly's indrawn breath at her audacity in cross-examining Caz. He grinned amiably enough.

'Nah, I pay rent for it, fair and square. Well, I've got a deal on it. I run a couple of stalls in the market, and the landlord knows me. Go on. You can have that room across the passage there.'

Dinah turned, eager to shepherd the girls away.

'Wait up. Twenty should see it right for the electric and that.'

Dinah took her purse out of her bag and handed him a twenty-pound note.

'Great,' Milly said. 'Thanks Caz.'

He winked at her.

The walls and floor of the room were bare and the windows uncurtained. There were two mattresses pushed together against one wall and an armchair disintegrating in a corner.

'This isn't very nice, is it?' Dinah whispered.

Milly turned on her. 'For fuck's sake, what do you *want*? It's dry, it's safe, there's light and hot water. Caz is all right, he's a good bloke. I used to come here when I bunked off school. The filth don't come in, no one'll ask us any questions. We can go out and buy all the stuff we need to fix it up, can't we? Look, I'll go if you want. You can stay here.'

Dinah shivered. But where else could they go? It was frightening to realise how easy it was to fall through the net of ordinary life, taking Sarah with her. In a matter of hours they had become displaced people.

'No, I'll do it.' Matt's money, Matt's credit cards. Where had her independence gone? Swallowed up by the slow years of guilt, was that it?

She added with a firmness that she did not feel, 'I'll get food and some clean things to lie on. Stay here and look after Sarah.'

'You sure?' Milly was examining her again, doubtfully, as if needing to be convinced of Dinah's capability.

'Yes. Why not?'

As she went out, Dinah checked the rooms separating theirs from Caz's. She found a kitchen and a bathroom, decrepit but not insanitary.

Leaving the car behind she walked to Inverness Street market, to Marks & Spencer, and the old-fashioned bed-linen shop in Parkway. She felt shapeless, disconnected from the throngs of other shoppers, like a bag-lady, more than a little crazy. She wondered how long it might be before she started shouting at passers-by.

At the top of the street Dinah passed a public telephone. She hesitated beside it. Matt would worry about where she had gone; his anxiety would transmit itself to the boys. Fourteen digits would connect her to him at the lab.

But she could not talk to him. He would be angry, shocked by what she had done. Like Eleanor, he would insist that Sarah be taken back home. Dinah realised that by holding on to her she put everyone else she knew, everyone except Milly and Sarah herself, in the enemy camp. Yet still, with her fierce and distorted logic, she clung to the one certainty in her mind. She wanted to keep Sarah.

Dinah blinked at her watch, trying to make sense of the time difference. Then she fed money into the slot and lifted the receiver anyway. She dialled the number of the house on Kendrick and heard what she wanted, Matt's steady voice on the answering machine. She left a message. She was quite all right, tell the boys. She was with Sarah and Milly. She was sorry about everything. Her voice trailed away because she couldn't think what else to say to him. There were two or three seconds while she stared at the smeared glass enclosing the payphone, and then she hung up.

The receiver was still in her hand. Dinah reached into her bag and took out her address book, bound in navy-blue soft leather, a present from Matt. She looked up Lavinia Jackson's office number. She had promised Milly and this connection would have to be made now, at once, before the news of the kidnapping became public. She fixed on the importance of it with overblown determination, knowing all the time with part of her mind that she was losing reason and sense of proportion.

But Lavinia was pleased to hear from her. Yes, it had been far too long. They must have lunch. And she listened attentively while Dinah volubly explained about Milly. Yes, she understood the problem. Yes, she would see Milly tomorrow evening, at her flat in Wigmore Street. Just across the park from Fortinbras Mansions.

Dinah was grateful for the other woman's crispness. She felt herself to be so far and so finally out of control. When she hung up again she was shaking so much that she dropped her bag and the contents spilled on the ground. As she scooped them up again she was possessed by a terrible wave of fear for Sarah. She had brought her to this place, and left her. What wickedness was she capable of?

She gathered up her shopping and ran, wildly threading her way through the crowds. She ran until she was sobbing for breath and pulled over almost double by the pain in her side. Empty taxis cruised past her, but it never occurred to her to hail one. Cabs were not for criminals and fugitives.

At last she reached Fortinbras Mansions. It all looked exactly the same, even down to the dog and the two boys sitting on the steps. They eyed her armfuls of purchases but Dinah hurried straight past them and ran up the stairs. Loud hard music throbbing with bass came from behind Caz's closed door.

To her great relief, Sarah was sitting passively on one of the mattresses. Dinah let go her armfuls of shopping and dropped to her knees in front of her. She kissed her and stroked her hair, unwillingly recognising that Sarah's stillness did not indicate calm, but the opposite. Her child was bewildered and uncomprehending, and Dinah could not make anything better for her except by taking her back to Pauline. A window of pain opened inside Dinah, letting in the light of logic that she had denied.

'Everything is all right,' Dinah whispered, uselessly.

With stubborn hope and apprehension hammering together in her head, Dinah told herself that she and Milly and Sarah would be warm and fed tonight, and somehow she would find a way to take care of tomorrow. In the kitchen she made the girls a simple meal, soup and sandwiches, and gently helped Sarah to eat.

*

Fortinbras Mansions changed with the coming of darkness. Caz's place filled up with people and the same thumping music, growing ever louder. The newcomers drifted up the stairs, huddling in from the cold outside. They were almost all very young, although there were one or two men of indeterminate age. They sat on the floor with their cans of beer and roll-ups, or drifted into the various rooms, even into Dinah's. Dinah made an ineffectual attempt to bar the first ones, but soon understood that she had no territorial rights in this kingdom.

'Wha' d'you mean, is it like this every night?' Milly demanded. Her face seemed to have contracted and her eyes widened. Dinah wondered exactly what it was she had taken. 'It's just a party. I know these people, right? I'm glad to see them.'

Sarah had brightened up, in her unpredictable way. She sat in the kitchen, eyes and mouth wide open, watching the shifts of scene. Dinah wanted to intercept her gaze, selfishly to divert all her attention to herself, but she was forced to recognise that she couldn't. Sarah was more interested in Milly, more responsive to swaggering Caz.

So Dinah watched with Sarah. There were so many shaven or matted heads, pairs of boots and tattoos and rings in ears and noses, so many outfits and attitudes. Milly did seem to know many of these people. They greeted each other laconically, without expectation. There were a dozen near-Millys of all sexes, some of them no older than Milly herself, and in each of them Dinah saw Milly's aggression and hesitancy exaggerated. It heightened Dinah's sense of alienation to recognise that here Milly's appearance and behaviour were the norm, and her own remarkable. She felt old, and odd, and afraid.

But she also understood that on this little island of Fortinbras Mansions, in the middle of the hostile city's decay, almost nothing was too bizarre to attract attention. Certainly not an odd trio of fugitive women, whoever they were and wherever they might be heading.

298

Fortinbras Mansions, threatening as it seemed, was also their place of safety.

Dinah found herself suddenly laughing at this peculiarity. Every perspective had changed, snapping reason at the roots and leaving her exposed and unsecured.

Out of the thick of the noise Milly herself came by, following Caz. She almost clutched the hem of his waistcoat. Caz sat down next to Dinah and Milly perched at the other side, grinning disjointedly at Sarah.

'Here,' Caz said. He passed Dinah a short, squat bottle of cider and she drank from it, not wanting to refuse.

'She yours?' he asked, nodding at Sarah.

'Yes.'

'Right. What you really doin' here?' He was looking at her, calculating dark eyes, the whites bloodshot. She felt the precariousness of him, his tight and delicate balance between friendliness and aggression.

'Just passing through,' Dinah answered.

'Yeah. *Hey.*' Suddenly he leaned across her. Her muscles seized and the hairs of her neck icily prickled in response. Only she saw that he was smiling. 'Babe. Want to dance with me?'

He was talking to Sarah.

'Dance,' Sarah answered thickly. She glanced uncertainly at Dinah and then she wagged her head with the slow dawn of pleasure. 'Dance.'

'C'mon, then.'

Caz helped her to her feet. She lumbered after him into the dead centre of the room. Half a dozen people had already begun dancing. One of them was the silent boy from the front steps with his dog still on its string, and another was a broken old dosser who swayed and chuckled with his bottle of Newcastle Brown held clamped so as not to spill a drop. They cleared a respectful space for Caz. Caz lifted his arms in the air above his head and rhythmically twisted his body. Milly's eyes followed his every movement, and after a little while so did Sarah's. She copied him, and the swing of his hips and the way his wide shoulders turned and hunched and the curve of his dark fingers in the smoky air.

Soon, after a minute or two, everyone was dancing. The room filled up and the scrappy furniture was kicked aside.

The music was thick, as pungent and inescapable as the smoke, penetrating Dinah's lungs and brain and body. She let the crowd edge her aside and then absorb her, so that she was dancing too.

In the middle of the room, a yard away, she could see Sarah.

Sarah was dancing with all the others. Her arms waved and her hips swayed. She would never look or be like any of these fierce, independent child-adults. She would never be able to fend for herself as they did. Nor would she ever have to sleep in a doorway with only a mongrel dog to protect her. She had had Pauline and Malcolm, safe in the quiet village beside the sea. That was what Dinah had snatched her away from.

But for now, she was dancing too. She was one of them tonight.

Dinah had done that, also.

Dinah saw her face. It was radiant, transfigured with happiness. She looked as she had done at her sister's wedding. Complete.

The noise went on and on. Quite soon Dinah developed a crushing headache. Milly had vanished, in Caz's wake.

Sarah danced on for a while, seeming not to notice when Caz turned away from her. But she was soon tired. Her shoulders slumped and she edged to the corner of the room. She looked round at the looming faces with dawning anxiety but when she found Dinah her eyes did not fix on her. Her clasped hands made a small, pale knot under the shelf of her jersey and her head turned from side to side. She was blinking behind her glasses and the soft triangle of her lower lip stuck out.

Dinah took her arm.

'Let's sit down and have a rest.'

300

Sarah seemed not to recognise her. She pulled away.

'Where's my *mum*?'

'Your mum's fine. You're in London, with me and Milly.'

'Milly . . .'

Sarah's hands made a little stroking, patting shape.

'Let's have a little rest. It's been an exciting day.' Dinah guided her to the mattresses in their room. The grinning boy from outside stood over them for a second.

'You sorted?' he murmured, winking.

'Just leave us alone,' Dinah snapped.

In the passage outside, the silent boy took one match after another from a box. He struck one and watched it flare, then blew it out with a long controlled exhalation and dropped it on the floor before striking the next. His friend pulled at his shoulder and they went away together.

Dinah closed the door and spread new blankets on the mattresses. She wedged their few belongings and her purse behind the mattress, at the corner farthest from the door. She poured Sarah a drink of juice from the supplies she had brought back and then settled her under the covers.

Sarah took off her glasses, carefully folding them and patting their place with alert fingers to make sure that they were safe. Exactly as Jack did.

Dinah's eyes burned with the sudden rush of helpless tears. Turning her head away, she switched off the overhead bulb and the room subsided into shadows licked by the orangey light of the street lamp outside the window. The darkness was filled with the creaks and rustles of an unfamiliar place. The music had subsided to a mere bass vibration, sensed rather than heard.

Sarah sighed and snuffled a little. Very carefully, Dinah lay down next to her.

'Mum,' Sarah said forlornly.

'I know. I know.'

Dinah reached out in the cover of the darkness and found her hand. She had wanted to say, *I'm here*. But her presence was no reassurance.

She could not usurp another woman's place.

She fended off the realisation for a moment, trying to obscure it with memories of her first pregnancy, and Sarah's birth, and the days after it in the hospital. It was like sticking little coloured fragments of gummed paper to the larger outline of a picture. Jack or Merlin had been given something similar, a long time ago. But the coloured pieces were too small, and the picture too large and complicated.

Pauline was Sarah's mother. It was wrong that they were here. Everything was wrong and she had been too blind and too needy to understand how it would be.

Dinah could not trust herself to say anything. Not to Sarah; her birth child who was also unknowable, unconnected as they were by history or language. That was the link in the chain, stretching from Sarah's conception to this moment, that Dinah had fatally allowed herself to overlook. She warmed the hand instead, uselessly and fervently caressing the short, thick fingers between her own.

Sarah fell asleep almost at once. Dinah knew she must be exhausted. Soon, she dozed herself.

She didn't know how much later it was when she woke again. The orange-patinated darkness seemed thicker, but she could just distinguish that the door was slowly opening. She stiffened, ready to jump, and then recognised the shape of Milly. Even in the dark, hurt and defiance were plain in every contour of her. Poor Milly, Dinah thought. Rejected by her hero. But Milly was no longer a little girl; no longer even quite the needy daughter Dinah had interpreted. She was closer to adulthood, more nearly a woman than Dinah had allowed.

And *I* worried about *her*, Dinah thought in bewilderment.

Milly had become the responsible adult, able to make her own choices and distinctions, and Dinah was the unpredictable child.

All the pillars of Dinah's strength and rationality, all the supports that she had erected to hold herself up in the world that somewhere, elsewhere, also contained Sarah, were softly and terribly crumbling away.

Milly found the far edge of the mattress. She sat down and unlaced her heavy boots. When they were off she sat for a moment or two with her arms wrapped around her knees, her head resting on them. Dinah kept still, trying to breathe evenly. She could hear that Milly was crying. And Milly would not welcome her eavesdropping.

Then, with a sharp sniff, Milly sat upright. Dinah heard the soft crinkle of her coils of hair as she shook her head, and felt around gingerly to define her own area of mattress. And finally she stretched herself out, pulling up the blanket that Dinah had left for her.

It was later again when Dinah woke once more. The russet blackness had begun to fade into dirty grey, although it was still night.

The blankets were twisted, but they held the soft warmth of sleep. Dinah listened for music and the dull cadences of unfamiliar voices, but there was nothing. Very gently, the woolly nap of the blankets scraping her knuckles, she reached out to either side of her. Her fingertips found wrinkled clothes, heated and musky, and the solid resistance of sleeping bodies.

She listened harder, and now she could hear them both breathing.

Dinah lay on her back, looking upwards into the arcs of unfamiliar space. The smooth breaths continued, sweetly antiphonal.

Tenderness and calm descended on her. For that moment, Dinah knew neither guilt nor regret. She simply listened to her daughter sleeping. Her mouth widened into a smile, and tears ran out of her blinded eyes and soaked through her hair into the shared blanket.

In Franklin, after the boys were asleep, Matt played and replayed Dinah's message on the answering machine. He listened, as if he could tease some further meaning out of the words and then punched the button to hear them again, over and over.

He had never heard Dinah sound like this.

She was all right. Tell the boys. She was with Sarah and Milly. She was sorry about everything. And then a yawning silence was cut short by the click of the receiver being replaced. It was the silence that frightened him.

Matthew sat with his head in his hands. She was not at the hotel. They had not seen her since the early morning.

I'm sorry about everything. Where was she, and what did she need?

Something was badly wrong. He felt his limbs twitching. His impulses dictated that he should jump, run, do something to find her, when all he could rationally do was sit and wait. The minutes stretched into silence as he sat beside the telephone.

Dinah was woken finally by Sarah. She was crawling away from the mattresses, dragging the covers with her. All that was visible of Milly was a knot of hair and a hump of blanket. It was properly light now.

Sarah crouched in the middle of the floor. All the round contours of her face drew into crimson knots and then she opened her mouth and began to howl. Her fists clenched and then drummed on the floor.

'Mum, Mummummum*mum.*'

Dinah leapt to her. Sarah swiped her away with one blow of the arm.

'Mum', she screamed. 'Nowowowow.'

'It's all right. Sarah, Sarah, hush now. You're with me and Milly, don't you remember?'

The heap of Milly stirred and groaned. 'Shit.'

Sarah's whole body was rigid. She roared and beat her fists and tears of frustration ran down her face.

'Shut up,' Milly shouted at her. Dinah tried to take hold of the stiff body and soothe it with hugging and patting, but she might as well have been a fly on an elephant's hide. Sarah

304

would not be calmed. She wrenched herself from side to side in Dinah's grasp as though she wanted to throw herself somewhere. The force of her fury was unstoppable.

Dinah had no idea how to deal with her. When Jack and Merlin had had tantrums as little children she had always been able to break through to them with calm reasoning. But Sarah was different. Her difference was suddenly apparent as if it had hardly been noticeable before. The screaming went on, rising in volume.

Milly scrambled out of the bed. She knelt on the floor in front of Sarah. She didn't say anything, simply knelt and waited.

Sarah's head wagged from side to side, and then gradually stilled. Her body shuddered with huge sobs. Swollen-faced she gaped at Milly.

'Hi,' Milly said quietly. Sarah snatched at her hand. She looked down at it, and found the crude tattooed flower. Suddenly, extraordinarily, her face crumpled again, this time into a smile. She rubbed at the flower with her thumb.

Milly asked, 'Do you want something to eat? Are you hungry?'

Sarah nodded, sniffing. Damning herself for her own lack of initiative, Dinah hurried to the place where she had hidden yesterday's shopping. But everything had gone. Her handbag had gone too, with her purse in it. The money, Matt's money, and credit cards. There was nothing left.

Dinah felt herself falling. Through the net, into nowhere.

'It's all right.' Scared-faced, Milly held on to her. 'It doesn't matter, look, I've got all these dollars of Ed's, hundreds.' Streetwise Milly, with the bills zipped in a belt under her clothes. 'Let's go and get food in the cafe by the market.'

There was a tourists' currency exchange opposite the tube station. The street outside was littered with vegetable stalks and cardboard boxes and fruit wrappings, reminding Dinah of the old flat over the greengrocer's.

The cafe was half-full, with a mixture of market traders

and single men who sat alone, smoking over single mugs of tea. Dinah and Sarah huddled in a corner by the window until Milly came back with the rest of Ed's dollars changed into sterling. 'More than three hundred quid,' Milly whispered.

Sarah hungrily ate a bacon sandwich and Milly gnawed at a piece of toast. Dinah drank tea. As they had come in she had caught sight of the three of them reflected in the steamy mirrored wall behind the counter. They were dirty and grey and weary-looking, as if they had slept rough. As they more or less had done, Dinah thought. Because of her.

There was a smell of fried food and cigarette smoke. Thin sunlight struggled through the plate glass and warmed them, glinting on cutlery and strips of chrome. The man at the next table was reading the *Sun*. Dinah tilted her head to see the front page. Something to do with Diana. Nothing about a kidnap. Not yet, of course. But how long would it be? Already, she was certain, there would be police and questions and descriptions inexorably reaching after them.

Milly finished her toast. She rested her chin in her hands and looked across at Dinah. Sarah chewed and stared expressionlessly out into the street.

I know, Dinah thought.

'What are you going to do?' Milly asked.

Without money, except what Milly had stolen from Ed Parkes, without any ally except Milly, without even the anchoring thread of her own sane judgement, Dinah wildly considered the old question again. Only now, out of some recess of clarity locked in her brain, she did know the answer.

She said slowly, 'I'm going to take her back home.'

Sarah's head turned. 'Mum.'

Dinah smiled, the artificially bright and inarticulate smile that she had developed for Sarah, and wanted to strike from her own face. 'That's right. Back to your mum.'

Only, Dinah thought frantically, only I want to have today. If I can just have today with her, knowing that is just and all it is, a single day free together.

After that, I'll take her back to Pauline. Where she belongs.

She waited an instant and felt the expected clutch of pain. But it was different now, the dull and featureless ache of inevitability instead of the roughness of longing.

'Yeah.' Milly nodded her approval, like a mother to an obedient child. 'Yeah, I s'pose that's right. When?'

Dinah stared down hard at the chipped surface of the table. She could see other pictures framed in it but she refused to let her mind's eye linger on them.

'Tomorrow,' Dinah said. 'And we must also call Ed and Sandra and tell them where you are. I suppose they'll be in Hampstead by now, won't they?'

It was a mark of her disorientation that she could no longer properly work out time differences or easily reckon how many hours had elapsed since the fog and the road to Wivenham.

'I guess,' Milly said. She looked coolly at Dinah from under her black eye make-up. She had no need to accept Dinah's strictures now.

Dinah was thinking, I will just have today. A single day can't be too much to ask.

The swimming pool was Sarah's idea. When they had finished their breakfast Milly asked her what else she liked doing, apart from painting and dancing. Sarah's face split into one of her sudden smiles.

'I like swimming,' she said distinctly.

They went to Marks & Spencer and exchanged some more of Ed's money for three swimsuits.

The pool was new, the pride of the borough leisure services. There were sloping beaches of yellow-painted concrete, fountains and plastic palm trees and giant slides, and a wave machine that sent breakers crashing on the beaches for ten minutes out of every thirty. The temperature under the huge glass roof was tropical. There were also scalding hot showers that restored the three of them to the same pink scrubbed state as all the other swimmers.

Sarah ran into the breakers in the red and white swimsuit she had chosen for herself. She lay down in the shallows amongst the splashing toddlers, spreading herself like a starfish and letting the waves break over the dome of her stomach. Dinah followed, hovering as anxiously as any of the other mothers. Droplets of bright water beaded the smooth white skin of Sarah's shoulders and thighs. Without the focus of her glasses she blinked up at the blue-grey dome of insulated sky above her head.

The echoing shouts and slapping water and the chemical-scented heat intensified for Dinah her sense of other-worldliness. She was taking her daughter swimming. They were clean and warm, and enclosed within a make-believe tropical paradise. One unreality permitted all the others, for now.

The wave machine was switched off and the water slowly subsided. Surprised, Sarah stood up and launched herself forwards, churning through diamond-sparkling arcs of spray. Then she fell with her arms outstretched and Dinah's breath stopped in fear until she saw that Sarah was swimming. She turned and rolled. In the water, all her ungainliness was gone. She was sleek and solid, as confident and splendid as some big sea mammal.

Dinah and Milly swam alongside her. Milly's hair soaked into thin black tails and Sarah laughed and pulled at them.

'You're a beautiful swimmer,' Dinah called to Sarah. Pride swelled inside her and with it a reluctant, envious admiration of Pauline. Pauline had taught her to swim, and how much else that she couldn't even guess at?

Pauline was suddenly there, within the envelope of their tropical haven. Dinah could see her carefully protected hair, her ironbound bathing suit. Pauline would always be there. How could she have imagined that she would not be?

'Lovely,' Sarah crowed. 'Lovely lovely.'

In the deepest water at the centre of the pool there was an island crowned with a single palm tree. They reached it and triumphantly climbed the steps. There was just room for the three of them to perch on a yellow ledge with their feet hanging in the water. Dinah sat in the middle, with one arm around each girl. Milly's shoulders were rigid and bony, Sarah's meaty and slick with water.

'Castaways,' Dinah said.

Matthew was woken by the telephone. He lifted himself on one elbow and tried to focus on the bedside clock. Six a.m.

A man's voice at the other end, British, with a regional accent, identified itself as a policeman, a DS somebody. He was sorry to be calling so early.

Matthew sat up, fear jerking him fully awake.

'What is it? What's happened?'

The policeman explained. A missing teenager. A woman matching Mrs Steward's description. Yesterday morning. Did Mr Steward have any idea of his wife's whereabouts?

Matt understood at once. While he sat upright with the early-morning cold on his naked shoulders he remembered a hospital corridor, and himself half running, with the white bundle of a baby held close in his arms. Had he been running towards something, or away from it? He knew what Dinah had done. A cold arrow of dismay pierced him. He was dismayed not by Dinah, but that he had not been there with her.

Dinah had had or was having a nervous breakdown. How could his attention have been so occupied with insulin and Kathrin Pang and his own concerns that he had failed to understand?

She needs me now, he thought. And realised in the same instant that he had not been with her for so long, and that his absence had hardened and solidified into a block between them.

'No,' he mumbled to the policeman. 'I haven't spoken to her since, since Tuesday evening. Yes, she was at her hotel in Cromer then. A young friend of ours had just arrived to join her.'

Be careful, he warned himself.

A powerful determination took hold of him. It was Dinah and himself against the rest, the police, whoever they might be. Dinah had taken Sarah because she could not help herself. He knew it as clearly as he knew anything, and he understood that every separate step they had taken since the birth had led them irrevocably to this moment.

'I will,' he promised the policeman. He took a notepad from the bedside table and wrote down an Ipswich number. 'As soon as I hear anything.'

After the swimming, Milly suddenly lost patience. She flung on her clothes much quicker than Dinah could help Sarah and dress herself.

'See you,' she muttered at the doorway of the changing cubicle.

'Where are you going?'

Dinah didn't want to be left; the three of them should stick together. She wasn't sure what direction she might take without Milly.

'Nowhere. Just, you know.'

'Wait . . .'

Milly was already sidling away.

'You've got to see Lavinia, you asked me to arrange it . . .'

In her own ears she sounded childish, accusatory.

'Yeah. No problem. I'll be there, right? Here, look, take this.'

She thrust some money at Dinah, and wretchedly Dinah took it. Milly went. Sarah was sitting on a slatted bench holding her soaking wet socks. They had fallen on the floor.

'Just you and me for now,' Dinah said brightly to her. She squeezed as much water as she could out of the socks and rolled them on to Sarah's broad feet. Sarah sat uncomplainingly, her lower lip stuck out.

They ate a hamburger lunch in the swimming pool cafeteria.

Outside, the London afternoon was murky. It was not quite

raining but the pavements and taxis and shopfronts sweated a shiny film of cold moisture. Dinah stood holding Sarah's hand under the canopy of the pool entrance.

'Shall we have another ride in the car?'

Sarah nodded without enthusiasm.

It was not far away. The street was almost exactly the same as Dinah remembered it. Some of the brick façades had acquired cladding of pebbledash or fake stone, others had sprouted porches or new bay fronts or Regency-style doors. But there was the same line of tiny front gardens insulated from the street by low walls and scratchy shrubs, the same sloping skyline running towards the looming height of the football stadium. She drove to the end, where Matt and she had lived.

There was the house.

The front door was the same colour, pillar-box red, but faded under the street dust. There were window boxes on the lower window-sills, unwatered and neglected. Brown stalks curled and shrivelled. The curtains of the bedroom overlooking the street were drawn, revealing torn linings.

Dinah switched off the engine. In the quiet that followed she heard Sarah breathing through her mouth, mucus in her throat catching with each inhalation.

'Are you cold?' Dinah asked softly.

Sarah shook her head. She seemed to be retreating, moving even further from Dinah and into some place of safety within herself. The happiness of the swimming session had evaporated. She had not spoken since they were eating their hamburgers.

'Let's get out and walk a little way.'

With hands linked they moved slowly away from the car. Dinah looked up at the closed windows of the house. She wanted to show Sarah: here, this is part of your history. Up in that room in our bed you were conceived. You are a part of us, each of those living cells within you, and each of the forty-seven chromosomes within those cells. Which make you what you are.

After you were born I came back here to the four walls and curtains and the same view, without you. I gave you to Pauline. It is what *I* did. And consigned myself to a waste of guilt. And you to all that you know, and love, and have benefited from.

I know I must take you home.

As they walked slowly, hand in hand, Dinah was visited by a sense of the formless vastness of the world. She imagined that she could see the seething cells of life itself, the hectic and ceaseless dividing and multiplying that made and modified herself, her children, all the crowded universe.

It was random, entirely random. What had happened was history. It was not a judgement or a punishment. Matt and she had chosen, and the outcome was theirs to experience.

With the acceptance of her small place and Sarah's in the illegible pattern, Dinah's eyes turned themselves to the smallest details. She saw the bud swelling on the blackened twig of the shrub that poked itself over a garden wall. She saw the twinkle of a speck of mica in the paving stone beneath her feet, and the halo of pinkish fuzzy light surrounding a single unravelled thread in the smooth weave of Sarah's jacket. She saw her own trajectory. Moving forward, not retracing itself to try to recover what was already spent.

Sarah walked with her head hanging, eyes fixed on the ground. Dinah looked around, at the other houses and their gates and windows and doors, but nobody emerged. If any of their old neighbours remained, they were not visible now. She had walked this way so many times, to the bus or tube or the local shops; it was easy to imagine that then was not separated from now by fifteen years, that she might shrug or lift her head and find that her earlier self and the present one had merged and none of this history had intervened.

Only there was Sarah's unresisting hand in hers. Bones, flesh and skin, the fruit of her own flesh, and another woman's child.

They reached the opposite end of the street. With the last few steps Sarah had begun to drag her feet and now she groaned. Dinah stopped, alarmed. Sarah groaned louder. She stood with her legs wide apart and her face turned red. Then she howled aloud in dismay and anger.

In a panic Dinah cried out, 'What is it? What is it? Tell me what's the matter.'

Then she saw. An ugly dark patch spreading down the front and legs of Sarah's jeans.

When Sarah had stopped howling, she began to cry. Shame and confusion were clear in her face. Her jowls wobbled and her eyes squeezed shut. The worst thing had happened.

Dinah was stricken. She had been so preoccupied with her own meditation on the universe that she had neglected the most basic of Sarah's needs. For a long moment she was frozen with despair. She wished for Milly with her sharp common sense to come and rescue them. Milly would be able to deal with this.

Then, mercifully, Dinah had an inner glimpse of how they must look. A sobbing, humiliated teenager and a middle-aged woman, rooted helpless to the spot, holding on to the girl as if she were the supporter and the woman the sufferer.

She led Sarah back towards the car. She whispered to her that no one had seen – the street was empty – that it didn't matter, that she would have dry clothes in a minute. That it was her fault, not Sarah's at all. That she was sorry, again, the ineffectual and only postscript.

Sarah cried wretchedly. Dinah bundled her into the passenger seat, cursing her heavy immobility, her own clumsiness. The car filled with the sharp ammoniac stink of fresh pee.

Dinah stopped at the nearest line of shops and ran into a sports outfitters and then a chemist's. She came back with jogging pants and socks and disposable pants and towels. And in a deserted cul-de-sac, struggling in the confined space of the car, she helped Sarah out of her soaked clothes and dried her and dressed her in the fresh ones.

It was both a reproach and a solace to perform these

intimate services. Sarah gave herself up to the ministrations, with a kind of humble and weighty resignation. It was as if a baby had been handed to Dinah, and she tended to her with clumsy care and with mute, hopeless love that would never animate itself.

When the job was finished Dinah bundled the wet things into a plastic bag and left them in a kerbside litter bin.

'There,' she soothed Sarah. 'Nothing happened.'

Only it was clear from the child's face that it was not forgotten. Dinah held her cheeks between her hands.

'I'm sorry,' she whispered again.

They drove slowly back to Fortinbras Mansions. Dinah could hear the chorus of reason swelling against her; Matt's voice, Eleanor's, Francis's, even Lavinia Jackson's. Telling her to turn about at once and take Sarah back to her mother and father.

No. Dinah slapped her hands on the wheel. The car swerved and she forced it straight again, adrenalin tightening her muscles.

She stared ahead at the meaningless traffic. She only wanted today. She would never see Sarah again, they would not let her. She wanted to sleep beside her once more. Hear her smooth breathing in the night.

This whole day, and then tomorrow's atonement.

Fortinbras Mansions enclosed them like a sanctuary. One more night, Dinah repeated to herself. Over and over again. Then they can have her back. Then they can. Then.

Milly came back later. Her face was gathered into a scowl that overlaid disappointment.

'Well?'

'Your friend was okay. For, you know, someone like that. She gave me tea and *scones*.'

'Yes,' Dinah nodded, thinking of Lavinia. 'She would have done.' The world of tea trays and warm scones and folded napkins seemed very far away.

'But she said I can't do anything until I am legally of age.

All in due course of time kind of stuff. Like, when I'm eighteen, she said, I can apply for a full birth certificate which will give my mother's name and where I was adopted. Then I can try and trace her. She told me how it all happens. There are people to help you, if you want.'

Milly shrugged with the words and turned away to hide her face. Sarah sat passively on her mattress, watching the two of them.

'Is that too long to wait?' Dinah asked.

'It isn't that,' Milly answered at length, her voice muffled. 'What if she doesn't want me to find her?'

Dinah's certainties were breaking up and dissolving. 'She may not do,' she admitted.

Milly looked exactly as she had done when Dinah first met her. She had resumed the full eyepaint and blackened lips and Fortinbras Mansions had added a layer or two of authentic grime. She swung round now and went to look out of the window. She stood with her thin arms wrapped around her ribs, meditatively scratching her side with one black fingernail.

'It's funny. I suppose it's the same except the opposite way for you with her, isn't it?' She jerked her chin towards Sarah.

'Yes.'

'And you can handle it.'

Handle it. Was that all it meant?

'I haven't, up till now. From now on, perhaps.' She thought of Matthew and in the same instant the dingy room and the walls of Fortinbras Mansions rocked and then steadied around her as if a hideous earthquake had threatened and subsided. She realised that she was not crazy. The threads and knots of reality caught her and held her with blessed security.

'If you can, I can.' Milly sighed and turned back into the room. 'You are going to give her back, aren't you?'

'Yes.'

Milly passed by her.

'Are you all right?' There was the appraising look again, telling Dinah that she must look otherwise.

'Yes.'

Milly waited, but Dinah did not offer anything more. She gave her characteristic shrug. 'Right. So can we have something to eat now?'

'Of course we can.'

Dinah cooked a hot meal and fed Sarah, repeating the pattern of the night before. The fragment of an established routine seemed to reassure her and she chattered and laughed with Milly.

The evening at Fortinbras Mansions hatched people and noise from the day's shell, but this time there were fewer and they did not penetrate into Dinah's room. Milly slipped away again. Sarah was lethargic and tired so Dinah helped her to bed and she lay down gratefully between the blanket covers.

'Tomorrow we'll see your mum,' Dinah promised her.

Sarah's smile broke through the fog of her confusion. Once she had fallen asleep, Dinah sat beside her on the mattress. She rubbed her shoulders and back, watching her, preparing to say goodbye.

Dinah could not remember afterwards if she had already woken, or if the sound penetrated her sleep. She opened her eyes on the darkness, the reassurance of Sarah and Milly on either side of her, and an immediate certainty that there was something wrong. She turned her head, trying to identify what it might be if the two girls were safely there and asleep. Then she heard it once more. There was an urgent thumping from somewhere lower in the building, followed by confused shouting. She could not distinguish the words, but the frightened hoarseness of it was enough. She sat bolt upright, straining to hear, and at the same time she caught the acrid whiff of smoke.

Fire. Something was on fire.

316

Dinah scrambled over Milly and crawled to the door. Its opening by no more than a crack brought a thick coil of smoke into the room. Gasping with shock Dinah slammed it shut again. She flung herself across the room to the sleeping girls. Milly mumbled and swore at Dinah's efforts to rouse her. Sarah slept heavily.

On her hands and knees beside the mattresses Dinah shook and shouted at them. Long minutes seemed to elapse before Milly struggled even into semi-consciousness. Dinah ordered her to find clothes, bedcovers, anything that would soak up water. Milly heaved herself up, groping in the half-dark, to do what Dinah ordered. Dinah hauled Sarah into her arms and stumbled to the door with her. She resisted Dinah's efforts all the way, arms and legs bumping as she gave little guttural grunts of fear.

It's all right, Dinah tried to soothe her between her own gasps for breath. *It's all right,* although it was not.

In the bathroom she doused the clothes under the tap and dragged the sopping bundle back to the two girls. Dinah wrapped Sarah's head and face.

'Do the same,' she panted to Milly.

Then she pulled Sarah down on to her hands and knees. Milly copied her. Caz's door was open. The room was empty, and so was the rest of the apartment.

Dinah put the back of her hand to the wooden frame of the apartment door. She could not feel any heat.

'Are you ready?' She could just see Milly's frightened eyes. Milly nodded.

'*Go first. Crawl for it.*'

Dinah inched open the door. Thick smoke rolled in over their heads, filling the room, burning their eyes and throats so even Sarah clutched at the protection of her wet shroud.

'*Go on,*' Dinah screamed at Milly. '*Down.*'

Coughing, half-blinded, with Dinah pushing Sarah, they began to crawl. Out of the door and down the stairs.

Fourteen

The smoke was everywhere.

It poured into their eyes and throats, suffocating, a blinding stinking pall of it.

Trapped in that first infinite second on the stairs Dinah understood, *this is how it happens.*

They would choke and die here in Fortinbras Mansions.

Out of nowhere the spectre of death swung close. It was in her own breathing, it clung around them in the smoke, a solid presence which she had never properly regarded and which struck her down now with its effortless proximity. *Fool.* The knell of her own voice rang in her head.

Dinah heard Sarah choke on the first breath she took. The sound made her jerk forward and she realised that she had been collapsed on all fours, frozen motionless with fear.

Pressing her wet cloths to her mouth and nose with one hand and blinking back burning tears she dipped her head. There was perhaps a foot of clearer air just above the floorboards. One-handed she snatched at Sarah's arm and pulled her down to her belly. Behind her, she caught a glimpse of Milly. Her eyes were staring wide, white in her blackened face.

There was a light on somewhere, Dinah realised. Incredibly, through the murk, a dim bulb was still glowing. Quick. *Oh, quick.* Before the dark leapt to consume them . . .

Too breathless to speak, scrabbling backwards on her knees, dragging Sarah after her and with Milly pushing behind, Dinah slid down the stairs.

There had been an impression of noise, pressing inwards on her ears.

Now Dinah realised that the cacophony had all been within her own head, the drumming of panic. There was silence under the swirl of smoke; no more banging or shouting. No help. Everyone had escaped. Except them. No. That was wrong. There was something. The terrified whining and scratching of a dog. Below them somewhere.

How many steps to go? Dinah shook her head, thickly gasping for breath. Sarah coughed more feebly.

Down, where the smoke seemed thicker.

Dinah lost all her bearings. She could hardly tell if they were going up or down. Her lungs burned with each inhalation. All her efforts became no more than a painful bump, drag, slither, step by step. Each movement cost her more strength and determination than she believed she possessed. Every inch felt like the last. Sarah was whimpering, a low fluttering bleat that dragged into a groan.

Dinah had no words, no breath to spare.

There was a long, flat expanse. The first-floor landing. It was fearsomely hot. Her knees burned on the floorboards. Sarah moved faster, under her own volition now. Once their foreheads cracked together in the blind smoke and Milly swore, behind them, dimly surprising Dinah with her fluency. And then the stairs began again.

Suddenly, the smoke thinned.

The scent of almost fresh air made Dinah faintingly gulp a huge mouthful. Fumes raked her lungs and she choked, spitting and retching on to the filthy wood an inch from her mouth.

'Go on,' Milly screamed at her.

Obediently, with no impetus left of her own, Dinah began again, bump, drag, slither. Down and down. She could not tell if it was thirteen steps or three hundred. Only the air must be clearer. Because Sarah was moaning louder now, a rising ululation of pure terror that surely cost more breath than Dinah possessed.

No stairs now. Obstacles everywhere. The boxes and rubbish that littered the hallway.

And the dog again, a scrape and a frantic whine.

Dinah found a last reserve of strength. Pushing, shouldering her way over the detritus. She knew where the door was. Beyond it was air and life.

For the last half-dozen feet she was upright, stumbling, her breath held close in her chest. She reached the heavy door and pulled, wordlessly praying.

The door swung inwards. A draught of sweet air rushed into her face. There was a flood of orange light from the street lamps. And a circle of faces, drained of colour, punched with the black holes of mouths and eyes.

Sarah and Milly were on their hands and knees, a yard behind her. Dinah took a handful of each of them and hauled them forwards. An instant later they broke out of the door and into the wet, cold heaven of the night.

Dinah staggered down the steps, pulling the girls with her. Hands caught at them, offering help and support, but violently she shook them off. Her cracked lips drew back from her teeth in a warning snarl. She crossed half of the pavement, trying to run, before her legs gave way beneath her.

Dinah sank to her knees, and then crouched in a heap. The wet slabs under her scorched knees and palms were wonderful, cold and greasy. Sarah and Milly tumbled beside her. They were coughing and kneading their fists in their eyes. She reached out and pulled them close to her body. She pressed her mouth against each face in turn. She could see nothing because she was blinded by tears. But with her lips she felt the padded resilience of Sarah's cheeks, the bony ridges of Milly's nose and brow. Her fingers wound in their hair, tightening, pulling their heads closer to hers. She kissed them and cried.

Dinah wept. She cried in horror and relief, wordless, the sobs breaking out of her like bursting bubbles. Someone had run to them and now helping hands intruded again. She knocked them away with her arms, holding the girls tighter. Sarah was heavy and helpless, but Milly was rigid. A second later Milly broke out of her grasp.

She was on her feet, looking back at the Mansions. Dinah's instinct recognised what her mind was too disconnected to follow. And recoiled from it.

The dog. The horrible, whining, frantic dog, trapped somewhere in there.

'*No*,' Dinah howled at Milly. She pulled at the thin wrist. '*No. No. No.*'

Milly hesitated. Then she was gone, breaking out of Dinah's reach, running back across the road. The crowd in front of the Mansions ate her up. Smoke was coiling from the upper windows now. The underbelly of the cloud was licked into the colour of a bruise by the street lights.

Dinah did not see the small knot of people who had gathered around her. Caz was amongst them, and the boy, not grinning any longer. But she only saw the fuzz of Sarah's hair in front of her eyes, and the place where Milly had gone. Back into the smoke. Dinah's mouth opened wider. She held the one daughter, rocking her in her arms, and looked wildly for the other.

Dinah had no control or reason or dignity left to her. They bled out of her eyes and mouth and flowed away. She was no mother or mentor. Everything had melted down and run away.

She moaned, and tried to cover Sarah's ears with her hands. There were no words or thoughts, only moans. She sounded like an animal, crying for relief. Thin rain fell on her lips and tongue and she turned her hollow face up to the sky. Someone put a clumsy arm around her shoulders.

Dinah's moment of abject crouching within her punctured skin stretched on for ever. Time was suspended, collapsed, meaningless. Nothing in the universe moved except for Sarah and Sarah was weakly crying, her mouth blubbery, her round face marked with the filth of smoke.

Then there was a surge in the crowd on the steps. From the midst of the people Milly re-emerged. She was dragging the mangy dog on the end of its string. It skidded to the kerb and stood stiff-legged, whining.

Milly flung down the string. She ran back towards Dinah and Sarah. Halfway across the road Caz caught her.

'What you doing?' he bellowed at her. 'We're all here.'

'Where's Mick?'

Mick, the silent boy.

'Went out for chips, or fags, or summat.'

Milly screamed into his face. 'You left us in there. You knew we were there and you left us.' She swung her fist weakly, trying to hit him. Caz held her off and then sullenly pushed her away.

Milly dropped to her knees beside Dinah and Sarah. Faintly at first and then louder, sawing through the moist air, they heard the first sirens.

'We've got to get away from here,' Milly muttered.

Dinah clutched at her. Her fingers knotted in Milly's clothes, too tightly to be torn loose a second time.

'Listen to me, Dinah. Do what I tell you.'

Dinah was no use. She felt her impotence, her weakness like a child's. 'Stay here,' she whispered. 'Milly, stay with us.'

'Christ. Don't you understand? You're as bad as *her*. Move. Come on. Run.'

'I can't.' She was too shocked.

Milly's hand whipped back and cracked hard against Dinah's cheek. Dinah's head jolted. She became aware of the circle of onlookers, the sirens growing louder, the nauseating smell of smoke. She hauled herself to her feet, pulling Sarah with her. Her jaw rattled and stung, focusing her attention.

'Don't leave us.'

'Jesus. For fuck's sake.'

They began to move. Arms around each other's shoulders. Their steps lengthened, carrying them away from Fortinbras

322

Mansions. At the end of the road, the first fire engine hurtled past them. Another turning, and there was the wide benign expanse of Chalk Farm Road. Dinah had no idea where they were going. All her trust was in Milly now. Milly was the mother. Milly was what she was not.

A yellow light cruised towards them. Milly flung up her arm. The cab braked and swung in to the kerb. The chrome handle smooth and cool and the door opening for them. Inside the familiar taxi scent. They fell into the miraculous mundane safety of it.

'Where to then?' the man asked over his shoulder.

Milly said clearly, 'Gainsborough Gardens, Hampstead.'

Dinah lay with her head back. There was a girl on either side of her. Sarah was breathing fast, staring around, wide eyes in her dirty face. They were insulated in the commonplace bubble of a black cab. No smoke or fire. No death.

The world began to connect and coalesce again. It was still remote and fragile-seeming, but it streamed past the windows, gathering depth and brightness.

Gainsborough Gardens. Ed and Sandra.

Where did Milly the privileged daughter turn, when real need finally came upon her?

Of course. She turned for home.

Dinah was weak and shocked. The more so when she heard cracked laughter seep out of her. Milly turned her head.

'You don't even like dogs,' Dinah gasped.

'Shut the *fuck* up,' Milly snarled at her.

Milly helped Dinah out of the cab. The immense dark bulk of the house in Gainsborough Gardens loomed above them. Dinah drew Sarah after her. Her hand felt burning hot.

'You'll have to wait while I wake up my parents,' Milly said to the driver.

A moment later Ed stood in his plum silk dressing gown under the light of the porch. He looked down at the three of them.

'Christ,' he whispered. And ran down the steps.

He held open his arms and Milly flung herself into them. Ed lifted her effortlessly, holding her against him.

'Honey, you're okay, honey. You're safe, your Dad's here. Nothing can hurt you.'

Over her head he looked at Dinah holding the Down's syndrome child by the hand.

'Who's this?'

'She's my daughter.'

He gaped at her, startled out of his self-assurance. Then he mumbled uncertainly, 'Come on. Come on inside.'

In the Parkeses' kitchen white tiles and grey marble stretched as far as Dinah could see. The lights were bright, all the surfaces were clean and smooth. It reminded her of a hospital and she wondered if that was after all where they had ended up. For safety – and without distinguishing for whose sake it was – she held on to Sarah. She had the sense that her hands were black claws, digging into her. Nobody had said anything much, yet.

Ed and Sandra were here, moving to and fro in their night clothes and dressing gowns. Sandra's robe was ice-blue satin. It wasn't a hospital, of course. Somehow they had escaped from Fortinbras Mansions. They were unhurt, safe. The magnitude of this and the connected links of what might have happened set Dinah uncontrollably shivering.

Ed brought her a glass with a finger of whisky in it but Sandra moved it away again.

'Not alcohol,' she whispered to him, 'not now. Shock.'

Dinah had not been supposed to hear this but her hearing and each of her other senses were painfully sharpened. Light bounced in her eyes. Sarah's rounded shoulders within the crook of her arm shifted in response to Dinah's smallest movements, like part of her own body, as if the two of them were at last a single ungainly hybrid.

Milly huddled close to Ed. She held on to the slab of his hand, shivering, chewing at the corner of her mouth.

324

Smeared black make-up and smoke made a piebald mess of her face.

Sandra brought mugs of hot milk. Dinah took hers and drank, looking down first at the bland moon face of it. The taste in her mouth was chalky innocence, the flavour of infancy.

'You'd better tell us what's been going on,' Ed said loudly to Dinah, taking control once more. 'We get here yesterday morning, and you've gone. No one at the hotel, not a word to anyone except a message to Matt that you're off somewhere together. Now you turn up looking like you've been in a war zone.'

Milly suddenly turned her face and hid it against Ed's shoulder.

'I'm sorry. It's all my fault. We were at Caz's place and there was, there was a terrible fire. We had to get out in . . . all the smoke . . . it was . . . so . . . frightening.'

Ed's horror overcame his anger.

'I told you to keep away from that place. And those kids who hang out there. They're crazy and they're dangerous.'

'I know that now,' Milly whispered.

She burrowed against her father as if to obliterate the memory with the powerful bulk of him. He stroked her thin shoulders with his big hand, his belligerence softened.

'It's not Milly's fault,' Dinah said clearly. Ed and Sandra swung to look at her. 'Nothing is. It's only because of Milly that we are safe here now.'

The clock on the kitchen wall told her that it was two-ten in the morning, only forty hours since they had met the bus on the fog-bound road. Light and dark images of the last hours slid before her inner eye as she tried to explain what had happened.

'I haven't seen my, seen Sarah since she was a baby. I was in Norfolk looking for her, when Milly came. The next day I just took Sarah. I stole her. We came to London, the three of us. There was a fire in the place we were staying in. We only just . . . got out.'

She had lost her containing skin. The stuff of her inner being was spilling out, a cell without its membrane. All her careful defences and the guilty subterfuges with which she had long held and manœuvred her adult life were stripped away, with Ed and Sandra Parkes as her auditors. She had no pride left. All Dinah felt was gratitude that she and Milly and Sarah were safe in this big clean house.

Ed and Sandra listened until the story was told.

Ed held Milly tighter. He was telling her in an undertone, *Don't worry any more, no one's angry. We love you.*

And it was plain from his face how much he did love her.

Sandra released Sarah from Dinah's grasp and led her to sit at the table beside Milly and Ed. She went uncomplainingly with only a little frown of bewilderment. Milly rubbed her face and made room, and Ed offered his free hand. Sarah cuddled up to them.

Sandra drew Dinah away. Leading off the kitchen was another room, black-roofed and furnished with opulent tendrils of green-black foliage. It was some kind of conservatory. Dinah sat in a creaking wicker chair. The corrugations of the arms were minutely painful to her sore fingers.

'You must tell me about what happened before all this, before yesterday,' Sandra said.

Must. The tender-stern voice of authority. Dinah recoiled from it and at the same time it unpinned her. She hid her face in her hands. The words came out painfully slowly, and then faster, spilling away into the space between them.

'After Sarah was adopted, when she was a baby, Matthew and I never could talk about her. I couldn't talk about her to anyone. And I thought about her all the time. When we went to live in Franklin the loss of her grew inside me until I couldn't bear it any longer. Then I met you and Milly, and she told me she was adopted and in return I found myself telling her what I had done. Somehow Sarah and she slid together in my mind. You knew what I felt for Milly was something wrong, hidden, didn't you? It was then I under-

326

stood that I had to come back to find Sarah. And then when I saw her, I did this terrible thing.

'I think what happened was that I went mad.'

There was a long silence.

Then Sandra came to Dinah and held her, kneeling on the floor in her blue robe. Dinah had not expected sympathy.

'I understand,' Sandra said.

There was a rich scent of damp conservatory earth mingling with the residue of Sandra's perfume. But still the stink of smoke clung around Dinah. The smell of it would always bring terror, and if it did so for her what would it mean for Sarah? Dinah began a reflex lunge towards the kitchen but Sandra held her.

'She's all right. Ed's looking after her. She's drinking her milk now.'

Dinah insisted, 'You must believe that what I did wasn't anything to do with Milly. She has been so strong and determined, and brave in the end. Everything I have failed to be in the last two days. She's remarkable.'

'I knew you and she were keeping a secret from me. I was jealous of you. I thought you were trying to insinuate yourself between Milly and me. I'm not very confident in myself as a mother. I'm not really a very good one, am I?'

Dinah had misjudged her. She had fended Sandra off, preferring to dismiss her brittle manner and her overdesigned clothes and houses, because she was fearful of intrusion and exposure. Now that there was no guilt to conceal and no greater shame to suffer, Dinah needed a friend. She told her the truth now as she plainly saw it.

'Sandra, you are a good woman and a good mother. You're as remarkable as Milly is.'

Sandra said, 'I have often imagined . . . been afraid, in the way you fear something unknown . . . that Milly's birth mother might appear. One day, a face at the window looking in. I never met her, but I'd know who she was after one glance.'

As I appeared at the wedding, Dinah thought. A face across

the windswept churchyard. It was Pauline's fear too, and she was right to be afraid.

'Now you have told me about Sarah I understand better how it might feel to be the face at the window. To be outside, looking in at another woman with your child.' Sandra added softly, 'Milly often talks about tracing her real mother. It makes me feel jealous and bitter. A failure. As if we both know I haven't been good enough for her. Do you understand?'

'You have been better than good enough,' Dinah repeated. 'I know that, knowing Milly. But I do understand.'

'Milly feels betrayed by both her mothers. Given away and not given what she believes she deserves. It's why she is always so angry,' Sandra stood up. Kneeling on the floor had stiffened her knees so that she lurched a little, and Dinah steadied her with her blackened hands. They looked at each other for a long moment.

'I introduced Milly to a woman lawyer I know. She wanted some advice about tracing her mother. Lavinia told her she can do nothing until she's eighteen. I'm very sorry. It was wrong of me to interfere.'

'Maybe it was. But I think maybe you're right too. Ed and I should let her, help her to trace her birth mother if she wants it so badly. We may have to . . . let her go, if we want to keep any of her.'

Sandra stood at the black glass, looking into the invisible garden.

'We love her very much.'

'Yes,' Dinah said.

She could hear Sarah saying something in the kitchen, a stream of liquid syllables. She sounded like herself, newly curious about this magnificent new place.

'I don't want Sarah's mother to have to worry any longer about where she is,' Dinah said.

'We'll telephone,' Sandra assured her. 'We'll tell her that Sarah is safe with us.'

*

In the kitchen, Ed and the two girls were still sitting at the table.

To Milly, her father had the rumpled, middle-of-the-night look that reminded her of waking up as a little girl, to be soothed and settled to sleep again.

'I'm sorry for running away,' she mumbled.

'You did run back again, anyway. How did you get all the way to England by yourself? I'm not surprised you did it, I'd just kind of like to hear the details.'

Milly told him, exactly as she had described it to Dinah.

'Not bad,' Ed admitted. 'Couldn't have done it in better style myself.'

'I took a lot of your money. There's some left, not much.'

Milly squirmed inside her clothes and produced her body belt with its zipped purse. She took out some crumpled notes and pushed them into her father's hand.

'Thanks. I always like to get some change from a deal.'

Milly stared at him. She shook her head from side to side.

'The fire was so horrible. I thought we were going to die. What would we have done if you and Mum hadn't been here waiting for me?'

'We're always here,' Ed assured her.

Milly suddenly folded her arms on the table top and laid her head on them. Glassy tears of exhaustion began to roll out of her eyes.

Sarah's mouth formed a round O of concern. She leaned forward to see better, blinking without her glasses. Then she touched Milly's shaking shoulders, patting them softly with her thick fingers.

'Never *mind*,' she murmured, the words only slightly entangled. 'Never never *mind*.' And then a minute later her attention was caught by a set of copper pans, tiny to huge, hanging on the wall behind Milly. She jumped up to touch them, exclaiming in wonder.

'It's ringing now,' Sandra said. She had called directory

329

enquiries for the Greens' number, and then dialled it. She held the receiver out to Dinah and then walked away.

'Hello?'

Pauline woke at the first ring. Her voice was sharp with fearful anticipation.

'It's Dinah Steward,' she whispered. 'She's safe, Pauline. She's here with me in London. She will be home with you tomorrow morning.'

'Oh God,' Pauline wept. 'Oh God, thank God.'

'I'm so sorry. I'm so sorry for everything I've done.'

Sandra came back and held Dinah. She put the telephone receiver into Dinah's filthy hands again.

'Now tell Matthew everything is all right. It's only ten p.m. in Franklin.'

After the policeman's call on Thursday morning Matthew rang the hotel in Cromer once more.

This time the receptionist told him with acerbity that Mrs Steward and her young friend had definitely not checked out, but neither had they been seen since going out after breakfast on Wednesday morning. Exactly as she had explained to the police, the woman added.

Matthew gritted his teeth and exerted as much charm and reassurance as he could command. He extracted a promise from her that she would telephone him immediately she had any more news, either from the police or Mrs Steward herself.

After that, bracing himself, he spoke to the Parkeses in Hampstead. He told them that Milly and Dinah were together, somewhere, because Dinah had left him a message. He wasn't quite sure *where* they were, just at this minute, but he was certain that Dinah would call back again soon.

They were not to worry, anyway.

'Worrying about Milly is a fact of life for Sandra and me, Matt. I'm just glad she's with Dinah as of this moment.'

'Good,' Matthew said, and hung up as quickly as he could.

330

He could not think how to convey to Ed Parkes what was really happening. He would have to unpack for his overbearing scrutiny so much of himself and Dinah that had been laid away out of sight.

Matthew thought of this portion of their history as a suitcase. It had been closed for a long time; he could almost feel the smooth brass catches under his fingers. The clothes inside – no treasures, just flat shapes, sad and unworn, no longer in mode and creased along the fold lines – would have to be shaken out of their tissue wrapping and spread out in the air, for Ed to shake his head over.

The idea of such exposure mushroomed inside him like a pain.

Matt rolled over in the empty bed, curling himself double to contain the ache of it. He lay diagonally across the space where Dinah should be. The sheet on her side felt smooth and cold to his heated skin. From the clock on the bedside table he saw that it was six-thirty a.m. He felt as if he had already lived through a full day, but he pushed back the covers and set about getting dressed.

The boys would not wake for another hour.

Downstairs, Matthew fed Ape and let him out of the back door. He stood at the kitchen window and watched the dog run across the yard in the chilly half-light. His tail rippled behind him like a flag.

Turning back again Matt noticed how sordid the kitchen looked. The table was a mess of newspapers and crumbs and coffee mugs, and there were dirty pans and drinks cartons and food wrappers spread over the counter between the cooker and the sink. In front of the fridge, the floor was sticky with spillages, and it was marked all over with footprints and Ape's pawmarks.

Dinah had not yet been away for a week.

Matthew missed her in every moment. The possibility that she might not come back seized his throat with panic.

If, he thought. If he had known when he blindly stumbled into Kathrin's bed that he risked Dinah, risked even her safety and sanity, he would never have glanced at another woman. The spectre of his carelessness shocked him.

He remembered her telephone message with numbing anxiety. The voice had been unmistakably Dinah's, and yet had not sounded like Dinah at all. *I'm all right, tell the boys. I'm sorry about everything.* And then silence, before she hung up.

I'm sorry. It might mean that she no longer loved him, and hadn't yet found the words to tell him. Or perhaps some *thing*, some horror that he shied away from imagining, might have overtaken her.

Matthew's legs and hands twitched with the effort of suppressing his fear. He was accustomed to doing and solving, to making happen what he wanted to happen, and now his ignorance of the truth jammed him into a stale corner of impotence.

I won't lose her, he insisted to himself. I won't let her go. If she's ill, she will need me. If she's hurt . . . if something worse has happened to her . . .

Dinah.

The telephone mounted on the kitchen wall blinked its reproachful silence at him.

Matthew went to the sink. He pulled on the yellow Marigold gloves that Dinah kept clipped inside the door of the unit and filled a bucket full of suds and hot water. He swept the debris from the table into a rubbish sack and left the crusted saucepans to soak before he began on the floor.

The activity was a partial balm. As he worked, he thought about her. Once or twice, out of the corner of his eye, he caught sight of his blurred reflection in the glassy door of the oven or in the lightening windows. In her household gloves, doing these chores, he might have taken his reflection for Dinah's. It was almost as if their physical entities had slid together and coalesced in the humming space of the kitchen. He began to think as if he were Dinah, about how she must feel to have come here to Franklin, about the contract they had made to give his work every priority, and about the other silent contract, concerning Sarah.

332

Matthew paused for a moment, breathless, resting his hands on the Squeegee mop. Then he began again, working faster, as if he could erase much more than the stains on the floor.

How strong Dinah had been, he thought. She had absorbed so much, and contained everything within herself. She remained composed and logical and unshakeable.

He could not even remember her ever being ill. Or only once. It must have been quite a long time – months, at least – after Sarah was born. Dinah had taken to her bed for a week and had lain there, gazing out at the square of urban sky beyond the window.

It was flu, she had said.

He remembered that he had been grateful for her self-diagnosis. He had brought her Disprin and hot drinks, and after a few days she had declared herself better again.

But apart from that he could not remember that Dinah had ever even faltered. Once Sarah had been formally adopted. Dinah made lists and fixed them to the fridge door with jaunty magnets. She shopped and cooked for them all, and made their house comfortable. She cut out Hallowe'en party costumes, and constructed Christmases, and picnics, and birthday surprises.

And much more than that, Matthew reprimanded himself. Those were only the superficial things. Dinah held himself and the children and their lives secure in a net of love and generosity.

Only lately, when she had begun to talk more about Sarah, had Matthew become aware of the drop that yawned beneath the net. And understanding that it was there, the danger had begun half to threaten and half to entice him. He had almost thrown himself into the chasm.

The kitchen was suddenly empty of Dinah's almost-reflection. Matthew knew that he was there alone.

He bundled the mop away into the utility room and went upstairs to wake the boys. The first thing Jack asked when he opened his eyes was,

333

'Did Mom call last night?'

'No. She did lunchtime yesterday, remember? I'm sure she will later. Come on now, we'll be late for school.'

Jack looked sourly at him. Matt knew that the boys were blaming him now for Dinah's absence. He bumped around the bedroom, making a show of tidying and picking up discarded clothes, as if this might reassure or compensate.

'It looks nice down here,' Merlin said, surveying the kitchen. He was trying to be kind, filling in for Jack's silence.

'Yeah. I thought I'd better have a bit of a clean-up,' Matt said, taking the box of Cheerios out of the cupboard.

While the boys were eating and Matt was drinking his coffee, Ape came bounding in through the open door of the utility room. It was muddy and damp out in the yard and the dog trailed a pattern of pawprints across the clean floor.

Matthew banged down his coffee cup and leapt out of his seat. He chased Ape across the room and the dog barked gleefully, anticipating a game, his tail whacking against the cupboards and whisking over an open milk carton that Merlin had left on a chair. Milk flowed across the seat and down the legs to spread in searching fingers across the pawprints. Matt heard himself swearing at Ape, in the same enraged and ineffectual cadences that Dinah used against him. *Bloody dog. Filthy. Menace.* He swiped at the dog's hind-quarters too, failing to connect with the bristling fur, in just the way that Dinah did.

The boys stared, spoons held halfway to their mouths.

Ape bounded away with something between a whine and a snort, and disappeared back where he had come from.

Matt knelt down on all fours to mop up the milk.

'You sounded like Mum then,' Merlin said.

Matt wrung the greyish milk out of the cloth into the sink. 'Did I?'

Her absence squeezed at him and the kitchen's discovered emptiness beat in his head.

'That was a dumb place to leave the milk. Come on, guys. Let's get ready for school.'

After he had dropped off the boys, Matthew did not make the regular circuit onwards to the lab. Instead, without having planned it, he drove home again. Franklin had become a different place, no longer a tranquil academic community into which he fitted smoothly, but somehow alien. Foreign, he thought, as he pulled up in the Toyota at the traffic lights in the main square. That was it. It had become a foreign country.

When the lights changed, he had to pause for a second to remember which was the way to turn for Kendrick.

The house was silent and stale-smelling. Ape was sulking out in the yard. Matthew cleared the breakfast dishes and switched on the dishwasher. The telephone rang and he snatched it up, but it was only a message from a parent in Jack's class about an expedition. Matthew was already writing down the information for Dinah before he reconnected the fact of her absence and the meaning of it. He completed the remainder for his own benefit, and thumbtacked it to the kitchen pinboard.

At a loss with himself in the shell of the house, he went upstairs to the bedroom. He picked up discarded shirts and newspapers and tidied them away, then made the bed, straightening the undersheet and plumping the pillows in the way he usually only did when on the point of getting back into it again. Out of one window he could see the side gable of the Kerrigans' house. The timbers were freshly painted, and the storm shutters securely fixed. The domestic castle, Matthew thought.

Dinah had told him once that all homes were like castles, secured against the outside world behind the drawbridge of the front door. And then when something went wrong with the marriage within its castle it was like an invisible rot gnawing until the walls crumbled from the inside.

Matthew wandered across the bedroom. He opened the door of the closet and looked in at her clothes on the bones of hangers. He remembered different occasions when she

335

had worn the various dresses. The red one she had worn for Christmas eggnog at the Pinkhams', the night of the department Christmas party. The same night Kathrin had worn a little velvet coat, with stars in her hair.

As Matthew slid his fingers between the folds of the fabric, the ghost of Dinah was the more vivid to him. He caught the breath of her scent, preserved beneath collars and within the facings of necklines. Kathrin was paler, evanescent. He could not remember the smell or the texture of her now, nor did he wish to, although at other times he had been all too easily able to conjure them up.

Matthew knelt down. On racks at the bottom of the closet were Dinah's shoes. There was a black suede pair with high slim heels, the heeltips narrower than a little finger nail. He turned a shoe in his hands. The sole was still caramel-colour, hardly marked. Inside, in the pale lining, he could just see the print of Dinah's toes and heel. In his mind's eye he could see her walking in the shoes. The high-heel walk, from the hips, calves and insteps taut.

The shoe in one hand, Matthew reached out with the other and slipped the red dress off the hanger. Rubbing the flimsy silk of it between his fingers, he sat down on the bed.

He had thought he might enter into a fantasy. He lay back with the dress in his arms and inhaled the mosaic of scent. He thought of Dinah walking in the suede shoes, the long groove that ran inside her thigh muscle from groin to knee contracting and lengthening with her steps. But the image as it came to him was fond, tender rather than sexual. It pierced too deep within him to be merely erotic. He held the dress against him, lying still, allowing his thoughts to drift backwards.

Something in the faded scent trapped in the dress's folds made him think of Eleanor. Dinah's likeness to her mother had at one time been striking, and then as Eleanor had aged it had diminished a little. Matthew had not seen Eleanor for

336

some time, but he guessed that the resemblance must be growing stronger again.

And then, entering his head as if the reverie had been all in preparation for her, came Sarah. He didn't pinch out the thought as he had always done before. Did she look like Dinah, and therefore like her grandmother, continuing the thread? Matthew retained only the dimmest memory of her as a baby, a little bud of a face within a white blanket, and in time the Down's features had been superimposed with Jack's and then Merlin's. Sarah had sunk within him, unacknowledged.

Yet she was complete, Dinah had said. Herself. Not a shadow or a memory.

And now, as clearly as he knew that he loved Dinah, Matt knew that he wanted to see his daughter. This *wanting*, then, was what Dinah had known. He understood why she had been unable to deny it.

After a little while, Matthew dozed. He allowed himself the unfamiliar refuge of daytime sleep to hold his own discomfort and his fears for Dinah at bay. But he soon woke again, with the sour taste of worry in his mouth.

The day was very long.

In the mid-afternoon he was working in the yard, cutting and tying back the overgrowth of shrubs, when he heard the front doorbell ringing. Dee Kerrigan brought the boys back from school and looked after them until Matt came home, but now he found the three of them standing on the porch.

'Dad, are you okay?' The boys' tight-skinned, winter-pale faces blinked identically at him. Their anxiety reproached him and gnawed his own into fresh life.

'We saw the car was here and they had to come straight over,' Dee explained. 'You're not sick or anything, are you?'

'No, no, nothing like that. Working at home today. Thanks, Dee. Come on in, you two. You can help me out in the garden.'

'Heard from Dinah?' Dee asked.

'Yes, she called yesterday. She's fine.'

How much longer should he claim this, Matt wondered? For whose sake was the pretence anyway – the boys', his own, their neighbours'?

The boys trailed listlessly into the house, Merlin exaggerating his limp, and dropped their bags before switching on the television. Watching their dejection, Matt felt the fabric of his own capability stretch to the point of ripping.

It was Dinah who kept the threads knitted together. Without Dinah it seemed they were separate, patternless, weak in their singularity.

Matthew roasted a chicken for supper. He took trouble with vegetables and roast potatoes, but neither of the boys ate much. The evening dragged by and even Jack did not protest that it was too early when bedtime came. By nine-thirty they were both asleep. Sitting in the den with a scotch, Matt tried to feel angry with Dinah for her silence, for subjecting them to this much worry. But his anger was stillborn. He knew that something had happened to her, something that had carried her beyond the boundaries of what was safe and rational and considerate.

At ten o'clock the telephone rang.

'Matthew. I'm here with Ed and Sandra. Matt, I've done something so terrible . . .'

His head jerked back with the force of his gratitude for the sound of her voice alone. His relief was so great that he didn't even listen to her words.

'Dinah, tell me you're safe. It doesn't matter what's happened so long as I know you're safe.'

Her voice was small, weary, a long way off.

'You had better hear it first.'

She told him and he listened with his eyes closed. Dismay and regret bled out of him. It need not have happened.

He wouldn't fail her again.

'Listen, darling. Listen to me. Stay where you are. Stay with Ed and Sandra until we get to you. The boys and I will be there . . .' his mind was leapfrogging hours and miles '. . . on Saturday morning.'

'Please come. I'll be waiting to see you all.'

Dinah lay in the bath. Her arms and legs seemed to float apart from her, under the skin of water, reflecting the disconnection of her rational self. Water reminded her of the pool and Sarah's majestic swimming. Was it only fifteen hours ago? She turned her head against the hard white slope of the bath, checking the solidity of her surroundings, anchoring herself.

The Parkeses' guest bathroom was unsurprisingly splendid. There were planes of pale grey marble and a small white cliff of folded towels. There were restrained soaps in glass dishes and infinitely reflecting mirrors, curves and flares of polished chrome, and the sweet scent of fern bath oil. Sandra had run the bath for her.

The opulence of it all made the memory of Fortinbras Mansions and the last two days the more sharp and fearful. Dinah's ruined clothes lay in a heap by the door. Sandra had given her a nightdress and a robe.

Dinah had nothing. No money, no clothes, no belongings. For a moment the realisation made her feel curiously easy, as if she was free to start something afresh.

Dinah sat up. Water ran off her shoulders. She turned her hands over and looked at the reddened palms. There were no blisters. Only scorch marks that would fade.

She had undressed Sarah in the bedroom next to Milly's, bundling her black clothes out of her sight. Sarah was unresisting, her arms hanging loose and heavy over her mottled thighs. Without her glasses she fumbled and blinked, her round face shy and vulnerable. Dinah examined her as carefully as she dared.

'Is anywhere hurting?' she asked. 'Is anything sore?'

Sarah shook her head.

Dinah dressed her again in a roomy T-shirt of Milly's, and folded back the white covers on the bed. Sarah lay down under the covers with a small sigh and Dinah smoothed them over her. She sat down on the edge of the bed, not quite within the hollow enclosed by Sarah's knees and arms.

'You aren't frightened, are you?' Dinah whispered.

No answer.

'Shall I stay with you?'

No answer again. But Sarah turned her head a little on the pillow so that she looked up at Dinah. It was a look of assessment, seemingly quite clear and cool, but it contained neither recognition nor acknowledgement.

Dinah gently touched her shoulder. Then she stood up and moved quietly to the chair at the foot of the bed. She sat there until she was quite sure that Sarah was asleep.

In the bath, Dinah soaped herself with one of the tablets from the glass dish. The lather was slick and soothing to her hands. All of this was real, marble and scent and soap. Somehow the net had closed beneath her again. The terrible confusion was subsiding, leaving in its place a weight of gratitude.

Sandra and Ed were so kind. Kinder than she could ever deserve.

She hoisted herself out of the bath and wrapped herself in a scented towel. She saw that her clothes had left a faint sooty mark on the marble. Dinah pressed the towel to her face to hold the tears.

The one other person she wanted to telephone was Eleanor, to try to explain to her what was inexplicable and to be comforted for it.

But it was nearly four o'clock in the morning. Dinah remembered that she had crossed the threshold between being cared for and providing the care. She couldn't wake her mother in the middle of the night.

Tomorrow, Dinah comforted herself. Tomorrow, that and everything else.

Fifteen

In the morning the officials took Sarah away.

A policewoman and a social worker came for her in an unmarked car. She was dressed in clothes of Milly's, a navy-blue jogging suit that looked unworn, and a long ski-jacket. The suit was too tight for her, pulling across her stomach and exposing her ankles and the rings of flesh at her wrists.

This morning her face did not betray any sign of distress. Her short sight seemed to limit even further the dimensions of her awareness and so to permit her the security of some internal and reassuring world. While she was eating her breakfast she saw a yellow Walkman on top of a pile of glossy magazines in a wicker basket.

Sarah pointed at it with a delighted shriek of recognition. 'My Warmer. *Mine.*'

Sandra unwound the headset, installed a tape and gave it to her.

After that, head rhythmically bobbing, she retreated further into the music.

Dinah sat at the opposite end of the table. She had woken in yet another unfamiliar place, but with a sense of recovery. She felt thin-skinned, brittle, as if she had been seriously ill, but clear-headed. Covertly she watched Sarah as she waited for whatever must happen next. And found herself thinking, with a new hard-edged clarity that seemed to have grown out of yesterday's final disablement, *I don't know her at all.*

She knew the face now as well as she knew Merlin's or Jack's, the round-knobbed pink features, even the scent and the texture of her skin, but the real knowledge of Sarah was denied to her as absolutely as it had ever been.

The two days they had spent together, all the raw-rubbed poignant and fearful hours of them, had in the end uncovered no more than the first half-hour in the Greens' house at Wivenham.

Dinah understood that she had been irrational, wishful and presumptuous to imagine that she ever could have gained that knowledge. As if the long-ago umbilical connection gave her some magical right, over and above the real links of history and proximity.

No wonder Pauline had been so angry with her.

Dinah felt a weighty, complicated sadness for Sarah. The connection with her daughter was like sand in an hour-glass, the last grains compressed in the translucent neck of this bright morning, running steadily and silently away.

But she also understood one other thing. Some long standing and steely constraint of her own had been finally lifted. She was weak and unsupple without it, like a broken limb at last released from a cast, but she was also free.

When they arrived to take Sarah away the policewoman and her companion came into the kitchen, shown in by Sandra. They looked at the acres of bright white space, the glass-fronted cupboards and the fingers of sunshine reaching in from the conservatory, and then at Sarah standing with the Walkman held tight in two hands in front of her, like her bridesmaid's bouquet.

I am glad Pauline isn't here to see all this, Dinah thought. Gainsborough Gardens was too opulent.

'Come on, Sarah, love,' the policewoman said, in a cheery loud voice that reminded Dinah that she had also spoken to Sarah in the same way. 'Let's go home to your mum, shall we? She's waiting for you.'

But Sarah with the headphones clamped in her ears was deaf to them all equally.

When they led her away, Dinah and the Parkeses followed them out to the front door. Sandra stood close to Dinah, anticipating some need, and Dinah in her turn understood this and did not edge away from her. She accepted Sandra's concern gratefully.

As she was buckled into the rear seat and realised that she was being taken away, it was Milly whom Sarah reached back for. Her fingers flapped in the air like a baby's. After a glance at Dinah, Milly skipped down the steps and leant into the car. When she stood back again the social worker closed the door and the car moved away. Dinah watched it, with Sandra and Milly on either side of her. Her face showed nothing. In her heart, she had already done the work of letting Sarah go.

When the car had turned the corner, Sandra and Milly linked their arms with Dinah's. The three of them walked up the steps together.

Inside the house, Dinah said, 'I'd like to make another call, if I may.'

'Of course,' Sandra said.

Eleanor was at home. She answered the telephone on the second ring and Dinah knew that she was sitting in her armchair beside a window that looked out on to the garden. There would be the first knobbed growths of spring showing in the flower borders.

Eleanor said, 'Darling, I've been thinking about you so much. Are you all right? Where are you, at home?'

Eleanor did not even know she was in England.

Being with Sarah had removed Eleanor from her reach. Dinah had longed for her mother, and at the same time feared her intrusion. Everything that she was doing made Eleanor one of the enemy, one of the voices who would insist, *You must take her home.*

She had warned Dinah, *Be careful. I am afraid of the hurt that this might cause.*

Dinah hesitated. The hurt and the damage were done

343

now, and would have to be made good. But even as she took the measure of this, she recognised a separate relief. The proper balance was restored, this far at least. Her wish and her instinct were to reassure her mother, not to be a child in need of Eleanor's protection. Somehow she had regained control of herself. Renewed strength bubbled up within her. To hear her mother's voice was an infusion of it.

'No, I'm in London. With some friends.'

'Are Matt and the boys there?'

'They're coming tomorrow.' Gratitude for that. She heard from the silence that Eleanor was waiting for what she would say next.

'I saw her,' Dinah said simply.

'Did you? Tell me what she's like.'

No how or why or expression of amazement or anxiety; just the wish to know. Dinah understood how admirable her mother was.

'She is like herself.'

Eleanor listened while Dinah talked. She heard about the wedding and about the visit to the Greens, and then the fog that had descended on the coast.

'Mummy, I took her. I put her in my car, with Milly Parkes, and drove her to London.'

Another silence extended itself. Dinah stared unseeingly at the little study Sandra had shown her into. There were white cushions and shelves of art books and white lilies in a vase. A clock on a marble mantel. Dinah would not be able to talk for much longer.

'Tell me,' Eleanor prompted, in the same level voice.

And when Dinah had finished she said immediately, 'I'm coming to London. Give me the address. I'll be there this afternoon.'

Dinah smiled, then. That's what her mother would say.

'There's no need. I promise. Everything will be all right.'

Eleanor thought for a moment. 'It's very odd. It does sound as though you *are* all right. Better than you have been.'

344

'I know. I am. I promise I'll ring you this evening or tomorrow.'

'You'll need a solicitor, of course. Have you got one?'

'A very good one.'

'Dinah, what about Matt?'

'He'll be here tomorrow. It's not long.'

'You need one another,' Eleanor said. It was the only pronouncement she had made.

'I know we do.'

A little later, as she had been told it would, another car came to Gainsborough Gardens. Dinah went with the police to Hampstead police station.

Lavinia Jackson responded to Dinah's call at once. She came to the police station and sat beside Dinah in the interview room while she gave her statement. In the windowless room, Dinah could smell the other woman's floral perfume mingled with the indigenous stale cigarette smoke and disinfectant. The police treated Dinah with patronising sympathy. Dinah understood that she was to be regarded as a harmless housewife probably goaded by her hormones.

Two hours later, with Lavinia's help, Dinah was free again, pending a medical examination for Sarah and the Greens' decision whether or not to press charges.

They stood together in the sunshine on Rosslyn Hill. Dinah was compressed in a beige outfit of Sandra's, with narrow suede shoes that pinched her feet. Cars and buses flooded past them. She felt dazed by all this bustle, as if she had been out of the ordinary world or unobservant of it for a very long time.

They began to walk down the hill, to get away from the police station. There was a graceful church with a white steeple standing against the oyster-white sky, and trees with their branches uncertainly tipped with green. The heels of Lavinia's black court shoes clicked smartly on the pavement.

'Thank you,' Dinah said.

'It's what I'm here to do,' Lavinia answered crisply.

345

Dinah had not known her well even when they were neighbours in Sheldon, and even though it was disturbing to re-encounter Lavinia like this she felt a difference, a lightness in herself. The chilly air was like silk against her face. Sandra's too-tight shoes lifted as she walked, as if they were sprung. She did not any longer have to keep a secret pressed tight inside her. She was part of the world, she could let herself be helped.

'Will I have to face charges?'

Lavinia considered. 'I don't know the parents, of course. But I think it's unlikely. You may have to give some formal undertaking to leave the family alone in the future.'

Dinah bent her head. 'I could do that, now.'

The olive-grey space of the heath rose ahead of them. The sun in the pallid sky shone on their faces.

They stopped walking at the edge of the open space. Dinah thought she liked Lavinia Jackson, and trusted her. It was good to feel the elasticity of friendship.

'I could ask you back to the Parkeses' for some lunch,' she offered uncertainly.

Lavinia smiled. 'I've got to get back. And it might be awkward, if I'm going to act for Milly when the time comes to look for her birth mother. How is she, by the way?'

'Milly is extraordinary. I don't know anyone remotely like her.'

'Yes, bit of a one-off, isn't she?'

Lavinia raised her hand to a cab. As it rumbled to the kerb beside them she kissed Dinah on the cheek.

'You take care of yourself,' she ordered, in her authoritative way.

'I will,' Dinah murmured, although Lavinia was already out of earshot.

As she walked back towards Gainsborough Gardens, she thought about Matthew.

She did want to see him; sharp edges of longing for it nudged through her. She flexed and stretched her fingers in

346

the pocket of Sandra's coat, remembering the way his hand fitted hers, the exact drop between the crest of his shoulder and her own when they walked in step. And other things: most of them from a long time ago. The way he had made her laugh. The way his precise hands touched her. These things seemed less remote than they had done.

What felt uncomfortable was the prospect of their reunion in Ed and Sandra's house. Matthew was not a public man. He would not want their private reunion to take place where other people might observe it, and Dinah also knew that he was not quite socially adroit enough to engineer the circumstances differently.

As she turned into Gainsborough Gardens and looked across at the assertive red bulk of the house, she was certain that her instinct was correct.

There was the hotel room in Cromer, facing the sea; it contained her clothes, it was at least partly familiar to the boys. The safe anonymity of it drew her strongly. And there was Francis, too. When she was with him she had thought of an end in their beginning, but the end was still to be properly defined with its final cadence and full stop. She owed Francis that definition.

Dinah decided as she climbed the steps. She would go back to Norfolk and wait for Matt and the boys to join her there. They could walk by the sea again together.

'Back to *Norfolk*?' Ed expostulated.

He had come out of his study with a pair of spectacles slung on a cord around his neck. In the room behind him Dinah could see the pale square of a live computer screen. Ed was working. Sandra hovered in a doorway and Milly was nowhere to be seen. The status quo had been restored in the Parkes household.

'Yes. If I speak to Matt right now, before they leave for Boston, he can arrange to pick up a hire car and drive on after me. It makes everything much simpler.' Dinah surprised herself with her crisp conviction.

347

'No, come on, stay here with us. Look, there's plenty of space. We can look after you all, you don't want to go off to some dismal hotel.'

Ed was kind and Dinah knew that his goodwill was genuine. But she shook her head.

'I think she should do what she wants,' Sandra said softly. 'Use the phone in the drawing room, Dinah.'

Dinah spoke to Matt, and to the boys. Once they had heard her voice Jack and Merlin were able to enter properly into the excitement of this unscheduled trip to England.

'See you tomorrow,' they yelled into the phone.

'Okay,' Matt agreed at once, relieved not to have to include the Parkeses in their plans. 'Cromer, then.' He was not sure what Dinah would want, and his uncertainty made him sound unfamiliar to her.

'I love you,' he said, before he rang off.

'I know you do,' Dinah answered.

Ed could only direct his organising energy into finding the best mechanic to accompany Dinah back to Camden Town and the hire car. It was parked where she had left it the day before, outside Fortinbras Mansions.

While the mechanic fiddled with duplicate ignition keys, Dinah stood on the opposite kerb and looked up at the block. On the first floor, the glass had burst out of the windows and the brick was blackened with smoke. With the smell of it in the back of her throat again, Dinah relived the fear. The skin crawled over her neck and shoulders and she shivered, wrapping her arms around herself.

Pictures of what might have been began to form in her head.

But Dinah turned sharply away, dismissing them. This is what would happen; she would have to learn to live with the aftermath of the fire. The mechanic glanced over his shoulder at her. The door of the building had already been

348

boarded up with rough planks. Everyone had got out of there, by some miracle. The police had told her that.

There was no one sitting on the steps. Caz and the others had gone. Even some of the soaking debris had been cleared away.

The clean little spring of relief bubbled up in Dinah again. They had escaped. Sarah would be home with Pauline by now. It was all right. It was all right to be happy. The images were no more than that: her fears. She let the relief wash them away.

As she came level with the car again, the engine turned over and then fired.

'There you go,' the mechanic called. 'One ignition key.'

Dinah thanked him. She settled into the car and carefully reversed it, not looking in the mirror at Fortinbras Mansions. She drove back up the hill to Hampstead.

Milly was in her bedroom. It was tidy, almost bare. There was a huge tree outside her window, and a view through the branches across roofs and gardens. Dinah leant on the sill and rested her head against the glass, looking out. The private backs of houses descended away from her, purplish slate roofs and plump-curtained windows and balconies with spring pots set out. Orderly, prosperous, like everything that surrounded Ed and Sandra.

'You're going, then?' Milly said.

Dinah faced her. 'Yes. Back to the hotel, to get the rest of my things and to meet Matt and the boys.'

Milly nodded.

'Will you miss her?' Milly demanded abruptly.

'Yes. But I'm glad that Pauline has got her back.'

After a moment Milly muttered, 'I'm sorry it was, like, me she said goodbye to. I felt crap about it. What she wanted was to look at this again, right?'

She held out her hand to show the crude tattooed flower. 'She rubbed it with her thumb and, you know, blinked at it. She couldn't see it very well. Anyway, I'm sorry.'

349

Dinah was going to say that there was no reason to be sorry, but then she saw Milly's face. It went dark and tight with what Dinah first thought was anger. But then Milly put her hands up to cover her eyes.

'*I* will miss her. Oh shit,' she groaned. 'Shit. Dinah I was so fucking scared. I was so fucking scared in that place. I thought we were all going to die.'

Dinah took her in her arms.

Milly shook her head violently. 'Poor old fat Sarah half-blind without her glasses. That pig noise she was making. And all of us choking.'

Dinah hugged her. With her hand under her hair she cupped the back of her neck. It felt brittle, a thin stalk. Her shoulders were so narrow and thin. Milly felt the aftermath of terror, too.

'It's all right. You were brave, Milly. We got out together. You even went back for the bloody dog.'

'I thought it was my fault that we were there. Even that the fucking dog was in there. I was so scared I ran back to get it out.'

'It wasn't your fault. It was mine if it was anyone's. I'm the adult. I should have said we weren't staying there and that was that, and then taken you both somewhere safe.'

'*Yes*,' Milly sobbed out her sudden anger, rolling her head on Dinah's shoulder. 'Why didn't you? Why?'

'Because I had disintegrated. Can you think what that means? I'm ashamed of what happened. But I thought you were taking charge of me.'

'*Me?*'

'Yes. And you did, didn't you?'

'Dunno.' But the thought clearly meant something to her. Milly looked up, sniffing and rubbing her nose with the back of her hand. 'I suppose, in a way.'

Dinah said softly, 'You did. You were admirable. And we were also lucky. Those are the two things to remember when you can't help thinking about the fire. You were admirable, and we were lucky. No one was hurt. Will you be able to remember that?'

Slowly, Milly nodded her head.

'What about you?' Dinah asked her.

The shrug. 'I'm staying here I suppose. Because they want me to, you know?'

Dinah could read her more clearly now. Milly was confused by the contrast between this place and Fortinbras Mansions; there were insoluble contradictions all around her and she shielded herself with indifference or aggression.

'Is it what you want?'

'I did last night, didn't I? I couldn't come home quick enough.'

'And?'

'I dunno. Well, yeah, I suppose I do, really. It was, like, how would it be if there wasn't this place, and them? Like, what would I do?

'They're okay, Ed and Sandra, basically. Even though they can piss you off properly. This morning when you were at the police station we had a talk, you know? One of those *talks*?'

Milly's eyebrows went up into the tangle of hair. She couldn't tell even this story quite straight.

'I do know.'

'Anyway. They said that if I really want to look for my mother, they won't stop me. They'd help me if I want. If it means so much, right?'

'That's good, isn't it?'

'I dunno. Yeah, I guess. I'll think about it, anyway. See what happens. I kind of feel a bit different, seeing you and old Sarah. It wasn't like you were her mother, was it?'

'No,' Dinah said, 'it wasn't like I was her mother.' She smiled suddenly at Milly, unfolding her arms. 'I have to go now.'

'I know. Will we see each other again?'

Dinah was astonished. 'Of course we will. All the time, probably. Try and stop us.'

'Okay then,' Milly leant forward and awkwardly pecked

Dinah's cheek. 'Does it matter if I don't come down to say goodbye?'

'No, it doesn't matter at all.'

'See you then.'

Dinah left her leaning her elbows on the window-sill and staring down at the houses on the hill.

Ed and Sandra pressed their concern on Dinah. But Ed's overbearing manner seemed merely solicitous now, and the membrane of reserve between the two women had broken down. Dinah kissed them both goodbye with real affection and gratitude.

Somehow, the truth that it was not Dinah who had rescued their daughter but vice versa had never quite dawned on the Parkeses. In some safer time, Dinah thought, they deserved to know the truth.

They came out into the street to wave her off, still pressing on her money and extra clothes and emergency phone and fax numbers.

'I'll be okay,' Dinah assured them. 'Thank you for everything.'

She drove away. Through the London traffic and then north-east, back in the direction they had come.

In the morning, Redemption Street was deserted, bleached colourless by a chill salt wind coming in off the flat slate-grey sea. Even the tobacconist's shop on the corner was closed, with sun-faded blue blinds drawn down in front of the display of plastic toys in the window.

Dinah had found two messages from Francis waiting for her at the hotel. Could they meet again? He was beginning to worry, no one knew where she was. But she was exhausted. She could do no more accounting for herself today. She went to bed instead and slept for twelve dreamless hours, and then was woken by the telephone ringing. Matthew and the two boys were at Heathrow. They would be in Cromer before the end of the afternoon.

She walked slowly down the silent street towards Francis's house. She noticed that the first green spears of dandelion leaves had begun to unfurl in front of each front door, in the cracks between the hollow steps and the gritty paving stones. Even in the four days since she last walked this way spring had advanced. The recognition made her feel light and optimistic, even though the wind was cold. She was on her way to him, but she did not know what she would say when she saw Francis again.

The door of the house seemed more faded and splintered by wind and salt. As soon as she had knocked, he opened it. Meeting his eyes, Dinah saw the leap of delight in him, and looked away. He wanted more than she could give, and had done so from the beginning. What could she say, after all?

'Come in,' Francis said.

There was the little room, the ashes in the grate and the table heaped with books. Beyond it, of course, was the steep staircase and the bedroom overhead. Dinah remembered the details of the night they had spent. She wanted to look at Francis again, to make amends, to try to explain something, to recover their understanding. But she did not trust herself.

'Perhaps we could go out somewhere? To have a cup of coffee or something?'

'If you would prefer that.'

He took his long coat from the hook behind the front door. He closed the door and locked it and then turned, offering Dinah his arm. After an instant's hesitation she took it, folding her hand beneath his.

They walked down to the sea front. There were seagulls perched on the groynes, facing out to the oily waves. The shingle was shiny-wet, with occasional combs of thick foam caught in the bladderwrack at the tide line.

'You've been away,' Francis said.

Dinah felt the filaments of mutual responsibility, of trust that had now become misplaced, and a poignant sense of need and longing stirring between them, failing to connect.

She took a breath. In a low voice she told Francis everything that had happened since she had left Cromer with Milly.

'I see,' he said at length, looking out at the sea. 'That makes a difference to everything, doesn't it?'

'Yes,' Dinah admitted. There was no secret now, only a history. She was not hiding anything or wishing for a miracle.

Already, she understood, there had been a stepping-forward on his part and a retreat on hers. Before she had seen Sarah there had been a knot of pain and bewilderment within her that had snagged and affected everything else she saw or touched. Francis had been knotted into the confusion, and in seeing him she had been able to see only the clarity of his quiet desperation. She had mistaken it for calm and strength. And then the knot had been severed, severing them also.

At the end of the promenade stood a wooden kiosk with a canvas awning. The shutters that had protected the front all winter stood optimistically open, and bottles of sauce and a glass sugar-shaker with a chrome dispenser tube waited on the counter shelf. Apart from the kiosk attendant and Dinah and Francis there was no one but a couple of fishermen, and some chin-tucked pensioners in the shelter overlooking the sea.

'Sumer is icumen in,' Francis murmured.

He bought two cups of coffee in flower-printed paper beakers with circles of card that folded back for handles, too small to accommodate thumb and index finger. Anticipating the taste of the coffee, smiling at each other a little, they took turns with the sugar dispenser.

They sat on the sea wall with their fingers laced separately, identically, around the paper cups. The spot they had chosen was not far from where they had first met, and this section of the wall and its backdrop of houses appeared in the pen-and-ink drawing that he had given her. The drawing still lay in her drawer in Franklin, between its protective sheets of paper.

354

Dinah thought back to the night and day they had spent together.

It seemed a long time ago, although her memory of each detail was vivid, as if for those hours she had achieved hyper-consciousness. She remembered the craziness of her reflection in the spartan bathroom mirror, the cold bedroom, the unexpected happiness that had briefly engrossed them both. The happiness remained with her now, but it was in the past tense. Begun, and ended.

She ventured a glance at Francis, daring to hope that it might be the same for him.

He stared straight ahead at the sea. The tiny seams at the corner of his mouth held a gleam of coffee, before he reached up with the back of his hand to rub it away. On the horizon Dinah saw that he had been watching the blocky white shape of a big ship, perhaps a ferry heading from Harwich to Esbjerg or Gothenburg. Francis would know for sure.

'What now?' he asked, not moving his head.

Dinah manoeuvred temporarily within the intent of his question, disliking her lack of directness where they had been direct before.

'Sarah is already back at home with the Greens. If I don't have to face criminal charges I shall probably have to give an undertaking not to interfere with her life in future.' And then she added clearly, 'I don't feel proud of what I did, but I don't regret it either.'

That was the baldest version of the truth as she saw it now. Except for the fire. And perhaps even the fire, for the sense of relief, of almost magical reprieve with which it had left her.

'Good,' Francis nodded. Then, after an interval just decent enough, 'And?'

There was expectancy in him, more apparent than before. It altered Francis, and her perception of him. Guilt murmured in her again but she remembered that they had each taken what the other had offered, and promised nothing more.

355

'Matthew and the children will be here this afternoon.'

'Is that what you want?'

The whisper of the flat sea and the gulls' cries seemed to contain his fading hope. Francis's sadness became palpable, but Dinah did not want him to be sad. She had admired his apparent contentment and his self-sufficiency.

'It is,' she answered, with much more conviction than she truly possessed, to make herself clear.

Francis crumpled his empty cup and aimed it accurately at a green municipal litter-bin.

'Do you have time for another walk?'

Dinah made herself not take the automatic glance at her watch.

'Yes. I'd like that.'

He led her by a different way, to the point where the sea front petered out on to a scrubby headland. They took a path along a low cliff between gorse bushes and stunted trees, one behind the other because there was no room to walk abreast. After a little way, as if this was too obvious an acting out of their position, Francis swung inland across a field. They had to negotiate rough ground, and scramble under and over wire fences.

'I'm sorry,' he said at one point. 'Not such a good route.'

Dinah faced up to him, made faintly breathless by the pace he had been setting.

'No apologies, all right?'

He seemed suddenly taller, spectrally thin, and in his black coat with the pale sunshine behind him almost threatening. Dinah caught her breath, then moved to one side so that the easterly light caught his face when he turned to look at her. And she saw him clearly, with a little shock of recognition.

Francis was tired, and there was a hunger in him that their connection had briefly obscured.

Dinah had noted and then fixed upon his strengths, because those were what she had needed and wanted to see. But they were not all of him. He had even told her: he was washed up here, hard by the sea, with nowhere further to go.

356

There was nothing straight or simple, Dinah thought, except her own wish for it. There were only the layers and folds and puckers of truth, and the half-truths and secrets and deceits that were concealed within them.

Dinah understood that it was not Francis who threatened her, but her own fear and guilt. And she did not want to be fearful or guilty any longer.

She smiled, suddenly, squinting because the sun was in her eyes.

The constraint between them melted with the smile. Dinah put out her hand to touch his arm, and at the same moment Francis bent his head to kiss her mouth. Their lips touched briefly before they drew back again. Then he caught her face between his hands and looked into her eyes, minutely examining her.

'Did you expect more than this?' Dinah asked.

'No,' Francis answered at last, with the difference between expectation and hope left unqualified between them.

'Was it enough, in a way?'

They began to walk again, towards a field gate that led into a road.

She was asking for reassurance that no damage had been done, but he didn't give it.

'You're expecting me to recognise what's enough of what I like?'

He asked the question lightly, and they both laughed. Dinah understood that she was warned off.

The road beyond the gate curved back towards the town. Soon they were in the outskirts with its petrol station fore-courts and anonymous brick warehouses. Once Francis hesi-tated at an unmade roundabout and another time he took a turning that led them into a cul-de-sac of new brick-built houses. It had become a walk of obstacles and dead-ends.

'I'm sorry,' Francis said again. 'I don't usually come this way.'

Nor would he have to follow the route in the future and encounter the turns that they had taken today, Dinah knew.

At last they saw the wrinkled expanse of the sea ahead of them again. They passed the end of Redemption Street without looking down it. They walked round to the front door of the hotel, the wind catching them briefly unawares as they came out to face the sea.

They stopped on the hotel steps. A couple came out, the man buttoning his car coat and the woman patting her hair under a printed headscarf. They nodded at Francis and Dinah and walked away along the front, not quite in step, the man impatiently half-turning after fifty yards to wait for the woman to catch up.

Francis said, 'Will we see each other again?'

Asking as Milly had done. Only now Dinah had a brief vision of a family party, of social introductions to be negotiated. My husband, my lover . . .

Inwardly she stopped short. Was that what Francis had been, a lover? Not quite. A little less than that, perhaps, and also more. More than a tit-for-tat to Matthew, less in the sum than Matthew had always been. Francis had lent her happiness and insight and she loved him for that, as well as for what he had revealed of himself.

Only now, with quick certainty, she wanted to be away from him. The beginning and then the end. No other promises.

'I think we'll be going back to the States quite soon.'

Even now she could not bring herself to deliver the flat truth.

'Is that all? Is that everything?' Francis demanded with sudden disbelieving bitterness.

He needed more from her, and Dinah was sure that there was no more for her to give. How inevitable it was, she thought, that this unequal expectation should be the eternal pattern between men and women. What was more surprising was that anyone ever found the satisfaction of giving and getting in equal proportion. Probably even for Matthew and his Kathrin Pang there had been less of the illicit delight than Dinah had painfully imagined, and more of the same untidy and clumsy mismatching of needs and desires.

Dinah nodded her head. The wind stung her eyes, making them water.

Francis was disappointed in her, finally and inevitably so.

He stood back, one step, still looking at her. She resisted the conciliatory urge to follow him, motherly, to make sure that after all he was all right.

'I still have your picture,' she said.

He lifted his hand. He did not say goodbye. Dinah watched him walk briskly to the corner, the unkempt hem of his coat flapping around his legs. He turned the corner without looking back.

Walking away, Francis crossed the road at the rear of the hotel and went diagonally across the park to the doors of the supermarket. Inside, he took a wire basket from the pile beyond the checkout and began a methodical working of the aisles. He passed up and down each side, once or twice taking a tin or a packet from the shelf and reading the list of ingredients. Each time he replaced the item, almost regretfully aligning it with its fellows, and passed on. Once he nodded to an acquaintance who greeted him but his pre-occupied air did not invite casual conversation.

The aisle farthest from the entrance was the wines and spirits section.

Francis walked more slowly here, examining the ranks of bottles with a critical air. But he did not stop until the very end, when he took two bottles of Bell's whisky from the shelf and placed them in the basket. Then he put the basket gently on the floor and took out his wallet. He studied the contents for a moment, seeming to hesitate over the photographs contained in the transparent flap. But after a moment he picked up the basket and carried it over to the nearest check-out. He paid for his purchases and scooped them into a plastic carrier. With the bottles inside their bag in the crook of his arm, held safe against his chest, he walked home again to Redemption Street.

*

359

Someone knocked lightly at the door of Dinah's room. It sounded as if the chambermaid was tapping with the plastic key-tag against one of the panels. She put down the book she had been pretending to read and went to open the door.

Matthew stood there with Jack on one side of him and Merlin on the other.

There was a second while Dinah stared at them as if they were a picture or a mirage that she had conjured up out of the seaside desert. And then they moved and flowed into the room, a tidal wave, engulfing her with warmth and life.

'Mom, are you surprised?'

'Merlin slept in the car. I didn't.'

'Do you want to see my foot? There was a hole in it from the spike but it's closing up now.'

'Of course she doesn't want to see the hole in your foot, Mer, don't be such a klutz.'

The boys' vitality made Dinah remember how they changed all the time, almost from hour to hour. They seemed larger, stronger, more vehement than they had done only a week ago. For a week she had kept the notion of them frozen in her mind, a pale and static version of the two of them that took no account of their growing. Now this exuberant sprouting and reshaping seemed joyous, more than merely alive, entirely amazing. They swarmed against her and she hugged them, willingly trampled by their feet and elbowed by their hard bones.

And then, over their heads, her eyes met Matthew's.

'You're here much earlier than I expected.'

'We made good time on the road.'

He was smiling, but with a touch of awkwardness. He was unshaven, tired and crumpled.

There were no trumpets sounding. Dinah was glad she had not expected any, and gladder still that none of this was happening in Gainsborough Gardens. Matthew was her husband. There were dark pouches beneath his eyes and the short hair above the line of his beard was noticeably grey. His face was entirely familiar to her, and behind the bones and skin was the plain fact of him, known to her in the same intricate detail as the features of his face. His breath when he kissed her was slightly stale. Dinah let her cheek rest against his. She cupped the bony curve of his head in her hand, holding him there.

Watching them, more alert than their parents would have wished to acknowledge, the boys hung silent for a second. Then they glanced at each other with a flicker of triumph.

'I'm hungry,' Jack said. 'Can we get tea?'

Tea was served in the hotel lounge, where Milly had waited for Dinah. There were pairs and trios of leathery old wing chairs and moquette sofas drawn up around low tables, and Saturday-outing couples and groups being served by the pensionable waitresses. The tea came in a chrome pot, too little of it, with hot water in another identical pot. The boys pounced on the plate of white-bread triangle sandwiches, and Matt and Dinah faced each other with their teacups. They were both smiling. The faded room with its polite occupants and the low murmurs of conversation and the afternoon light on the lamp brackets and dim water-colours were safe and unremarkable.

They were a family taking tea, also safe.

Matt looked at Dinah. Her hair was arranged differently. She had twisted the thick lock at the front and pinned it back off her face in a hurried way that made her look young and eager. She was not wearing any earrings. Dinah always wore earrings, saying that she felt undressed without them, and this difference also seemed notable. Her thin left hand with his rings on it rested in her lap, inclined backwards slightly from the wrist. The four tendons fanning from the wrist to the base of each finger stood out sharply. Matthew wanted to reach out and trace the tendons with his own finger, to feel the warmth of her skin and to see it wrinkle a little where it was beginning to lose its elasticity. Instead he sat motionless in his creaky leather chair.

This was a good moment, he thought.

361

One of the moments when life slows, and then gathers momentum in a new direction.

Jack finished the last scone. He laid his plate back on the table.

'Mum? Where's Sarah?'

The pit-pat of conversation continued on the next table; a waitress shuffled by with a fresh pot of hot water for the group of Americans sitting by the fireplace.

'She's with her family. They live not far from here, in a place called Wivenham.'

'Have you seen her again?'

'Yes.'

Dinah looked imploringly at Matt. *Don't tell them what I did.*

'Will we see her?'

Matt leaned forward and the cushions creaked under his weight. He took Dinah's hand, but waited for her to answer the question.

'No, Jack. It was my mistake to think that we might, that we could share a part of her.

'The truth is that she doesn't belong to us, however much we might like it to be otherwise now we also have you, now we understand what it is to be a family. But Matt and I decided long ago to give Sarah to the people who are her mother and father now. They love her and understand her, and she is happy with them.

'It might have been a right thing or a wrong thing to do. I don't know which. But the point is that it's done. And now it might be more comfortable for me, for us, to see her and reassure ourselves of the rightness of what there is today. But it isn't what Sarah wants, or her family.

'It's very simple, really. She doesn't need anything. She didn't ask to be found. The need was all mine, and I made a mistake.'

Jack blinked solemnly behind his glasses.

'Would she understand we are her brothers if we told her?'

'No, she wouldn't. She knows she has a grown-up sister of her own.'

Merlin drew arrowheads in the air with the tips of his fingers.

'Is she like Jack and me?'

'Not at all. She's like herself.'

'We'd be just other people to her?'

'Yes, Merlin, we would.'

The boys looked at each other. After a moment's thought Merlin said, 'I don't want to see her if she doesn't want to see me. I'd rather keep the imagine of her in my head, just for myself.'

'The idea of her,' Jack corrected.

'Jack?' Dinah prompted him.

He answered more slowly. 'Yeah. I guess. We can't just go there, anyway, can we? A whole other family? It'd be like saying, "Hey, look. Here's us, and there's you".'

His sensitivity pierced her, and she bent her head.

Matthew spoke for the first time. 'I think you're both right in what you say.'

And Merlin and Jack appeared to be content with that much, still being at the age when adult assurances were absolute, and trustworthy. For how much longer? Matt wondered.

When they had finished all the tea the boys announced that they would go and catch up with the day's football results on television.

'Soccer,' Jack murmured with relish.

Matt was still holding Dinah's hand. He did run his finger over the back of it now.

'Thank you,' he said.

'For what?'

'For telling them that we made the choice together.'

'We did, Matt.'

'Shall we go upstairs?'

Dinah nodded. He tried to tuck her hand under his arm as they walked to the lift, but she edged an inch away from him. He thought that she didn't want to be made to feel like an invalid, needing support. The lift seemed to hold the smells of all the hotel cooking trapped within its steel walls.

In their bedroom they sat on the bed, propped against the padded headboard. They were both reminded of weekend mornings with the newspapers spread over the covers, of evenings when they retreated to watch sloppy films on the television, of longer ago times when the boys were babies crawling in the blanket spaces between them. Matthew took off Dinah's shoes and patiently rubbed her feet.

'Inquisition time?' she asked him.

'No. Just tell me what you want to.'

He listened to her as she described again what she had done. He tried to knit up the spaces and the imagined omissions between the words as well as the bare story.

'I understand,' he said once, and Dinah turned her eyes sharply on him, to gauge whether he did or not.

At the end she lay with her head back and her eyes closed. He could see the steady pulse beating in her neck. He rubbed her feet, spreading the toes and kneading them in his fingers. She sighed, letting the breath drift out of her.

'I feel weak,' she confessed.

Matthew was amazed. 'No. You are so strong.'

Later, when they were in bed in the dark, he took her in his arms. They rested with their faces just touching.

'Are you too tired?' he asked her. He wanted to feel the contraction of her muscles, the slither of her skin beneath his, the workings of her hands and tongue. His wife.

'No. Aren't you?'

'It's only just gone teatime for me, remember.' Too early yet for jet lag, although he felt the beginnings of the stretched, slightly other-worldly detachment.

'So it has.'

He slid his hand over her shoulder and downwards, to rest in the hollow of her waist.

'Are you interested in the teatime of my desire?'

364

'Could be.' He felt the turning up of her smile against his mouth.

Sixteen

'I want to do it,' Matthew said.

Matt and Dinah were walking on the sea marsh, a great curved tongue of sand and seagrass exposed at low tide to the wide, pale sky. The air was thick with salt and the low-water reek of mud and weed, and the voices of their children faded and grew thin in the distance. Jack and Merlin had taken out a pair of canoes to paddle in the brown river channel. The water was barely deep enough to float the canoes and the boys had been shouting and protesting as they ran aground on sandy shoals. Now they were further off, following the inland winding curves of the channel with the first sluggish flow of the incoming tide.

Matthew and Dinah were diminished by the breadth of the sky, made into tiny but determined figures as they steadily progressed across the ribbed sand. They had been separate in their thoughts, and isolated in the great space, with the children carried away from them on the river. Then they had begun to talk again, about Sarah.

'I want to see her,' he repeated, with increasing vehemence. 'I can't go away from here, not having seen her. You can understand that, can't you?'

'Yes, I can,' Dinah said.

And then, unconsciously echoing Eleanor, she confessed,

'I'm afraid, that's all. I'm afraid of what you might feel, and of what the Greens might do.'

'Don't be afraid. You're strong. The weakness has been in me.'

Matthew was cut by the knowledge of having failed Dinah before. Now, since their reunion, there was a sense of new fragile skin forming over the healing wound. He did not want to bruise the skin, nor did he want some infection to begin and to be sealed in all over again, under the tissue of their dishonesty. If he failed to admit to his own needs now, might not the decay begin once more?

'I'll just go and see her. No more than that.'

He was possessed by the intention. It had become vital for him to go to Wivenham and see Sarah and her parents.

It was not for his own sake alone. He wanted to defend Dinah, too. If he could see the Greens, talk briefly to them, Matthew thought he could make the truth clearer than a hundred communications between lawyers and police. And he could make his own failure clear to them, for Dinah's sake.

Dinah nodded. 'I can't argue with your need to go, can I? What about Jack and Merlin? If they don't see her, will she become a ghost to them, like she was to us?'

Matthew thought about his sons with a new twist of tenderness and pride. The days he had spent alone with them in the house on Kendrick had drawn them closer and opened them up to him in a way that all the years before had never quite done. They seemed now to possess a resilience and understanding that he had not valued highly enough. And they seemed also now to belong fully to him.

They stopped walking. The spit of sand had narrowed and the sea was properly visible ahead of them, with a white line of waves feathering the shingle. It was time to turn, ahead of the incoming tide. Matthew put his arm around Dinah's waist and drew her against him so that her head rested on his shoulder. They had become connected again. To touch one another now was to acknowledge the link between them, whereas before it had only emphasised the distance.

With his eyes on the breaking waves Matthew said carefully, 'They are only children themselves. Ghosts are made up of loss and longing and guilt.'

'I believe you're right,' Dinah said at last.

They turned in the opposite direction, with their faces to the land, and began to walk back along the sand spit.

Matthew had always known that there never would be a bridge built between themselves and the Greens. There was no hope that for Sarah's sake the two families might establish some kind of friendship. How could he and Dinah take their sons and introduce them, and then stand beside the Greens to watch their children together?

There were two families, and there was Sarah and there were the two boys. That the division existed at all was his responsibility. Walking across the glittering sand, with Dinah beside him, Matthew accepted the weight of the responsibility.

'When will you go?' she asked him.

'This afternoon.'

'I'll take the boys to the big swimming pool. They like it there.'

He linked her arm through his, and this time Dinah did not draw away from him.

They reached the end of the sea wall and climbed the steps. There was the sound of pounding feet, and Jack and Merlin came flying towards them. They had left their canoes drawn high up on the shingle. Jack was ahead but Merlin was running flat out to catch him. The injury to his foot was forgotten.

Matthew drove to Wivenham without thinking in advance what he would do when he got there. He watched the low horizon instead, and the trees hunched against the wind, and the patterns of crops and livestock in the immense fields.

The village was full of visitors' cars and Sunday trippers in sturdy anoraks. He left his own car down at the quay and walked the length of it. The tide was rising and the moored dinghies bobbed upright, rigging cables slapping musically against the masts. There were groups of children peering over the quay into the swirling water, and sailing people in deckshoes, and elderly couples enjoying the warmth of the mid-afternoon sun. Matt slowed his pace. Further down the estuary there were white sails beating across the water.

At the end of the quay a flight of half-submerged wooden steps led down into the brown estuary. There was a bigger knot of people gathered here, with nets and buckets. As Matthew came up to them there was a shout of triumph and excitement. Three or four people were crouched on the steps with lines let down from wooden frames. They were crabbing with baited hooks. He waited and saw one of the lines gingerly lifted from the water. A fat, dark crab clung with its eager pincers to the bacon bait.

'Go easy with 'im now, and you'll have 'im,' someone called out.

A girl was hauling the crab in. It slipped and spiralled on the end of the line and there was a gasp from the onlookers. A man knelt on the steps to reach down with a shrimping net.

Matthew gazed at the girl's face.

She lifted the crab on the hook another few inches. She was frowning with the effort of concentration. The pink end of her tongue protruded catlike between her clenched teeth.

The man with the net stretched as far as he could, almost overbalancing. The loop of wire slid underneath the crab just as it released its hold on the bait. It fell straight into the net and the man quickly swung the bamboo pole up and over to the quay. The crab plopped straight into the waiting bucket and there was a loud shout of glee.

The girl lifted her face to her father's. Her eyes closed almost to slits and her tongue emerged further between her teeth in a great beam of delight. She dropped the crabbing hook and clapped her hands. Several of the onlookers patted her on the back.

'You got 'im. Good crabbing, girl.'

'That's a beauty, that is.'

Matthew knew that the man with Sarah was Malcolm Green, although he could only see his back in a grey anorak. Malcolm lifted the bucket by its wire loop handle so that Sarah could peer in at her catch.

'Big,' she said.

Matthew stood still, a yard away from her.

The other crabbers resumed their fishing. A motorboat swished past the quay, the putter of the diesel engine amplified by the walls and the ripples of the wake slapping against the dripping wooden steps.

There was no pause or jerk in time for him to wonder at.

He saw a healthy, excited child with Down's syndrome. The features of the condition were characteristic, even familiar to him. He could not see in her any resemblance to anyone else.

Sometimes, in the innermost recesses of his imagination, Matthew had painfully envisaged a distorted replica of Dinah. But Sarah did not look anything like her mother, or in any way like Jack or Merlin. As the moment stretched, and the strollers passed by and the motorboat's gurgle faded, Matthew saw that Sarah looked like herself. She was, as Dinah said, complete.

And sensing Matt's stare Malcolm had already turned around.

He grasped the crab bucket with one hand and with the other caught Sarah against him. Matt and he gazed at each other until Matt stepped forward, some neutral phrase of reassurance on the tip of his tongue.

'No you don't,' Malcolm said loudly. One or two of the people nearest to them on the quay glanced at them. 'Sarah, it's time you and me went home for our tea.'

He led her away, walking quickly, the crab bucket and net awkwardly held in one hand. Matthew saw that Sarah's crabbing hook was still lying on the cobbles where she had dropped it. He scooped it up, one of the barbs digging into the ball of his thumb, and ran after them.

'Wait,' Matthew begged.

Away from the quay there were fewer people within ear-shot. Malcolm stopped and reluctantly turned. Matt saw a mild-looking man with sloping shoulders, a home-knitted pullover showing under his unzipped coat. Sarah still tugged his arm in the other direction.

'I wondered if we could talk,' Matthew said.

'Hasn't there been enough trouble?'

Malcolm was not angry or aggressive, Matthew saw. He was anxious and protective, a shy man unwillingly forced into a confrontation. He made Matt feel an intruder, bringing his urban insistence weightily to bear where it did not belong.

'I don't want to make any trouble. Please? Just five minutes' talk.'

Sarah released her father's hand and came round between him and Matthew. She turned her back on Matthew and rubbed her face against Malcolm's shoulder, mumbling something to him. Then she tried to push him on up the village street away from the quay and Matt.

'She wants to go home,' Malcolm said.

'May I walk with you?'

'*No.*'

Matt saw the man's red hands ball into awkward fists. It might run against everything in his nature but Malcolm would still offer whatever defence he could for Sarah and Pauline.

'I don't want her to have to see you.'

Malcolm meant his wife. He even squared himself up, as if he could block off the village street. Matthew nodded his understanding. Malcolm's determination made him feel all the more miserably deficient himself.

He realised that he was still holding Sarah's crabbing hook. He wound the orange nylon cord around the frame

371

and hooked the triple barbs securely within the coil of cord, then handed it back to her.

He reached forward and let his hand rest for a second on her shoulder.

And Sarah rewarded him with a smile that broke through her owlish solemnity and turned her face into pure overlapping circles of happiness.

'Mine,' she said.

'Yours,' he agreed.

Malcolm said abruptly. 'I'll take her indoors. Then I'll come back if you want. But you keep away from the house.'

'I will.'

'There's a bench, the other end of the quay. It's round the corner, a bit out of sight, overlooking the water.'

'I'll wait for you there.'

Malcolm took Sarah's hand. She had already tucked the crabbing hook away, out of sight, in the pocket of her coat. It was a hooded ski-jacket with a leaping skier and *SkiFun Aspen* embroidered on the back. The two of them walked on up the street, past the souvenir shop and the pub, and the café open for the first cream teas of the season. Neither of them looked back at Matthew, although he stood still and watched Sarah until she was out of sight.

The corner with the bench was sheltered. Matthew leant his head against the stone wall behind him and closed his eyes.

He thought of Dinah, imagining her seeing Sarah as he had just done. He had listened to her carefully, even humbly, when she told him about the wedding, the house in Church Walk at the moment when Sarah had walked into it. And he knew there was a lack within him, some deficit, that made him unable to feel the same amazed pride and relief that Dinah had known. All he did have was the hollowness, the faint whisper of regret for its absence.

Sarah had looked as he had known she would. She was happy and cared for.

There was a faint throat-clearing sound. He opened his

eyes and saw Malcolm standing in front of him. Matt moved a little sideways on the bench.

'Sit down.'

They sat and looked out at the sea. Matt was minutely conscious of the other man beside him. He looked down at his grey trousers and grey woollen socks, and his serviceable laced shoes. He could even hear his breathing, a regular and quietly emphatic inhalation and exhalation that for some reason reminded Matt of his father.

Malcolm broke the silence with sudden surprising vehemence.

'It's been very hard for her. Sarah's all the world to her, you know. And when your wife took her, well. Even though we were told by the police and them she'd come to no harm, that we'd get her back. I thought Pauline would make herself ill. Or worse. I've never known her like it, not in all the years we've been married.

'When I saw you over there, I wanted to . . . Well, I won't tell you that I wanted to do.'

His plain sincerity and lack of articulacy touched Matthew deeply. There was a space between them that seemed filled with the musty useless lumber of Matthew's own acquired knowledge and opinions and attitudes. He thought of the lab back in Franklin and Jon and Sean and his team and the insulin programme and all the white-lit humming technology of the world he came from and he wondered, What does that *mean*?

'I'm sorry,' he said. And then rubbed the heel of his hand against his mouth. Useless words. 'You know, Dinah couldn't help herself. It wasn't to hurt you or your wife, least of all to harm Sarah that she did it. It was just that, that she couldn't stop herself.

'She told me, almost as soon as she had taken Sarah she knew she should bring her home again. But she wanted just a day with her. One day.'

Malcolm twisted the ring on his wedding finger. His knuckle bulged purplish above it.

'Does she know you're here?'

'Yes. I told her I was coming. She didn't want me to. She thought you and Pauline had been through enough. But I wanted to try and explain something to you.'

'It's all right for the likes of you,' Malcolm said, with a flare of resentment that mottled his cheeks with dull colour. 'It's plain sailing for you, isn't it?'

'No. Nothing is plain sailing. Believe me.'

Matthew's low voice made Malcolm turn his head. Their eyes met.

'There's one other thing I wanted to say,' Matthew added. 'If there is a villain, if you want to point a finger, you should do it at me.'

'I don't want to.' Malcolm dismissed him.

'Just the same. Let me tell you the truth.'

Matthew studied the arm of the seat. The wood was weathered to silvery grey and the cracks in the grain were whitened with salt. As he traced them he felt the minute grittiness dissolve beneath his finger. He made his confession to Malcolm Green.

'I forced Dinah to choose.

'As soon as we were told what was wrong with Sarah, it seemed to me that a choice was exactly what was involved. I thought I couldn't accept the child she was. And I made all the leaps of conjecture about our future there and then, sitting beside her hospital bed. I could see all the disappointments and compromises lined up ahead, waiting for us.

'I didn't want to have to meet them. I thought we would fail, and that we would run the risk of losing all we had that seemed so precious.

'So I made Dinah choose. The baby or me. That's the truth, if you want to know it.'

Malcolm said, 'And they reckon you're a brilliant man. You're a professor, now, is that right?' He spoke without rancour, merely incomprehension.

Matthew smiled. He felt the complicated mechanics of it, his lips and cheek muscles moving, the thin inner skin of his

374

mouth sliding against his teeth. It was as if all of this, the inner workings of him as well as his mistakes, was exposed to Malcolm Green's scrutiny.

'It isn't always an advantage,' he said, meaning cleverness. 'It doesn't always guarantee courage or insight, or humility.

'But I loved my wife. Not to acknowledge imperfection, not even to allow the threat of it into the circle we made, that seemed the way to protect her and me and keep our love intact. And having rejected Sarah, the only way to deal with the fatal flaw itself was not to acknowledge it either. Never, never. Dinah and I entered into a fourteen-year conspiracy of silence.'

Matthew looked up and turned his head to Malcolm. There was a tension in the muscles beneath his jaw and in his throat that made him wonder with sudden shame and panic if he might be about to cry.

'I don't mean to excuse what Dinah did. Even less to excuse myself. But the loss of her child stayed buried inside her because that was the way I saw for us both to deal with it. And at last her desperation swelled up and burst out of her.

'She came here, and saw Sarah standing beside a bus in a thick fog on a country road. And she took her.'

Malcolm nodded his head, very slowly.

Matt went on, more hurriedly, as if he were afraid that he might not be able to say everything that he wanted.

'I love Dinah very much, and our two boys. That is the central truth, you see, the most obvious one that I had some-how not allowed proper weight. And everything that has happened since Sarah was born, all the accumulations of omission and silence, tiny and massive, have brought me to the edge of losing them.'

'I see.'

Malcolm's hands rested on his knees. For all his physical slightness there was a solidity about him, a reassuring absence of diversity or nuance that reminded Matthew again of his father.

'You know, Sarah means everything to my wife. And to me

as well, for that matter.' He put the consideration of his own feelings into a distinct second place. 'She's a grand little girl. 'She's . . .' He splayed his fingers over his grey-covered knees in an attempt to put her qualities into words, and failed.

'Grand,' he said softly.

'I know that.'

Matthew felt once again the whisper of loss, the echo from a place he could not see, that was his own failure to know her or grow to love her.

Malcolm shifted his position and then abruptly stood up.

'She thinks I've only come out to the shop for a couple of bits. I'd better get back home.'

Matthew stood too. They faced each other. An awkwardness had crept between them, as strangers who had revealed more of themselves than decency permitted.

'We won't be taking it any further. Pauline and me, with the police, that is. We both know why it happened, and we know that's all there is to it.'

'Thank you,' Matthew said. He held out his hand to shake Malcolm's but Malcolm had already slid his left hand into the inner pocket of his anorak. He took out a rectangle of creamy-coloured card, and still holding it he extended his free right hand instead. The men touched and then clasped hands uncomfortably, hastily, and then drew back again.

Malcolm said, holding it out, 'I brought this. It's for your wife, really.'

Matthew took the thing, whatever it was, without examining it.

'I'll be off, then,' Malcolm announced. He zipped his jacket up to the neck, and pushed his hands into the pockets.

'Goodbye,' Matt called after him.

For a long moment after he had disappeared, Matthew stood holding the paper. Then he sat down again on the bench. He saw that Malcolm had given him a folder. The outer edge was a little shorter than the one underneath. He flipped it open to examine what was inside.

376

It was a photograph, an enlargement, mounted in diagonal slits in the card.

The photograph showed a wedding group. It was conventionally posed, outside what looked like a church porch. The bride was dark-haired in a puff of a white dress with a bouffant veil. The bridegroom was red-faced in a high tight collar. There were two other couples, parents, in wedding clothes. And the senior bridesmaid, in a dress of shiny turquoise satin, was Sarah. She held a posy stiffly against the folds of her skirt, and she was crowned with a circlet of yellow daisies.

Her smile beamed out with complete impartiality. To Matthew she looked just as she had done when she had lifted the crab out of the cocoa-brown water below the quay wall.

Matthew looked down at the print of her face on the glossy paper, waiting for some moment of recognition.

But all he saw was her smile, and the radiation of her well-being, and the other smiles of the other people who were also unknown to him.

He smoothed the folder again to cover her face. The photograph was for Dinah, not for him. He slipped it into his pocket, careful to avoid creasing it. For a moment he lingered, stroking the salt-crusted arm of the bench with the tips of his fingers. Then he stood up, stiff-jointed.

With his eyes on the grey line where the sea met the sky, he walked along the quay, back towards his car, and Dinah.